J.S. Barnes

DRACULA'S CHILD

J.S. Barnes

DRACULA'S CHILD

TITAN BOOKS

Dracula's Child
Print edition ISBN: 9781789093391
E-book edition ISBN: 9781789093414

Published by Titan Books
A division of Titan Publishing Group Ltd.
144 Southwark Street, London SE1 0UP
www.titanbooks.com

First Titan edition: May 2020
10 9 8 7 6 5 4 3 2 1

A CIP catalogue record for this title is available from the British Library.

Printed and bound by CPI Group Ltd, Croydon CR0 4YY.

For Heather

'My revenge is just begun.
I spread it over centuries, and time is on my side.'

Count Dracula

EDITOR'S INTRODUCTION

The first dozen years of my life were spent in near-absolute ignorance of those bizarre and terrible occurrences which had, immediately preceded my birth. Although my childhood was predominantly a happy one I was nonetheless consistently aware of the existence of some great unseen shadow, the details and particulars of which were kept from me at all times.

The papers which follow make plain both the painful process of my enlightenment and the horrible reassertion of that murderous past which many close to me had long believed to have been forever buried. A number of the dramas and incidents which are described in this collection of journal entries, clippings, telegrams and letters may strike the doubtful as being at times at variance with the limits of twentieth-century belief. I give you my word, however, that every part of this narrative is accurate, authenticated and exact.

You may also wonder why, at more than a decade's distance, I have decided that this is the proper moment at which to prepare my account. For the time being, it must suffice to say that I have of late, against all hope and better judgement, become in awful increments persuaded that the spectre which for so long haunted my family may still in some form be with us, even as the whole of Europe cries out in pain and grief.

Lieutenant Quincey Harker
Dover
13 October 1914

PROLOGUE

MINA HARKER'S JOURNAL

———————◆———————

6 November 1903. Many years have passed since last I thought to set pen to paper in this modest journal of mine. In part, this apparent dereliction has been due to varied and hectic happiness, as our little family – Jonathan, Quincey and I – has grown and thrived. The demands of being both wife and mother have, quite naturally, kept me from daily composition.

Yet there is an additional and more sober motive for my long silence. Namely, that I have come to associate the very business of diary-keeping with those events that overtook us more than a decade ago, which wrenched from us our dear friends, Lucy Westenra and the gallant American after whom our son was christened, as well as bringing us all into association with that implacable creature whom I shall certainly never name here.

Those horrible months are not ones on which I have ever wished to dwell. For years, I have pushed them from my mind. I know that Jonathan feels as I do, though we have not spoken of it often, not, at least, since our boy was very small. For several years, we have preferred to look only at the present and towards the future; to speak of summer rather than of winter things.

Yet the seasons cannot be held back for ever, any more than

our history can be entirely hidden. I am afraid to say that it is tragedy which has occasioned this return to my journal – a tragedy which unfolded scant hours ago, at the finish of an evening which ought to have been marked only by good cheer, with generous merriment and quiet joy. The melancholy truth of my words will become apparent soon enough.

Our day began most pleasantly. As it is his birthday, we made something of a fuss of Quincey. He is still young enough to relish such attention, for all that he is embarking now upon that difficult stretch of years which will lead him out of childishness and into manhood. We are fortunate to have him with us at present, back from school for the half-term holiday. I shall be sorry indeed to lose him again in a few days' time, for all that Jonathan – without, I suspect, much conviction – chides me for my sentiment in such matters.

In the afternoon, the three of us went for a long and meandering walk, through the outskirts of this little village* where we have made our home and into the countryside beyond. Jonathan and I enjoyed the opportunity to take the air and engage in some light exercise while Quincey, ever watchful and unusual, seemed inspired by the starkness of the landscape. There is a wildness to it which speaks to his young soul, derived, no doubt, from his parents. For all our outward respectability, we possess a strain of bohemianism that sets us apart from many of our peers and neighbours.

We walked down shaded lanes and across chuckling brooks, skirting the edges of farmers' fields and strolling through copses and the scattered remnants of the old wood. Returning

* Shore Green, Oxfordshire

14

by another way to the village itself, we passed the site of last night's Guy Fawkes celebration which many of the villagers had attended. We had not joined them, for Jonathan's nerves are delicate and he finds the constant merriment, the roar and crackle of the blaze, and the almost pagan committal of the guy to the flames, to be profoundly upsetting. For the first tranche of our marriage, he was – and I can admit it here at least, where nobody but I shall ever read it – very bad in such matters indeed but there has in recent years been a modest, steady improvement.

I dare say that Quincey might have enjoyed last night's spectacle. I am myself by no means averse to such harmless entertainments and I fear that our continued absence from those festivities lends us in the eyes of the people a disagreeably aloof appearance. Yet, for the sake of my husband, we continue to decline such invitations.

We stepped without comment about the edges of a great circle of scorched earth where the bonfire had been laid. As we did so, Jonathan made a show of fixing his gaze upon the horizon, and delivered some remark concerning the unusual motion of a flock of starlings. Quincey played along with this piece of mummery, kindly feigning interest in matters ornithological while I kept my own counsel and considered how pleasant it might have been to have walked the night before amongst a throng of revellers, to have taken part in their exuberance and gaiety.

At home again, we gave Quincey his presents – a volume of poems by Mr Lear, a new suit of deep aquatic blue and, yielding to his repeated entreaties, a small, gingery kitten with whom he was delighted.

He named him – who knows from where it originated? – 'Auguste', and set about immediately making of the animal the firmest of friends. At his uncharacteristically expressive pleasure, Jonathan and I exchanged glances of contentment and pride. We held each other's gaze in a most meaningful fashion and I even found within me, for the first time in too long, a sudden and unanticipated resurgence of desire. My husband smiled, as if he knew, or at least suspected, the nature of my thoughts. As our son played with Auguste and as Jonathan and I seemed to sense something in the way of a rekindling it seemed that all might yet be well amongst us, that things might go on in just this mode of agreeable serenity.

Yet even as I had these thoughts, as Quincey stroked the kitten's small and vulnerable head, as Jonathan and I looked at each other with half-sleepy longing, it was already growing dark outside. Shadows were falling.

The first of our guests arrived with the dusk – dear Jack Seward, as kind and as decent a gentleman as ever he was, for all that he is a little stouter now and greyer in the temples than when we first met him, in the old century, when Quincey was yet to be thought of.

'My dear Mrs Harker,' he said as he was shown into our parlour by the maid, his words tumbling over each other in their haste to be heard. 'You must forgive my early arrival, for I somehow contrived to quite misjudge the length of the journey to this most charming spot.'

'Please.' I rose to greet him. 'You are welcome indeed. Your arrival here is always a cause for celebration, however early.'

'But not the chief cause tonight, I think,' he said and, from behind his back, he presented a small package, bound in red paper. 'Happy birthday, Quincey!'

At this, our son jumped up. Whereas in the past Jack

might have ruffled the boy's hair, the two of them now, with a seriocomic solemnity, shook hands.

'Thank you, sir. How generous of you to remember.'

Quincey unwrapped the parcel to discover that it contained a copy of Mr Darwin's The Descent of Man. Our son is intelligent and thoughtful but I suspect that such a volume may prove, at least for now, beyond him.

'I think,' Jack declared, 'that that book will prove of considerable interest to you. For it has to do with the interrelationship of all life. With the processes of evolution. And with the nature of predation itself.'

Quincey thanked him politely but, almost at once, he set the thing aside and went back to the kitten, who mewled and wriggled in shy delight.

My husband spoke. 'We ought to get you a drink, Jack,' he said and the two men busied themselves in a discussion, which there is no need to describe here, concerning various wines. I was grateful for the interruption, for Jack is not always the easiest company. Jonathan finds it all rather uncomfortable, I know, and his relief at the appearance a few moments later of decanter and glasses caused an expression of relief to flit quite visibly across his features.

We stood awhile, we three adults, each with a glass of wine in hand and watched Quincey and the kitten.

Jonathan, rendered more sociable by the application of alcohol, endeavoured to make small talk with our guest, enquiring as to the state of Jack's practice which is now situated prestigiously, and, I dare say, lucratively, in Harley Street.

'Oh, it's interesting enough,' said Dr Seward, taking at least as swift and punctual sips as did my husband, 'but it lacks variety.

The cost, you see, being so very prohibitive means that my patients are derived solely from a particular stratum of society.'

'I suppose,' said Jonathan, with a heartiness which I know does not come to him naturally, 'that you have to suffer a stream of monied hysterics? Nerve-wracked countesses? Elderly dukes who wish to be hypnotised in order to recover a sliver of their vigour and youth?'

Jack managed a thin smile. 'There is more truth in your words than you know.'

'Come now,' I interjected, 'surely you cannot miss the days of the asylum?'

Dr Seward smiled again and for a moment seemed very far away. 'The particular difficulties of that time of course I do not miss at all. But there are occasions, yes, when I do miss certain elements of the past.' He frowned, as if remembering. 'Certain fascinating puzzles and challenges. And perhaps also the sense that one's life possessed a... purpose.' His gaze passed away from us and went instead to Quincey, who was still engrossed in the kitten. At this sight, I saw the doctor's features arrange themselves in an expression, doubtless unconscious, of considerable dolour and regret.

The silence that ensued was interrupted by a brisk tap upon the door and the entrance, first of our maid and then in her wake, of two further guests – Lord Arthur and Lady Caroline Godalming.

At their arrival, the atmosphere improved. Arthur, as befits his rank and education, has about him a courteous bonhomie as well as a rare quality of being able to set all but the most disordered souls at their ease. As soon as he made his entry there was an outbreak of greetings, congratulations, kisses and embraces. It was all quite wonderful and even Jonathan seemed caught up in the simple sweetness of the scene. Carrie, as exquisite as ever, and beautifully dressed in the most fashionable way, was quite the essence of grace.

Truly, she has risen above those irregularities in her upbringing and early life to become as splendid a wife to Arthur as one might possibly have wished. Poor Lucy would have been pleased at his hard-won happiness. Indeed, I often like to think that she might look down now from a better place to see how the man whom she loved with all her young and tender heart has found, in his middle years, a generous measure of joy.

In this manner we were happily caught up for some minutes. Jonathan insisted on refilling all our glasses and a small draught was given to Quincey, diluted liberally with water. There ensued much merry clinking and declarations of pleasure at seeing one another again after so many months apart.

Excited by this pleasant commotion, Auguste scampered nervously about our feet. So taken up were we with this that we did not notice the arrival of our final guest until he had crossed the very threshold of the parlour and had announced in tones of jocular outrage: 'And what is this? Who dares to start such celebrations without me?'

'Professor!' I cried, and the others followed suit.

For reasons which I am not entirely sure that I care to examine too closely, I always feel profoundly secure in the company of Professor Abraham Van Helsing. I flung myself girlishly into his bearlike arms, caring nothing for decorum but only breathing in the comforting scent of him.

Jonathan too held him briefly in a manly embrace, as did Arthur. Even Jack was grinning broadly as they shook hands, and Quincey ran with feverish pleasure over to the old

Dutchman just as though he was again an infant and not on the cusp of a new maturity.

The Professor beamed. 'What a wonderful welcome! How splendid it is to see you all again, on this most auspicious, this most notable of dates, this singular and remarkable anniversary!'

He breathed in before continuing and in the lull I saw, as if in a cinematograph reel, a flurry of images from this very day thirteen years ago: the ranks of dark trees in a Transylvanian forest, the road to the castle, the mad chase to its gates, the band of gypsies and their deathly cargo, the final confrontation with the —,* and the sacrifice of our American companion as the light in the eyes of that monster was finally expunged.

I fancy that the Professor must also have been thinking at least some of these thoughts. He stayed silent a moment too long for comfort. 'The anniversary in question,' he went on, 'being, of course, the birthday of our young friend, Master Quincey Harker.'

There was applause at this, I thought, of a somewhat relieved variety. I do not know how much of his past Arthur has disclosed to Carrie, though I suspect there is a good deal of which he has not seen fit to inform her – wisely, given her own history.

Quincey as yet knows nothing of it. We have chosen to delay telling him anything of those circumstances in which his parents and their friends – our little crew of light – were first brought together. Tonight, at the conclusion of the Professor's soliloquy I saw my son look at me with something like doubt, even suspicion, in his eyes. The moment passed, however, and the air of general celebration resumed.

* There is one word here, crossed out so intently that the paper is torn and blistered.

At dinner, more fuss was made of Quincey, this being the first occasion on which he has been allowed to sit up so late with his seniors. Despite attempts to separate them, his new kitten crept in beside him and gambolled a while longer. Then, having exhausted his tiny body, he fell into a deep slumber upon the lap of our son.

Many families would doubtless forbid such a thing, but it was the boy's birthday and I saw no real harm in it. Had I the chance again, I would, of course, make a different judgement.

The food was bountiful and rich, the wine of excellent quality, and as I looked about me, I considered how fortunate I have been for the great majority of my life and how various and diverse are all my many blessings. Tonight everyone spoke, everyone had their moment in the sun and, for a time, our circle seemed to exist in something like perfect equilibrium.

'So, Arthur,' said Jack once the food was set before us, 'I read often of your doings in the House. How fares your battle to propel the place into the twentieth century?'

Lord Godalming smiled generously. 'I'm not altogether certain what it is that you're reading in the press, Jack, but to say that the House of Lords is institutionally indisposed to the process of modernisation would be to singularly understate the case.'

There were some wry expressions of agreement at this, together with a single snort of solidarity from the Professor.

'Let it suffice to say,' Arthur continued, 'that the challenge is in the nature of a life-long task.'

'You are, my lord,' said the Professor in his tone of old-fashioned deference, 'doing so much good work. Why, only last week I heard your name in connection with this rum "emergency law". You are said, sir, to be its most determined opponent.'

Jonathan gulped, rather greedily, at his wine. 'What law is this?'

'Have you not heard?'

'Oh, as a mere country practitioner I am afraid that such legal developments lie far beyond me.'

Lord Godalming waved his hand. 'It's rather a grubby and disreputable business.'

'Go on,' said my husband. 'Please.'

'I am not even altogether certain of the origin of the thing. But there is at present a growing impetus to restore an ancient law: that, in the event of a crisis, municipal power might be taken from the authorities and handed to a cabal known as the Council of Athelstan. As it happens, I am by birth a member of that committee. Though I stand against the very notion of it.'

'Quite right, my lord,' said the Professor.

Arthur would have said more but Carrie touched her husband's wrist very lightly. 'Let us now speak of happier matters,' she said. 'Mina? Jonathan? Are you still enjoying country life as much as ever you did?'

Amid such significant issues as Arthur had described, our own lives seemed rather stately and free of incident, but our friends listened as we spoke of our rustic happiness here, of Jonathan's practice, of Quincey's success in the schoolroom and of my own carefully guarded existence as a wife and a mother.

Afterwards, emboldened by supper, Jack Seward spoke up and amused us for a time with several anecdotes concerning his clientele, including one about a duchess who had convinced herself that she would be happier living as a Pekingese which bordered on gossip of the most mischievous sort. Then the Professor spoke of his partial retirement and travels. On the exact nature of his continuing research and the purpose of his many journeys, he did not, out of respect for us and tact towards Quincey, choose to elaborate.

We had finished the main course and were waiting for its successor when, at the end of a story concerning Van Helsing's surprisingly wayward youth in Amsterdam, Carrie, doll-like and nervous, cleared her throat and said: 'Everybody.'

We turned to look.

'Thank you all for tonight. To the Harkers for being such wonderful hosts. To Quincey on his special day. To Jack for being so steadfast a friend. We are so very glad to be amongst you.'

'Hear hear,' Jonathan said, too noisily, and tapped the side of his glass in a way which made me wince.

Caroline continued. 'Now my beloved Arthur and I have something in the way of an announcement. A happy and somewhat overdue announcement.'

'My dear?' I asked, recognising at once in Caroline's voice that familiar tone of elation which I well recall from when first we understood that I was carrying our child. 'Can it be?'

She nodded and Arthur beamed, as boyish an expression as I have ever seen upon that nobleman's face. 'There's no doubt,' she said. 'He is due in six months.'

Arthur chided her affectionately. 'He or she.'

'No, no!' A single line appeared on Carrie's features as she furrowed her brow with certainty. 'It will be a boy. An heir at last for the Godalming estate.'

At this, unbidden, a great roar of approval went up from our assembled company and there followed a cavalcade of good wishes, praise and congratulation.

The Professor was on his feet and, in his eccentric way, applauding uproariously as if giving an ovation at the opera. Jack was pumping Arthur's hand with unfeigned delight. Jonathan was filling glasses and making toasts and promising the menfolk cigars after supper. Quincey was grinning and offering Arthur his felicitations. I took Caroline in a tight embrace, holding her slender form firm against my body. I could feel her warm breath against my cheek as I dare say she could feel mine on hers.

'I'm so very happy for you both,' I said. 'I'm delighted beyond measure.'

'Thank you. But, Mina?'

'Yes?'

'Will I be...? That is, do you think it is within me to be a good and proper mother?'

'Oh Carrie. You will be wonderful. Just wonderful. I promise you.'

She seemed relieved. 'Thank you. You are such an inspiration, you know.'

I squeezed once, then let her go as all around us that happy uproar continued. Even the kitten, woken by the ruckus, seemed to dance and caper on the floor as if paying homage to these gladdest of tidings. I dare say that any stranger seeing us at that moment would think the entire party quite mad.

If only one could elongate that happy instant. If only one might luxuriate in those moments of joy. For an instant later, everything changed.

We heard, amid the clamour of celebration, a horrid, strangulated cry from Van Helsing.

All other sound ceased, save for a single perplexed mewl from the animal. We turned to the Dutchman to see that his face had gone quite puce, that his hands were shaking and that his whole body trembled violently.

'Professor?' asked Jonathan, his own face now quite white.

A single gout of blood trickled from the left-hand corner of Van Helsing's mouth. He took in a wheezing breath and murmured the following words, quite meaningless and indicative of whatever mental contortions were at that moment tormenting him. 'Beware... Strigoi... the White Tower... the one-eyed man...'

He staggered forward as Dr Seward told us all to stay back, not to crowd the Professor and to give him some air. But Van Helsing stumbled again and fell with hideous violence on his back. His eyelids fluttered and he moaned. Now his gaze was turned solely upon poor Quincey. 'You,' he said. 'You are to be the vessel, my boy. But you must fight. You must... do battle for your soul.'

This weird message delivered, he shuddered once and lay still. Seward was already by his side, reassuring us that the Professor still breathed, that he had suffered some manner of terrible seizure and that he should be laid down at once in a quiet place and a medical doctor summoned immediately, regardless of inconvenience and cost.

And so our merry party ended in the utmost misery. The Professor lies now in the best of our rooms on the first floor. He has yet to regain consciousness. The local physician, Dr Scott, has visited and done what he can. We must leave Van Helsing to sleep and hope that nature may heal him yet. Scott did not attempt to hide from us the gravity of the situation.

The Godalmings have, at my insistence, left for the night. I feared for the effect of such sights upon Carrie. Jack is still here, at his most coolly professional, doing his utmost to calm us. Jonathan busied himself with the physician, taking notes and thanking the fellow with unnecessary effusiveness for his time and trouble. My husband sleeps now too, a state no doubt abetted by that wine which he continued to consume even after the Professor's collapse. I have sat and written these words in large part as a distraction. I find slumber to be impossible while that heroic old man lies above us, hovering between death and life.

As for Quincey, that poor child for whom this ought to have been the happiest of days, he concerns me the most of all. He has not cried, nor has he shown any outward sign of grief. Rather he has taken to his room alone, his face pale and drained. Not only has he seen a man – the closest that he has known to a grandfather – laid low before him in the most upsetting of circumstances, but that horrible collapse had its own sickening sequel. For it was only when we lifted the prone body of the Professor from the ground that we realised that the kitten, Auguste, had been beneath him when the Dutchman fell, and that its little life had been at once snuffed out, its skull crushed, its contents spread upon our dining room floor in a pitiful smear of crimson.

PART ONE

THE
SHADOW
FALLS

FROM THE PRIVATE JOURNAL
OF MAURICE HALLAM

———◆———

6 November. Tonight is to be my last in the ancient, charming, thoroughly wicked city of Bucharest. These past three weeks I have drunk deep of its pleasures; like some new Epicurean, I have descended into its fantastic depths. This sybaritism has been frank, absolute and altogether without apology. As a result of such conduct, I shall tomorrow continue my wanderings at the rim of this great continent and head still further east, towards Brasov and beyond. Until then, in the next few hours, I shall endeavour to make my farewell a memorable one.

As to the precise reason for my departure, I yawn to admit the truth of it. Until now, this hotel has been largely accommodating but, following an interview with its bourgeois manager this afternoon, it has been made plain to me that my behaviour during my stay (together with a certain languidness upon my part when it came to the prompt settling of their innumerable tariffs) has made me decidedly unpopular. And so I shall go on, just as I have these past years, journeying deeper into the recesses of the world.

As I write it grows dark outside and so I am called to the evening, to take my final bow in this place of murky pleasures. I shall go to the oldest part of town to walk amongst those narrow, cobbled boulevards which speak of dreadful cycles of invasion and resistance, but where today the music is loud, the hashish plentiful and cheap, and where the boys are cheaper still. There do rare blooms flourish amongst the scrubland of poverty, there all things are possible, there a man might for a time cast off the robes of middle age and failure. Divested temporarily of the mask of ordinary life, he may be as he was meant to be, unruly and unfettered.

Later. The evening was a wonderful one. In the candour of its dissipation, it showed me once again, as though through a polished looking-glass, my own soul. These few lines I scribble just before dawn, in the pleasantly heightened condition of one who has feasted upon all those many vices which are here manufactured with such industry and verve.

Of course, in the aftermath of such indulgences, coming back alone to this temporary room, it would be unnatural indeed not to consider the choices of the past and of those opportunities – a wife; a cottage; a schoolteacher's calling – which, as a much younger man, I spurned out of the noble desire to live a life devoid of hypocrisy. In this I have largely been successful, although many necessary sacrifices have been offered up. The compensations for my decision may best be represented by the diversions of the night, which included food and drink of a rough-hewn peasant kind, stimulants of a sort which, in more supposedly advanced climes, would be considered illicit, and the lightly-purchased company of an exquisite street Arab. Once the deed of darkness was done, I kissed him and recited a poem by Gide, concerning which he was good enough to feign enjoyment.

Afterwards, when I thought that the evening could become no more pleasurable, just as I left the dosshouse into which the ragamuffin had taken me, I had the privilege to behold the most striking young man whom I have seen in the whole of this century.

The stranger was tall, slender and possessed of rather Roman features, with sleek, glistening blond hair. He stood opposite the establishment which I had lately vacated with a boy on each arm. He was evidently English and educated, for I heard the crisp clear accent of our public school system rise up in that benighted alley. He must have seen that I was staring, for he caught my eye and smiled, revealing rows of perfect white teeth. In mock salute, he touched the fingers of his left hand to his temple. I was about to reply in kind – even to try to strike up some conversation, as one émigré to another – but he turned his back and, flanked by shameless boys, vanished into the shadows.

I cannot say precisely why, but at the thought that I might never again see this beautiful creature I felt a profound heartsickness, as if some great and wonderful thing had been forever lost.

7 November. And so, in that atmosphere of infamy to which I have grown accustomed, I left Bucharest this morning, settling up and departing early to frosty goodbyes from the proprietors. My head was sore, my throat dry and my heart perhaps just a little tender – all states attributable directly to the delights of last night. By a rare stroke of good fortune, I was able to board a coach shortly after ten that was headed further east. With my little suitcase on my lap, I found myself sandwiched between an elderly matron (black-clad as though deep in sorrow) and a young girl who, in England, would be at school but who in this place of primitivism is doubtless already a mother of three. I drowsed as we passed, with sublime unconcern for speed and punctuality, out of the city and into those wilder lands which lie beyond.

When I woke, about an hour ago, the last vestiges of Bucharest were receding into the distance and the countryside was opening like a pearl before us. The road is very long and very straight and I dare say that in sunnier seasons the view might prove to be delightfully picturesque. Yet today, the lone and level fields which lay on either side of us were minatory and grey.

After a time we passed from this blasted landscape into considerable stretches of forest. Tangled lines of tall trees, of immeasurable antiquity, towered over our little coach. I wished again that I might be seeing the kingdom in some more verdant season. Winter in this place serves to exacerbate the shadows, to darken every horizon, to lend even the most harmless piece of rustic frippery an air of profound ominousness.

Typically, in such circumstances, I am able to slumber with aplomb. Now I find myself too awake and so I gaze, as if compelled to do so, at the scenery outside. In between such surveys, I have managed to pen these remarks. No doubt my handwriting is rather more unsteady than is usual.

The young woman beside me has surprisingly good English and she has made it plain that we are to stop in several hours' time in the town of Brasov.

'A charming place,' she assures me, in an accent which

somehow contrives to be both jagged and lilting, 'with much in it that is old.'

Just a moment ago, we passed across the border from relative civilisation into the ancient province of Transylvania.

Later. I write now in Brasov – an unexpectedly delightful town. This place is full of quaint beauty and has in its atmosphere a pleasing kind of rural floridity.

As soon as the coach stopped I knew that I must tarry here awhile. The town is small yet clean and well kept, its neat streets centred all about its picturesque square, from which the rest of the community emerges like spokes from a wheel. It is a carefully tended place and has something about it of the mittel-European stage set. I should say also that it nestles almost at the foot of the Carpathian Mountains, colossi which loom towards the sky and dwarf this settlement, lending Brasov itself (as if it needed any further such lustre) the air of a sanctuary, a vulnerable camp amid a savage landscape.

Something in this painterly scene made an appeal to my soul so that, having disembarked, I did not board the coach again but found instead, at the edge of the square, the town's only hotel, the name of which, according to its stout, aged proprietress, can be translated approximately from the Roumanian as 'The Most High and Treacherous Mountain Path'. It is a peculiar name for such a humble establishment, if charmingly whimsical and old-world.

Having stowed my bag in my surprisingly comfortable room, I left to take a stroll about the town. The place is quiet and peaceful. There is little enough to see but its strange, beguiling character is easy to imbibe. The people are mostly of peasant stock, though there are some tradesmen, merchants and commercial travellers. They view me with curiosity but without any suggestion of suspicion or hostility. I dare say that I represent to them, in my frock coat and cravat and my hair worn down to my shoulders, something of a figure of fascination and glamour – a dash of the '90s in this forgotten corner of the world.

A little beyond the square, facing, as if in defiance, towards that cyclopean mountain range, stands what is known to these people as 'The Black Church', so called because of its charred exterior, the result of a terrific fire some two hundred and fifty years ago, a conflagration which, so far as I can tell, all but scourged these streets. No doubt in its costly and destructive fashion it was also a boon in its eradication of the plague, which still at that time lingered here.

The charred walls of the temple lend it a forbidding aspect which is not supported inside – a large, light and rather graceful space, if, at least to my metropolitan eyes, a trifle lurid and idolatrous. A statue of the suffering Christ upon the cross seemed even to me, one who has never shied away from any dramatic flourish, to be so overstated in its depiction of that brand of agony which dwells at the extremities of human endurance that I doubt I shall sleep altogether soundly for some time. The expression upon our Saviour's face seemed too authentic, the blood with which his sinewy form was daubed too realistically painted. I hurried on with my tour of the place and it was with some relief that I emerged from the Black Church into the world beyond, just as twilight was falling.

The atmosphere in the shrine must have affected my imagination more than I had at first believed, for when I came into the street I could have sworn that there was a young man standing in the shadows upon the edge of the footpath and that he was watching the entrance to the house of prayer. I blinked in the fading light and rubbed my eyes. When I looked again there was nothing at all to be seen.

I write in my room, shortly before I am to go down for dinner, in a state of complete sobriety. I stress this point in order to make plain that the following claim is not the product of any excess or indulgence. I am almost certain that the watching figure whom I glimpsed was the selfsame Englishman who so arrested my attention yesterday in that grimy, sin-sodden avenue in the old town.

8 November. The first spokes of a new dawn are slanting into my chamber. I am joyful and inflamed. Yesterday I discovered a wholly original passion; strange fire now surges through my veins.

Returning to the hotel after my visit to the Black Church, and having composed a few paragraphs concerning the chief incidents of my day, I fell into a light doze from which I woke dry-mouthed and cobwebbed, tired from the journey and, I dare say, from sundry diversions also. As I approach my half century I find that I am no longer as robust in my constitution as once I was. Struggling upright, I anointed my face with cold water, dressed for dinner as best I could – my supper raiment being by now just a little threadbare – and went down to eat. What awaited me was both profoundly improbable and entirely thrilling.

The room in which the good proprietress serves her repasts is darkened and narrow. Its walls are bedecked with mountain views and gloomy forest landscapes. The food offered here is, as is the case throughout the kingdom, composed in large part of numerous meats (with especial emphasis placed upon the versatility of the sausage) accompanied by a great many dishes of cabbage, alternately boiled and stewed. All this – from furnishings to victuals – I might have guessed before I had even descended the staircase. Yet there was one element in that mean dining hall of which I would hardly have dared to dream.

The room was quite empty of any other visitor – entirely predictable in this autumnal and isolated burgh – save for one gentleman whose face, form and charming mien were to me immediately and marvellously familiar.

The young man from the back street in Bucharest and from the church yesterday afternoon looked up as I entered. He glanced over in my direction. I found that I paused, even that I stumbled for a moment, at the sight of him. Righting myself, I managed to form the words 'good evening'.

He smiled in return. 'You are English?'

'Yes,' I said. 'I am.'

'Well…' He gestured about the empty room. 'Would you care to join me? One Englishman, breaking bread with another in a foreign land.'

'I should be delighted.' I drew nearer and offered the youth my hand. 'Please, let me introduce myself. I am Maurice Hallam.'

'Charmed.' His grip was firm, his skin soft and smooth. 'Gabriel Shone.'

'How splendid.' I relinquished his hand with some regret and took the chair that was set opposite him. 'How splendid to meet you properly at last.'

Shone looked at me with some bemusement. 'Have we seen one another before?'

'I do believe we have,' I said as coolly as I was able. 'Perhaps...
Yes. By the Black Church?'

'Oh! Of course. I think I remember that now, Mr Hallam.'

'No, no,' I said, leaning forward. My manner was confidential
while striving simultaneously for wry charm, 'You ought to call
me Maurice.'

'Maurice it is, then. And so to you I shall be Gabriel.'

'The greatest,' I murmured, 'of all the archangels. Most
revered and exalted of divine messengers. Chief consoler of
Adam before the Fall.'

He smiled at me as we sat down together, a pair of Anglo-Saxon
pilgrims in this land of blood and shadow. There was wine upon
the table and we drank our fill of it. At first, the conversation, at
least in my half of the equation, was a trifle halting and unsure
(unaccustomed as I have lately been to conversing with anyone
other than tinkers, hoteliers and guardsmen). Nonetheless, I saw
at once that Mr Shone was cut from singular cloth. In addition
to the glory of his youth, he possessed both a radiant humility
and true, impermeable glamour.

'So how did you come to be in Brasov?' I asked as I settled
upon the chair. 'You seem – forgive me – almost as much out of
place here as I.'

He lowered his head in acquiescence. 'There is some truth in
that.' His voice was smooth and well-modulated, yet without that
braying quality which so often marks the aristocrat. 'My story
is perhaps too ugly for the dinner table. At least in its specifics.
Suffice for now to say that my birth was a low one, that I was
rescued from the penury of the orphanage by a noble benefactor,
Lord Stanhope, whose recent demise has granted me both the
motive and the wherewithal to leave England and explore.'

Intrigued by this unusual sketch I was considering ways in which I might enquire further without appearing too eager or impertinent, when our landlady bustled once more into the room.

'Gentlemen!' she declared in her charmingly broken English. 'I trust that you are both being fully settled in this so humble establishment?'

Naturally, we insisted that we were. Glowing with pleasure, she disappeared almost at once, departing amid voluble promises of the excellence of our imminent supper.

When she had gone, Gabriel looked me in the eye and said: 'And you, Maurice? How came you to Roumania?'

'Oh, I dare say that my tale is common enough. It is the narrative, perhaps, of all émigrés. Towards the end of the last century I simply came to find England too small in its imagination, too unkind in its attitudes and too unbeautiful in its aspect for me to countenance remaining within its limits. While my own country convulsed in pettiness and intolerance, I struck out for continental climes and fresh adventure.'

Gabriel inclined his blond head again at this speech of mine and, at the gesture, I felt that he had somehow understood me and my motives entirely.

'How interesting.' He raised his chin once more so that I might admire without difficulty that delicious profile. 'Well, what is a loss to the motherland is doubtless the continent's gain.' He paused and peered. 'Forgive me, Maurice, but it seems to me that, notwithstanding our recent, glancing encounters, I seem also to recognise you from the past. That is to say, from England.'

I managed a brisk shrug of world-weary unconcern. 'I suppose that such a thing is possible.'

'How so?'

For emphasis, I moved my plump left hand through the air. 'Long ago in the old country, back when you were very young, it is true that I enjoyed some small renown.'

'In what capacity?'

'As an actor, dear boy, upon the London stage.'

'Oh,' said Gabriel Shone. 'Yes. Of course.'

'Perhaps you saw me as a child? As a boy, awe-struck from the stalls? My Petruchio? My Berowne? Or perhaps,' I went on, thinking of the description which he had provided of his earliest years, 'perhaps you simply glimpsed my likeness upon a playbill or spied me upon the street, pursued by admirers, spectators and gentlemen of the press.'

'I dare say that might be so,' said Gabriel and, at the thought of this intertwining of our biographies, a silence fell between us. 'Strange, are they not,' he said at last, 'the invisible patterns of our lives? And their unseen connections?'

I was about to reply that my own thoughts were running upon very similar lines but then, our hostess was with us again, bearing platters of meat and another carafe of wine, providing copious felicitations and good wishes, full of a slightly clucking concern that all should be well with her pair of English guests. In the wake of this intrusion, our conversation shifted into less philosophical territories and we spoke, with increasing ease and comfort, of more general matters – touristic, gastronomic, historical, geographical and pecuniary. I spoke a little of the old days, of London in the '90s, and of my now slumbering career, while Gabriel talked not at all of the past but exclusively of the future.

'I am,' he announced when our plates were empty and almost all the wine was drunk, 'that most dangerous of things – a man with a fortune in want of a purpose.'

'So there is nothing in particular,' I asked, 'which you wish to achieve? No especial goal?'

'There must be,' he sighed, and seemed for a moment suffused with sadness, 'but I have yet to find it. This great objective of mine.'

'You want, I imagine,' I said, 'to do good in some fashion?'

'Perhaps,' he said, sounding most uncertain, 'although I think that it might be rather more accurate to say that I desire some manner of change. And change, after all, has no morality. It is neither benign nor maleficent. Merely transformative.'

'Fascinating. I had thought you some new Adonis. I see now that you are, in truth, the very spirit of Proteus.'

At this he smiled, more widely than he had all evening. He locked his gaze onto mine and there passed between us some manner of silent communication. I saw that we were in some essential fashion the same, twin spirits in this distant and isolated place, drawn together – let it simply now be said – by some Uranian magnetism.

The hour that followed this wordless exchange was one of painful anticipation, a gavotte of pleasantries and play-acting, of glances and proximities, of more wine and cigars and instances of physical contact, designed to appear inadvertent but possessed instead of warm-blooded intent. At last, the old dance done, we both retired to our chambers.

I waited for almost a quarter of an hour, trembling and heart-sick, before I stole along the corridor to Gabriel's room. There, as I had hoped with every fibre of my jaded soul, he was waiting for me, disrobed and upon his bed, with only a strip of pale white cotton to ensure his modesty.

'Gabriel,' I breathed, worshipful in my approach and prepared utterly to submit.

He smiled. 'Sit down, Maurice.'

He pointed to a chair beside the bed which would provide me with an ideal vantage point.

'You may never touch me as you wish to touch me,' he said at once and with firmness. 'Never. But you may, according to my own desires, be permitted to watch.'

And as he slid away that white shroud he began to speak, not of those courteous things which had engaged our attention downstairs but rather of the truth of his life, his secret life. He told me of his days as a child upon the London streets, of his time in the orphanage and of the terrible mercy of his benefactor, Lord Stanhope. I did absolutely as Gabriel had instructed and, aflame with desire, I watched and listened and gave more of myself to him than I have given to any other human being for more than a quarter of a century. As I write at the brink of dawn I feel a surge of such feeling, unknown to me for so long, that I had almost forgotten the taste and the tang of it.

I cannot even say for certain precisely what the nature of that emotion may be. Yet this seems to me to be beyond question – that if Mr Gabriel Shone wants me for any purpose or reason then I am his, body and soul.

Later. A strange postscript to the above. As the light of morning illuminated my chamber and as I put down those preceding lines of fervour and desire, I heard from somewhere in the streets beyond what seemed to be the barking and snapping of a wild dog, a phenomenon by no means uncommon in this country, where such unhappy creatures are often to be spied languishing dolefully in public places or begging by restaurants for scraps. Having finished the last of my sentences

– that ringing, heartfelt exhortation – I flung myself, in a kind of frenzied and exhausted joy, into bed where, amongst those tangled sheets, I fell at once into Morpheus' arms.

When I woke, only a few minutes ago, the noise of the dog had not ceased or diminished but had rather grown very much louder, sounding so uproarious and proximate that it seemed as if the animal must be almost at the very doors of this establishment.

Rising with as much alacrity as I could muster, I hurried to my little leaded window and peered into the street below. What I saw there inspired within me a shudder of atavistic fear. For, standing on the road outside was a great grey wolf, bigger than any that I have ever seen in captivity.

The creature's appearance was wild and unkempt, desperate and so hungry. Its eyes, doubtless bloodshot with fatigue (for it must be frantic indeed to have ventured so far into this municipality), seemed to flash crimson as it turned its head upwards, as if to meet my gaze. At the sight of me it loosed a howl, chilling and terrible to hear. I cannot rightly say whether it was a sound born of fear or despair, or of some weird triumph I have yet to wholly understand.

MINA HARKER'S JOURNAL

———————◆———————

8 November. How unhappy have been the hours that have passed since last I wrote here, and how sorrowful is my duty to record now the details of that time. It is as though a great, glowering cloud has descended upon our once happy home. Van Helsing lies upstairs, breathing but otherwise lost to us, comatose, fading and weak. What a procession of medical men have there been through these doors! Godalming's London specialist, two friends of Jack Seward's and, again, our local physician from the village, Dr Scott, who arrived this time with the unmistakable scent of liquor on his breath.

Amongst our circle there is certainly no shortage of funds, though not a penny of it seems capable of offering the slightest comfort. Indeed, it serves only to emphasise the puniness of man and his devices when set against the irrefutable laws of life. Such thoughts are often with me when I visit with the Professor and see with what awful swiftness the attack has reduced him. He looks so very frail, lying in that narrow bed as if in state, unshaven, untidy, breathing with a dreadfully pained quality as if every exhalation is for his old body a desperate exertion. The others have been kept informed of this, though all have stayed away. It would distress poor Carrie, I know, to a near intolerable degree, so I understand well her and Arthur's absence. Van Helsing has no surviving family of whom I have ever heard.

I do not know how long our household can continue in this state of constant alertness and utter impotence. The strain is visible on us all. Jonathan says little and drinks more than he ought, but I see in his eyes the sorrow which he struggles to contain. Quincey has reacted with a kind of exaggerated stoicism. There is a blankness in his face and, when he speaks, an extreme neutrality of tone which I find most troubling. He will not talk of it, nor of the calamity which claimed the life of his kitten. We have promised to buy him a replacement although, at least for now, he insists that he does not wish for one.

He was due to return to school but has not done so. Jonathan and I made this decision – much, I suspect, to the baffled irritation of the Headmaster, Dr Harris – for it seemed more important to us that he stay at home awhile longer, at least until we know the fate of Van Helsing.

Jonathan and I both possess regrets as to our absences from the death-beds of loved ones. If it comes to that in this instance, we would not wish such guilty confusion upon our boy. So we wait for some sign about the noble Dutchman. We all owe him our lives. Such a dutiful standing guard as that upon which we are now engaged is nothing less than just and fitting. We wait. We keep watch, and we pray.

I dare say that it is the entirely explicable consequence of recent events, yet these past two nights I have been troubled for the first time in years (almost, indeed since motherhood) by bad dreams, much like the dreams of old. I woke this morning, too early and fatigued, from a nightmare of the most vivid sort, in which a wolf, a great grey beast, its eyes blazing with fire, howled with appetite and desire.

Such things belong, I know, to the last century, to that portion of our lives of which we do not speak. Yet it troubled me greatly and it has lingered in my mind.

9 November. Our state of siege continues. Van Helsing remains lost to us. An atmosphere of dark disquiet is felt throughout the house. Jonathan went to work this morning – the reading of a will in Summertown and another difficult family to placate and console – after which I persuaded Quincey to leave the house, practically for the first time since the tragedy, and to take a constitutional with me about the fringes of the village.

I fear that his is not an age at which one might expect communication with his mother to be conducted with any degree of open-hearted ease. Nonetheless, as we stepped beyond the bounds of Shore Green, and as we circled those fields which lie beyond it, we managed something in the way of meaningful conversation.

Neither a child any longer nor yet quite a man, Quincey's behaviour slides between one state and the other with curious speed. At times, as of when we spoke again of the horrible demise of poor Auguste, he might be almost half a decade more junior than he is in actuality. At others, when we talked of his schoolwork and of those mature labours which will succeed it, I could have been speaking with a young man freshly come down from the university. He seems nowadays to envisage not a career in the law, of which he once spoke with a boyish enthusiasm, derived, no doubt, from frank admiration of his father; but rather, following in the path of Jack Seward, to specialise in the treatment of the human mind.

As what was once called a 'New Woman' (how quaint an expression that seems today!) I believe that the destiny of each individual is their own to form and shape as they see fit. I am content to encourage our boy in any direction that he chooses. Nonetheless, I find myself wondering whether his new enthusiasm is born not wholly from his intellectual interests but rather from a growing disappointment with Jonathan, who has in recent months seemed ever more listless and disengaged. Perhaps our son, by charting this change in course, means to arrest my husband's attention? My own task is to listen, to understand and conciliate. It is important work and I do it gladly. Is there still a part of me, however, that feels something like wistfulness for those days when I was so much more than a domestic diplomat?

These are foolish, girlish thoughts.

Those parts of the conversation done, our discourse first faltered, then flagged, then ceased altogether, for Quincey would not speak of the fate of that dear old gentleman who slumbers in our home, but rather grew sullen and withdrawn.

When we arrived home, Jonathan had returned from his professional errand but had already taken recourse in what he called an aperitif but which looked to me rather more like neat gin. I went upstairs and sat beside the Professor. I watched the rise and fall of his breast, his ragged irregular breathing, the spittle at the edges of his lips, the utter reduction of that great personage. I felt an overwhelming sadness at the necessary progress of time, its inexorable forward motion, and I wondered at the injustice of it all.

Yet I knew someone once – as did we all – who had, through diabolic means, been placed above such processes and beyond the reach of time. He was in essence immortal, for all that his weird gifts allowed him to choose different forms: a bat, a rat, a column of mist. But what had that availed him save for fathomless misery? What had agelessness granted him except for the opportunity, across long centuries, to inculcate within his soul unmatched wickedness and hunger?

Later. Jonathan lies beside me, sleeping too heavily and perspiring, dead to the world. I do wish that he would not lean so upon the bottle at times such as these.

I think that there is at least a partial explanation for such a resort. Although he has spoken of the man but rarely, I do believe his late father made of strong drink a similar crutch. I try to understand. Yet how, at such moments, do I miss the best of my husband. For I have just woken from another startling dream.

I dreamed again of howling and of sharp white teeth and, silhouetted in the moonlight, the crouched and feral outline of the wolf.

LETTER FROM DR JOHN SEWARD TO JONATHAN AND MINA HARKER

10 November

My dear Jonathan and Mina,

I am sorry indeed to be still from your side at this difficult juncture. My work at present is seemingly without end – how very various and inventive are the maladies of the mind! – and I must fulfil my responsibilities. Nonetheless, I should hope that it needs no restatement from me that my thoughts are often with you, your family and the Professor.

May I take it that there is no change in his condition? Please let me know by telegram of the slightest sign of any alteration and I shall leave London immediately to be with you all.

Without the presence of Abraham Van Helsing my life would be infinitely poorer. Nonetheless, I am quite certain that, above all else, my old teacher would wish me to discharge my professional obligations. Yet it is from concern for his wellbeing as well as for the sanctity of your household that I write today.

I have a proposition. In my practice there is a very fine and dedicated young nurse by the name of Sarah-Ann Dowell. She has been in my employ for the whole of this year, in which time she has proved herself to be of an admirable character: patient, gentle, resourceful and skilled. She is a sober-minded young woman, with a considerable facility for healing and a desire to do good in the world wherever she is able.

Her family were, as I understand it, a somewhat deprived

and troublesome brood, yet she has set aside these awkward beginnings and is determined to make her own way in society. I suggest that I send her to you forthwith, on secondment, to aid you in your continuing care of the Professor, a medical feat which must be placing strain upon yourselves and your servants. Miss Dowell's fee and expenses will, of course, be paid in full by me for such time as she is to reside with you. I do hope that you will allow me to do this small thing in the name of our friendship.

Today it is my fervent consideration, as I know it is Arthur's, that our circle remain unbroken no matter what manner of shadow may seek to engulf it.

Yours always,
Jack Seward

PS. Do give my warmest best wishes to your son. He is a sensitive soul at an uncomfortable age and I dare say that the events of his birthday feast were profoundly upsetting to him. That poor kitten! What a senseless waste. I find that I cannot quite rid my imagination of the streak of scarlet that it left upon the ground. It made me think for the first time in years of an odd proverb much beloved of that unhappy madman, R.M. Renfield. Do you recall? It was spoken by him over and over, as though it were some beneficial incantation. 'The blood is the life,' he used to say, all of a tremble, his mad eyes gleaming. 'The blood is the life.'

FROM THE PRIVATE JOURNAL
OF MAURICE HALLAM

———◆———

10 November. I cannot recall, at least in this drab century, experiencing so great a concentration of animal pleasure as that which I have these past two days enjoyed in the company of Mr Gabriel Shone.

Not, I should hasten at once to make clear, that there has been any shift in the nature of things. Hellenic matters still stand between us just as they did two nights past and just, I suspect, as they always will. I shall be permitted to drink my fill of him solely with my eyes and any more intimate congress will be perpetually out of bounds.

Under ordinary circumstances, I should refuse to accept such a ruling and seek sustenance elsewhere. The Shone case, however, is sui generis. In his company, whether strolling about the town or dining together in the hotel, my chief sensation is contented peace of the profoundest sort. With him, I have found an unfamiliar calm and, although our acquaintance can still be measured in mere hours, a curiously deep-rooted loyalty.

All this has emerged in the time that has passed since the night when first we spoke. In recent days, we have both played at being the idle traveller, washed up by chance in this place and determined to explore its every cranny. We have acted as fast friends and gone about together, quite inseparably. We know these shadow-dappled streets better, I dare say, than has any other Englishman in the whole history of the place.

Nonetheless, it would be accurate enough to state that Brasov has a finite set of attractions; a few days are sufficient to exhaust them all. If I – a man, surely, with a great deal more life behind him than that which lies ahead – feels this thing, then it is a certainty that Gabriel, so many years my junior and filled with the impatience of youth, does so with a still greater degree of intensity. He has within him a wanderlust, a questing thirst for fresh experience which will not lightly be sated.

We shall not be long now in Brasov. Mr Shone wishes to move on and I, God willing, intend to go with him wheresoever that may be.

He has my heart and all that it might contain.

TELEGRAM FROM JONATHAN HARKER
TO DR JOHN SEWARD

11 November

Letter received with thanks. Kind offer of service of Miss Dowell accepted. No change in Professor. Doctor visited earlier. Diagnosis: the longer VH sleeps, the less likely he will ever wake again.

FROM THE PRIVATE JOURNAL
OF MAURICE HALLAM

———————◆———————

11 November. My prophecies have come to pass. In the morning,
we are to depart for those deep forests which lie upon the dark
side of this quiet settlement and, from thence, into the Carpathian
Mountains. Yet the manner in which these prognostications of
mine came to pass was wholly unexpected.

A trinity of curious events took place today. The morning
and afternoon were passed largely without incident, either in
languid pleasure or else in conversation of an agreeably high-
minded sort. Yet as twilight began to fall, we both came to
realise that – a tray of meats which our landlady had brought
to us shortly after noon aside – we had eaten very little for
hours. We have taken many meals at this hotel but we elected
tonight to eat at a tavern upon the opposite side of the town, a
goodly walk from our accommodation. Its name translates into
our own tongue as 'The Gored Stag', a strange title for an inn,
for all that such oddities are in this land commonplace.

The decision to sup there was Gabriel's. I should have been
happy enough to linger once again in familiar haunts, but I
am coming to understand that the search for novelty is a key

constituent of his nature. In the first oddity of the day, our landlady became more animated in her opposition to our plan than I have ever seen her yet.

'Please, good sirs. Be not going to that den of wickedness. It is no place for Englishmen. Or for any who still be having a shred of goodness in their hearts.'

Her face seemed to me to be suffused with vexation. As she spoke, she touched a small wooden cross which hung about her neck. The theatrical quality of the gesture rather appealed to me, though the poor woman seemed to be entirely in earnest. Her sincerity had not to do, I think, merely with the loss of that trifling sum which we would, had we stayed in the hotel for supper, have granted to her. Rather, it seemed derived from what appeared to be fear in its most potent form. Hearing her voice, Gabriel wore an expression of amused scepticism and, at the sight of his beauteous lips curled into something not so very far from mockery, I felt quite certain that her words had provided only fuel for the fire of his curiosity and added only weight to his compulsion to explore.

An old truth of the world is here presented: that to make a thing forbidden is to fill the souls of those who are warned against it with unquenchable thirst. Such I beheld then in the demeanour of Mr Shone.

Older than he and perhaps in possession of some accidental wisdom, I asked our hostess why she was so very adamant in her opposition to our visiting The Gored Stag.

'I shall say, sirs, only this. The place is not itself a source of wickedness. But it is being an outpost of evil. It is an echo of the past. It is a gateway through which no man or woman may be passing unchanged.'

With these peculiar sentiments delivered, she turned away while my companion adopted a scoffing expression. At the door, she looked back: 'I will be keeping my hotel open for you, sirs, but only tonight until midnight. After that hour I will grant entry to none. Not even, most noble sirs, to you.'

She vanished from our sight before we could reply, shutting the door with decided emphasis. When I glanced up at him again, Gabriel Shone was beaming.

'Look lively, Hallam. For we leave at once for this site of immorality. This temple to transgression!'

'Are you quite certain? There is much to value, is there not, in local knowledge?'

'For men such as we, Maurice, I doubt that there shall be anything in this place which will shock or startle us in the least. Some illicit lust, perhaps, amongst the peasantry. Some overindulgence dressed up by superstition. I grow tired of Brasov. This bourgeois little town. Let us drink tonight from blacker waters. Let us indulge ourselves and see what lies in the shadows.'

Of course, in the light of his ideal smile, I could refuse him nothing.

Once we had dressed as extravagantly as we dared for this supposed bazaar of iniquity, we left our residence (the landlady doubtless sequestered prayerfully within) and set out for The Gored Stag. Although it was entirely dark and the evening was crisp to the degree that our breath billowed from our mouths, the promenade proved pleasant enough. I moved through the silent streets of Brasov with this remarkable man whose earlier display of petulance had not in me invoked – as it would surely have done had the perpetrator been any but he – irritation or regret, but only an exaggerated indulgence.

That the formation of such an attachment upon my part will lead only to heartbreak and loneliness is plain to me, even now, at this early moment, the acme of infatuation.

Old actor that I am, I find myself quite content to speak the lines that fate has written. I will stand wherever destiny wishes for me to stand and I shall give my bow at the very instant that it is decreed by that unseen dramatist.

As we walked to the far side of the town the houses became more humble in aspect, more rickety and indicative of poverty. Away from the calm of the square and the melancholy grandeur of the Black Church, the atmosphere underwent a further modulation. We were the object of gazes from the shadows which were frank in their hostility. We were peered at by peasants who seemed of quite a different class and stock from our homely landlady. The menfolk slouched against walls and looked at us with envious contempt, while their women peered despondently from beneath their heavy lids. All was dispiritment, hopelessness and the dreadful ugliness of poverty. I should have been more than happy to turn around and go back to safer streets, yet Gabriel Shone strode on with such gleeful resolution that I knew better than to suggest retreat.

We reached the outskirts of the town and I saw a large square building, almost a barn, outside which stood a cracked and faded sign, swinging in the cool night breeze.

Beyond the establishment there was but a thin, unwelcoming road, scarcely used and disappearing into dense, dark forest. After this were only mountains.

From the tavern came a low hum of conversation and merriment. I was put in mind not of any joyous celebration but rather of an insect hive angered by the approach of human beings and set to roaring with pent-up fury.

We paused before the place, whose very exterior made plain its nature. For a moment, I even thought that Gabriel might be considering a volte-face, that his languid brand of bravado might dissipate in the face of simmering menace. In this I was incorrect, for Shone had turned his gaze towards the mirk of trees and seemed almost to be sniffing the air, like a creature scenting the approach of peril.

'Fascinating, isn't it? Dark and deep and lonely.'

'You mean the forest?'

He nodded. 'What would it be like, I wonder, to step into that ancient realm? To move with utter liberty in so wild a place?'

I was about to suggest that the dream of such a thing might very well prove to be superior to the experience itself when we heard, from somewhere beyond our sight, a low and guttural sound, unmistakably the growl of an animal.

I moved closer to my companion. 'Gabriel?'

Out of the darkness it padded then, the great grey wolf. Its fur was thick and matted. Its eyes blazed in the night. Its jaws were open wide to reveal sharp, yellow teeth and thick ropes of saliva hanging from its maw. So absolute a terror seized me at the sight, so primitive a shrinking fear, that I could do nothing, neither move nor speak.

To my horror, the wolf growled again, tensed and sprang forward. There was in my mind no uncertainty that the animal meant to kill us both. An absurd thought flashed like a magnesium flare – that I was meant to die in some London gaol and not in Transylvania at all, not so achingly far from home.

Yet something curious took place. For Gabriel Shone

stretched out a hand and, in his high and eloquent tones, cried: 'No! This is not for today.'

The effect upon the beast was extraordinary, for the wolf behaved as though it had leapt not into the air but rather directly into some invisible wall. It fell at once upon the earth, snarling in frustration and anger. Shamed, it loped away, as if it had just endured a rare humiliation.

I looked at Gabriel, whose face was now slick and shining with perspiration. I breathed his name with something like reverence.

'What happened?'

'Maurice, my dear old fellow, I have not the slightest notion. I acted instinctively, thinking that the beast might be startled or distracted. Such results as those we have witnessed were by me wholly unthought of.'

I saw that he shook. His hands and arms trembled in the aftermath of our sudden, unheralded proximity to death. He smiled again with what I took to be relief and I was able to reply in kind.

'Well, I suppose,' remarked my saviour, 'that after such an encounter the very least we've earned for ourselves is a drink. Shall we?'

Without waiting for my answer or even looking back, he walked towards the entrance to The Gored Stag and stepped with unmistakable purpose inside. I followed, dutifully, in his wake.

So rackety a life as mine has necessitated the visiting of numerous unsavoury haunts and low meeting places. Almost since boyhood, I have been an habitué of deep and secret rooms, an aficionado of the hidden, the dishonourable and the louche.

With such experiences at my back, the interior of The Gored Stag seemed at first to be a considerable disappointment.

In spite of the florid protestations of our landlady, it appeared to be nothing more than a peasants' tavern, patronised by farmers and labouring men. It was a little dirtier, perhaps, than its several cousins in the town but otherwise – with its rough trestle tables, its scents of sweat, warm ale and cooked meat, its sullen, spluttering fire and straw-strewn floor – it struck me as being wholly unremarkable. Furthermore, our arrival seemed to excite little interest from that proletarian throng, who barely glanced up from their flagons at the arrival in their midst of two fashionable strangers.

The roil of conversation dipped in volume not at all and such curiosity as they possessed drifted almost immediately away. In other circumstances, on an evening less wreathed in portent, so marked a reaction might have struck me as peculiar. Tonight, however, I thought little of it, grateful simply for the rustic ordinariness of the place. There was a small table unoccupied by the door and it was into a chair beside this that I flung myself. Gabriel did the same. We exchanged glances which spoke chiefly, and, I think, creditably, of rueful amusement. We said nothing – no words were necessary – until a stout woman nearing old age approached us. She was dressed in black as though in mourning and she mopped her sweat-jewelled brow with perhaps the filthiest handkerchief I have ever beheld.

She spoke no English but only her mother tongue. Through a system of mime and gesture, we were able to place a basic order: an ale for us both and a plate of what I think that she referred to as the speciality of the house. Once this performance was done, she managed a slatternly smile. As she turned to go, I caught something in her eyes and in the almost girlish set of her mouth which gave me to understand that she was nothing like so mature in years as I had first imagined. In actuality, she was very much younger even than my companion. How hard life is in this place. How pitiless. And how unstinting.

As the excitement of the evening began to fade, and as even the memory of that rapacious beast started to drift into anecdote and reminiscence, we settled into something like calm. It was a lull which was not to last. As we sat, overlooked by our fellow drinkers, as we relished the cheap but honest beer that was brought to us and, upon its heels, the platters of meat, we spoke together of many things. I talked of the past – of the grand theatres of London, of roles that I had played and of those that I wished I had played, of scandal and rumour, of unwise liaisons and faded loves, and as we picked with increasing recklessness at our plates, as we ordered more strong drink and began to sink into our cups, Gabriel Shone spoke to me, not as I had spoken of history, but rather of all that he hoped was yet to come.

'Since the death of my benefactor,' he began, speaking the words with an absolute neutrality of tone which I knew to mask a very much more complicated web of emotion, 'I have found myself in want of purpose. With very few financial limits I have travelled and explored, in part that I might yet discover some great goal or objective. Some just and noble design for my life.' As we spoke there crept into his voice a speechifying – one might almost say a rhetorical – tone as of a nascent politician honing his craft upon some provincial stump.

'I have seen much of the world,' he went on. 'More than I would ever have thought possible. From the fleshpots of Marrakesh to the salons of Paris, from the beauty of the Swiss valleys to the untarnished peace of the Italian lakes. Yet nothing in all these sights has ever satisfied the longings of my soul. I have been nowhere and seen nothing that several thousand rich men have not done before me. I want novelty, Maurice. Novelty and unseen things. True wildness! I want to saunter into forbidden territory and flout the rules of civilisation. I want to step away from the well-trodden path through the trees and plunge madly into the depths of the forest.'

This pretty soliloquy was approaching its end when I came to sense in the hostelry a palpable alteration in its temper – a sort of gathering hush, a shrinking back as if some unhappy accommodation were being made.

A shadow fell upon our table, just as my companion had ended his speech. We looked up as one, expecting the return of our barmaid or the arrival of some emboldened churl.

The vision that greeted us was altogether unexpected, a sight more befitting the odd carousel of a dream than the patient linearity of real life. The arrival was a stranger, a woman, but as far removed from our hostess as is the most exquisite lily from the lowliest hedge-nettle. She cannot have been more than three-and-twenty. Tall and slender, she had eyes of blue, long raven-dark hair and a remarkable physique, visible even beneath her huntress' garb.

She carried herself with grace and hauteur but in her motion one could perceive the lithe elegance of a cat. Her presence was galvanic, as if she had stepped from a florid mural of times past and walked, with all the richness of history, into the drabness of the present. She gave a close-lipped smile in greeting. She exuded sensuality and eroticism of the most flagrant kind, an aura of carnality, the power of which even I – whose tastes have been forever Grecian – could sense quite clearly. Her influence upon the majority of gentlemen would, I imagine, be entirely irresistible, analogous to the effect of the ripest provision of nectar upon the innocent honeybee.

With this in mind it struck me as peculiar that not one of those moribund revellers could bring themselves to look upon her. Instead, they bent further upon their libations, cast their gaze upon the ground or fixed their eyes upon some median point in the air.

So marked an antipathy to this vision seemed to me to stand in opposition to all the reproductive laws which have ensured the continuance of our species. When she spoke it was in very good, if thickly accented and antique English.

'You will be forgiving me, gentlemen, for my intruding upon you, but my senses are acute and I could not help but overhear your words.'

I thought that her hearing must indeed be quite superb if she were able to make out our sentences amid the hubbub. Gabriel seemed immediately charmed, sensing in the stranger someone possessed of a magnetism still greater than his own.

'Madam, you are most welcome. My name is Gabriel Shone and this is my associate, the actor Mr Maurice Hallam. Will you not join us?'

'Thank you,' said the lady, 'but I cannot tarry and I do not sup. I am pleased to be making the acquaintance of you both. My name is Ileana.'

We both murmured some polite platitudes about our being gratified to meet her.

'You said,' Gabriel went on, 'that you had overheard our discourse? May I take it, then, that something of what we said attracted your attention?'

She bowed her dark head in what seemed to me to be mock-supplication, a parody of solicitous modesty. 'You are correct. For I heard you speak of the longings of your soul. Of your craving for the forbidden and the dark. Of your desiring to see the secret places of the world.'

'That is so. But what is it to you?'

'I am being occasionally employed,' said the woman, 'as a guide. As a leader for those curious persons who wish to be venturing into the forests and the mountains and to what lies beyond. It seems to me that if you long for the fulfilment of your desires you will need such a one as me to be showing you the way.'

Gabriel and I traded glances. Whereas I was all scepticism and uncertainty, his mind evidently seethed with possibilities.

'Tell me more.'

She smiled her predatory smile. 'There is a place, several days from here – ancient, terrible and unvisited. Long ago, it was owned by a great nobleman of our people. A bloody ruler who inspired both fear and loyalty. He lived far beyond his allotted time and there grew up about him many strange stories. Even now it is said that the structure – ruined and overrun – hides within its crumbling walls a great and wondrous secret.'

'And what is that?' I interjected, with a single eyebrow raised.

'Eternal life,' said she, speaking with a fantastical coldness.

Gabriel looked enthralled. 'What is the name of the place?' Hunger pulsated in every syllable.

She turned her deep blue eyes upon us both and breathed two words: 'Castle Dracula.'

And so, in this uncanny fashion, is our new course set.

★

It is late now, very late, and we have returned to the hotel, abiding by our hostess' dictate that we be back by midnight. Once we had made an arrangement to meet Ileana (her surname remains unknown) at the hour of dawn tomorrow, the young woman bade us farewell and took her leave of the drinking establishment, to the palpable relief of the revellers. After her departure we felt altogether less welcome. We finished our ales swiftly and came here to our beds.

Gabriel is consumed by a puppyish brand of radicalism, seeing in our forthcoming expedition the chance to give the kind of thumb-bite to conventionality for which he has long been searching. I am considerably more wary, seeing too many oddities in the scenario and too many suggestive ellipses in the woman's reasoning to feel anything other than acute trepidation. However, I have pledged myself to remain by Gabriel's side – a decision made not purely, I think, from carnal curiosity but from something else, something akin to a desire to protect him.

I shall go with him tomorrow and meet with Ileana, and together we shall travel beyond the town, into the forest and ascend the mountains, there to behold for ourselves this mystical castle, this rumour-shrouded ancestral seat. Everything that is within me cries out that it is folly, yet all the same I shall walk with Gabriel without hesitation or question. For that is the nature, is it not, of love?

I have written for too long and I am tired. To bed now and to sleep. Pray God that I do not dream of the wolf, of his deep and blazing eyes.

NOTE LEFT ON THE PERSONAL WRITING DESK OF ARNOLD SALTER*

11 November

Dear Mrs Everson,

I suppose it must be you who finds this message. No doubt its contents will cause you some distress. For this – sincere apologies.

At least I have chosen to do the deed far from home. I know how you hate surprises and unexpected mess. Besides, you have always been a loyal servant to me. I would never want to burden you with the discovery of my corpse.

I hope you are not too shocked by all this, Mrs E. Two years now I have been without my Mary and deuced hard years they have been.

There is no love in my life. My career is behind me. I have grown old and weary. I scarcely recognise this country as the England of my youth. The present generation have none of our resourcefulness and fire, and the nation is sliding into slothfulness, incompetence and disarray.

I want you to know that my decision was not taken lightly. By the time you read this I shall be at the bottom of the Thames, sleeping soundly, my pockets filled with stones.

In the top drawer of this desk you will find an envelope, which contains instructions for the disbursement of my estate. Please place this in the hands of my solicitor. Beneath that, you will find a particular sum of money

---

*Deputy editor of *The Pall Mall Gazette* 1888–1901.

in cash. This is for you with grateful thanks for all your service. I hope it will let you consider retirement at last.

With thanks,
Arnold Salter

FROM THE DIARY OF
ARNOLD SALTER

———◆———

12 November. Now here is a surprise. I am starting a diary.

D—n me and d—n my eyes, but this is an unexpected thing. Mostly (and not to put too fine a point on it) because I fully expected by now to be dead.

I had my final resting place all mapped out. It was to be a spot on the Embankment from where I could take a single forceful leap into the Thames. I even believed myself to have written my own last words by way of a note to the stalwart Mrs Everson.

I have to say it was with relief that I set down those last sentences and laid my pen aside. But here I am in the light of next morning, writing on the first page of a fresh journal and about to begin what looks like a new chapter in my life.

I should explain.

Having put my affairs in order, I took myself down to the Embankment, stopping now and again as I walked to pick up any stone I happened to see on the ground. I selected only the smoothest. In spite of the solemnity of my expedition I made a bit of a game of it: careful each time to pick the best flints and pebbles, weighing each addition carefully in my hand before tucking it away in a jacket pocket. In this simple diversion I took an almost childish pleasure.

But then how rare it is nowadays, I thought, to see real children abroad and so easily diverted, let innocently loose upon the streets. We live in a sad and cynical world that has come to mistrust such harmless pastimes.

Weighed down, I arrived at the spot I had chosen. It was as secluded as I had hoped, with few pedestrians, poor light, and railings which had been partly torn away. I dare say there was even a jauntiness to my step as I approached the place where I had intended to abandon myself to the mercies of the river.

I halted, glanced about me, climbed onto the ledge and looked down at the surging water of the Thames. In the distance, I saw a tug towing a string of barges. And at the sight I felt a peacefulness, knowing I was shortly to be set free of all of the cares of this world.

For a moment, I thought about the past and how things used to be. I thought of the happiness which has been taken from me. I felt no particular doubt, or anything in that line. In fact, a brief survey of my present existence served only to persuade me that I should jump right away and be done with the business.

I was about to do just that when I heard from somewhere close at hand five unexpected words, delivered in a cool, patrician drawl.

'I say, sir, excuse me?'

On the very edge of leaping, I had first to correct my balance before, arms flapping like a d—n chicken, I was able to turn around with even the slightest dignity.

A stranger stood a short distance away, looking up at me. A lean and weathered man with great, arched eyebrows, he was dressed in a frock coat that had not been fashionable since the early '80s.

At his side was an elderly Irish wolfhound. It growled with disapproval.

In spite of the circumstances, I did my best to be sociable. 'Yes? How can I help you?'

'On the contrary, my dear Mr Salter, I think that it is you who will be able to assist me. Or, at least, that we may yet in several ways help one another.'

'Do I know you, sir?'

'To the best of my knowledge, Mr Salter, we've never met before tonight. But I fancy that it is possible you know me by reputation. You may have heard my name a time or two in the course of your brilliant career. I am Lord Tanglemere.'

Now, this rang a distant bell. A member of the Upper House. A politician but a decent enough representative of his class, honest and of the old school. What he could want with me, I had no idea. 'What is it? I was about to... Well. Let's say: I'm busy.'

'Mr Salter. I think we are all very well aware what it is that you are contemplating. Nonetheless, I should like to beg your attention for a moment so that I might be permitted to propose an alternative.'

Tanglemere crouched down and rubbed the back of his dog's head with affection.

'What do you mean?'

'It has of late come to my attention that this once mighty nation of ours is falling into a most regrettable state of disrepair. The grass grows long, Mr Salter, and the barbarians surge at our gates. We all of us need to return to a stronger time. We must restore ourselves by any means within our power.'

'I don't disagree,' I said as a seagull swooped noisily by.

'And, as it happens, I know of an ideal mechanism by which it might be achieved. I can see how this necessary restitution might be wrought. Though I shall need your assistance in order to achieve it.'

'Me?'

'Yes. You.'

I looked down again at the murky water.

Behind me, I heard the dog yelp.

'But… my decision…'

'Can be overturned,' Tanglemere murmured. 'Your country, Mr Salter, has need of you. You still have duties, sir, and obligations to this great land which sired you.'

'But I…' I heard the chuckle of the river, calling me to it. A breeze pushed, casually but with some persistence, on the small of my back.

'You must, Mr Salter. After all…' Lord Tanglemere stepped closer. 'Would not your Mary have expected you to do your duty?'

'How do you—' I began, then stopped and nodded firmly. 'Yes, my lord. She would.'

'Well, then. You are needed, Mr Salter. We have much work still to do if we are to save this country from wrack and from ruin. If we are to save her from men who apologise too often for being as we naturally are. From those who would weaken our nation with limp and impractical softness in the name of their so-called modernity.'

At his words, I stepped back with some determination from the brink. 'My lord,' I said with unexpected eagerness. 'I agree upon every point. How often have I looked around me and thought the state of this nation comparable to the last days of Rome. But how will this great task be brought about?'

Tanglemere seemed pleased. I felt a pinch of happiness.

'Tell me, Mr Salter. Have you ever heard of that remarkable – and, I've always believed, rather overlooked – public body that is known as the Council of Athelstan?'

'The Council...' I said. 'Yes. But only dimly. As a rumour. A whisper.'

'We are a hereditary group which can, in certain circumstances, be permitted to circumvent Parliament and the Upper House and take control of the state.'

I swallowed hard. 'In what circumstances, my lord, could that possibly come about?'

'In conditions of... emergency.'

'But, my lord, from where would such an emergency originate?'

Tanglemere smiled as the dog beside him growled, low and deep. 'Can you not sense it, Mr Salter? Can you not feel it on the wind? The emergency we need is already on its way.'

LETTER FROM MINA HARKER TO DR JOHN SEWARD

13 November

My dear Jack,

I write to you today, hardly for the first time in our long acquaintance, with a marvellous sense of gratitude. What a treasure is Miss Sarah-Ann Dowell! What a diligent, sweet-natured girl. Thank you for your generosity in sending her to us and for your touching, though quite unnecessary, insistence upon paying her wages.

She arrived late yesterday afternoon, shortly before nightfall, and we all took to her at once: to her kind nature, her demureness and eagerness to please. Both Quincey (and even Jonathan) are quite smitten, I think!

She is very young (not more, I would venture, than nineteen?) but she seems to me to have a wisdom far beyond her tender years. She has already proved herself to be an excellent nursemaid, and her very presence has cheered considerably our beleaguered household and provided a most welcome restorative.

There is, alas, no change in the Professor's condition. He remains wholly insensible. One of us is always with him – dear Sarah-Ann in particular – and, although we all hope that his strength is, by some miracle, being restored as he slumbers, the prognosis is poor. Our sottish local doctor visited this morning and, very grave in his manner, informed us that the Dutchman's powers continue to fade. Another stroke, even one half so potent as that which felled him upon our anniversary night, will, said the physician, prove fatal.

Do come and visit us soon, dear Jack, whenever you can.
We should all be delighted to see you (Sarah-Ann speaks of
you as the very kindest of employers) but, more than that,
it is now quite clear to me that any future opportunities to
see the Professor are dwindling by the day.

Until then, believe me to be your good and faithful friend,
Mina Harker

PS. Would you be so kind as to tell Arthur the latest
news? I cannot seem to bring myself to write two such
sad letters in a single day.

MINA HARKER'S JOURNAL

———◆———

13 November. I have written to Dr Seward to tell him of recent developments. I will not rehearse again those dispiriting details here. Suffice to say that while I have given Jack the facts – the arrival of Miss Dowell; the sad continuance of the Professor's condition; the practitioner's mournful diagnosis – I could not provide him with the complete truth. That is to say, the truth about my fears, concerning the Professor's ominous last words, the sense that his death is but a single sudden shock away, and, above all, of my inexplicable disquiet concerning Miss Sarah-Ann Dowell.

Dear me, but she is so very pretty and so young. She seems to me to resemble some little doll whose surface hides an awful vulnerability. Jonathan noticed this at once, for all that he tried to hide it. With something like a rush of indignation, which I know does me no credit, I saw the way in which he looked at her. I glimpsed the appetite in his eyes. I feel – and I would not entrust such thoughts to any pages but these – as though we are surrounded by an air of impending disaster, that we are living through the long, hot, arid days which prefigure the coming of a storm.

And why do I find myself thinking with such frequency of the last words of the Professor before his collapse? Surely they were meaningless and phantastical? Yet they had the ring, did they not, of a warning? There can be nothing to them. Nothing at all.

FROM THE DIARY OF
ARNOLD SALTER

————◆————

14 November. The instincts of a good journalist never fade away. They might hibernate awhile but, in any hour of need, they always come roaring back to life.

I am nobody's fool and nobody's catspaw. And so today, in advance of a meeting due later in the week with a certain noble lord of my recent acquaintance, I made a familiar pilgrimage, to Number 14 Eden Street and the house of Mr Alistair Clay.

He was little changed since last I had seen him, at the end of the '90s when he had provided me with that crucial item of information about Lord Ernsbrook and his dalliance with his neighbour's cook. A slim, attentive man with the capacity for a sort of blank charm, Clay remains the ideal source for any inky-fingered excursion which might be necessary when dealing with the upper echelons of society.

He received me as graciously as ever, though I noticed he was shaky on his feet. There was an occasional tremor in his hands, and lines about his rheumy eyes which I had not seen before.

D—n me, if age isn't a savage and uncaring business!

★

'I was surprised to receive your note,' he said once we were both sitting down, with a small glass of something strong set in front of us. His servant is a tall, handsome fellow who moved between us throughout the conversation as a model of discretion. 'I thought you had retired.'

'Who's to say I haven't? But I like to remain informed. I like to keep my ear to the ground.'

Clay looked at me thoughtfully. 'Are you planning something?'

'I'm too d—d old,' I protested, 'for planning anything except my own d—d funeral.'

He smiled, rather unhappily. 'Tell me what you want from me.'

'Lord Tanglemere,' I said. 'You know the man?'

Clay winced. 'I know his reputation. And I have met him. On no more than four occasions. He moves in the very highest of circles, including several from which even I am perpetually barred.'

'And what's your appraisal of the fellow?'

'A decent man. A patriot. Singularly determined...'

'But?'

'He is perhaps rather too old-fashioned in certain of his views.'

'No such thing,' I said stoutly.

'And more than that...'

'Yes?'

Clay hesitated, and in the moments that passed before his reply the young servant came again to both of us and replenished our glasses.

'Of course, this is nothing more than a rumour – and of the most scurrilous kind...'

'Tell me,' I said.

'It's rumoured that he longs for a master.'

'Sorry. Don't follow.'

'His life has been one of service, you see, and he longs now to be led by another. The Council of Athelstan, of which he is a member, seemed once to offer such a possibility in the shape of Lord Godalming.'

'I've heard of him,' I said. 'I remember his father. And I've heard the son is not all he might be. So who then is working with Tanglemere? Who is amongst his faction? And from where is this great leader meant to spring?'

Clay spread wide his trembling hands. 'Who can say? I've not quite the connections I used to have, you know. I hear nowadays only gossip of the most ephemeral sort.'

'But can you trust him?' I asked. 'Be honest now.'

'I would,' Clay said carefully. 'I would trust him, but only if your ambitions happen to accord with his – namely, to turn back the years and see this England as she used to be.'

'Then to that,' I said, 'I can most certainly drink.'

We made a toast and clinked our glasses. Even this action seemed to tire poor Clay and he sent me away not long afterwards, declaring himself to be exhausted. By the end of our conversation, his whole form seemed to twitch and shake, all quite beyond his control.

Yet what he said about Tanglemere and the Council stayed with me. I spy distinct possibilities. Yes. Distinct possibilities for change.

DR SEWARD'S DIARY
(kept in phonograph)

———◆———

15 November. During these past three days, I have observed within me to a marked degree a quality of melancholia. This I ascribe to the following events:

(i) The sad decline of Professor Abraham Van Helsing

(ii) My interview with Lord Godalming yesterday evening

(iii) Hardest to admit: the absence of a certain Miss Sarah-Ann Dowell.

There is not the slightest doubt in my mind that, in sending her away, I have made the only morally correct decision that was available. I could no longer continue to avoid acknowledging those feelings which she invoked in me or to accept how the sight of her sweet face, haloed with blonde tresses, kindled in my breast passions which have slumbered ever since I was widowed. To have acted upon those emotions in any way would have been thoroughly wrong and against my professional responsibilities. Even were this not so, she is more than twenty years my junior, and so strikingly pretty that even were I a very much younger man I should have had not the slightest chance of winning her.

I have sent her from me both so that she might do good at the Harkers' home and to spare myself from acting in the manner of some latter-day Malvolio. There is no doubt – no doubt at all – that I have behaved with decorum and made, if perhaps a little later than might ideally have been the case, a correct and proper judgement.

Concerning point (ii) – my meeting with Lord Godalming. We had supper together last night at Boodle's, just one of a clutch of clubs of which the noble lord is a member. It struck me at once how pale and ill at ease he seemed, how unlike his usual self. He is, naturally, kept extremely busy by his duties in the House. Indeed, he was late to the table, having had to chair a meeting of some Council or other of which he is a hereditary member. Yet this alone is scarcely sufficient to explain his visible diminution. I had no wish to add to his burdens, yet in her letter Mina did give me my orders which I should never have dared to disobey.

Over wine, I provided him with a précis of Van Helsing's persisting condition.

He nodded gravely and, speaking with that thoughtfulness which has in recent years come to characterise him, said: 'I suppose that his life has been a full and a rich one. He can have few regrets. He has wrought much good in the world and done more than most to stamp out evil.'

At this, he gave me a level, meaningful look – for we both knew full well to what he was referring. For an instant it was as though our surroundings had dropped away and we were back in the thick of our battle against the Transylvanian, both of us young once more. Then the effect vanished and we were in the twentieth century and again sober, sensible, methodical gentlemen of middle years.

I could tell that something troubled him beyond what was set before us. He has, after all, lately received the very happiest of news, although his behaviour is far from that which might be expected of any imminent father. Indeed, he seemed unwilling at first to respond to my enquiries concerning Caroline's wellbeing, or their future hopes and plans. As our supper was brought to us and much was drunk, Art would speak only of work matters, his labours at the parliamentary coalface, his efforts to reshape and modernise the system.

To all this I listened with that brand of calm patience which has for a pair of decades formed the cornerstone of my professional practice. At length, however, I grew tired of his prevarications and asked him, with a directness and intensity which would have been impossible were it not for the nature of our shared experiences, to state the reason for his sorrowful and distracted air. My words were almost harsh in tenor yet his response was dazed, like a man awakening.

'Forgive me, Jack. I ought to have been candid with you from the first.'

'But what is it? Tell me.'

'It's Carrie and the life which grows within her. Being with child... it does not seem to suit her. Not to suit her, you understand, at all.'

'Oh? What exactly are her symptoms?'

'She weeps often. She insists on being by herself for great stretches of the day. And she says... she says the very strangest things.'

'To you?'

'No, not to me. To herself, I think. Or perhaps to God. At least she does so when she believes me to be out of earshot.'

I gave him my most reassuring look. 'Such cases are not uncommon. The process is always a vexing one, all the more so for a woman with the history that your wife possesses.'

At this, Art looked but little comforted.

'Would you like me to see her?' I asked. 'To speak to her? To see if I can't get to the root of the problem?'

This was evidently the suggestion for which he had been waiting.

'Thank you,' he said, then added anxiously: 'There's nothing unorthodox in it, is there? I mean. After all...' He paused, swallowed and seemed almost to flinch before continuing. 'You were her doctor once before.'

'Of course,' I said. A silence settled between us, most uncomfortable in nature.

Eventually conversation resumed and we spoke of other things, general and impersonal, although with a feigned carelessness which would have fooled none but the most casual observer. We arranged for Carrie to visit me at the surgery on the morning of the seventeenth. Arthur mentioned a desire to see the Professor in the very near future, an event which, for obvious reasons, I was considerably less than helpful in fixing immediately in my diary. Of this, I am far from proud.

We parted early, on good terms but, as is ever the case, with a very great deal left unsaid. I have busied myself since with work in the hope that these exertions will dispel the cloud which seems to hang over me with such malign insistence.

★

Later. I have just woken from dreams of the most frank sort. I cannot recall having experienced such lurid intensity since I was a boy. As I speak, I am all but quivering with shame. What a fool I have become. What a prematurely aged fool.

FROM THE PRIVATE JOURNAL
OF MAURICE HALLAM

——————◆——————

15 November. Love leads one to the strangest of places, into the darkest dells and to the highest and most windswept plateaus.

The day after our meeting in The Gored Stag, everything proceeded as had already been decided. We settled our bills in the hotel (in this, Mr Shone was most generous) and we both did our utmost when replying to the landlady's questions concerning our next destination to deploy only tactful evasions. Even with the use of my own rusted talent, I doubt that she was entirely fooled, though she wished us well and made us promise – like schoolboys! – to say our prayers every night before bed.

As we left, each with a single suitcase (how very light we travel for modern men!), I saw that simple, stout-hearted woman make the sign of the cross, floridly and with feeling.

We spoke then only of fripperies and of beauteous things, the last such conversation we have to date enjoyed. We met Ileana at the appointed place and at the appointed hour. I believe that I hid my disappointment successfully when her svelte form stepped from the shadows and she smiled hungrily at us both.

'Are you ready? Truly ready in your hearts to step out of the known world and go into the wild? Are you prepared to be thrusting aside the veil of civilisation and entering the forbidden?'

'We are,' Gabriel declared, at which her smile only widened.

For myself, I said nothing, and she must have taken silence to betoken my consent. She turned away from us, then beckoned us to join her and almost hissed the words 'Come with me'.

We walked out of Brasov and into what lies beyond.

How to describe the days that followed without recourse to needless drama or to language of a garish sort? I shall do my best to be both accurate and brisk. Yet the task is not so simple, for time in this dark and rustic place seems to run rather differently than it does in the well-lit thoroughfares of the town. It seems tangled and mirrored, and many details of the last days seem now to me to be distant and confused, almost as if I had not lived through them at all.

Of any discourse that was shared between we three I can recall but shreds and fragments. Ileana, when she turns her full, attentive gaze upon you, has in abundance a soothing quality which makes all of one's fears and concerns seem trivial and transitory.

This is how our journey began. We moved from the outskirts of the town, past The Gored Stag, off the stony road and onto grass which lies towards the edges of the forest.

As we approached the trees, Ileana warned us: 'Stay on the path. Never be leaving it except with my permission.'

Beneath that canopy was another world entirely. It was quiet and damp and cool. At first, the silence was broken only by the busy rustlings of the undergrowth, by the small creatures dwelling there who, startled by our arrival, fled at our approach.

Ileana strode ahead, a lithe, determined silhouette amongst

the trees. She beckoned. 'Come. You must be made ready before we go further. You must be prepared.'

Gabriel and I traded glances, and I felt instantaneously something in the way of a resurgence of that species of amused and witty kinship which had characterised our first meeting. His expression soon hardened as he pressed on and I followed.

We must have walked for two hours along the narrow path, through thick-penned ranks of trees, at the end of which Ileana was still just as she had been when we had set out, just as pale and beguiling. Gabriel perspired lightly and showed some signs of slight fatigue, while I was wheezing and desperate to stop. My suit had been made sopping and gross. We came at last to a clearing, at the fringes of which there seemed to be an encampment.

The place was arranged in an approximate crescent, a shape made also by a trinity of wagons, all of them painted a dark shade of red. A fire smouldered in the centre, and around it slouched four young men. At our arrival, more such strangers appeared, most of them male although there were amongst them some careworn women. A dozen of these individuals watched our approach with suspicious eyes. All were dressed in filthy clothes, tangle-haired and unkempt. They were dirty-faced and low-browed, a study for Lombroso in the cranial characteristics of those people whom we prefer to call—

'Gypsies,' Gabriel breathed. There was a distinctly boyish note in his voice, as though he thought himself the hero of the kind of story in which a white man journeys into darkness to gain treasure, and in doing so earns the respect of the natives.

'They are the Szgany,' said Ileana, raising her hand imperiously to keep us where we stood. 'They will be giving us what we need. But I alone must talk with them.'

She spoke then in the harsh, angular tongue of the Roumanian peoples. A vein of beauty was audible in the hard lines of its syllables. As she talked, the gypsies – how strangely she had named them – drew back, their manner one of exaggerated respect. She gave more orders (or, at least, what sounded to my ear like commands) and several of the women loped away from the fireside and into one of the caravans. There were no words that I recognised in the lady's monologue, although one in particular seemed to recur with unusual frequency: 'Strigoi'. I have no notion of its meaning, yet something in the shape of it seemed, somewhere deep within me, to resonate.

Ileana's speech done, she stepped back and took up a curiously choreographed position, facing the Szgany but with one hand, palm outwards, placed before the two of us. I could not be certain – though now I have my strong suspicions – whether this was intended as a gesture of protection or as a symbol of ownership.

To break the silence, one of the men produced an old violin and began to tease from that flaking, battered fiddle a tune which seemed to speak of lonely roads and treacherous mountains, of lost lives and the impossibility of true love. I turned to Gabriel and, having by now recovered at least something of my breath, spoke some words of Shakespeare's: 'Be not afeared, the isle is full of noises, sounds and sweet aires, that give delight and hurt not.'

He nodded but, fascinated by our surroundings, did not reply. I was, I confess, made extremely nervous by our having walked into the heart of such a place. Had the formidable Ileana not been at the head of our party I have no doubt that matters would have turned out differently indeed.

At last, one of the women emerged from a caravan, now

carrying in her arms a pile of clothes and a pair of battered packs. Ileana pointed towards them and said: 'These are for you. Change. Stow your possessions. Your old clothes are to be a gift to the Szgany.'

I began to protest at this indignity but Gabriel silenced me.

'If this is how it must be, dear Maurice, then this is how it must be.'

I acquiesced and agreed that, given the nature of the quest, the proffered raiment did seem rather more appropriate than did our city costumes.

'But where,' I asked, 'do we change?'

I expected to be shown to one of the caravans, or at least to some secluded paddock. Instead, Ileana smiled.

'Here,' she said. 'You are to be changing here.'

I must have looked appalled but Gabriel laughed.

'Come, if this is their custom then let us honour it. Let us be gentlemen in this matter. Let us be civilised.' And in defiance of all English decorum, he began to disrobe. At this sight, the music took a jauntier turn, almost mocking in its cadences. Reluctantly, to the sullen delight of that gypsy band and the inscrutable smile of our guide, I followed suit.

We left shortly thereafter, dressed in the drab, durable clothes which are worn by all the peasantry in this province and with our few possessions encased in those crudely fashioned sacks which are affixed now to our backs.

'So you are ready,' Ileana had purred, and it was true that I felt as if some preliminary change had been wrought in us both, one which should make us acceptable to the wild.

There is little enough to say of the interminable hike that followed, the long, exhausting, repetitive hours of walking, as we ventured farther and farther into the forest, less like explorers, it seemed to me, than children in some grisly fairy tale.

We stopped only once, for luncheon. Bread and cheese was provided by Ileana, who watched us tear and rip at our repast with notable disdain.

She must eat in private, when our backs are turned, for I have seen her take no food at all. She bristles with secrets and invokes in the breast of any observer a multitude of questions, the answers to which I fancy it might be best never to learn.

We walked on. There was nothing to be seen in any direction but trees. All was bark and leaf, root and bough, an arboreal profusion which seemed to eat the light and which rendered our existence in this primeval woodland one of near-perpetual dusk. The three of us were made as shadows, moving ever farther into a kingdom of shadow.

Eventually, we made camp. We built up a small fire around which the three of us lay.

'Do not fear,' Ileana said as we slumped miserably in blankets, watching the flames crackle and rise, 'you are being quite safe here. No animal will come close. The fire drives them away. You fine English gentlemen are both under my protection.'

So profoundly fatigued were we by the labours of the day that Gabriel and I went to sleep that night almost at once, heedless of the dreadful wilderness into which we had, with such cavalier abandon, delivered ourselves.

The following day was just the same as our first, a trek along a rarely trodden path, much grown over.

Little was said between us, although Gabriel and I occasionally exchanged glances of substance. We had no time alone in which to renew so much as an echo of our former confidentiality.

Once, in the afternoon, Ileana stopped beside the track and crouched to examine a trampled patch of grass. She brushed it – indeed, she seemed almost to stroke it – before returning to an upright position, murmuring: 'There is another in this forest. A stranger who is not yet known to me.'

'You can tell so much from a few twisted blades of grass?' Gabriel asked.

Her eyes flickered up and down his form with the expert's contempt for the amateur. 'My senses are acute, Mr Shone. I have honed over many years all the skills of the huntsman.'

He looked at her with a frank admiration for which I did not care.

We made camp again just before darkness fell. Gabriel and I busied ourselves with the fire. He avoided any conversation or intercourse with me. For a few moments we lost sight of our dark-tressed guide. She returned just as the conflagration was taking hold, with two plump, sleek rabbits in her arms, their necks neatly broken.

Precisely how all this might have been achieved in so short a space of time I have no plausible notion, for all that I recalled her earlier remark concerning the talents of the hunter. We ate well that night, though Ileana herself once again abstained. Instead, as we ripped with our teeth at the soft flesh of the animals, she spoke more and in far greater depth and detail than she ever has, before or since. She spoke of the history of Transylvania, and of its peoples, of the Boyar princes, of the aggression of the Turks and their empire, of the courage and resourcefulness of the Impaler.

In spite of our exhaustion we listened with keen attention, as though at the feet of a storyteller. Again we slept well, warmed by the fire, our heads full of tales of warfare and bravery, heroism and blood, although I felt a little troubled in my mind by what seemed to be a growing sympathy between Gabriel and the woman.

Another day of hiking passed and we drew near at last to the edge of the forest. The trees began to thin and we caught glimpses of increasing duration of the sky above our heads. I noted that our little group was beginning to divide into two. Gabriel and Ileana walked ahead, talking more and more often, while I, old and aching, struggled to keep pace and, often, even for breath. I felt within me an uneasy queasiness, not wholly unfamiliar, as of that which presages betrayal.

Again, last night, we made camp, now at the very fringe of the forest, at the foot of the Carpathian Mountains. As we ate by the fire, Ileana spoke once more of the past, this time of the family that had resided in the stronghold which we were endeavouring to reach.

'The Dracula line,' she said, her liquid voice rising above the crackle of the flames, 'was once courageous and true. In ancient times they were devoted to the care and protection of their people. Yet, over the ages, something in them grew sick and withered. They became ruthless, avaricious and lost all vestiges of mercy. There was being said about them many strange things and many wild rumours flew. Who knows the truth of them now? The last of the Draculas died in the old century. There are no living heirs. His castle has been left to rot and ruin. The common people, they dare not go there out of superstitious fear. But we, my friends, are being far from common. We despise the ordinary. We spurn the everyday.'

In the course of these accounts, I observed not the lady but rather my friend. Gabriel's face was a mask of delighted attention, his expression one of adoring credulity of which I would not hitherto have believed him to be capable. Although I remain in a state of near-absolute exhaustion, I found last night that I slept only fitfully. I woke often from bad dreams and stirred awkwardly upon the ground, assailed by doubts and fears.

I cannot be certain even now that I saw what I believed I saw after midnight or whether it was simply the product of sleep-fancy, an hallucination born of exhaustion and unease.

Nonetheless, I do believe that, as Gabriel slept on, I woke in the deep of the night to witness the most outré of sights: that of our guide standing, entirely without her clothes, before the fire, her arms outstretched in some hieratic incantation. I am by no means an aficionado of the denuded female form but even I could tell at once that she was altogether remarkable. Her lean, athletic body gleamed with perspiration, yet was she possessed of softness also – firm, high breasts; large erect nipples; a posterior of smooth curves; that mysterious darkness beneath. At the sight I felt breathless, as though, like Pygmalion, I had witnessed a perfect statue come to impossible life. What man of the majority's persuasion would ever be able to resist her?

She was murmuring strange words in what I took to be her own tongue, all of them unknown to me save for one: 'Strigoi'.

I lay still, filled with obscure and nameless fears, watching this weird tableau through half-closed lids lest the woman realise that she was being watched. My attempts at deception were doomed. I had recovered consciousness for but a few moments before she sniffed the air and turned to face me. I saw then that some liquid substance trickled in the deep valley between her breasts. In seconds she was over me, crouched by my side, closer than she had ever been before. I smelled her then and I understood that there was something metallic in the taste of her, something sour and ancient.

I could not move. I was made helpless by her proximity. Her soft fingers caressed my face. Her breath, oddly cool, danced upon my skin.

'Sleep,' she breathed. 'Sleep, Maurice Hallam. There is nothing here that is for you to be witnessing.'

Even as she spoke, the world grew distant and all that was about me began to dim. I swooned and I drowsed.

I am not yet sure quite what it was that I witnessed when I half woke once more in the long hour before the dawn.

Now I tell myself that it must have been some manner of nightmare, one that was unusually realist in nature. Yet I am not certain. I am not certain at all.

This is what I believe that I glimpsed as I rose up briefly through my slumber: Ileana, still nude, athwart Gabriel, both of them crying out. Their bodies were lit by the wild capering of the flames and I saw upon them blood in considerable quantity. It glittered in the firelight. Strange shadows were cast about them, so bizarrely capering that it seemed for a moment almost as though the lady possessed upon her back nothing less than a pair of vast black wings.

Yet the moment passed, as in a vision, and I knew no more.

When I woke again it was first light and all in our camp was as it should be. Gabriel slept, looking as though nothing in the least could have disturbed him. Ileana was dressed again (if, indeed, she had ever been otherwise) and was sitting close to the fire. She smiled.

'Good morning, Mr Hallam,' she said, to which I replied in kind. She gestured behind us to the great wall of the mountains. 'Today we climb. Are you ready to come with me to the Castle?'

My mouth was dry. I swallowed hard and replied with a single, pitiful, croaking 'Yes'. I was about to ask her more – I swear that I meant to confront her about what I had seen – but then Gabriel awoke and the day began in earnest and my courage, such as it was, melted away.

We are to leave in minutes. This account I have scribbled during our last hour in camp. We are well prepared. Ileana beckons. The climb is to commence and we have a dread appointment with the ancestral home of the late Count Dracula.

It may be folly, but if I still believed in the divine wisdom of God, then I should most assuredly be praying to him today.

FROM THE DIARY OF
ARNOLD SALTER

———◆———

16 November. To Great Russell Street and to a sad little tea-room in the shadow of the Museum. According to the flaked and speckled sign that hangs above its door it is called 'The Pony's Trough'.

It was here I met Lord Tanglemere just after five o'clock this afternoon. He must have been early for our appointment as he was waiting when I entered, sitting in the corner of a surprisingly large room, with a pot of tea already set before him.

The air was clammy and stale. There was a smell of steam and second-hand tobacco smoke. The place was all but deserted except for two elderly matrons, lost in conversation, and a sallow fellow with a sloping, protuberant forehead who cast his gaze lazily about the room, interrupting his survey only to take fastidious bites of a thin slice of fruitcake.

Tanglemere waved me over. As I came closer, I saw that his old wolfhound lay on the floor by his feet, stretched out and sleeping. Close up, it is an ugly brute.

'My lord,' I said, trying to make sure I had the proper deference in my voice.

'Mr Salter. Do take a seat.'

Tanglemere indicated the chair opposite. I sat down, taking care not to wake the animal between us.

'This is a fine cafeteria,' I declared.

'On the contrary, Mr Salter, the Trough is thoroughly and drearily undistinguished. One could hardly imagine a less memorable site for our rendezvous. All of which, of course, makes it ideal.' He smiled briskly. 'Tea?'

The question was delivered as if it were a statement: a trait that is typical of men of his breeding.

He poured me a cup without waiting for a reply. I was about to thank him when he held up a hand to silence me.

'Ah!'

In a single, deft motion he pulled from his pocket an expensive silver flask which he proceeded to tip up briskly into my cup. I reached out and took a sip, identifying the spirit as brandy of a d—n fine sort.

'Thank you, my lord.'

He waved a hand. 'My pleasure. Besides, I really should be thanking you for turning out on so bleak an afternoon to so unpromising a venue.'

'But, my lord... you saved my life.'

He pouted. 'After a fashion, perhaps.'

'The least I can do now is offer you my loyalty.'

'Then that's splendid, Mr Salter. Truly splendid. Good man.' Tanglemere quaffed from his cup then placed it again on its saucer, its polite chink sending a signal that our preliminaries were done. 'Mr Salter, have you given any thought since our last meeting to the question of the present state of our nation? Of that creeping weakness which we see in every area of public life? Of that moral uncertainty which seems to breed in every strata of our once-great state?'

'My lord, I have.'

'Have you thought of the work that might be done by the Council of Athelstan?'

I saw no need, of course, to mention my researches in the company of Mr Clay. 'I have, my lord. Of course.'

'And have you thought also about the great good that they might do in the alteration of this nation's destiny if only they might be permitted to stand once again at the helm?'

Just as this question was being asked, the pair of matrons rose to their feet and began their various, complicated preparations for departure.

'I have, my lord,' I said, as discreetly as I could. 'Often I have thought since our fortunate meeting how much better might the future look if only the Council held the keys to the kingdom.'

'We are of one mind, then?'

'We are, my lord.'

'Well, the Council will have their day again. At least if you and I and certain friends and allies place our shoulders to the wheel and work towards that happy end.'

The two matrons stepped heavily towards the door and lumbered out of the premises.

'Thank you!' one cried with unexpected gaiety.

'We are most obliged to you!' trilled the other.

These words got for themselves no response at all.

'Mr Salter?' Tanglemere was peering at me. 'You seem distracted.'

'Not at all.'

'Concerned then?'

'How?' I said abruptly, for liquor tends to make me blunter than usual. 'That is my question for you, my lord. How might it be done?'

'This... restoration?'

'You'll forgive me for saying so, my lord, but it strikes me as all being something of a pipe dream. Surely nowadays the Council are very far indeed from real power?'

'Oh, but you must have faith, Mr Salter. You must believe. In truth, the Council is not so very far from power at all, not at least in strictly constitutional and legalistic terms. That, I grant you, is not reflected in the public's perception. Which is, I should have thought, rather your own area of expertise.'

'I see. And what would you have me do, my lord?'

'Only that at which you have always excelled, my dear Mr Salter: at speaking to the common man in his own language and persuading him to see the truth of things.'

'About the Council?' I said. 'Is that what you want? To tell the people about what they could do?'

'About what they must do, Mr Salter. About their inevitable return to the very centre of public life.'

I took another long sip. I was thinking hard.

'Already you perceive possibilities, Mr Salter. I can see that you do. Why, yes. The old energy is visible once again in your eyes.'

'Maybe, my lord. Or at least... yes... I can see where I might begin.'

MINA HARKER'S JOURNAL

——————◆——————

16 November. We have settled now into something like a routine which, if not precisely agreeable, is nonetheless sufficient to steer the ship of our family through these arduous times.

Miss Dowell has proved to be something of an angel in human form, a tender nursemaid who has become quite devoted to the Professor. She begins and ends her days by the Dutchman's side and she sleeps in the room adjacent to his lest he should, at long last, awaken. In all this she is unflagging and makes not the slightest suggestion of any complaint. Whatever Jack is paying her, it cannot possibly be half so much as she deserves.

The Professor himself sleeps on, drifting, I fear, ever farther from us and nearer to the undiscovered country. Only occasionally – in the fierceness of his beetling brows or in that benevolent smile which passes sometimes fleetingly across his lips – do I glimpse anything at all of the man whom I used to know and admire. Otherwise, he is fading still, passing from us in sad instalments. Our duty is to protect him until the end as once he shielded us and led us all together into battle.

So have our recent days been spent, in watchful care. Jonathan has been kept busy by his work although I think that this business has affected him more than he might like to admit. It has stirred old and unspoken memories. We have reached a point in our marriage at which sustained familiarity may have rendered necessary the revivification of certain now-buried aspects. I have tried to talk to Jonathan of these concerns, yet he hides in his solicitor's duties or else in the comfort of wine. This morning I said to him that if he will not confide in me then he ought at least to unburden himself in some diary or journal as he did once long ago. He said only that he would consider such a course of action. We all need some distraction. I hope that Arthur and Carrie will visit with us soon, and Jack too, although his practice seems now to absorb almost all of his time.

It is, however, Quincey for whom most of my concern is presently reserved. He remains with us, still free from his schoolwork on compassionate grounds. I know how devoted he was to the Professor, who was a grandfather to him in all but blood. Yet the boy seems remote.

He spends hours by Van Helsing's side as if the sheer fact of his presence might serve to heal the patient. When not in the sickroom he has taken to walking the grounds alone. In the company of Miss Dowell, he seems all but overcome with shyness, his face stained with scarlet. I am given to understand that all of this is common enough in boys of his age, yet there are moments in his silent observation when, although I do not care to admit it, he makes me almost nervous.

Motherhood is a most curious experience, about which no woman whom I have ever known sufficiently well as to even approach the discussion of such matters, has ever felt herself to be truly prepared. There are such changes, both external and also within, in the depths of one's emotions.

After Quincey was born, the bleeding seemed so very prolonged. Even the physicians were startled at its persistence.

They always say, the wise women and the old mothers and those who have no longer any daily contact with their progeny, that one feels love from the moment of birth, that one is somehow filled up with it, to a hitherto undreamed-of degree, like a chalice filled to overflowing. There is in this much truth but, somehow, not quite as much as I would once have hoped.

It is normal enough, I suppose, that one may not always like one's children. Yet is it ever to be considered natural that one might, in one's darkest moments, come actively to fear them?

LETTER FROM SARAH-ANN DOWELL TO THOM CAWLEY

17 November

Dearest Thom,

Here is a letter as I promised you I would write when we parted. I hope you will keep your end of our bargain and write to me too. I think of you often, dear Thom, and of the future we've talked of. I hold you in my heart like I hope you hold me in yours. I suppose you ache for me as I do for you. How long it has been since we were alone!

Now I must write a few lines on my news. I am safely arrived at the house of Dr Seward's friends, Mr and Mrs Harker. The place is big and lonely. Far from the village, it is surrounded by fields and trees. Though I am pleased to have been set free by the doctor, for (as you know) he always looked at me the same way a cook looks at the best joint of meat, this new arrangement is almost as strange. The patient is a Dutchman, very ill and not bound long for this world. He sleeps always and is easy enough to tend to.

The head of the household is a stern fellow who I hardly see. He seems troubled, for he was (so I believe) much loved by the dying man. He drinks too. I can smell it on his breath. Smell it like I once smelled it on my father but how as I never smell it now, dear Thom, on yours.

His wife is very kind to me and says as she is grateful for my arrival. She sometimes seems doubtful and I have even seen her hide from my approach in other rooms and wait till I have passed before she cares to emerge. And then there is their son: Quincey. He is but lately turned twelve years old but he seems so grave in his manner that he might be a deal older. He has noticed me and that I do not like. He looks at me with a hunger in his eyes which he does not yet completely understand. But it is a hunger all the same. He stares when his parents are not with him. I admit it puts me out of sorts. Sometimes it is even as though he looks at me with the lechery of an old man and not with the confusion of boyhood at all.

Do write soon, dear Thom, and tell me you is well, working hard at the shop and keeping out of trouble.

I love you and I miss you. All my kisses,
Sarah-Ann

LETTER FROM LORD ARTHUR GODALMING TO MINA HARKER

18 November

Dear Mina,

I hope that all is as well as can be expected at the Harker home. I met Jack in town some days ago, who told me of the Professor's sad lack of progress. Might Carrie and I pay you a visit soon? The twenty-first would be ideal for the two of us if it is also agreeable to you. We would see you all again after that sadness which truncated our last visitation and I should like once more to hold that noble Dutchman's hand and to thank him for the good that he has wrought.

In that spirit, we are still as we ever were, a crew of light with shared responsibility, each for the other. It is my understanding that Jack is paying for the services of a nursemaid. It would be our privilege if you would permit Carrie and me to account for all those further incidental expenses which are bound to arise as a consequence of Van Helsing remaining in your care.

I do hope that we shall see you soon. Carrie wishes in particular to speak to you. Her condition is a delicate one and I know that there is much that she longs to ask you concerning the mysteries of new motherhood. She is finding the transition more difficult and considerably more painful than she had imagined.

I remain, your very good friend,
Art

FROM THE PRIVATE JOURNAL
OF MAURICE HALLAM

———◆———

19 November. Three days! Has it truly been three days now? Or four?

Four. Yes. Is that correct? I think that, surely, it must be. Four days, since last I committed my thoughts to paper. Three – perhaps – since we have been trapped in this dreadful place, prisoners in an unending nightmare.

I write in an agony of desperation and despair, surrounded by horror and lost in a miasma of hopelessness. Time has no order here. It defies, wilfully and with contempt, the natural way of things.

From the last page of my diary I see that I described our encampment and that weird, half-glimpsed congress between Ileana and Mr Shone. What I wrote then may seem strange enough – fraught with confusion and fretful desire – yet my pronouncements are, I know it, those of a still sane man, albeit one who has been weak and foolish. But these fresh scribblings, if ever they be read by any living person, must seem nothing less than the ravings of a Bedlamite.

I feel all but certain that I shall die here, lost in this place of madness and disease. Yet perhaps these final lines of mine will one day be discovered and the full truth known or guessed. Might this ragged testament not even perform some useful public service, to act as a caution for the unwary? Might it not, if there be any justice, provide at last the necessary justification for this infested edifice to be burned to the ground?

But I should put things in order. Yes, I should strive to forge some sense from this awful, whirling chaos. I must urge myself to write the truth, even while my dearest friend in all creation screams and wails by my side.

Our hike through the Carpathian Mountains was arduous and long. Gabriel, quite naturally, fared better than I for he is a stronger, younger and more supple man. Yet even he, as we ascended and ascended, was seen often to shine with perspiration and to breathe laboriously. On four separate occasions, I even saw his hands shake at the prolonged and unstinting nature of our ordeal. Often I wished to stop and endeavour to recuperate but I was in this granted by our guide not the slightest quarter. Indeed, Ileana forced us onwards as we wound towards the summit. She seemed tireless, inexhaustible, and – it might as well now be admitted frankly – something more than human.

I do not know how long it took, that terrible climb. Did we pitch camp for one night? Two? All to me is murky and unclear, as swirling and treacherous as mist. Yet somehow I can see us – in my mind's eye – three puny pilgrims ascending the peaks.

At last – after who knows how long – we reached the Borgo Pass. From here lay before us only more climbing, still steeper and more harsh than before. We had no choice but to go on, to go higher still and to move ever upwards.

Once I laid a hand upon the shoulder of my friend. I know not from where I gleaned the courage yet I found it within me to say: 'Gabriel? Please. Must we? There is still time, is there not, to turn around? To go back to civilisation.'

He did not look at me or slow his pace. His voice, when he spoke, was oddly light and even approximated cheerfulness. 'Oh, but it's too late. Have you not yet realised, Maurice? It's far too late now for any of us.'

I said nothing but only sighed, dropped back and lagged behind. In pain, and weary as I was, I still followed, caught up in the irresistible field of his gravity.

At long last we reached a plateau. The mountains still rose on either side of us, and I felt as though we were as the smallest, squirming life in the midst of that range. Nonetheless, there was a palpable levelling out as well as a sense that we were again in a place that might at least be habitable, if far from desirable.

In the distance, we saw a vast and ruined structure: a great courtyard, and beyond it the tumbledown turrets of an ancient castle, stark against the horizon.

We stopped for a moment, so that we might savour the occasion.

'It is almost being upon us now,' said Ileana, 'the castle of the king.'

As she spoke, it began to snow, gently at first, then with increasing urgency. Most unexpectedly of all, the scene about us seemed suddenly beautiful – as though we had stepped not upon a desolate elevation in the depths of a forsaken country but rather into some old and elegant painting, as though we were moving into a panorama drawn from myth. Without feeling the need to say more, the three of us walked on, yielding without question to our destiny.

I have no wish to write – not here and not now – of what we discovered in that dreadful place, in the castle which had been, for generations, inhabited by the line of the dragon. I have no wish to write of what we found in that dank courtyard, nor even less of what we saw within, in the labyrinth of those filthy, echoing hallways, in those long-abandoned banqueting rooms which smelled of ancient smoke and ashes, of the bats which flew up at our approach or of the spiders that lingered too long in the light and seemed to me almost as big as fists. No, I shall say nothing either of the library with its odd English books, all of them horribly moist with fungus. The London Directory. The lists of the Navy. Whitaker's Almanack. It was as though the present were in some fashion the subject of mockery from the past.

Nor can I be persuaded to describe in any detail those empty – yet somehow still resonant – crypts beneath the upper levels, in which the memory of death was everywhere, in which we heard the rustling of rats and other vermin. And where we heard what was assuredly – but impossibly – something like laughter in the dark.

As to what occurred after the hours of our initial exploration, I cannot, if truth be told, now recollect each individual incident. Time, as I have said, is not honest here and I am granted only flashes of what occurred. This is what I can recall.

Something falling, some shadow, over us.

The smile of Ileana and the cries of Gabriel. The look upon his face as he clapped his hands like a child.

Then, the letting of blood.

Her teeth. Her sharp white teeth.

Something which befell me, of great pain and simultaneous ecstasy.

Something pressed to my lips – a silver cup, a vessel of antiquity, an unholy Grail – from which I was forced to drink.

Burning, burning in my throat. The sensation of something starting to unfurl within me, something old and hungry.

The howling of wolves, the children of the night, so much closer than before, as I lay, suffering, upon the ground.

A shout – of mingled triumph and pain from Shone.

Did we descend, all of us, into a fever? Into some nervous attack? Might this explain our present predicament? Surely it must be so. For to countenance anything else would to be invite absolute insanity.

Less than one hour ago I regained consciousness to find myself in an old, four-poster bed in a chamber in the castle, feeling more fully awake than I have for too long. Of Ileana there is now no sign. She has left us, I think. What her true purpose may have been in bringing us to this evil relic I cannot and dare not contemplate. As for Gabriel, my once-beautiful, once-perfect, once-angelic boy there is only a husk, an echo of what he was.

For I woke, less than an hour ago, to find him beside me, groaning in pain, his hands and face covered with blood and offal. I cannot coax him to speak. He is driven mad, I think, or at least he has ventured as near to that precipice as any man might go.

Something has been done to him. Some terrible wound. Some outrage.

Dear God, but his left eye has been removed! Now a gory socket gazes sightlessly out. He is frantic with agony. He seems not to know me. His whinnies of terror rise high in these uncaring mountains to mingle with the dreadful shrieks of the wolves.

What is to become of us now? What?

How blissfully easy it would be for the two of us – the actor and the one-eyed man – to fall together into insanity and death.

Jesus of Nazareth, if you have the slightest shred of reality, I call upon you now to save us!

Or the other – the Fallen One – if you will rescue us, then I am yours.

LETTER FROM ARNOLD SALTER TO CECIL CARNEHAN[*]

20 November

Dear Mr Carnehan – or Cecil (if I may),
I trust that this message finds you in fine spirits.
Certainly, I hear nothing of you but good things. The
Paper thrives under your guidance. The choices you have
made might not have been those I would have selected
were I still in your position, but that is the nature of
change. The old must give way to the young. 'Tis the
order of things and nothing to be scared of.

Though let it not be forgotten by the newer generation
that those of us who have gone before and have yet to
pick out a tombstone, may still have a store of well-earned
wisdom to share.

With this in mind, I wonder if I could visit you soon
(at your convenience)? Retirement suits me well enough
but I wish to bring a proposition. I trust you will indulge
an 'old dog' in this request.

I look forward to your prompt response.[†]

Yours,
Salter

---

[*] Deputy editor of *The Pall Mall Gazette* 1901–1904.
[†] I have been unable to find any trace of a response from Carnehan. I wonder if one was
never sent and that Salter, tired of waiting, simply presented himself at the younger
man's office. Such an act would have been altogether in character.

MINA HARKER'S JOURNAL

———————◆———————

21 November. I am so very tired, yet I know that I must write at least a few lines before bed.

Tonight, Arthur and Carrie Godalming paid us a visit. Art spent some considerable time alone with the Professor. He emerged from his vigil looking pale, forlorn and very much older than his years. He said little save to remark that he would tell Jack, with some measure of urgency, to visit us again at his earliest convenience.

We ate supper together. It was agreeable enough, though Quincey remained all but silent throughout. Sarah-Ann was invited but did not join us, wishing instead, she said, to attend to some correspondence of a personal nature. I suspect that she has a sweetheart to whom she writes, no doubt staining the pages with tears while declaring her deathless love. How well I remember the earliest days of our courtship, when so sharp was the desire to communicate with one's beloved that it was all but a need. Not, of course, that one would ever be desirous of living the whole of one's life at quite so heated a pitch!

After supper, as Quincey went to bed and the men retired to smoke, I took dear Carrie aside and did my best, as her husband had requested, to speak to her. Poor thing – she should be so excited at their news yet she seems positively cast down by the prospect of motherhood. I asked her why she felt as she did. Since she is young and healthy and in an excellent position, the reverse ought to be the case. She gave me a curious look and in reply would say only this: 'I am so fearful, my dear. I am so awfully afraid.'

'Of what?' I asked, as kindly as I could.

'Why, of the world he will be born into, Mina dear. Of the black and evil universe he will inherit.'

LETTER FROM DR LEON WAKEFIELD TO
DR JOHN SEWARD

22 November

Dear Dr Seward,

I trust that this letter finds you satisfied and well. We hear often of your work and, perhaps undeservedly, are pleased indeed to see that your reputation has continued to flourish and grow.

Here at the asylum we have striven since your departure to make improvements in order to ensure that the institution is a credit to the twentieth century. I dare say that you would hardly recognise the place now, so extensive have been our refurbishments. All the cobwebs of the '90s have been entirely swept away and I am pleased to say that our asylum can now be considered to exist upon the very frontier of modern medical science.

It is as a direct, though unexpected, consequence of these necessary changes in the fabric of the building that I write to you today. We have recently completed a thorough renovation of what was once the most secure wing of the hospital. In the course of this rebuilding something was uncovered which we had all thought long lost. It is a relic of sorts which dates back to your heyday at the head of our institute. The details of the matter are too delicate to commit to print.

I wonder whether you might care to take a trip to Purfleet before long so that we might discuss the issue in person? It may interest you greatly – the very strangest of connecting tissue from the present to the past. Besides, it would be pleasant to see you again, the éminence grise of our asylum family. I do not think we can have spoken for several years, not since the party that was held for your departure.

Yours sincerely,
Leon Wakefield

LETTER FROM LORD ARTHUR GODALMING TO DR JOHN SEWARD

22 November

Dear Jack,

Please forgive the brevity of this message for it is being written in haste and with no small degree of concern.

Carrie and I visited the Harkers yesterday.

Van Helsing continues to fade; you really ought to see him once more while you are still able.

I write to you now, however, concerning my wife whose behaviour, rather than being mollified by an evening spent in the company of friends and having spoken alone to the redoubtable Mina, has instead grown still more distracted and strange.

She cries often about the future. She fears the inevitability of the birth. Many of her complaints strike me, I am afraid, as existing once again upon the cusp of that particular kind of illness which is your own specialism.

Jack, I am bringing her to London two days from now. Will you consent to see her? There is no one but you, my dear fellow, to whom I can turn.

I remain, your very good friend,
Art

DR SEWARD'S DIARY
(kept in phonograph)

————◆————

23 November. Two letters of interest received.

(i)   From Arthur, insisting that I see Carrie tomorrow, in which duty I should be very happy to oblige. I have sent him a telegram to confirm that fact. He seems anxious and I must do my best to allay the worst of his fears.

(ii) From Dr Wakefield at Purfleet, his manner as sly and oleaginous as ever, determined to remind me in every line of his precocious ambition. They have found, it seems, some old souvenir in the rubble of the asylum and he wishes me to see it for myself. I have no notion what this queer antique may be but I have agreed to make the visit soon. It will be a little odd to return to that place, which was once filled for me by drama of the wildest sort, yet I dare say that sufficient time has passed that I can approach it in a spirit of nothing more than mild nostalgia.

In truth, these distractions are all most welcome, for they keep my thoughts from wandering into unwise spaces – in particular, those unhappy realms of the imagination which have to do with a certain young lady, now resident in Shore Green.

Her blonde hair. Her sweet smile. The delicate curve of her neck.

LETTER FROM SARAH-ANN DOWELL
TO THOM CAWLEY

24 November

Dearest Thom,

As it has been one week since last I wrote to you and as I have not yet got a reply I thought as I would write again. Thom, I love you but I know how you is easily led when I am not with you by your side.

I hope you is working hard at the shop and not falling back into any of the old trouble. Please do not be cross for I know you swore to me that such bad things are all now in your past. But I know what a pull the life you used to live can have on a man. The easy money and excitement. But keep honest and keep true, Thom, and keep at the shop. Above all, stay away from the Giddis Boys and your sweet Sarah-Ann will come to you soon and soothe you and care for you and we will be so merry together.

I think of you often here in this big gloomy house, though I am happy enough with my duties. The old man sleeps on and Mrs Harker is very kind. But it is the boy, Thom, the boy who goes on upsetting me. He still looks at me in that greedy way yet it has grown worse since last I wrote to you. He waits for me so that we might pass close together in the hallways. Twice I have caught him watching me from the corridor. I try never to be in the same room but, this is often hard as he is much with the patient.

Then there are his eyes. Much of the time he is an ordinary child but there are moments when his eyes

glitter and gleam and something old and wicked seems
to me to be gazing out of him.

Write to me soon, my love, and tell me all is well.

Your devoted flower,
Sarah-Ann

LETTER FROM DR JOHN SEWARD TO
LORD ARTHUR GODALMING

25 November

Dear Arthur,

It was pleasant indeed, in spite of the nature of our meeting, to see you both in my surgery yesterday afternoon.

As promised, here is my formal report upon your wife's condition. Following a thorough physical and mental examination, I should like to make the following seven observations:

(i) Your wife is suffering from abnormal degrees of anxiety and fear.

(ii) I would diagnose also incipient hysteria.

(iii) The cause is wholly mental and any physical symptoms are illusory.

(iv) I would recommend that she spend the duration of the outstanding period at home, in the most tranquil state. Surround her with peace and calm wherever possible.

(v) She must sleep long and deeply. Slumber can prove to be profoundly restorative.

(vi) To assist in this process I have prescribed strong pills, the first of which I gave to you yesterday. These have considerable potency. Make sure that she takes no more than five a day. I hope that these medicaments will staunch in her that torrent of disturbing nightmares of which she has complained.

(vii) I would for now suggest keeping her away from the house of the Harkers. It is an unquiet place at present and seems to distress her greatly.

I trust that the above will prove to be of some comfort. Please do not hesitate to ask for help from me of any sort. This and any further consultations will, of course, be provided entirely gratis.

My lord, these months before the birth will not be easy ones. They may be made more difficult by the odd resemblance of Lady Godalming's symptoms to some – although by no means all – of those which once afflicted a certain dear lady who was most precious to our hearts.

I have noted these echoes, my lord, and I have dismissed them. I would urge you now to do the same. The nature of our shared ordeal is that we see shadows where there are none and that we jump at the most quotidian of sounds.

In contrast to her predecessor, Carrie has always been acutely sensitive and unusually vulnerable to those travails which are inevitable in even the most cosseted of lives. I recall that I said as much to you shortly after the two of you first met, not long ago after she had emerged from my care. I know that you both have suffered in the past and that this forms part of the bond between you but, Art, I say this not only as her doctor but also as your friend: she is amongst the most fragile individuals whom I have encountered. She will require from you much love in the days to come.

I stand ready, as ever I have been, to assist in any way that I am able.

Yours,
Jack

TELEGRAM FROM LORD ARTHUR GODALMING TO
DR JOHN SEWARD

26 November

Thanks for letter. All assistance received with gratitude. C has taken to pills with relief. Says the dreams are fading. Hope worst behind us. I pray that all will yet be well.

Art

FROM THE DIARY OF
ARNOLD SALTER

———◆———

27 November. To Fleet Street, to the premises of my old employer and to the office of my successor, Cecil Carnehan, where there was waiting for me a conversation of the pretty b—y difficult sort.

Carnehan had agreed to see me, mostly out of courtesy. Even then he required a good deal of chivvying. Few things in the wide world seem to the young fellah quite so ridiculous as the pensioner, especially if the point which represented the high-water mark of the old man's career has already been reached (and, one may reasonably expect, is soon to be exceeded) by the upstart.

And Mr Carnehan is young indeed, being barely more than thirty: a tall, pointed person with a calculatedly firm handshake and a spurious layer of maturity.

He waved me into his little sanctuary (which once, of course, was mine) and asked me to sit on a new chair opposite his desk. The fact that he made me clear away a sheaf of copy which had been laid on top of it was not lost on me.

'So,' he began, once we were settled and after much

ostentatious checking of his no doubt d—d expensive pocket watch. 'To what do I owe this pleasure? Or had you merely a yearning to see the old place again?'

Everything in that young cub's manner, from his knowing deference to the impatience which flickered in his eyes, made me want to do nothing so much as ball up my right hand into a fist and plant it firmly into his face.

Oddly, this sensation roused in me not frustration or fury but surprise that I could again be capable of such emotion after years of numbness. I felt again the welcome sense that blood is thundering once more through my veins.

'In part, Mr Carnehan,' I said, 'you are correct.'

'It is always a pleasure to see you here again, sir. You are, after all, something of a legend in these halls. Fleet Street, Mr Salter, salutes you.'

I humoured him in his flattery. As though his opinion matters a tinker's cuss!

'You're kind,' I said. 'You're very kind.'

I managed a grizzled grin. I dare say the sight was a ghoulish one. 'But, you see, the truth of it is this: I don't believe that I am altogether done with the inky-fingered newspaper business. Nor it with me. At least – not yet.'

At this, young Carnehan played dumb. 'Now whatever do you mean by that, Mr Salter?'

'I mean I want to write for my paper again. Regularly and often. That is what I have come here today to ask.'

He smiled impudently. 'Oh, but I am afraid our books are quite full at present. As you are no doubt aware, the desks of this newspaper are all manned by a staff of eager new voices.'

'That, of course, I appreciate. But isn't there still space for a veteran? Can't the voice of experience be allowed to speak from time to time?'

The smile on Carnehan's face did not falter as he tugged free his pocket watch and glanced down at it. 'Pray tell, Mr Salter.' He stowed away the timepiece. 'What kind of writing did you have in mind? You are now a little too advanced in years – don't you think? – to be walking the beat or scouring the streets like a new-born pencil-pusher?'

'I had thought rather: a view from the hill. My own thoughts and opinions. We could call it… I don't know… how about "Salter Says"?'

Carnehan looked politely sceptical. 'Upon what topics, sir, do you intend to discourse?'

'The state of the nation. The follies of the current century. The dire and urgent need to learn the lessons of the past.'

My successor favoured me with a look of indulgence. 'I see.'

A long pause came which neither of us cared to fill.

At last, I said: 'I take it the notion does not enthuse you?'

'Not at all. It's only a question of…' He leaned back and steepled his fingers. 'The demands of business. I'm sure that you understand perfectly such commercial necessities. We have to give our readers what they want.'

'I always thought we ought rather to give them what they need.'

The smile began to fade. 'Everything changes, Mr Salter, and the world moves on.'

'You think there'd be no appetite for my opinions?'

'I think there is at present no appetite for sermonising. Nor for lectures from the elderly.'

'Perhaps that's where the problem lies. Perhaps that's why society has taken the wrong d—d path.'

'Perhaps, Mr Salter, perhaps.' His tone suggested that he thought my supposition an unlikely one. 'Yet the fact is that the public taste is for scandal, rumour and innuendo. Not, you understand, for morality.'

'Oh, I understand. Believe me.'

'I'm most glad to hear that.'

I looked him in the eye till he looked away. 'That's your last word?'

'I am afraid it must be. We have to run the tightest of ships here, Arnold. You know that there can be no place in a press room for sentiment or for old loyalties, no matter how individually worthy they may be.'

After he had said this, the d—d pocket watch came out again and he cast an appreciative eye at its face. I stood up and extended my hand.

'I'll take up no more of your time, sir. I know there must be many demands upon it.'

Carnehan agreed that these were indeed plentiful. 'Thank you so much for visiting,' he said, 'and more than that, Arnold, thank you for understanding.' Insincerity flowed through every vowel and consonant.

'Not at all.' I turned to go, eager by then to be back in the open air and away from this palladium of memories.

'Of course...' said Carnehan.

'Yes?'

'If you were to have something of quite another order for me... If you were to bring me some scandal, say, some grand, exciting story... something which would enthral our readers... then things would most certainly be quite different.'

'You'd put me back in print?'

'And be glad to do so.' His smile did not falter. 'But of course you don't happen to have anything for me of that nature at the present moment. Now do you?'

MINA HARKER'S JOURNAL

———◆———

28 November. It would seem that matters have come to a head with Miss Sarah-Ann Dowell and, I regret to say, with our son. The poor girl visited me this morning shortly after breakfast to confess her deep discomfort.

'It's not that I is ever one for speaking out of turn, ma'am,' she said, flushed in her face but determined in her manner. 'It's not that I ever want to make a fuss where there isn't no fuss to be making. Ask Dr Seward, ma'am. I'm sure he will vouch for me.'

I assured her that there would be no need for such a course of action. 'Go on, Sarah-Ann.'

'It's your boy, ma'am. I am sorry but it really is getting impossible. The way he looks at me. The way he follows me round the house and… lingers about the grounds. The way he watches me, hiding in the shadows.'

I shook my head in sorrow, a gesture that the nursemaid at once misunderstood.

'Please, ma'am, I'm telling you the truth.'

'Of course.' I did my best to soothe her. 'And I believe you.'

'His age is difficult. I know that. And it cannot be easy for him living out here just with you and with the old man dying so slowly.'

'Quite.'

'But he fair gives me the shivers, ma'am, the way he looks at me. He gives me the horrors.'

I nodded sadly. 'You're very pretty, Miss Dowell, and I am sure that you are well accustomed to the unwelcome gazes of men. So you must be discomfited indeed to come to me now. I shall ask my husband to speak with him. Better, I think, that such a discussion is had with his father. You have my word that we will in this matter be most stern. This is not how young gentlemen behave and we shall make that fact quite plain to him.'

'Thank you, ma'am. I do appreciate you trusting me.'

'Sarah-Ann, you have made this most difficult time more bearable for us all. I would not have you be unhappy here.'

The girl smiled bravely and bowed her head. When she looked at me again there was anxiety in her eyes.

'What is it?' I asked. 'You know that you can speak to me of anything.'

'You do know, ma'am, don't you?'

At her tone, I dare say my own smile grew a little tighter and more forced. 'Know what, my dear?'

'What's happening here. Under your own roof.'

There was, of course, great discomfort in her voice as she spoke, but also – unpleasant to relate – an odd note of amusement too.

'Thank you,' I said. 'There is little that happens in this house of which I am not very well aware.'

'Is that right, ma'am?' she asked, and, almost grinning now, turned to go.

And so, in this fashion, it was left between us. I shall speak with Jonathan when he returns from his office. There lies already about this place a pall of death and sadness. I will not have it darken further.

DR SEWARD'S DIARY

(kept in phonograph)

———◆———

29 November. What a curious day it has been, full of strange echoes and resurgences.

Intrigued by the letter of Dr Wakefield and, more than anything, I suppose, eager to be free for a while from this consulting room, I made a journey to Purfleet and to the old asylum there.

As I travelled away from the city, first by train and then in a fly from the railway station (driven by a coachman of the gnarled and taciturn variety), it felt almost as though I were travelling back into the past, deep into my personal history. Memories stood at every crossroads. They sauntered along each lane and haunted every field. These memories I had long considered faded things but, revisited now, they seemed rather to be infused horribly with life.

As we approached the madhouse along the familiar winding driveway, and as the place itself hove inexorably into view, I saw that Wakefield's boasts of modernisation had been well founded. The very shape of the building appeared to have changed. Whereas once it was squat and barrack-like it looked now, following its recent renovation, rather as though it had been elongated, stretched into something sleeker and less distinct.

Alighting from the fly and thanking my sullen driver, I saw that Dr Wakefield stood waiting at the entrance.

'Seward!' He stepped forward, with one hand outstretched. A small, neatly maintained man, he is more than a decade my junior, although (with a surge of schadenfreude of which I am now ashamed), I noted that he is in possession of considerably less hair than I. His always scanty straw-coloured thatch creeps backwards across his pate like a retreating tide. 'Thank you so much for coming,' he said. 'I appreciate that we at Purfleet are a little out of the convenient way of things.'

'Not at all. I am quite accustomed to the journey. In the old days, I made it often enough. But I confess myself curious as to the precise reason for your invitation.'

'Come in, my dear fellow, and I shall make everything plain.'

I stepped over the threshold, into what was once my asylum. Even the smell of the place had changed since my time. The hallway was clear, clean and well kept and there was everywhere a scent composed in equal parts of turpentine, soap and some unfamiliar fragrant polish. I dare say that there are a goodly number of reasons why such surroundings might be deemed more conducive to the recovery of the sick in mind than those of my era. Nonetheless, I found myself missing the character and spirit of the old place. All at once I felt, not for the first time, achingly aware of my years.

'Well now,' Wakefield went on, his manner briskly seigneurial, 'I thought we could begin with tea in my office, followed by a tour of the facilities. We shall hardly lack for conversation.'

'Dr Wakefield. I know how hectic your job can be. So why do

you not simply tell me precisely what it is that has caused you to bring me here today?' I tried to smile. 'I make the suggestion, you understand, purely in order to provide a mechanism by which I might inconvenience you to the smallest possible degree.'

He looked startled by my candour. 'Very well. If that is what you wish. Naturally, I appreciate your consideration. Nonetheless, I believe that I can do more than simply state my reasons for this invitation. I can show you. Please. Come with me.'

He strode away. I followed, purposely leisurely in my gait. Wakefield led me out of the entrance hall and into the main body of the asylum. We passed a succession of antechambers of a sort more befitting a clerk's office than a realm which had purportedly been built with the objective of making whole shattered minds.

This region conquered, we moved into the engine room of the institute – the cells in which the patients were kept. Unlike in my own time, many of these now possessed a clear glass frontage and I was able to perceive, as clearly as one might penned animals at a zoo, the lunatics themselves. Their conduct surprised even me – one who has seen all that any practitioner in my field might be expected to see, as well as a good deal else which lies beyond the general run of experience.

For tears, anguish and exhortations of every kind I was quite prepared, my heart having been hardened and my sensitivities dulled by experience. What I encountered, however, as we passed along the rows of these clinical quarters was wholly without precedent.

With no exception, every patient was silent and still. They stood at the edges of their rooms or, more commonly, sat as though at the commencement of prayer upon their narrow cots, closed-lidded or with blank and incurious stares. All, to a man, were singularly listless.

'How have you done this?' I asked the keeper of these convalescents as he trotted with self-importance before me. 'Indeed, sir, why have you done this?'

'Medication,' he said, neither slowing his pace nor looking back. 'A very considerable dosage for all concerned. I find it keeps them docile and allows the necessary time for their wounds to heal.'

'So you simply maintain them,' I protested, 'in this state of dulled compliance?'

'The results have been significant,' said Wakefield, as mild as a curate rebuking a parishioner over some liturgical wrangle, 'and the benefits have gone beyond all reasonable expectation. You may have seen a paper of mine upon the subject in the Lancet last year?'

'I'm a little behind with my reading.'

'Ah, well. Do let me know what you make of it once you catch up.'

We reached the end of the corridor and paused before one last cell. It was immediately familiar.

'You will notice,' said Wakefield, turning to face me once more, 'that this particular room is unoccupied.'

'I know...' I said softly. 'I remember... And I believe that I can guess the reason, even now, for its vacancy.'

'You recall then its former inmate?'

'I am most unlikely,' I said, 'ever to forget Mr R.M. Renfield.'

I pushed away those disagreeable memories which clamoured for my attention. I tried not to think of that zoophagous madman who had acted both as a servant to the Count and as an uncanny barometer of his movements. A sad, crazed fellow, who had communed with the evil one in all his forms, as bat, rat and pale mist, and who had met his end at the Transylvanian's own hands. Such was the grisly fate of the vassal who longed in vain to be raised above that state.

Wakefield bowed his head. 'I wonder if you believe as I do, Dr Seward, that there are some people who are so potent and so forceful, and some brands of wickedness that are so pervasive, that they linger long after the physical death of the malefactor, permeating places which had for them a particular significance. Something in the way of...' He paused, searching for the mot juste, '... quality or atmosphere. Some etheric aura.'

'I understand your meaning. You believe that some such process has taken place here, in the late Mr Renfield's cell?'

'Dr Seward, we have tried our utmost... We have cleaned and swept and washed and tidied. We have stripped it bare and we have repainted. We have done everything within our power to make this cell habitable to those who have fallen into our care. Once we even invited a priest to speak some words of cleansing and bless our endeavours. Yet the situation became intolerable. Any patient we placed in this room, no matter how disturbed they were upon entry, had increased in that state tenfold by the time they left it. My attendants would skirt the edges of the room, avoiding it at all costs, and several workmen walked out unpaid after a day's labours rather than face returning on the morrow. Oh, nothing was ever heard or seen. Rather, there exists a sense of some malevolent presence. Of some sinister, invisible watcher.'

'I see.'

'Do you believe me?'

'I think so. Yes. Certainly I have heard of far stranger things. So what, in the end, is your solution to this... disturbance?'

'We intend to use it as a storeroom. We want to leave it to be rarely used and overlooked. So that its memories might be allowed to fade. But – and this, Doctor, is the crux of my invitation today – in the course of that renovation work something was discovered.'

Wakefield opened the door to the cell and stepped with obvious reluctance inside. I followed. Although the place looked rather different than it had in the time of my own tenure, I felt once again the power of history, seeking to submerge me.

As I blinked I seemed to see the tortured face of Mr Renfield, pale and trembling, screaming his allegiance to his master, with his half-meaningless insistence that 'the blood is the life'. My throat was dry. 'You said that something was discovered?'

Wakefield nodded. 'We found that a portion of the wall had years ago been patiently removed, creating a narrow space in which something... secret was kept.'

'And what was that?' I asked, feeling an odd queasiness within me.

Wakefield gestured to the sill of the barred and narrow window which let into that unhappy space a bare modicum of light. 'We found this,' he said and he pointed, warily, as though at some toxic substance.

I saw that to which he gestured: a slim brown book.

'A capsule from the past, Dr Seward. A message in a bottle from long ago.'

'Whose book is that?' I asked.

'I think you know whose book it is.'

'Is this why you called for me?'

'Yes.'

'I see.'

'Please. You must – that is, we want you to take it.'

I stepped forward and moved to the window. As I came closer I saw that a white label, yellowing at the edges, had been fixed to the cover. Written there in spidery ink were the words: 'The Diary of R.M. Renfield'.

Unable to help myself, caught in the riptide of the nineteenth century, I reached out and touched the book itself. As I did so, unexpectedly and without the slightest warning, we heard the most terrific uproar from outside: a sudden cacophony of bestial screeches and hopeless cries. It was as if – and we learned later that this was not so very far from the truth – all the inmates of the asylum had awoken as one and were screaming their rage, anguish and despair, their dreadful comprehension of the pitiable hopelessness of the future.

FROM THE PRIVATE JOURNAL
OF MAURICE HALLAM

———◆———

30 November. When one is an infant one possesses not the slightest accurate notion of time. Rather one swims through existence much as might the hero of a fable, in which whole aeons pass in a sunlit afternoon or a single look of longing lasts for millennia.

As one leaves boyhood and enters that most gilded passage of life, time no longer seems magical but merely leisured, as if this happy period shall be yours for ever, an eternal moment of grace and beauty. Such thoughts are an illusion, however, and one day, time speeds up, first quickening its pace, then doubling in speed, then hurtling frantically towards the waiting grave. Years pass by so fast that one is unable to savour them or to appreciate their variety until, without warning, one rises to discover that one has grown old.

These thoughts I record here both as a way to order my own opinions and as a means by which I might approach the setting down of what has occurred to me since last I put pen to paper.

I am told that this period has been of eleven days' duration, though it seems to me as if months have gone past in scarcely any time at all, so tangled and confused has their chronology grown in my mind. There is much that is simply darkness, a void about which I can recall nothing. Whether this is due simply to unconsciousness or whether there are things that I cannot remember because my mind has blotted them out in order to spare my sanity, I cannot be sure. In daylight, I am able to believe the former. When night begins to fall, however, it is the second possibility which seems to me to be the only true reading of events.

Suffice it to say, I have little enough to offer posterity concerning my memories of the time that we spent in Castle Dracula. The last thing that I remember from that doomed expedition is the tortured face of Gabriel Shone, the bloody gash where his left eye ought to have been and my own plaintive shrieks for mercy. Before that are only images and glimpses as of a shattered kaleidoscope.

It is a dear hope of mine that no clearer or more detailed memories from that period are ever returned to me.

In my first real memory after the ordeal I woke in a soft clean bed and blinked into the light. Someone sat beside me, a stranger: a small, neatly attired man with dark hair, delicate pince-nez and an exactingly trimmed Mephistophelean beard, all of which served to put me in mind of that remarkable gentleman, M. Toulouse-Lautrec.

He must have noticed me awakening, for he looked down with a smile that seemed both unguarded and benign.

'I think,' he began, 'that you must at last be back with us. Welcome, Mr Hallam. I wanted to wait, you see, and to delay my departure until I was certain that you had been returned to the land of the living.'

Naturally, I had a hundred questions concerning his identity, our location and the wellbeing of Mr Shone... Yet when I tried to form the words I found that my body had turned traitor, that tongue, mouth and teeth would not conspire to permit communication. The man beside the bed seemed kind.

'Do not struggle, my dear fellow. Your recovery is likely to take time. Do not risk relapse by endeavouring to speak.'

I could only look at him, striving, by the intensity of my gaze, to suggest my gratitude.

'I saw you once upon the stage,' he said, as cheerful and as conversational as though we shared some old acquaintance, 'playing Banquo in the Scottish play. How well I recollect the feasting hall when the new king was surprised by your apparition.' He warmed to this reminiscence, growing wistful. 'You, Mr Hallam – all caked in white – a vengeful spirit from the past.'

There must have been more, and this bearded enthusiast must have talked on, yet I can remember nothing more. For as he said these words of welcome praise, oblivion surged up again.

There was afforded to me one further glimpse before I regained my faculties in their entirety. When I again became aware of my surroundings some considerable time had elapsed, for the light in the room was of quite a different hue than before. It seemed to me also that I lay in fresh sheets. As I struggled free of the darkness, I understood that I was not alone. Of the eager man with the beard there was no sign at all.

Instead, conversing a few feet from me and paying me not

the slightest mind, stood the figure of a stout stranger whom at first sight I took, being passingly familiar with the genus, to be a medical doctor. His interlocutor? None other than Mr Gabriel Shone, who stood with his back against me. I caught a fragment of their conversation.

The Englishman to the physician: 'But he has to be made well. He is vital to our plans.'

The doctor, nodding: 'It shall, mein Herr, be done just as you command.'

'Money is no object and no treatment may be considered out of reach. Maurice has to be returned to us.'

I struggled to speak but the effort exhausted me and produced not the slightest effect. As I sank once again into a vacant sleep, my eyes played the very oddest of tricks. For an instant, before the curtain fell, the shape and substance of my young friend appeared to shift and I seemed to see the outline of a very much taller, older man, clad entirely in black.

The apparition began slowly to turn as though it meant to face me. With a thrill of horror, I understood that I could not bear to see his face, knowing that it would no longer be the visage of my companion but rather that of some altogether malevolent outsider.

As before, my mind proved merciful. It snatched away this grim hallucination and in its place deposited the inky, starless void of my own internal night.

Then, this morning, I woke again in the bright light of a new day. My small room was empty. I must have lain alone for almost an hour as consciousness crept over me. As I grew again to know all my body's aches and plentiful discomforts, I swallowed, cleared my throat and realised that I was able to move and make sounds. At this understanding I felt surge through me a feeling akin to exultation.

I was on the brink of attempting to rise from my sickbed when the door to the chamber was opened delicately and Gabriel Shone stepped inside.

The first thing that struck me about my friend was the large and messy bandage which had been applied to the left side of his face, an alteration which, while certainly disfiguring, lent him also a certain wounded nobility. My second observation was that he was smiling widely.

'Maurice!'

He closed the door and strode eagerly towards me, taking up the chair beside the bed. 'Welcome back to us, my dear fellow.'

'Yes.' My voice sounded frail and hoarse and faraway. 'Thank you. But I... have... so many questions. Your... eye...'

Gabriel shrugged. 'A terrible accident in a treacherous place. Dreadful to be sure. It's all rather hazy now but I think I must have slipped and fallen. Ileana meant to rob us, you see, and perhaps much worse than that, but somehow – yes – the bloodshed must have startled her into flight.'

'We ought...' I began haltingly, '... ought never to have trusted her...'

'I know that, and I've learned the very harshest of lessons in the most unpleasant of circumstances. But we should put such grisly matters firmly in our past. We should improve ourselves by our mistakes and place our trust in the possibilities of the future.'

'Where...' I said, still struggling, 'exactly are...'

'We are back in Bucharest. At the hospital of the Children of

Delilah. And as you can see, we have both been well cared for.'

'How did this come to pass?'

'We were not alone in the forest. There was another man – another Englishman – close by. He is an expert naturalist. A specialist in bats, who was searching for new specimens. His name is Haskell Lynch and he heard from that dread castle our cries of despair. Oh, courageous man! Oh, brave and mighty naturalist! For he entered alone and brought us safely to civilisation. We both owe him our lives.'

'I believe that I have seen him,' I said, 'at least if he is a small man with a pointed beard…'

'Aha! Then yes, that was most assuredly he!'

'I must… thank him…'

'Alas, he has returned to the forest. His work is far from complete.'

'Then we have been the beneficiaries,' I said, struggling with every syllable, 'of some terrific miracle.'

'We have indeed. The Lord has offered us both a second chance – an opportunity to make good use of our lives. It is a chance that I for one do not intend to squander.' Almost absently, he brushed a cool hand against my brow.

'What will you do?' I asked. 'You sound so… determined.'

'I mean to go to England, Maurice. To return home and there to busy myself with work of the most important kind. With labours of redemption.'

'How…?'

'I intend to enter the political sphere. Already, as it happens, a place for me stands ready. For as Lord Stanhope's only heir, I am entitled to take up my hereditary position in the Council of Athelstan.'

'The Council of...'

'Athelstan.'

'But... I thought that was merely a ceremonial body. A relic of older times.'

'Oh it is. At least for now. Still, it will be enough to give me that purpose for which I have so long been seeking. And my question to you, my dear fellow traveller, my comrade-in-arms, is this: will you come with me? Will you stand beside me and lend me your experience, your wisdom and your knowledge? Will you be my aide, my factotum, my conscience and my guide?'

I was about to reply, to give him the only answer of which I was capable and to swear that I would not leave him, when I saw a line of crimson creeping down his face, dirty, trickling red slime emerging from beneath his bandaged eye. I gestured helplessly.

'Gabriel...'

The young man smiled, dabbed his finger in the scarlet and, most strangely, placed that finger in his mouth. 'Oh, but there is nothing to be concerned about, Maurice. The doctors have assured me that some leakage at this stage is still perfectly usual. Besides, a great truth has lately been revealed to me.'

'And what...' I stammered. 'What is that?'

'Why, Maurice, haven't you heard?' His smile widened still further. 'The blood is the life.'

PART TWO

THE
SHADOW
GROWS

POSTCARD* FROM RUBY PARLOW TO
CHIEF INSPECTOR MARTIN PARLOW

1 December

Dad,

I do hope this card reaches you. I prayed and sought guidance and thought it best to send it. Mum has been taken badly ill and I have come home from the factory to care for her. I think she has not long left. She is full of sadness and regret. She is asking for you. I think you should come home again. I know you have many duties in the city but if you do not come now I fancy you shall regret it.

Still, and for always, your loyal daughter,

Ruby

---

* The front of this card depicts the wreck of an old fishing boat upon the beach at Wildfold. The shattered remnants of its hull, looking something like a giant's ribcage, have been left to moulder on the sands.

FROM THE DIARY OF
ARNOLD SALTER

◆

1 December. I believe I have found my story or, to be more accurate, that my story has found me.

It was late, almost midnight, but I had yet to go to bed. Sleep holds little interest for me nowadays.

Awake, I was reading through a great variety of newspapers and magazines, hopping from one to the other without ever finding much to engage my attention or delay my eye.

How diminished are the journals of the present era and how far away seem the glory days. Take the Strand Magazine, Punch or Taylor's Almanac – pale shadows every one of what they used to be.

Then the doorbell rang and I was startled. I was already on my feet and making to answer the summons when it rang again, briskly and impatiently. Mrs Everson had long ago retired for the night.

For the third time the bell rang. I reached the door and heaved it open. There was a young man – or young enough – standing on my threshold with a shining bald head and a sly demeanour. I disliked him at once but I paid the emotion no mind. No man could have enjoyed a career like mine had he resolved to do business only with individuals of whom he approved. I often used to say that no reporter should be frightened of supping with a long spoon.

'Yes?' I said. 'What is the meaning of your calling so late?'

He smiled simperingly. 'My name is Dr Leon Wakefield.'

I gave him a small, tight shake of my head. 'Never heard of you.'

'Wakefield,' he said again, 'the alienist.'

I spoke the next words slowly. 'I do not recognise that name.'

'Well. That's as may be. But we have a mutual friend, I think. The noble lord?'

I paused and breathed in slowly. 'Ah.'

'And I have… information,' he said with care, 'about a certain former patient. Her story may well be of interest to you.'

I glared at the man. He looked unblinkingly back.

'We are on the same side, Mr Salter,' he said, 'no matter the public faces that we wear. In private and behind closed doors, I assure you: we are on the same side.'

'We are part of… the Tanglemere Faction.' This new-minted phrase came easy to my lips.

'Yes,' said Wakefield. 'Yes, Mr Salter, I like the ring of that.'

'Then you had better come in.'

The head-doctor walked inside. We sat together in my study and, surrounded by all the sad flotsam of contemporary journalism, he told me the story that will at last restore me to my proper place.

TELEGRAM FROM ARNOLD SALTER TO
CECIL CARNEHAN, DEPUTY EDITOR OF
THE PALL MALL GAZETTE

2 December

Scandal uncovered. Public interest clear. Prominent nobleman at heart of mucky business. Full story to follow.

JONATHAN HARKER'S JOURNAL

———◆———

2 December. It has been a while indeed since I last endeavoured to keep a diary of any sort. In truth, little since those old blood-soaked days has warranted such expansive treatment, my life of late being spent largely in rural seclusion and divided, in approximately equal parts, according to my responsibilities as a country solicitor, affectionate father and dedicated husband. Recently, however, matters have seemed to shift and we are once again caught up in the current of events: the decline of Abraham Van Helsing, the arrival of Miss Sarah-Ann Dowell and the sad fraying of our little circle.

I suppose that this last occurrence ought not to form too great a source of surprise. Our party was always an unlikely convocation, a group which could scarcely have had less in common: a Dutch professor, a young medical man, an English lord, an American hunter and, of course, Mina and I. That the bonds endured for as long as they did is perhaps unlikely enough and the present state of dislocation ought to have been expected.

Life, after all, tends towards decay. Everything, in the end, falls apart.

But I should stir myself from such fruitless thoughts in which, Mina tells me, I allow myself too often to become entangled.

She has a way of looking at me, when she says such things, composed of puzzlement, concern and, I think, a lingering disappointment.

Today, I had no choice but to broach a sensitive topic with young Quincey. Miss Dowell has been with us now for several weeks and, besides proving herself to be a diligent and attentive nurse to the Professor, is also a most engaging and attractive addition to the household. To Quincey, of course, a boy on the road to manhood, she is simply a thoroughly winsome young woman who has appeared in our home without warning.

His reaction to her is typical enough in a boy of his age, though I am given to understand that he has exceeded the boundaries of good taste and decorum in his conduct. She has spoken to Mina of her profound discomfort while in his company. Of course, we cannot permit any guest of ours, let alone one who is such a boon, to feel any anxiety in the time that she is with us. And so, meaning both to chastise and to explain, I took Quincey on a walk this afternoon, on our usual circuit about the borders of the village.

We were a little uneasy in each other's company. I have been somewhat distracted lately and he is swiftly growing up. At first we spoke of sundry things – of the weather, of that initial tranche of schoolwork which he has received by post from his theology master, the Reverend Ogden, and, at his instigation and, I thought, somewhat unexpectedly, of the child who will next year be born to the Godalmings. There was also a good deal of silence between us and our conversation was rather unsatisfactory. It is not an easy thing to be father to a boy such as he, who seems always to be struggling with some internal conflict.

Only when our house came back into sight did I find it within myself to say: 'Quincey, I have been meaning to ask you about a matter which concerns Miss Dowell.'

I think he knew that of which I was about to speak, for, at the mention of her name, he flushed scarlet. 'Yes, Father?'

'You like her?'

He nodded.

'You admire the work that she has done on behalf of the Professor? And you admire certain of her personal qualities? Am I correct?'

He bowed his head and quickened his pace. 'Yes, Father.'

'I understand that entirely. Yet there are times, my boy, when one can be too frank in one's admiration and too candid in expressing appreciation.'

'Father? What do you mean?'

'I mean by way of looks and glances, you see, and of, well, of lingering too closely to the object of one's affection... of haunting her. Do you understand me, Quincey?'

He darted a look at me of odd collusion. 'I do, Father. Yes, of course.'

'Well then. Let us say no more about it and let us consider the matter closed.'

'Yes, Father. Of course.'

We walked on until, unaccountably nervous, I added: 'She is very pretty, I know.'

'She is, Father.'

'But the world is full of pretty women and, some day, when you are a man, you shall make one of them your own and call her your bride.'

My son did not look up at me but gazed down at the rutted path for so long, and with such intensity, that it was as though he were mesmerised by it. When he spoke again I had the most curious sensation that it was not my son speaking to me at all, but rather another personage altogether. 'Oh, there shall not be one bride,' he murmured. 'But many.'

The effect was most strange. I sometimes wonder whether alcohol numbs my imagination (Jack, no doubt, would say that this is my hidden intention) or whether it serves simply to inflame it.

All that I said to my boy, however, was: 'Quincey? Whatever do you mean by that?'

He did not reply, but rather, like a very much younger child, he took to his heels and fled back towards the house, pell-mell and helter-skelter.

The incident struck an ominous note. To Mina, for the present, I have elected to say nothing at all. She is already most concerned and I should not wish to vex her further. Instead, I have vouchsafed my thoughts to this journal in the hope that patience and perseverance may deliver us all from our present troubles and bring us, in time, to some brighter future.

NOTE FROM CECIL CARNEHAN TO ARNOLD SALTER

3 December

Dear Arnold,

Many thanks indeed for your story concerning Lord G—. I agree that the public interest is quite clear and that it will prove to be of considerable interest to our readers. We shall run the piece on the fourth and your payment will follow shortly thereafter.

Although your talent is as sharp as ever it was, I fear that there is no call at the present time for your notion of more discursive articles in which opinion is propounded. No appetite for it so far as I can see. Should this change, you will be my first port of call.

Yours, most sincerely,
Carnehan

LETTER FROM SARAH-ANN DOWELL
TO THOM CAWLEY

3 December

Dear Thom,
This is the third letter as I have written you and still I
have received no reply.

Let me know just as soon as you can that all is well
with you, dear Thom, and that you have not fallen again
into your old difficulties. The more I think of it (and I
think of it often) I do believe I am meant to keep you on
the path of virtue. This is not to say, my darling boy,
that it will not be a path filled also with merriment and
fun. Write to me and smooth away the worst of my fears.

Things go on here the same as before. The old man
is fighting every day to keep his hold on life. It is a
humbling thing to see and he seems fearful determined
but I know there is but one way the struggle will end.

Something odd happened yesterday evening. I passed
the son of the family in the corridor and he stopped and
said that he wanted to say sorry if he had caused me
discomfort in his looks and glances. They were meant
to be admiring, he said, and never to unsettle me. As he
spoke, he went very red and stumbled and stuttered with
his words. So much so that I felt almost sorry for him.

I said as I understood but that he must not stare at
ladies so. He told me he would do his best to be a better
boy from now on. I said we should shake hands but he
only blushed still fiercer and would not do as I had asked.
He fled soon after back to his room.

It's like he has two different ways of being. One is a sweet, clumsy youth while the other... In that one there is a knowledge and a hunger which seems so unnatural. Perhaps, darling Thom, you could set my mind at ease? Can't you tell me all is normal and that I am worrying myself unduly, like the silliest of geese?

But, dear me, what a strange household this is! It seems to seethe with secrets and things left unsaid, like water in a pot just about to boil over. Write soon, my love, I pray you. Write soon!

Your little one,
Sarah-Ann

DR SEWARD'S DIARY
(kept in phonograph)

———◆———

3 December. I have of late been much occupied, and my mind has been more clouded than it ought to have been, by the making of a single decision.

The book – the journal by the late R.M. Renfield, a man about whom, in spite of my attempts to cure him, I know so very little – is on my desk before me, still unopened since my return from Purfleet. It is a queer thing indeed to see it sitting there as though it is but an innocuous antique, its cover scuffed and damaged, its spine crumbling and cracked. It is an emissary from the past, a voice from history which I had long believed to have been silenced for eternity. It waits.

According to a small voice inside me, I ought not to open the thing at all. This is very probably wise. I have managed so far to obey it. The past is the past, says the voice, and all relics from that unhappy time should be abandoned. Why not throw the book away, without reading it? Why not toss it into the river or give it up to the flames? Let it fall away now or let it slumber. What possible good could come from so strange a visitor from the old century?

Yet another voice, one more strident, more passionate and more seductive than the first, urges me to open it and to read what lies within. What harm can it do? it asks. Surely your curiosity will be sated? Besides, the chances are that the diary will prove to be overly dull, merely the repetitive ravings of a lunatic. Why, I shall most likely glance at the thing only once or twice, before casting it aside for ever.

Open it, Dr Seward. Open it, Jack. Open it. Open it.

FROM *THE PALL MALL GAZETTE*

4 December

THE SECRET AGONY BEHIND A NOBLEMAN'S SMILE

To hear of great and sustained misfortune is always a cause for regret, yet never more so than when it is applied to a gentleman of noble birth and influence. When the personage in question stands at the very head of the nation's oldest and most distinguished governing body, then perhaps the sadness extends still further, from a strictly private misery to a matter of national concern.

Such is the case of Lord Arthur Godalming (formerly Arthur Holmwood), who seems to be bedevilled by tragedy, bad luck and women of a fragile sort, to the extent that to the unprejudiced observer it begins to look like misjudgement. The aristocrat has led a life dogged by madness and mortality. He inherited his title and vast estate while still a young man after the premature death of his father. That same year he lost his fiancée, the notoriously flighty Miss Lucy Westenra, in circumstances which some gossips still say remain suspicious.

Four years ago, it seemed that a new chapter had begun when he met and fell in love with a young woman named Caroline Brinkley. Caroline, who is known to her closest intimates as 'Carrie', is strikingly beautiful, blonde-haired and charming. Sadly this is just a pose. A fragile nature hides behind this alluring mask. Lady Godalming has suffered all her life from maladies of the mind, and she has on occasion seen no alternative but to seek residential care from several leading alienists, including the eccentric and very expensive Dr Seward of Harley Street.

Did Lord Arthur know of his new bride's mental weakness and moral frailty before they were wed? Or was this kept from him? Was he kept intentionally in the dark? Was this a deliberate subterfuge? The country should be told the truth or fears of a weakening in the bloodline are bound to be widespread. It is a matter of continuing concern. Close friends of the former Miss Brinkley have recently confided that her old troubles have recently resumed and that a new collapse seems probable.

These sadnesses are not only a source of personal grief for the noble lord. For Godalming stands at the head of the Council of Athelstan, an old and mighty cabal, rich in legacy and tradition. It still has considerable influence. Should a man with so many sad distractions truly be permitted to remain in so exalted a position? For the time being, of course, the Council remains a largely ceremonial body. Yet if it were ever to reach out and claim again those special powers which are still its own by right, then would we want a man like Godalming to be at its helm? Or would we prefer another, one whose life seems altogether less tainted? For us, as citizens of the realm and payers of taxes, these are questions which must be answered.

(story continues on pages 4, 5 and 6)

FROM THE PRIVATE DIARY
OF AMBROSE QUIRE,
Commissioner of Police of the Metropolis*

———◆———

4 December. Another day of trials and vexations, all of which are to be expected when one has chosen, as have I, the paths of responsibility and duty over those of enrichment and individual gain.

When I was at school there were boys whom I often outstripped who now take home a fortune from jobs in the City or on Harley Street, who fill their days with agreeable, profitable labours in order to spend their evenings with suppers at their clubs or at games of whist with their neighbours. I am grateful that their fate is never to be mine. Rather, my time is spent in service to society. I flatter myself that I have a higher vocation than they, a destiny which will lead me to be remembered and appreciated after their memories have gone to dust.

On such days as this, these thoughts are a comfort. The morning began, as it so often does, with the delivery of a report

*The Quire diaries came into my possession long after their author's unfortunate demise. I believe that the Commissioner hoped one day to see their publication, following his retirement. In a fashion, perhaps, I am honouring his wishes.

marked for my attention. I read it as soon as I arrived and found it to be an unsuitable accompaniment to my tea. The report concerns the present state of relations between the three main criminal gangs of London – the Sweetmen, the Pigtails and the Giddis Boys – who would seem to be growing distinctly fractious.

I am told that there is no obvious reason for this degeneration in their behaviour. None has displayed any desire to extend their realm or to diversify their trades. Nonetheless, the truce (unofficial in nature though long observed) does seem to be fraying.

It appears that there was some sort of struggle last night in Clerkenwell between representatives of all three clans. By the time our officers arrived upon the scene, the villains had taken to their heels. Only one arrest was made – that of a thuggish and surly young lad affiliated to the Giddis mob by the name of Thomas Cawley. He is but a minnow in that criminal shoal though we will hold him for as long as we can. He may be able to provide us with some information as to the cause of this unrest.

On reading these things, one of my headaches started up immediately and proceeded to worsen over the course of the morning. By lunchtime, having attended to a good deal of outstanding paperwork and after having chaired meetings of the CTOP, the Vigilance Committee and the Metropolitan Advisory Group upon the question of Combating the Rise of Civilian Munitions, it had become all but intolerable. I supped but found no relief and I was about to summon a sergeant and ask him to prepare a pot of what we refer to as our 'Blue Brew' when into my office marched the author of the report which had started all the trouble: Chief Inspector Martin Parlow.

He is a short, wiry man, thick-necked and full-featured, nearing retirement and running to fat. He is not educated but he has a certain innate cunning which looks at times like wisdom, allied to a beagle's determination to run his quarry to ground. It is these traits which have made him ideal for our profession. By his side stood a considerably younger man, not yet forty, brawny and, oddly enough, American. He is originally from New York, I think. His name I really felt I ought to know.

'To what do I owe this pleasure, Chief Inspector?' I asked, doing my best to sound not testy but gracious. 'Has this to do with your report?'

'No, sir,' said Parlow, 'it does not.'

He added nothing further. Silence descended. I caught the eye of the broad-shouldered Yankee but he looked back at me just as impassively.

'Well? Why have you come to me unbidden?'

'It is my wife, sir,' said Parlow. 'I fear she has been taken powerful ill.'

'Dear me. I did not even know that you were married, Chief Inspector. How is it then that I have not, so far as I am able to recall, had the pleasure of making her acquaintance at any of our Ladies' Days or Yuletide balls?'

Parlow looked stern. 'She doesn't live in London, sir, but in a little place on the Norfolk coast. A town called Wildfold. My work has kept me from her, and from my daughter too. Their lives are their own to be lived.'

Evidently, the poor fellow has long been estranged and so lives quite separately, doubtless sending back home each month a portion of his salary. Such cases are, sadly, far from uncommon. I nodded once to indicate both worldly comprehension and manly sympathy.

'I fear, sir, that she may not be long for this world. I have not been an ideal husband, Lord knows that, yet I would be with her at the end.'

'Are you asking for a leave of absence upon compassionate grounds?'

'Yes, sir. I am, sir. I've never asked for such a thing before and I dare say I'll never do so again, but it was my daughter, you see, who's called me and I must not say no.'

'Of course,' I said, 'you must go immediately. We shall make arrangements for your absence. How long do you suppose...?'

'Two weeks, sir. At least, no more than three. And I thought, with me gone, it would be best to leave my duties in the hands of George here.'

The man by his side stepped forward. 'Commissioner.'

Of course! I remembered him now – Sub-Divisional Inspector George Dickerson, one of our few immigrants and a man who possesses, in equal measure, brutality and intellect.

'Ah. Very well, then, Sub-Divisional Inspector. You are fully appraised of this present situation? The pressing matter of unrest amongst the gangs?'

'I am, Commissioner. And I mean to interrogate young Cawley tonight.'

'Very good,' I said. 'You must keep me abreast of any further developments. You may report directly to me.'

'Yes, sir.'

I gave them both a smile which spoke, I hope, of generous finality. 'Well, gentlemen, if that is all, I have a great deal of other business to detain me today...'

They gave me their thanks and went towards the door. Dickerson left first, no doubt eager to enjoy his new responsibilities. Parlow lingered on the threshold.

'Commissioner?'

'Yes, my man?'

He seemed suddenly very distant, his thoughts no doubt in that little coastal town in which his old bride lay dying.

'What is it?'

He looked confused, almost bewildered. 'Sorry, sir. But... that is to say... did you hear that?'

'Hear what?' I asked, as jolly as I could.

'I don't know, sir. I can't be certain. Yet it seemed to me just then, just for a moment, that I heard, close and clear, the sound of a woman laughing.'

I assured the fellow that I had heard nothing of the sort at all. He apologised, blamed the fanciful thought on his distracted state and left my office. Sorry old duffer. I trust he will settle his affairs satisfactorily in Wildfold and return to us renewed.

Following the departure of Parlow and Dickerson I busied myself with ledger-work. Shortly after dusk, I summoned my secretary so that we might examine together my forthcoming commitment in the time – dismayingly brief! – which remains before Christmas.

There was some confusion over dates and a number of overlapping functions, meaning that my working day finished with a flurry of petty irritations. My poor underling felt, I am afraid, rather the rough side of my tongue.

I had meant to dine at the club, but somehow my appetite seemed almost entirely to be lacking and so I took a stroll instead. I went into the heart of the metropolis and I spent a pleasant few hours wandering through the great roar and rush of London's humanity, passing anonymously amongst the throng and bearing witness to the whole of our society, from the highest to the very low. It is important for a man in my position never to become too haughty in his post or to forget those whom he protects: the vulnerable, the weak and the law-abiding of this nation.

As the purest chance would have it, my long walk took me ultimately eastwards and I found myself, at least before I eventually hailed a hansom home, in the lowest and most insalubrious of districts.

Ye gods, the people there! The coarse-looking men. The ugly, grasping children. And the women. The women in particular. All of them painted, shameless and desperate. Ignorant of my identity, they mocked me when they saw me and tried to call me to them. Naturally, I resisted, my visitation of that place being strictly anthropological. They seemed to take my refusal as some manner of dare or challenge and so they became still more forceful in their insinuations and blandishments.

As I turned away from them, I felt their gaze upon me still. And it was easy then, oh but it was so very easy, to imagine the looks of gloating in their eyes.

FROM *THE TIMES*

6 December

NEWS FROM THE LAND BEYOND THE FOREST

Word has reached us of a startling new discovery in the Roumanian province of Transylvania.

The celebrated naturalist Mr Haskell Lynch has reported that, in the forest which abuts the Carpathian Mountains, he has found what he describes as being an entirely new species of bat, one hitherto unknown to science. The creature is said to be larger and more bold than its cousins as well as being overtly predatory in its habits.

Unable to obtain photographic proof of his findings, Mr Lynch set himself the task of capturing a living specimen. This he has achieved and he is even now returning to England, where it is his intention to present his discovery before a closed panel at an extraordinary meeting of the Club for Curious Scientific Men. This newspaper will, of course, continue to report upon any fresh development in this intriguing story as it unfolds.

JONATHAN HARKER'S JOURNAL

———◆———

6 December. How strange and difficult life is at present. The whole household seems almost to be holding its collective breath, waiting as one for some imminent turning point.

As the Professor continues his decline, I confess that I cannot bring myself to sit with him for long, so diminished has he become. Miss Dowell remains a beneficial yet occasionally distracting presence. Although as diligent as ever in her ministrations she has in the last few days seemed to me to become rather preoccupied and distant, traits which are quite at odds with her ordinary demeanour. Meanwhile I have busied myself with legal work in order that I might remain profitably occupied during this long period of waiting. Tonight, however, certain other matters, pertaining, I am afraid, to young Quincey, were brought to my attention in the most unexpected manner.

Having dined, the three of us had retired, at Mina's insistence, to the parlour, there to read for an hour or so and enjoy one another's company. Mina was in a pensive temper and set about writing her journal entry for the day. I tried my best to look over the draft of a client's will but the words seemed to swim and grow faint before my eyes until I had no choice but to set it aside. Quincey, being of a lively and inquisitive temperament, had before him the newspaper of the day, through which he was leafing with the furrowed intensity of a boy who is eager to leave behind childish things.

We had remained in this domestic tableau for no more than twenty minutes before my son looked up from that page of The Times which he had been perusing and declared: 'Father? I think this might interest you.'

Naturally, I expressed some polite curiosity.

He passed me the paper and pointed to the article in question. 'There. See there.'

The piece was, I dare say, innocuous enough and of interest chiefly to amateur naturalists, yet its effect upon me was palpable and immediate. It was nothing about the details in the story itself so much as the combination of certain words – words of our buried past; words of the last century – which all at once caused me to turn quite white, stumble to my feet and cast the newspaper upon the floor.

'Why...' I stuttered. 'Why have you shown this to me?'

Quincey, surprised, answered: 'I only thought it a queer thing, Father. Queer and rather grisly too.'

I gazed at him and he looked back, wholly unabashed.

My wife appraised me with concern. 'Jonathan?'

'Forgive me, both of you. I do not feel at all well. I must, I fear, retire early tonight.'

I turned and fled from that room without waiting for any reply. I left Mina to deal with Quincey and retired to my study where, in order to combat the shock, I poured myself a single glass of brandy. I sat for a while quietly, endeavouring to clear my mind of the detritus of the past and to think of nothing at all, when I heard a soft tap upon the door.

'Mina?' I said, sounding, to my own ears, both hoarse and grateful. Yet when the door was opened it was not by the fair hand of my wife but rather by that of another.

'Forgive me, sir. But I heard such a commotion...'

Miss Sarah-Ann Dowell stood upon the threshold, pale and disconcerted, yet, as ever, seeming almost to project an aura of sweetness and innocence.

'Oh, it was nothing,' I said. 'Really, you ought not to concern yourself.'

Without an invitation, the girl stepped inside and walked several paces nearer. 'You'll forgive me for saying so, sir, I hope, but just at the moment this whole house seems to be living on its nerves.'

Her remark took me a little aback. I swallowed and nodded. I think we both knew that her presence in my sanctum was not appropriate, yet I did not send her from me nor did she offer to depart.

'Mr Harker? The Professor... before he was as he is now. When all of you was young. What was he to you then?'

'Sarah-Ann... Why would you ask that? Have we not stated that he is a friend of our family?'

'You have, sir. Yet I know in my heart that there is more to the story than you have ever admitted. And, forgive me, sir, but I think your son knows that too.'

I said nothing.

She went on. 'The old man, he's not long for the world. I've seen so much of him. So much I've even dreamed of him. And I've seen fragments, sir, of some impossible story. About you, sir, and your wife. And Dr Seward. And something awful, waiting in the shadows.'

I looked the girl directly in her eyes and saw there only pity and understanding.

'When will you tell him?' She stepped closer still. 'Your boy?'

'We had wanted...' I said, each word now difficult to form. 'We had wanted to spare Quincey the truth.'

The young woman parted her lips. What she may have wished to say must remain unknown, for at that moment, without any warning or having made the sound of any approach, Mina was amongst us, striding from the doorway to my side.

'Jonathan.' Her tone was icy. 'I came to see if you were quite recovered from your... turn.'

'Quite, thank you,' I said. 'Miss Dowell was making the same enquiry.'

'I see.' My wife turned to the nursemaid. 'Thank you, my dear.'

'Not at all, ma'am.'

'Well, it is late and we must all be tired. I have sent Quincey to bed. Miss Dowell, you must want to see your patient before sleep. Pray, do not let us detain you.'

'No, ma'am. Thank you, ma'am.'

She bobbed a curtsey and left the room. Afterwards, Mina simply gazed at me and made no remark whatever. She is in bed now while I finish my brandy and write these words downstairs. It would be politic not to retire until she is sleeping. For there are, I fancy, awkward conversations ahead for us all and difficult waters indeed to navigate.

MINA HARKER'S JOURNAL

7 December. I find myself this morning feeling almost too cross to write. It is as well, perhaps, that nobody but I shall ever read these words, lest I should appear too easily vexed and fearful of my own shadow.

There was last night the most unappetising scene. Quincey had found something mildly curious in the newspaper which served, I think, to remind Jonathan of the worst excesses of our past. He flew into a kind of whirl of anxiety and, much to our son's perplexity, fled shortly thereafter from the room.

In this, quite naturally, he has my sympathy. We all saw terrible sights in that dreadful year but none more so than my husband. In the castle in which he was held captive, he bore witness to things that would have driven many another man into the arms of madness. Yet did he endure, altered for ever, certainly, but resolute and sane. Nonetheless, his ordeal lingers on and the world seems full of means by which he might inadvertently be reminded of it.

He has in this continuing struggle both my pity and undying support. This morning, however, he is also the object of my considerable irritation for, going in search of him after I had spent some minutes reassuring Quincey, I found him not in any agonised process of recollection but rather sequestered with Miss Sarah-Ann Dowell.

Both looked abashed when I entered. Jonathan blushed at my discovery. I had always hoped that men would grow less foolish with age. Instead it would seem that their weaknesses become only more deeply entrenched.

He crept into bed late last night, doubtless embarrassed. At breakfast, we exchanged scarcely a word. All shall pass in time but the business adds a most disagreeable garnish to these troubling days.

Later. As frost thaws gradually in the grudging sunshine of winter, so too have matters between my husband and I settled over the course of this long day.

I am quite certain that Miss Dowell possesses not the frailest sliver of desire for Jonathan and that any fancy upon his part is only fleeting foolishness. Besides, he wears a face of such sorrow and I can stand no more of his brimming near-tearfulness. It has been an unfortunate interlude in a household which already seems to me to be holding its breath. I am quite sure that such an atmosphere cannot be doing Quincey the slightest bit of good. I have suggested to Jonathan that he should be returned to school in time for the last week of term. In this we are in agreement. Our son will spend another two nights with us and will make the journey back on Sunday.

We told him together at supper. Quincey simply bowed his small dark head and said with that intensity which I cannot help but find a little disquieting in one so young: 'Of course, Mother. If you think that is best.'

'We do,' I replied.

Jonathan added, superfluously: 'You must keep up with your studies, my boy.'

'Oh.' Quincey looked perplexed at this and an odd expression passed across his face. 'Do you know,' he asked, and it was as though he were thinking the thought at the instant of its speaking: 'I do not think that schoolwork is to be all that important. Not in the future. Not any more.'

Jonathan and I exchanged a look of nervousness. 'Of course it will,' my husband said. 'It must be the foundation stone of your career.'

Our son seemed not to understand. 'Father?' he said. 'Now may I sit with the Professor, please? I should like to do so as often as I can before I depart. For it is possible, after all, that such opportunities are almost over.'

As he said these words, I saw him again, through the mists of the difficulties of his age and the strange emotions of this time, as he used to be – my brave, strong, clever boy. Then he rose and left the room and was gone.

Still, I do wonder quite why he should choose to spend so much of his time beside the body of a man who surely can no longer be aware of his presence. It seems a little morbid, somehow, as though he is bearing witness to an aberrant degree. Does he appear also to be in some fashion relishing the experience? His first true encounter with grief?

Oh, but what a mother am I! How suspicious and unnatural!

DR SEWARD'S DIARY
(kept in phonograph)

———◆———

9 December. It is most exciting to be caught up once again in a purely intellectual pursuit.

I say intellectual though it is, in truth, something else. A profound exercise in mental exertion, to be sure, but also more. The diary of the late R.M. Renfield seems to me – and seemed to be so from the moment that I first held it – to impart an effect that is analogous to a kind of electrical charge. Touching it, stroking its cover, leafing with growing excitement through its pages seems to bring to mind the sensation one experiences when on foot in the countryside before the coming of a thunderstorm, when the air itself feels alive, crackling with a coming power.

It seems to have moods, this book, to wax and wane in potency according to the hour of the day or night. It is a strange thing, to turn its pages, through line after line all written in a neat copperplate hand, which in itself evinces little evidence of the unspooling of the author's sanity. It is, in its own way, a kind of privilege.

Yet there is something most curious about the text. Something which has surprised me and taken up much of my time.

It has been written in code. I have, at least in part, succeeded in unravelling the cipher – drawn, I believe, from certain numerical arrangements in the earliest books of the Old Testament. I cannot read every word of it but I can discern enough to begin to make sense of the initial entries. I have discovered an oddly unsettling truth, which I would never have thought possible.

Renfield was once, long before his madness, a policeman of all things. He was a detective sergeant who worked at Scotland Yard back in the last century, alongside a gentleman by the name (half-familiar) of Martin Parlow.

Strange how the truth emerges only in glimpses and whispers, how it slithers out of the shadows into view, like a snake from long grass.

Much is still lost to me. The work of translation is tiring and complex. Yet, even from what I am able to glean – of the investigation of Parlow and Renfield into the society murders of '88; of their mutual determination to uncover the facts of the case under any circumstances; of that terrible corruption which took place in the tavern in Clerkenwell – I see that not only was his story very much stranger than I had ever imagined but that, in truth, I never really knew the man at all. I must read on. I must.

There are long hours of labour ahead of me. I will see it all now. The whole of the design.

POSTCARD* FROM CHIEF INSPECTOR MARTIN PARLOW TO SUB-DIVISIONAL INSPECTOR GEORGE DICKERSON

10th December

Dear George,

I wanted to write to let you know I must stay here a while longer. I was delayed on the road to the country and now that I am here in Wildfold I find that things are not altogether as I expected. I shall write again as soon as I have news. My daughter, Ruby, is with me and there is much I have to arrange. I hope that you are 'holding the fort' in London and that friend Quire isn't acting too much 'the horse's ass'.

Yours,

M.P.

---

* This postcard depicts the members of a circus troupe from the last years of the old century – jugglers, clowns, funambulists, a ringmaster, two caged and weary lions. The effect is inadvertently macabre, a quality that is exacerbated by a sepia tint. The expression of the ringmaster is especially disquieting. His face is blurred and he seems panicked, as though he has just seen something dreadful behind the camera's lens.

FROM THE PRIVATE DIARY
OF AMBROSE QUIRE,
Commissioner of Police of the Metropolis

———◆———

11 December. A week has gone by since his departure and it is becoming steadily more apparent to me what a lucky charm was Chief Inspector Martin Parlow. He had about him a sense of living history, a lifetime of experience in upholding our laws and a wealth of terrific stories, stretching back to the '70s. I dare say I never appreciated him as I should have done when he was every day amongst us.

How odd! I write as if the man has died instead of merely taking a temporary leave. I understand that Sub-Divisional Inspector Dickerson has had some brief correspondence with Mr Parlow stating that he is delayed and that our loss will continue to be Wildfold's gain. In his absence, our work goes on.

The American visited me this afternoon so that he might deliver his report on relations between that triumvirate of gangs who are, in spite of my very best efforts, still responsible for much of the vast quantity of criminality which takes place in our metropolis.

Amid my day of administrative responsibilities, the sight of the Yankee stepping into my office was welcome, for all that the frown on his handsome features meant only bad news. He is a patient man, discreet and determined. A good fellow, I think. Like Parlow, he is cut from stern and solid cloth.

He sat before me at my desk, uninvited. He settled himself there with such confidence that I could do nothing other than accept it. He told me of the news from Wildfold. Then, before I was able to ask him myself, in his deep drawl he said: 'Now, sir, the tensions amongst the gangs just seem to have gone right on rising. Tough to say how or why it's happening, but all our sources tell us it's getting real ugly out there.'

'I see,' I said, and I imagine that I must for a moment have allowed my attention to wander. The next thing I knew Dickerson was asking, not without a touch of reproof in his voice: 'Commissioner? It would be a real error for any one of us to underestimate the seriousness of this situation.'

'Of course it would. Yes, naturally, I quite agree with you.'

I paused, and in that instant I believe that I heard (though such a thing is all but impossible) the sound of female laughter, echoing down the hallways. As soon as I noticed it, the phenomenon ceased.

'When last we spoke of this,' said I to the foreigner, restoring my composure, 'you had in custody some young bruiser. Arrested after a gang affray.'

'That's correct, sir.' Dickerson was visibly impressed by my grasp of detail. 'He goes by the name of Thomas Cawley. One of the Giddis Boys.'

'I see. And what has he told you?'

'Very little. He ain't no mastermind. And he's a very minor figure in any case.'

'All the same,' I mused, 'I think I should like to see him for myself.'

'For yourself, sir?'

Some understandable incredulity was detectable in his voice at the unorthodoxy of my suggestion. I would be a liar if I did not admit to feeling at least a small tremor of pleasure at having impressed this young buck with my swashbuckling disregard for convention.

'That's right. If we still have him in custody then I've a question or two I should like to put to the lad.'

'I see, sir.'

'Don't look so doubtful, George. Who knows – at the sight of so high-ranking a copper he may unstop his tongue and start to squeal like a piglet on a spike.'

Dickerson said something in response to this, too low and too quick for me to hear. I have little doubt that it was spoken in appreciation of the plain boldness of my words.

The demands of paper business and the necessities of the ledger book being no less onerous than usual, it was past dark when I was finally able to spare the time to visit young Cawley in his cell. He was of a type that is thoroughly familiar to any guardian of justice: a straggle-haired unkempt thing, brutish, muscular and dressed in clothes very much more expensive than anyone of his station ought to be able to afford.

'Look lively, Cawley,' Dickerson said as we approached the fellow's cage. 'You're a lucky kid tonight. You got yourself a visitor.'

The prisoner scrambled upright and hastened over to the bars. On closer inspection, I saw that he was even younger than

I had assumed. The rigours of the life that he had chosen had aged him badly. Dickerson went on: 'This is the Commissioner. Stir yourself!'

The boy blinked.

'Thomas?' said I, gently. 'It's Thomas Cawley, isn't it?'

'Yes, sir.' His voice was higher than I would have imagined and I thought that I sensed beneath the bravado something much like fear.

'Listen, Thom,' I said, with all reasonable moderation. 'We are sensible men. We understand, in our different ways, exactly how the world works.' I meant to flatter, to woo him and win his confidence – a strategy which has worked on many previous occasions. 'Sub-Divisional Inspector Dickerson and me, we both know full well that you're a tiny cog in the Giddis machine. We know you're a foot soldier. A serf and a vassal.'

The boy looked down at the floor of his pen as I delivered this speech, but at its final word he looked suddenly up at me with surprise in his hazel eyes. 'Vassal, sir? What a... What a strange word to use.'

'It means servant,' I said gently. 'Or even slave.'

'I know what it means, Commissioner. I've heard it before. But not... not when I've been waking.'

'Whatever do you mean?'

The lad fell immediately silent.

Dickerson took up the task. 'We have to understand what is happening. The gangs seem suddenly at one another's throats. Why? What's the cause?'

Cawley sighed, an oddly feminine sound. He muttered: 'I don't know.'

'There must be something. Some reason for this unrest.'

'Someone getting greedy?' Dickerson asked. 'Someone looking to extend their territory?'

Cawley shook his head. 'Not so far as I know, sir. No. But I think it's… I mean we ain't any of us getting much sleep.'

'Sleep?' I peered at him. 'What the devil do you mean by sleep?'

Cawley sighed again. 'Like I say, sir. It's the dreams, sir.'

'What… dreams?'

'We've all had 'em. Rich and deep and terrible. I've seen things myself. A shadow falling… White teeth flashing in the moonlight… My sweet bubbin Sarah-Ann crying tears of blood…'

This speech done, he turned away and retreated to the far side of the cell.

'You want me to go in?' asked Dickerson. 'You want me to knock some sense into him? Oftentimes a bruise can help a guy locate his conscience.'

'No. That won't be necessary. I think the poor lad is just dreadfully confused.'

Dickerson looked frustrated at my command, but he agreed all the same and escorted me away.

I worked late again tonight – too late – toiling through a mountain range of papers. It was well after ten when I left the building and took a stroll into the darker regions of the city. On this occasion, I wore a bowler as a disguise, stained my face with burnt cork, and affected in my posture the furtive slouch of he who dwells upon the wrong side of His Majesty's Laws and Statutes.

I am confident that I passed amongst the ranks of Whitechapel's very worst without arousing the least suspicion. As I lumbered on, not dropping my guise for so much as an instant, I took a series of discreet glances at those beggarly villains who were abroad. Was it my imagination that I saw there, in an echo of young Cawley's words, the frequent signs of utmost exhaustion, as if derived from a marked paucity of sleep, as if they all suffered regularly and without respite from night terrors?

LETTER FROM LADY CAROLINE GODALMING TO MRS MINA HARKER

12 December

Dearest Mina,

I hope that this letter finds you as well as might be expected. I hope that you and your family are well and that the Professor is at least comfortable in his extended twilight. And I hope also that you will forgive the direct nature of my approach. I know, for all that you have done your very best to make me as welcome as possible in your little circle, that we have never been what one might truly call friends.

I write this letter in a period of relative calm in my mind. I am prone to nerves and I have never been robust in the face of vicissitudes and strains. Those confusions and uncertainties which seem to have clouded my thoughts for weeks may at any moment return. So I must be brisk.

Mina, my dear, I have a boon to ask of you.

I have, I know, imposed upon you before now, and more than once. Today, I fear I must do so again. Might you come and see me here in the great house? Arthur is away so often, dealing with matters of politics and the Council. All these things have served to distract him from the new life which swells within me. I may as well confess it, my dear: I have become much afraid.

I am frightened for the future and I am wary of the past. In spite of that legion of nannies and staff with which I am sure I shall be provided, I am afraid that I shall prove to be a very poor mother indeed to the little Godalming who approaches. You know something of my past, I believe, that I was once unwell and was placed by those who loved me into the expert care of Jack Seward. Those were difficult months. I am almost whole again now, however, for all that some fragility remains.

It is a state to which I would do anything not to have to return. Dearest Mina, do say that you will visit soon. I need your advice. I am in urgent want of a friend. We shall pay whatever it takes for you to travel here. I know that you have troubles of your own at present, but I would owe you a great debt of gratitude were you to consent to do this for me.

Yours, always,
Carrie

DR SEWARD'S DIARY
(kept in phonograph)

———◆———

13 December. The code. The code has shifted.

Ninety pages into the text and the cipher has grown still more complicated. I must solve it. I must read the entire manuscript, the whole of the story, or else the exercise is fruitless. So much I did not know! About Renfield and Martin Parlow. About the horror that they glimpsed by the railway siding. About the enquiries that that future madman conducted wholly on his own. About the laughter in the darkness and the prophecies of the Piccadilly gypsies. Yet I am only beginning. There is much more, I know it. So much to discover and to learn. The code can be understood. It must. I need only time.

Speaking of time, I am dimly aware that the days are passing more quickly than they should, and even that there are events which I have overlooked. The Harkers. Lady Godalming. The poor Professor. There are numerous duties and responsibilities which, I fear, I have ignored and thrust aside. I will return to them all, as I shall to my neglected patients, in due course. But first – the code, the diary and, at long last, the truth.

LETTER FROM MRS MINA HARKER TO
LADY CAROLINE GODALMING

14 December

Dear Carrie,

Thank you for your kind and heartfelt letter. Please forgive me for not replying by return of post.

Matters here are but little improved. The Professor seems a little better, perhaps in consequence of Miss Dowell's ministrations. Sarah-Ann herself remains stoical and determined, although she seems to nurse some private anxiety, connected, at least if I read the signs aright, with an absentee sweetheart.

Quincey, meanwhile, has returned to school for the final week of term. We thought this for the best, as the atmosphere in the house is scarcely conducive to the wholesome development of a sensitive boy. I wonder if it might not also be leading him into morbidity? Certainly, his behaviour of late (if I might confess such a thing in confidence to so excellent a friend) has not been all that it might have been. In addition, given the candour of your message, perhaps I might be permitted to confide in you that relations between my husband and I are now at rather a low ebb? He makes recourse far too often for my liking to the decanter and the hip flask.

But you must have small desire to hear my ill tidings when your own life is so crowded with concern. I am sorry to discover that Arthur has been so very absent. Though I should not be troubled overmuch by it. Men are both easily distracted and often dismayed by questions of the heart. They will always choose matters of politics and business over those which require that tender self-knowledge which is said to be our birthright.

I would urge you to set aside all fears and vexations upon the issue of motherhood. You should not have the slightest doubt that you will be as wonderful a parent as you have already proved to be a wife. It is my hope that the months ahead will make us even better friends. The difficulties of the present will soon enough seem distant things and the challenges of the future will serve only to bring our families closer together.

I should be delighted to visit with you. Could we say the seventeenth? Christmas is already bearing down on us and there is much to be done. Quincey is to be returned to us on the nineteenth. Do let me know if such a time would be amenable to you, and I look forward to our conversation in person.

Your loving friend,
Mina

J.S. BARNES

TELEGRAM FROM LADY CAROLINE GODALMING TO MRS MINA HARKER

15 December

Letter received with great relief and joy. Do come on seventeenth. Much to discuss and much I wish to ask you. All my love, C.

FROM THE PRIVATE JOURNAL
OF MAURICE HALLAM

———◆———

16 December. On the last occasion when I set down words in this modest diary of mine it was from a Roumanian hospital bed. How things change and shift; how events adopt the most beautifully strange of patterns. I pen these sentences in a Viennese bordello.

In spite of the unfamiliarity of the city, there is a sense in which I believe myself to be back once again where I belong: surrounded by the accoutrements of sin, luxuriating in the sensuous and the forbidden. Having survived the castle in the Carpathians (whatever the designs of the treacherous Ileana may have been) and to be once again at the side of Gabriel Shone, I ought by rights to feel only contentment and relief.

Yet, although superficial and transitory pleasure has been mine these last few weeks, any more abiding joy has waned like moonlight in the dawn. I feel a sense of burgeoning anxiety, a steady, rising fear which clings to me. It grows, this subtle vexation, insinuating itself within me, like ivy upon some ancient wall.

For a man who but lately declared himself to have discovered a grand new purpose, Gabriel, far from hurrying back to our homeland to pursue his stated destiny, has adopted a policy of leisure and carnal distraction.

Earlier, on the train, I asked him why his movements seemed now so languorous, when before he had spoken so loftily of his political ambitions, of his intention to take up his hereditary post in the Council of Athelstan. He only smiled, as if at a secret joke, then turned his face towards me, a face which somehow, according to the capricious laws of desire, seems only more striking as a result of that terrible damage which has been wrought upon it.

'We have time yet. We cannot return to England till something passes from the world. A force that, even in abeyance, still exerts influence. We are exerting caution, at this stage in our plans. Be patient, Maurice. Once the gateway is clear we shall pass through it and then everything will happen very quickly indeed. Until then, we are permitted to move at a pace of our choosing. The time will come soon enough for work and for action. The demands upon us will be strenuous indeed. For now, why should we not rest and enjoy ourselves?'

He fixed his gaze upon me, his expression filled with a kind of promise. In all our acquaintance, he has been a man of rare persuasiveness and personal magnetism – so much so that even I fell immediately into line behind him, obedient as a mastiff.

I cannot leave him, nor can I go back or ahead of him. And so I sit and I wait and I wonder.

We have been in Vienna for a day and a night. Whereas Brasov and Bucharest are thick with the legacies of the past, Vienna is surely a city of the future. All here is sleek modernity. Youth is abroad upon every street and down every highway. Everything is change and flux and is reflective of new perceptions of the world. Curiously, and to my surprise, I like it not, preferring instead the shadowed avenues of the east, the barely tempered wildness of Roumania. Perhaps this new century is not for me – at least, not for long.

Our current abode, situated in the ancien quartier of this brash and thrusting settlement, is a little more redolent of days that have vanished, although, of course, it has of necessity the tinge of youth.

It was Gabriel who found the establishment, sniffing it out with the air of the knowledgeable wanderer. Tonight I found I could not take my pleasure, tired as I am and in occasional pain from my ordeal. He is next door while I write in this antechamber. Therein lies also another reason for my voluntary absence. Since Roumania, Mr Shone has acquired new appetites, those which twist the ordinary into something troublingly outré.

For he has come, this amiable Englishman, to like to watch, unmoving, as a boy before him opens a vein. Time and again have I seen it, this weird ritual. Shone looks on inscrutably, first as the blood pours and then is staunched, as the very stuff of life itself is unstoppered, decanted and enjoyed.

FROM THE DIARY OF
ARNOLD SALTER

———◆———

16 December. Down to the Embankment again, close to the selfsame patch where I almost put a full stop to my own obituary. This time I walked farther on, strolling into a much more prosperous stretch where the railing is secure and the Thames less of a menace.

Cool winter sunshine. The reflections on the river were almost pretty. I was there to meet my associate, Lord Tanglemere, though, for the purposes of necessary secrecy, we were not to greet one another or show by our expressions any familiarity or recognition.

We met by a pre-arranged point against the iron fence. Pedestrians swarmed everywhere – all the pageantry of London, from city men to skeevers, flower sellers to fine society ladies. The air was thick with the stink of the river and the disagreeable smell of our fellow human beings. Odd how detectable that reek still is, even when you are surrounded by folk of the better sort.

As expected, our encounter was brief but significant. He was waiting for me with his dog, the wolfhound, on a leash by his side. The animal sat upright, panting. I approached, ducking through a line of schoolboys and their clucking, ineffectual master. Coolly, I took up my position and gazed down at deep, fast-flowing waters. The noble lord, meanwhile, crouched beside his pet and made a display of rubbing the back of the beast. No passer-by took the slightest notice, no doubt mistaking us for a couple of weary but unacquainted old men.

Without looking up, Lord Tanglemere said expressionlessly: 'I trust you are heartened by our progress.'

'On the contrary, my lord,' I said, staring fixedly at a tugboat on the far side of the river. 'I am frustrated and disappointed.'

'But you ought not to be. The piece in the Gazette concerning the unfortunate Lady Godalming was both striking and efficacious. It caused quite a stir. One hears much talk of it even now.'

'Yet nothing since!' I retorted. 'In spite of repeated efforts to secure a pulpit I've heard nothing at all. That young pup Carnehan has responded to not one of my messages. He has neither seen fit to summon me nor to give me leave to speak again from the paper I used to know better than the back of my own right hand.'

'I do sympathise,' Tanglemere murmured. He stroked the animal's back and cooed. The beast shuddered. 'But such things cannot be rushed.'

'And more than that,' I said, getting into my stride now, 'the way in which he is driving the Gazette in entirely the wrong b—y direction. His choices are dreadful – dunderheaded! He doesn't understand his own audience. He's never moved amongst them as I have.'

'I did hear tell...' The aristocrat craned his head upwards at the sky, as if examining the patterns of the clouds. 'I did hear tell that the figures of circulation have, in fact, increased rather markedly under Mr Carnehan's control.'

At this, I only swore, almost too quietly for anyone to hear.

'Have patience,' said Tanglemere. 'Hubris is the prerogative of youth. It won't be long now until your voice is heard once again all over this land.'

'And then the Council takes control?' I said, with what was almost certainly too great a degree of eagerness.

'Eventually,' said the lord, 'if all goes according to plan.'

'But when exactly?' I asked. 'And how, my lord? How?'

Tanglemere rose to his feet. His dog did the same. He tugged briskly on the leash, and together man and animal started to walk away. The lord called back to me over his shoulder in a manner which would have seemed brash in a younger fellow.

'The fire has already been lit, Mr Salter. You need wait only for the flames to start to spread.'

And with that enigmatical remark, at the present time it seems I must be content.

MEMORANDUM FROM REVEREND T.P. OGDEN* TO DR R.J. HARRIS†

17 December

Headmaster,

I write in a state of some anxiety concerning a boy.

He is a first-former (Simeon House) named Quincey Harker. I instruct him in Theology. I wonder if you can place him? He is a quiet and thoughtful child, rather watchful in his manner. You may, I fancy, more readily recall his mother, who has visited the school on several occasions and has about her a most striking manner and demeanour.

His name might also be familiar to you in consequence of his recent prolonged absence due to the illness of a family friend. The business was all most unorthodox. This ought not to surprise us, for, from what I have seen and heard, the Harkers are a most unorthodox group of people.

Yet this alone is not why I write to you today. The issue is graver still.

While Master Harker was absent from these halls I and others sent to him much of that work which he missed while he was keeping vigil by the bedside of this aged greybeard. Quincey is considerably behind in his labours and much overdue, although, to give the boy all credit, he is shewing signs of considerable industry in order to keep pace.

* Chaplain of Somerton School, 1899–1912
† Headmaster of Somerton School, 1878–1905

Yet the essay that he wrote for me while in absentia is perhaps the most troubling composition I have read in almost two decades as a schoolmaster. Its subject was to describe and to trace the origins of a ritual in our Christian tradition. Most of the boys, quite naturally, elected to write upon the sacrament of Holy Communion, others upon Baptism and others still (Cairncross, of course, and his partner-in-crime Archibald minor) with a little too much relish upon the possibilities of marriage. Harker, however, wrote something very different, a choice that was more than merely idiosyncratic (a trait which, in any case, I tend to discourage) and struck me instead as a matter of profound disturbance.

Headmaster, the boy wrote his disquisition upon no less a subject than the Rite of Strigoi.

It may be that you are unfamiliar with this dreadful ceremony. Indeed, I hope that you are.

Suffice it to say that it is a ritual of rare and most unChristian ferocity. It is meant to remove the last portion of a soul from the body of one who has, since birth, been used as a vessel to prolong life after death. The ritual is the final act in a vile resurrection. It restores a ghoul to the whole of its strength and results in the absolute destruction of the host.

Naturally, you and I well know such folk beliefs to be nothing more than rank superstition and foolish irrationality. There is something thoroughly absurd in the survival of these antique and pagan creeds into our century. Nonetheless, I find it most sinister that the Harker boy should be so drawn to such macabre topics.

He wrote, Headmaster, with such fervour upon the subject, with an almost wild enthusiasm.*

I cannot imagine where he first stumbled across such information. What manner of library does his father possess? For there is no book in these halls which might have guided him in such a profane direction. He is at present still more sulky than before and thus will not easily be drawn.

I think in this matter that we must tread carefully. I would be most grateful, Headmaster, for instructions on how best to proceed.

Yours,
T.P.O.

---

* How odd it is to hear at such a distance of my own peculiar behaviour as a boy. So many changes have taken place since that it is much like reading of the actions of another, quite different person. This is, I suppose, in part true.

MEMORANDUM FROM DR R.J. HARRIS TO
REVEREND T.P. OGDEN

17 December

Thank you for your memorandum of this morning.

This 'Rite of Strigoi' is not known to me. Harker, however, is. As you surmised, I find that I can most readily recall his mother. I shall speak to the boy forthwith. Let it not be forgotten that we are to these children moral guardians as much as we are scholastic guides.

JONATHAN HARKER'S JOURNAL

———◆———

17 December. With Quincey returned to school and Mina gone to the Holmwoods, I find myself somewhat at a loss. Such is the paradox of the married man: when one is in the bosom of one's family, one craves only sanctuary and individual space, but when they are away one misses them with unexpected fire.

When I saw off my wife this morning, upon the train to London, where she will pick up the branch line to Godalming, she confessed herself much concerned as to the wellbeing of poor Carrie. I think that she sees in her – as, of course, did Arthur – something of a surrogate for the late Lucy Westenra. The recent article in the Gazette has scarcely set her mind at rest upon this and other questions. Although I am not certain that I truly believe it to be so, I assured her nonetheless that all would yet be well.

Lady Godalming is a fragile and, I have always thought, rather a complicated woman. Yet she has the attention of Arthur and Jack as well as the considerable resources of the family fortune. Mina agreed with me but tentatively and I could tell that neither of us was wholly persuaded by the argument.

A weak smile, a passionless kiss upon my cheek and, amid much slamming of doors, clanking of machinery and voluminous clouds of steam, she was gone. The bulk of the day I spent in legal and professional business. For supper, feeling suddenly and most unusually eager to be amongst other people, I took myself to the inn in the village where I ate a serviceable pie and drank an abstemious pair of ales. I thought that it was rather pleasant to sit anonymously for a time amongst strangers and to think of nothing of any particular significance at all.

Nonetheless, guilt found me soon enough and I returned home. The house was still and silent. I went to the highest floor and sat beside the sad, recumbent figure of Van Helsing. How pale he seems. How frail. How profoundly reduced from the man I used to know.

I took his bony, liver-spotted hand in mine and clasped it tight. The only sound in that chamber of sickness was the heave of his breathing. I thought how greatly he would have hated this long indignity, how he would have chafed against these weeks of enforced silence.

The past rose up then and I felt a great sob surge through me. I stifled it as best I could but it left my lips as a kind of anguished sigh.

A moment later I heard footsteps by the door, a turning of the handle, and before I knew it, I saw before me Miss Sarah-Ann Dowell. As pretty as ever, she looked tired and sorrowful.

'I'm sorry, sir,' she said. 'I heard a sound and I suppose I wondered...'

'Only me, I'm afraid.' I tried a half-apologetic smile. It was, I am sure, the consequence of the alcohol that I had earlier imbibed, but as I spoke my throat and mouth felt dry. I swallowed uncomfortably.

She smiled. 'It's nice to see you, sir.'

I averted my eyes and looked down at the Professor. 'His condition?'

'Oh, quite unchanged, sir. No difference at all.'

'Well, thank you. For your hard work. It is greatly appreciated, you know. By all of us. And also, I fancy, if only he could say so, by him.'

She blushed at this, then exhaled, rather miserably.

'I hope you aren't too unhappy here,' I said. 'Yours is a fine calling and I fear we have not been the best of hosts.'

'Oh, you've been very kind to me, sir. I cannot say otherwise.'

'And yet,' I said, 'I think there is some sadness in you.'

'My sweetheart...' she began, then immediately stopped the flow of her words. 'I mean, that is to say, I've got some questions of a personal nature which weigh on my mind.'

For a little while a silence hung between us, before, conscious of something shifting, I said: 'Tell me then. Tell me everything.'

An instant later, I was on my feet and she was in my arms, clinging to me and sobbing aloud and unburdening the whole of her heart.

DR SEWARD'S DIARY
(kept in phonograph)

————◆————

18 December. I know, I know that I have been absent for too long from the tide of events. Yet this journal still fascinates me. More, I appreciate, than it ought.

I can feel it, rising in me. The power of obsession.

The new cipher is inexplicable and I can recognise only stray words. All I can see is the outline of how it was that a man might come to accept his own damnation.

I think – yes, I think that the key to this new iteration of the code may lie with another. With an old ally of Renfield's before his damnation. The old policeman named Martin Parlow.

I have no wish to abandon my friends or my responsibilities here. And yet I have to know the truth. I must know everything, if only to free myself from the python-grip of this awful need to understand.

Why should it matter, at so great a distance of time? The old monster is dead, after all, and his hapless slave gone to the great beyond before him. Everything is safely buried and covered over. Why should I be drawn to the snare, like some unwitting creature, by this most curious of books?

I have no answers except to say that this thing has me now. The only answer is to act like one who is lost and bewildered in a maze, to seek a path to the centre of the labyrinth so that escape might finally be realised.

With this in mind, would it be so very wrong of me to take a sabbatical from the world? To journey elsewhere? To find the truth about the diary, about Mr Renfield and the interconnection of the present with the past? I fear it must be done. I wish never to disappoint anyone at all. But I have a purpose now again, a true quest.

I shall leave this narrow room and seek out that which is hidden. I will find Parlow. I will know everything. And, then, at last, all the clamouring voices in my head will fall silent.

MEMORANDUM FROM DR R.J. HARRIS TO
REVEREND T.P. OGDEN

19 December

Reverend,

Further to our correspondence concerning the Harker boy, I wanted to set your mind at rest. I am uncertain, however, if I can achieve this aim entirely.

I summoned the boy in question to my study yesterday. He presented himself before me at the appointed hour in an apparent spirit of utter meekness. He shewed neither surprise nor curiosity. There was no sign about him of fear or trepidation.

I proceeded to interview him as to the question of this eerie Rite of which you spoke – the name of which now, oddly, eludes me.

'Whatever did you mean by it?' I began. 'Why, the Chaplain thinks it tantamount to blasphemy.'

'Truly,' said the child. 'I meant only to execute the work that had been set. It was never my intention to cause the least distress.'

Written down these words have an air of archness or impudence, yet none of this did I perceive in the boy when he sat before me. On the contrary, he seemed to be acutely earnest and open, even displaying some signs of naïveté which one might expect to have left him by his present age.

'But where,' I persisted, 'did you even hear of such a thing?' He murmured something about the library of his father (in this, Reverend, your suspicion was correct) and also about the contents of his dreams (which I chose in this instance to dismiss as childish folly).

'Then you must read rather less widely,' I said. 'Or, at least, you must read with greater guidance. For your mind is now at its most malleable. You must be sure not to fill it with flummery and nonsense.'

He seemed distinctly puzzled by my words. There is, indubitably, something strange about the lad – something also of the savant.

'You mentioned, sir, my mind…'

'I surely did, for it is the most precious part of you there is, my boy. You must treat it kindly and you must consider at all times its health.'

He blinked at me in the manner that is often described as owlish.

'My own mind is quite split in two,' he said solemnly. 'One side fights constantly against the other. Light against darkness. One father against the other.'

'What on earth do you mean by that?'

'I have two fathers, sir, and both of them speak to me… One in person… the other… in here…' In a weird piece of pantomime, he tapped the side of his head.

There was a good deal more of what he said, but I find that I am quite unable to recollect a word of it now. The rest of our conversation seems befogged in my memory.

In the end, of course, I beat him soundly for his own good. I gave him twelve lashes which he endured in manly silence. Afterwards, however, his air of discombobulation continued.

Let us hope that the boy took my advice. Let us hope

that the festive holiday is one that soothes and calms him. Let us hope that this unpleasantness is all done with now.

R.J.H.

PS. Chaplain, I cannot say quite why, but I should like very much for you to pray tonight for that strange boy's soul.

MINA HARKER'S JOURNAL

———◆———

19 December. Another hammer blow has fallen; another tragedy has struck and our circle is again beset by catastrophe. When will there be an end to it? When shall we be spared? Not soon, I fear. Not soon and not without much sacrifice.

Two days ago, I left Jonathan to his work and boarded the train to Paddington. This portion of the trip was pleasant enough and I was able, alone and peaceful in my carriage, to lose myself in several works by Mr Conrad which I had not hitherto had the leisure to explore.

Arriving in London on time, I had to travel some miles by means of that subterranean railway which continues to burgeon beneath the streets, a world of steam, grease and metal which remains just out of sight, like veins beneath the city's skin. As I submitted myself, standing amid the ranks of my fellow citizens, I felt profoundly tempted to ascend at the earliest opportunity, to seek out Arthur in Westminster, caught up as he is in all his politicking, to take his arm as firmly as I dared and drag him with me to the Godalming estate, towards his truest and most important obligation.

Yet I knew that authority to do so would not be mine, and

perhaps even that the time for such an intervention has passed. No, I decided that the best course was to press on and to offer Caroline any aid that was within my power to dispense. I wonder now if this was merely pride and whether, had I made a different choice, the tragedy might somehow have been averted.

At Victoria, I returned to the surface and, having fought my way through the ceaseless bustle of the station, boarded the service to that rural outpost where I would meet a fly to take me to the Holmwoods. The train was a little busier than before but I found myself a deserted carriage. The journey passed swiftly; more swiftly, somehow, than it ought to have done. The words on the pages of my book seemed after a time to swim before me as the grimy excesses of the city rolled by. There followed an intermission of soft oblivion before I was, once again, jolted awake.

I became conscious that the landscape outside the window had changed, from the smoke and industry of London to the timeless vista of the English countryside in winter – bare brown fields, bleak hedgerows, lines of leafless trees. I had, I realised, been dreaming. Of someone from long ago. Poor Lucy – my friend – whom dear Carrie in so many ways resembles. Is there not a strange symmetry in events? And does not symmetry suggest some manner of design?

As I sat and waited, rain began to patter and then to drum against the window. When I arrived at the final station, the downpour had become torrential. No fly was waiting for me, meaning that I had no choice but to hire, at considerable expense, a motorised hansom cab which I found growling on the concourse. Its horse-drawn rivals had no doubt retired for the afternoon due to the inhospitality of the weather.

My driver was a young man, his pale face still speckled with spots. He struck me as being a newcomer to his profession and seemed anxious in my company. In some indefinable manner, he reminded me of Quincey. When, having settled myself in the back seat of the vehicle and breathed its unfamiliar scent of stale air and engine oil, I told him the name of my destination he reacted with what I thought to be a most exaggerated form of shock.

'The Godalming estate?'

'If you please.'

'You're sure, miss? I mean, you're quite certain?'

'Bless you for the "miss",' I said, with a smile that was intended to set him at his ease, 'and yes, I am quite certain. So... if you would be so kind?'

He must have seen from my expression that I meant to brook no refusal. He turned to his wheel and we nosed out into the street and into the driving rain. Rain hammered hard on the roof of our vehicle, a drumbeat urging us onwards.

'Do you know Lord Arthur, miss?' asked the boy behind the wheel as he negotiated those treacherous country roads.

'I do,' I said. I had meant to restrict my reply to those two syllables, but for reasons which were opaque to me, I heard myself adding: 'Not so well now, I fear, as once I did.'

Oddly, the answer did not seem to strike him with any degree of surprise. 'You're not the first. They do say he never was the same after he lost his fiancée.'

'But his new wife...' I began. 'Caroline.'

'Very pretty, ma'am. Like a lady stepped from a painting. But not – how should I put it? – not one of us.'

I could think of no ideal response to this and so I settled back in my seat again as we went on into the storm.

At length, the familiar turrets of the Godalming estate

appeared. We left the main road and began to progress down the long, straight drive which leads to the manor house. The rain was worse than ever, heavy and persistent, hurtling downwards from the heavens with such excessive force that it seemed almost to rebound from the earth, creating a seething, obfuscating spray. So absorbed was I by this phenomenon that I failed to notice at first the queerness of the sights that were set before us.

The great manor house was all lit up, its windows blazing against the afternoon gloom. Yet this view, unusual and subtly disquieting, was not in any way the chief oddity. Rather, it was something quite different – the sight, sporadically situated, on either side of the wide stone path, of what looked at first like statues formed in the most lifelike proportions. There were two straggling rows of them.

Naturally, I thought this odd, but I considered that it represented only some eccentric addition to the grounds until we drew nearer and I glimpsed at last the truth.

'Wait,' I said. 'Stop the car.'

'Miss?'

'Please. Do as I ask. Right now.'

He slowed as swiftly as was possible in the downpour. By the time he had done so, several of the statues had already slid by. We came gingerly to a halt and, against the protestations of my chauffeur, I opened the door and stepped out into the storm.

I approached the nearest 'statue' – that of a tall, barrel-chested man of about my own age – and saw at once that my worst suspicions were quite correct.

'What are you doing?' I called out, raising my voice to be heard above the cacophony of the downpour. 'What on earth do you think you are doing out here?'

The statue shivered. Any remaining doubt left me that I was looking at anything other than a living man.

'We're doing as we were told, ma'am,' he said. His voice was low and deep and I detected in it undercurrents of frustration and shame.

'You're a servant here?'

'Butler, ma'am. Amory is my name.'

'Well then, Mr Amory, I am Mrs Mina Harker, and I would greatly appreciate an explanation at your earliest convenience of all of this foolishness.'

Rain dripped down Mr Amory's face. He must have been soaked through, right to the bone. 'Lord Arthur is in Westminster, ma'am. In his absence, Milady has grown...' He paused, weighing his next words carefully. 'She has become fretful and erratic. Shortly after luncheon, she sent out the whole of the staff to stand just as you see us now – like statues.'

'Then it's very much worse,' I said, 'than I feared. Amory, this rain is quite intolerable. Gather together all your staff and bring them to the hall. You must be frozen.'

'Yes, Mrs Harker. At once. And as for the mistress?'

I set my face into a frown. 'I shall deal with Caroline.'

Had anyone been sufficiently unwise as to brave the extremities of the weather that afternoon they would have been met by a peculiar sight: a miserable procession of bedraggled figures, marching through the rain to reach an almost-empty mansion lit up as though for the grandest of gatherings. I sent the car on ahead and, desiring solidarity, walked alongside the servants. We trudged largely in silence, although I did ask Amory one thing.

'Has she got very bad?'

The loyal fellow would not at first reply, until I urged him to respond. 'Mr Amory, please. Be honest. I give you my word that what you say shall go no further.'

He bent his head against the rain. 'We have been most concerned, ma'am. Yes, she is not herself at all. Or rather…'

'Yes?'

'Rather, she is something like her old self once again.'

At the entrance to the hall I held up my hand to address the crowd of servants.

'You must all be frozen. The priority of every one of you is to wash and to warm yourselves immediately. Pneumonia must be a real danger. I shall speak to Lady Godalming and ensure that nothing like this ever happens in this house again. Mr Amory?'

The butler stepped forward. 'Ma'am?'

'As soon as you have bathed and changed, come to me. There is a good deal of work ahead of us.'

'Yes, ma'am. Of course, ma'am.'

He led his staff away, into the house, chivvying them and taking charge. The throng cleared and the driver emerged, looking about him with considerable bemusement. I realised then that his continued presence here would do us no good.

'Go home,' I said. 'And I should account it a personal favour were you to say nothing to anybody of what you have seen here.'

I took from my purse a pound note and passed it to him. 'This should help with the failure of your memory.'

He looked rather sceptical. 'Yes, miss.'

I pulled out another two notes. 'As should these.'

He brightened. 'Yes, miss. Thank you, miss.' He looked about him one final time as though committing the scene to memory and went to clamber back into the car.

I did not wait to see him depart, but rather turned and crossed over into that ancestral seat. It seemed at first to me that the place lay in utter silence, save for the sounds of the torrent outside. There was a momentary lull in the noise of the storm, and I heard from some distance away, yet assuredly from inside the building, a peal of shrill female laughter. I determined to track it to its source.

In the end, I found her easily enough, poor Carrie,* for it was she, of course, who was the author of that delirium, sitting alone in the dining hall. She was at the head of the table, surrounded by plates of food which were spoiled and beginning to acquire corruption.

At the sight of me in the doorway she made no further sound but rose silently to her feet. There was a swelling in her belly, quite noticeable.

For a long moment, we merely gazed at one another. It was then that I took in other elements in the scene: a sweet, putrid scent, the ragged, dirty quality of Carrie's fingernails, her red-rimmed, bloodshot eyes. For a moment, I even believed that I heard something like the rustling of wings, as if a bird had become trapped inside the building.

Then Lady Godalming spoke and, such was my concern for her, all other thoughts left me. 'Mina? Mina Murray? Is that you?'

'I am Mina Harker, my dear, as I have been these many years.'

Carrie tried to move about the table and stumbled, righting herself but barely. 'There's something within me, Mina, my

---

* There is here an intriguing quirk in the manuscript. The name 'Carrie' is a replacement for another which my mother originally wrote before scoring it out: 'Lucy'.

dear.' She drew closer to me. 'Something growing and starting to bud.'

She took a further, faltering step and I hurried to meet her.

'Carrie...'

She stopped, swaying uncertainly on her feet. 'It is soaked in blood, this little marionette. It is rich in the stuff of life and death.'

'You're tired.' I went closer. 'You're exhausted and you've been left alone for too long. You must rest. You must pray. Above all, you must be hopeful for the future.'

She opened her mouth but no words came. She was looking behind me, over my shoulder, as if her attention had suddenly been caught by an object of considerable fascination, although we were, of course, quite alone in the room.

'Mina...' she breathed. Her eyes rolled up and she fell heavily forward in a deep and desperate swoon. I caught her in my arms just in time.

I come now to the worst part of this account. I have been dreading its setting down. Nonetheless, I shall be clear and I shall be thorough.

As soon as poor Caroline had collapsed I called for help. Amory – newly scrubbed, clean and dry – appeared almost at once and together we carried her upstairs and laid her in her private chamber.

Once Amory had left, I undressed Carrie and put her in a long white nightgown that I discovered in her chamber, making sure that she was as comfortable as possible. Leaving the room, I found that the servants were all abroad again, busying themselves with the brisk restoration of the manor. I sent one of them – a sombre, thoughtful and rather impressive young man by the name of Ernest Strickland – into town with instructions to wire Arthur immediately and to return with the local doctor. We will need Jack Seward soon too. I shall send a message to my husband to that effect in the morning.

Amory had prepared a simple meal, which he brought to me by the fire that had been made up in Arthur's study. It was all most unorthodox, of course, yet entirely fitting with the character of the day.

I tried to question the butler as to the details of his mistress' evident decline and his master's absence. He proved evasive. 'Let his Lordship come home, Mrs Harker, and he will tell you everything. He's done his best has Lord Arthur, in his way, but...' The servant's words tailed away. 'Forgive me, ma'am.'

'If something is troubling you, Amory, then, please, you must speak freely.'

'Only to say, Mrs Harker, that sometimes when a thing is broken it can't ever be mended, no matter how hard you try. And sometimes, in trying to mend it you only break it all the more.'

His short speech done, Amory bowed and left the room. Young Strickland came back soon after with bad news. The telegram had been despatched but the local doctor was himself in his sickbed, meaning that a replacement had been sent for who was unlikely to arrive before morning.

I talked a little with Amory concerning this and it was between us decided, in lieu of any response from the lady's husband, to leave Caroline to sleep for now and to urge the doctor to appear at the earliest possible opportunity. It seemed unwise to try to move her. Night had long since fallen and my eyelids were growing heavy. Amory had the room beside Caroline's made up for me and a fire within it banked high. I thanked him and, by extension, all his staff and took myself upstairs.

I was too tired to write in these pages then. Before retiring, I looked in on Lady Godalming, who lay silent and still and, it seemed to me, quite peaceful. I sat beside her and took her hand. I spoke a few lines of prayer, my voice sounding, even to my ears, rather feeble against the relentless rain outside.

Afterwards, I went to the adjoining room and to bed. The fire hissed and crackled and I tried, in opposition to the sad events of the day, to form within my mind happy, joyful portraits of those whom I have loved. Somehow I was not able to conjure them to my satisfaction. They grew first distant and then faint before fading altogether into darkness. In my mind's eye, I followed after them and, gratefully, let sleep claim me.

I woke again suddenly in the night with a profound feeling of dread. The fire had not died down but rather had grown higher and more fierce, and its madly dancing flames cast capering shadows in the walls of the chamber. From outside, closer than seemed altogether comfortable, I heard the high baying of dogs as if at the outset of the hunt. And standing over me, on the left-hand side of the bed, stood Lady Caroline Godalming in her long white gown.

For a moment, the years dropped away and I was once again in Whitby, and Lucy Westenra was walking in her sleep in those weeks which immediately preceded her transformation. Then I remembered where and when I was and precisely what was required of me.

'Caroline,' I said authoritatively. 'You need to go back to bed. You need to rest and recuperate and be yourself again.'

She shook her head, and when she spoke her voice was so flat that I found myself wondering, at least at first, if she was not, after all, a somnambulist.

'There is a shadow,' she said. 'A shadow from the East.'

'What do you mean? I have to say, I think you're worrying unduly.'

'It is moving closer,' she breathed. 'It brings such contamination.' She held out her arms as if to implore me, cutting a weird figure against the flames. 'The world that is approaching is no place for a child. Or, at least, for no child of mine.'

'Please.' I rose from my bed. 'Please, we need to get you back to—'

She held up her hand to command me to stop my speech, more forceful and decisive than ever I had seen her before. 'And so,' she said, 'the child is being taken from me. It is being stifled in the womb. It is being ripped away.'

The fire seethed, hissed and crackled behind her, and a smile of madness appeared upon her lips.

It was only then that I finally understood what was occurring. I saw upon the front of Carrie's nightgown, in the space between her legs, the awful shape of spreading blood. Blood billowing from her, blood and more blood, turning her gown to crimson.

'The shadow,' said Caroline. 'The shadow has fallen. The shadow which means to claim us all.'

But I could scarcely hear her words over the sound of that single, shrill and heartfelt scream which has been building within me for days.

J.S. BARNES

FROM *LA CROIX**

20 December

A CURIOUS DISTURBANCE ON RUE DE L'ANGIER

The gendarmerie were called last evening to a boarding house on rue de L'Angier following reports from the landlady, as well as from concerned fellow guests and passers-by, of a disturbance of the most bizarre sort. A great, shrieking ruckus was heard to come from a room which had been lately let to an Englishman, one who had claimed to be a commercial traveller on his way home to London.

The shrill cries were said to be utterly horrible. A crowd of neighbours soon gathered and knocked vigorously upon the door, demanding that the occupant of the chamber emerge and explain himself immediately.

No answer came, save for the uncanny wailing from within, and so concern grew. The landlady fetched the key to the room but discovered that her tenant had somehow succeeded in barring it from the inside, making any egress impossible.

When the police arrived, they had no choice but to force the door down and to push aside those heavy boxes which the guest had placed against it to buttress his sanctuary.

What they found was startling – the Englishman in a deep swoon upon the bed and, by his side, a barred crate in which was to be found an enormous, red-eyed black bat, the source of the horrible uproar,

* This translation, from the French, is my own. Please forgive its inexact and halting style.

its wings thrashing wildly.

The visitor was brought around and, although groggy, was full of apologies. He explained that he was a naturalist, freshly returned from an expedition to the Carpathian Mountains, and that he was bringing back to England a singular specimen. He said that he had fallen into an unusually deep sleep and that the creature had grown hungry. He was markedly generous in his finan-cial recompense to the landlady and to several of her followers.

With reluctance, the police departed, after receiving a firm assurance that the gentleman would leave in the morning and go back across the Channel.

Rue de L'Angier – indeed the whole of Paris – will no doubt be grateful that he and his questionable pet are shortly to be the concern only of the English nation.

MINA HARKER'S JOURNAL

———◆———

21 December. A terrible few days at the Godalming estate.

Poor, dear Caroline is so very distressed. Even now Arthur has yet to return home, being much preoccupied with affairs of state and with his Council in particular. I find this abandonment rather a poor show, though I do not doubt that he is grieving also.

Yet I wonder if something greater might not lie behind our recent misfortunes, this horrible agglomeration of events. The timing of the piece in the Gazette concerning the personal histories of our friends (of which Carrie herself is mercifully ignorant) seemed to me most pointed and odd. And then there is something else also.

I write these words upon the train from London to Shore Green. Already the soot-covered city has been left behind and we are sprinting through the Oxfordshire countryside. What was once a scene of comfort and reassurance (and, to Jonathan, one of happy and secluded isolation) strikes me now as a great deal more sinister in aspect.

This is not, I believe, only the nature of the season – for winter has turned the fields to promontories, the hedgerows to sparse delineations and the trees to blasted sentinels – but also a phenomenon that is indicative of my own state of mind.

Is there something behind our recent travails and those of our closest companions? Something which stands outside?

I must set down the truth of it before the keenness of the experience leaves my mind.

I had left the estate, seen off not by Carrie, who remained bedridden within, but by Mr Amory, that stoical manservant whose acquaintance I had made in the most troubling of circumstances. I can admit here without qualm that I was glad to leave. The house has about it a dreadful atmosphere which quite saps the spirit. I am also, of course, looking forward to being reunited before long with my husband, although perhaps, if truth be told, not quite as much as one might ideally wish.

It was with some relief that I found myself aboard the express, several miles from the station at Godalming and steaming back towards the metropolis. The landscape there was a little prettier than that which is being unfurled before me now. Specks of snow were falling. Falling but not settling.

I was alone in my compartment, snug and feeling grateful for those several hours of peace which lay ahead. I found that, without distraction or any immediate concern, my mind drifted back quite naturally towards elder days – the days, I suppose, of our youth when we were all first brought into contact. I pushed away such reminiscences, yet was my memory insistent. Certain images, most of which were decidedly unpleasant, pushed themselves to the forefront of my imagination. It was this unsought preoccupation that surely explains what happened next. Or, perhaps – and this is a thought which I find all but unbearable to entertain – perhaps it does not.

Our progress, in spite of the puffs of snow, had been smooth and unimpeded. For all the doomsayers who complain of national decline in this new century, the British railway service remains the envy of the world.

Yet all at once the carriage gave a great convulsive lurch. With the shrill and desperate keening sound of wrenching metal, the carriage rattled and shook and I was thrown forward violently onto the floor.

All this happened really very quickly indeed, so that I was scarcely aware of what had befallen me. I felt an instant's pain and discomfort before I fell into a swoon.

As I lay in that undignified posture, insensible to my surroundings, I saw certain things in a dream which possessed the clarity of vision.

I was in some distant, ancient castle, far from civilised lands, a place made of cold stone. I found myself descending a steep circular staircase. In the distance, I heard a clock strike one.

I felt a great and urgent desire to go down those stairs, yet my descent seemed unending. For all my exertions, I seemed materially to progress not a whit. The spiral simply went on and on.

After a time, although I felt certain that an hour could not possibly have passed, I heard the clock strike two.

As the echo of it faded away, I glimpsed something ahead of me, at the very edge of my sight, moving before me down the corkscrew. It was the figure of a woman, one I had not seen for many years. Struck by surprise, I hesitated and she who went before me vanished out of view. I hurried onwards, risking a fall in my haste.

After a minute, she came back into view and I saw more clearly her white form, clad in a silvery gown, and her cascade of sleek blonde hair. Joyfully, I called her name, forgetting in the dream that she had long been dead.

'Lucy! Lucy, my dear!'

She did not seem to hear me and only hurried on.

'Lucy!' I called again, more desperately than before. 'Lucy Westenra!'

At this, at last, she stopped and turned to face me. She was just as she had been all those years ago, in the days of the last century before the great darkness fell over all our lives.

She smiled to see me and there was in her expression all her old gaiety of manner. When she spoke, however, it was with an awful coldness of purpose.

'You need to wake up, Mina, my dear,' she said. 'You need to open your eyes and see what is unfolding around you.'

'Lucy,' I said. 'It is so wonderful to see you again.'

'I cannot,' she said, as implacably as before, 'talk with you for long. It is not... permitted.'

'I don't understand.'

'See the pattern, Mina,' she said, and the effort of speaking the words seemed to cost her. 'See the pattern of events which surrounds you and draw the only conclusion that you can.'

I protested. 'But Lucy. I do not understand.'

'You do,' she said, and her dear face creased into a smile, every bit as radiant as those of our youth. 'My clever Mina, of course you do. The truth is before you even now.'

The dream soured. There came an intrusion of horror. A gout of blood emerged from the corners of my old friend's mouth, first on the right side and then upon the left.

'Lucy,' I began, but it was already too late. A trickle became a stream and then a gush, a tide. Her features were covered in wet crimson.

I could not help myself but loosed a cry of terror and disgust, and it was this unseemly howl which, I believe, woke me.

I opened my eyes to find myself upon the floor of the carriage. There was a man standing over me, a ticket inspector dressed in the smart uniform of the railway. He had a kindly face.

'Let me help you up, miss. Please accept my apologies for this most regrettable incident.'

'What happened?' I asked as, with propriety and courtesy, he helped me to my feet.

'Something of a misfortune, miss. There was a trespasser upon the tracks. I fear we were not able to stop in time.'

'How... awful.' Upright once again, I felt a little faint. 'What a terrible thing.'

'If it's any consolation, miss, it would have been over for him very fast. I've often thought that such a death is really something of a mercy in a way.'

He said more which I cannot now recall. He made certain that I was settled and was good enough to fetch me a cup of tea.

After a while, the train moved on. We left the accident behind us. I felt a mild restoration and the details of my dream began, at least to a small degree, to fade.

Yet much still remains.

I wonder about the warning that dear Lucy rendered unto me. I wonder about the pattern of which she spoke. I wonder about the exhortation that I should see the truth. If it be not mere fancy and delusion, I wonder what all of it means.

Can it be? Can it be that He is returning?

I must think. I must investigate. And I must speak to Jonathan.

JONATHAN HARKER'S JOURNAL

——◆——

22 December. Guilt is, for me, scarcely a novel emotion but at the time of writing it is present in my breast to an unusually predominant degree. I should first state that nothing in the least unorthodox or improper occurred between Miss Sarah-Ann Dowell and I. As to whether there is at least a part of me which wished for such a Rubicon to be crossed, I cannot say. It must suffice me to record that we only talked, as the Professor lay somnolent beside us, of many things, but in particular of love and of those strange places to which that brand of madness might lead.

She spoke of her own paramour, a gentleman of dubious character named Thom Cawley, from whom, it seemed clear, she should disentangle herself at the earliest possible opportunity. We parted late in the evening but chastely, and as friends.

This unexpected encounter was as preface to the news which came the following morning – that poor Caroline's reason is largely unseated and that her baby is lost. That I should have been engaged in conversation with Miss Dowell while my wife dealt single-handedly with this tragedy served only to sharpen and accentuate those emotions to which I was already subject.

I sent a telegram in reply to Mina's,[*] pledging my aid in any way that she thought fit. Her cool, ordered response came in the afternoon. Go to London. Find Arthur and Jack Seward. And send them both to the Godalmings at once.

In all this, of course, I was immensely happy to oblige and, leaving Sarah-Ann in charge of the house and its contents, I departed without ceremony for the metropolis.

Yet my mission was altogether less clear cut than I had hoped. For it would seem very much as though Dr John Seward has disappeared.

There was no sign of him at his home. At his Harley Street clinic he has not been seen for six days, occasioning a great deal of cancellation and much disgruntlement and mild outrage on the part of Jack's patients. His employees, staff and even friends (such as they are) have not received word from him and concern is, quite naturally, growing as to his whereabouts and wellbeing.

Eventually, and acting on my own initiative, I reported him missing to the police, arriving at Scotland Yard around dusk on the afternoon of the twenty-first. I queued for the attention of the duty sergeant, behind a stout restaurateur who seemed worried for the security of his premises. When my turn came, I explained the nature of the emergency, giving both my own name and that of the missing alienist.

At this, the sergeant – a rather grimy sort of sceptic – gave me the oddest look and bade me come with him. He left his post and escorted me to a small, whitewashed room, curiously monastic in atmosphere. I was left alone there for some minutes with nothing to do save examine the weft of the walls.

---

[*] I have been unable to find any trace of this correspondence.

'Someone will be with you presently, Mr Harker,' the sergeant said, before closing the door behind him.

I do not care to be left alone in confined spaces and I had grown rather anxious by the time that the door was opened again and a different policeman strode in.

'Sub-Divisional Inspector George Dickerson,' he said, extending his hand. Somewhat to my surprise, he spoke with a pronounced American accent. 'Sincere apologies, sir, for keeping you waiting.'

'Not at all,' I replied. 'You must have much to occupy your time.'

'There's always a deal to do, sir. I understand you wished to report a man who's gone missing. Party's name is Seward?'

'That is so.'

'And your own moniker is...' At this, he drew from his coat pocket a notebook in the consultation of which he proceeded to enact quite a pantomime before delivering my name. 'Jonathan Harker?'

I nodded. In exchange he gave me a look, almost as if we had known one another a long time ago, as children perhaps, and he was endeavouring now to place my present appearance. He paused for a moment, seeming to consider the wisest course of action. 'Sir, I'll be plain. Fact is John Seward was here himself, not so very long ago.'

'He was?'

'Yes, sir. He was making, as I understand it, some independent enquiries of his own.'

'Good Lord. About what, may I ask?'

'About a colleague of mine, sir. A man called Chief Inspector Parlow.'

'And what the deuce,' I said carefully and quietly, 'did Seward want with the chief inspector? He's not, I trust, in any trouble?'

'No criminal trouble, sir, no. But he did seem anxious. What he wanted with Parlow had to do, as I understand it, with Martin's old partner, who's been dead now for years. And there was something to do with a journal.'

'Who was the partner?' I asked, thoroughly bewildered.

Sub-Divisional Inspector Dickerson took a deep breath as though he were about to embark upon something unpleasant. He spoke then a name which will to me be forever freighted with the most insidious form of evil.

'Why, it was Renfield, sir. It was the late and unlamented Detective Inspector R.M. Renfield.'

I left the Yard and the company of Dickerson in a fug of confusion and unease. My head sang with mournful images of sorrowful events upon the exclusion of which from my memory I have, in the past decade, expended considerable personal effort.

So absorbed was I that upon exiting the Yard and commencing a search for a hansom, I practically collided into the tall angular figure of a man whom, after a moment's confusion, I recognised.

'Arthur! My dear chap. Whatever has brought you here?'

On closer inspection, Lord Godalming looked rather paler and more haggard even than he had upon our last meeting.

'It's Jack…' he said, a faltering quality to his voice which I had never heard there before, not even in those dark days. 'Jack seems to have gone missing. Nobody's seen him for days.'

'I know,' I said. 'I know, and I am afraid that there may be a good deal more to the business than we understand at present. But, Arthur, look here – I am so awfully sorry, you know. Truly. For you and for Carrie. And for the baby.'

I offered him my hand and he shook it.

'Thank you,' he said at last, stiffly, looking very far away. 'Your condolences are most appreciated.'

'Not at all.'

'I hear that your wife has been most generous and compassionate.'

'I know,' I said, and a further sad silence descended.

'Have you eatcn supper yet?' Arthur asked at length.

I said that I had not, to which he at once replied with an unpersuasive sort of bonhomie: 'Well, then you must dine at the club. The food there is really quite adequate.'

I began to protest. 'Really, I ought to... Mina will be...'

The noble lord raised a hand. 'Nonsense,' he said. 'Besides, I should tonight appreciate some company and some friendship. And...' He paused and touched his temples as if to ward off the approach of a headache. 'Some necessary conversation also.'

Arthur's club (this particular one, at least) was entirely as I would have expected: a place of luxurious exclusivity. The food was first rate, the wine excellent and the conversation, though at the outset halting and uncertain, grew increasingly easy. Arthur spoke at some length of his regret that his commitments in the House had kept him from spending a greater deal of time by his wife's side.

He seemed quite implacable in the matter of his opposition to the Emergency Bill and the role to be played by the Council of Athelstan. 'It is,' he said, 'a piece of absolute chicanery – and dangerous chicanery at that.'

I wished him well with the enterprise, though I admit that the whole business seems to me to be rather academic in nature. We spoke then of other things – of Caroline, of Mina and Quincey, of the poor Dutchman who languishes still upon the precipice of death.

As to the whereabouts of Jack Seward we are both quite baffled. Such behaviour, for all the doctor's burgeoning eccentricity, is most out of character. Together, we pledged to do everything within our power to find him. As the evening wore on and as our consumption of strong drink increased, we spoke again even that old and terrible name – that of the asylum inmate who, it now transpired, had once been employed by His Majesty's constabulary.

Arthur sighed. 'Can't you feel it?' he asked.

'Whatever do you mean?'

'This sense of something closing in. Like a net. Pulling tight about us.'

I only nodded, not daring, I suppose, to examine the implications of my agreement. Wearily, Lord Godalming tried to rally and to brighten.

'Good Lord,' he said. 'I had almost forgotten.'

'Forgotten what?'

'The season.' He raised his chalice, still half full of dark red wine. 'Merry Christmas, Harker.'

I mirrored the gesture. 'Merry Christmas,' said I, more dolefully than I had meant.

And in that place of age and privilege, we touched glasses and tried to toast our future happiness, as all the while we were compassed round by the evils of the past and by a mighty fearfulness as to the coming days.

FROM THE PRIVATE DIARY
OF AMBROSE QUIRE,
Commissioner of Police of the Metropolis

———◆———

24 December. A mere handful of hours before Christmas, and who do you think is still a-labouring at his desk when half the force is lost to revelry? None other than your own correspondent. Such are the demands of leadership. Such are the wages of command.

My duties now seem more numerous than ever. Something is rising amongst the criminal classes and there is inexplicable vexation amongst the trinity of London gangs.

I have read of a similar phenomenon on the plains of the far-distant Serengeti. Carrion birds fight amongst themselves at the approach of a greater predator. Vultures gather when lions do battle.

Quite why so colourful an analogy should occur to me now, I have not the slightest notion.

More than three dozen reports have reached me in the past fortnight of violent fracas and extended scuffles between rival gang members.

None of those felons whom we have at present in custody are able to shed any particular light on the matter. Dickerson is working hard, I know, for all that he seems to have allowed himself to become distracted by some missing alienist who has no doubt run off with his mistress or houseboy.

As ever, Parlow's knowledge and expertise are sorely missed. The only villain who seems at all willing to confide in us is young Thom Cawley – that smallest of fish – still in our custody following an incident in the cells. He speaks about that which his more hardened compadres will not, namely that at least something of the skittishness which is sweeping his fraternity has to do with some recurrent dream or nightmare from which (he says) they are all of them suffering.

He sees a shadow. A dark figure approaching. White teeth gleaming in the moonlight.

Of course I thought it the purest melodrama. Yet here – aha! – yes, here is a curious thing indeed. Shortly before penning this entry, hard at work upon a stack of bureaucratic necessities, I suffered a momentary loss of concentration and drifted into something like a doze. There is much that I cannot now recall, but I can remember that as I dreamed, the images which flitted through my mind were the same in every way as those which young Cawley had described.

Coincidence, I am sure. Nothing more!

And yet.

A new year soon. Perhaps then these cobwebs and unhappy thoughts will be driven away. Yes. Surely? Surely they will.

FROM THE PRIVATE JOURNAL
OF MAURICE HALLAM

———————◆———————

25 December. The flower of jealousy I have never before permitted to bloom within me. The seeds of envy I have rejected and the spore of covetousness has never once taken root in my soul. Naturally, it is Mr Shone who has reshaped these life-long habits, who has fractured the old disciplines and who has within me nurtured 'the green-eyed monster which doth mock the meat it feeds on'.

Our wanderings have brought us to Paris, where Gabriel has made a new friend.

The fortunate gentleman's name is Jules Dumont and he possesses even, symmetrical features and a pleasantly muscular physique. He is to Gabriel as is a dray horse to a thoroughbred. Nonetheless, he seems to bring my friend considerable delight. Dumont is a police inspector in the Parisian gendarmerie, a fact which appears to add some perverse additional lustre in the eyes of my companion.

We are staying in an agreeably rackety hotel, within sight of the Notre Dame, a place devoted to discretion, institutional incuriosity and the absolute guarantee to make no enquiry of a personal nature. It was in consequence of these policies that, having woken late this feast-day morn, I sauntered into Mr Shone's boudoir to discover my associate all but in flagrante delicto with the brawny peeler. Although Dumont covered himself with alacrity, I glimpsed upon his left thigh the raw red mark of a recent incision.

Gabriel laughed. He reached to the cabinet beside the bed and threw me a single gold coin. 'Merry Christmas, Maurice. Here's your present. Now be a good fellow, won't you, and leave us be? Why not go out and find one of your own?'

Monsieur Dumont gave a jackal's grin and Shone dabbed absently at the healing socket of his left eye.

'Very well,' I said. 'Perhaps I shall.' I nodded. 'The compliments of the season to you both.' And I walked with as much dignity as I could muster from the room.

For a long time I trailed through the streets of the old city, drawn as if by some instinctive magnetism to its seamiest reaches.

Even on a day such as today I had only a trifle more trouble than is usual in locating that oasis from which I meant, a little disconsolately, to drink.

The boy was one and twenty. A firm-bodied loafer who stood at the corner of a cat's cradle of dreary streets and alleyways, eating an apple with shameless theatricality.

He caught my eye at once and favoured me with a wink of experience. He turned and walked away onto a nearby boulevard, moving in such a fashion as somehow to suggest a beckoning. Pushing away all thoughts of loyalty to Gabriel, I followed. Hearing my footfalls, he glanced backwards and fixed me with an expression of salacious coquetry.

Yet I was destined never to reach him. All at once I felt a terrific surge of agony, deep in my gut. I stumbled, fell and sprawled face first in the filth and dirt of the street. I believe that the inexplicable pain may even have caused an instant's unconsciousness.

When the torture ended I looked up and staggered to my feet. My boy had vanished. I breathed in deeply but shakily. It was only then that I realised there was blood about my lips and chin.

It dripped with a horrible insistence. From far away I heard the angry howl of a wild dog.

Trudging home in wretched defeat, I thought that I could not easily recall any more miserable Christmas Day.

MINA HARKER'S JOURNAL

———◆———

25 December. I cannot recall any more miserable Christmas Day. We have all rallied, we have all done our best, yet there is scarcely any joy still to be found in our home.

Quincey has returned to us from school in a sad and meditative mood. I am quite certain that the oppressive atmosphere of this place will already have affected him. Pensive and cast down, he has yet to speak more than a sentence to Miss Dowell, for all that he still casts stray glances in her direction.

Absences are keenly felt – the Professor who lies shrunken above us, our dear friend Jack whose whereabouts remain unknown, and that sad absence of a different kind for poor Caroline Holmwood.

Melancholia hangs about us like a shroud, though I have tried to make the day as full as is practicable of the jollity of the season. Jonathan sought solace once again in his usual recourse. He drank too much before our luncheon and stuttered as he spoke the grace. I note that, even when half in his cups, he cannot bring himself to set his eyes upon Sarah-Ann.

Later, after the girl was gone, and when Quincey had finally been persuaded to go to bed (for flashes of his old self were at times tonight quite heart-wrenchingly visible), I tried my best to speak to his father.

'Jonathan…' I began. 'There is a certain matter I have, for a while now, been meaning to discuss with you.'

'Oh?' There was an undercurrent of belligerence to his voice which I have not often heard in it before. I blame the festive drink (although not, in truth, entirely) for its appearance.

'It has to do,' I went on, as though I had not detected at all the altered timbre, 'with poor Caroline.'

At first, at these words, an odd sort of relief seemed to me to pass across his face. 'It's most regrettable to be sure. A great tragedy.'

'But – what – I mean, dear Jonathan, what if it is more than that?'

'I'm afraid I don't understand.'

'Her symptoms… her behaviour… Do they not remind you of anything?'

My husband shook his head. 'I'm not sure that I quite follow your logic.'

'You know,' I murmured. 'You know of what I speak.'

At this, his voice turned very cold. 'Poor Caroline has never been well. We've always known that. Such behaviour as she has of late exhibited was only ever a matter of time. Some people are broken early in their lives and can never be put back together again. It's very sad, but there it is.'

'But what…' I went on, 'what if there was some other force, something outside her, pushing her on? Making each fracture worse. Driving her into madness.'

There was a very long silence between us after that. When Jonathan spoke again, his words were quiet yet angry. 'That is quite impossible.'

'Who knows,' I said, 'what's possible where...' I paused, unwilling to say the words aloud.

'Yes?'

'Where he is concerned,' I finished, as firmly as I could.

Jonathan rose with furious vigour to his feet. 'He is dead,' he said. 'He is dead and gone and that is an end to it. All this – your concerns – are so much nerves and imagination.'

'Please,' I said. 'Listen to me. On the train home, I had a dream. More than a dream. Lucy came to me. With a message...'

With a single gesture of his hand, Jonathan cut me off. 'Enough,' he said. 'Enough of this nonsense. I will not hear another word of it. You understand me?'

I surrendered. 'Go to bed,' I said. 'Sleep it off. We'll talk again.'

'Indeed we will. But not,' he insisted, 'of this.'

He turned and strode out of the room. And so in this most unhappy fashion have matters been left between us.

FROM THE *ST JAMES' BUDGET*

27 December

STRANGE TRAGEDY IN RUPERT STREET, W1

At noon on Boxing Day police were called to the premises of the Antelope Hotel on Rupert Street, W1, to investigate reports of screams and a violent dispute. The scene that awaited them was a grisly one: a man of middle years dead upon his bed, evidently the victim of a savage assault. His skin was torn and lacerated and his face so badly disfigured that his features were barely recognisable. He had few possessions save for a valise of clothes and a great wooden case, which had been shattered and broken as if from within.

Sub-Divisional Inspector George Dickerson of Scotland Yard spoke to this reporter, stating that the victim has been identified as the prominent naturalist Mr Haskell Lynch.

Lynch had been travelling abroad for some months and was returning home in order to announce the consequences of his most recent research. The inspector theorised that Lynch had with him a specimen capable of unprovoked violence and that it was this animal which had escaped the container and committed the atrocity.

London Zoo has been informed and Mr Dickerson has appealed for persons in possession of any additional facts about the death to come forward at once.

On the question of Lynch's presence in a district which has in recent weeks been subjected to increasing outbreaks of gang violence, Dickerson would not – for now – be drawn.

FROM THE PRIVATE DIARY
OF AMBROSE QUIRE,
Commissioner of Police of the Metropolis

———◆———

28 December. Until today, in the course of a more than averagely distinguished career, I had come to believe that I had seen pretty much all that there is to be seen. In that surmise I have this very evening been proved – and I am perfectly comfortable in making the admission – entirely wrong in every way.

Crime is no respecter of the season. The past few days must presumably have been as busy as their immediate predecessors, though, oddly enough, I find that I cannot recall them in any detail, discovering in my memory only a certain haziness.

Not that there is time left now for self-justification. Instead, I shall simply state the facts, while I can.

I suppose I must have fallen asleep at my desk, although I can't think quite how this could have come about. I woke at twilight, perspiring and with a start, as though from another corker of·a nightmare. I had been slumped over a cache of papers and I was dressed in clothes which – unpleasant as it seems to admit it – felt to me as though I had worn them for several days, at the least.

My head swam as if in the wake of too generous festive consumption, though I had no recollection of such a debauch. My skin prickled and felt clammy.

For the record, I should state that I was not woken at my desk in this regrettably dishevelled state entirely of my own volition. Rather, I was woken by a noise – by a persistent tapping on my window. Not a thing, you may mark my words, which one ever expects to hear when one's office is upon the third floor. I wrenched myself from the chair and all but stumbled over to the glass. I peered into darkness and at first I could spy nothing there at all.

Then I saw it – emerging from the dusk – the hideous form of an enormous black bat. It beat its wings with a horrible fury against the pane and I realised that this nocturnal beast was the source of that which had interrupted my slumber. I cannot explain now why I did what I did next, except to say that some new compulsion had started even then to work upon me.

I reached out and opened the window and I allowed the creature, as willing as a house cat, to slip silkily inside. The bat glided to the floor where it seemed to crouch, and looked up at me with a baleful invitation.

I ought also to make clear that in all of this I felt nothing in the least like fear, but only a distance from my experience, as though mesmerism had rendered me quite numb. I watched the intruder and the bat watched me, and then a thing occurred that remains wholly inexplicable, being both marvellous and awful: the animal seemed to quake and shimmer and, in my very office, to be transformed into the figure of perhaps the most beautiful woman I have ever seen.

She is tall and raven-haired, physically remarkable in every way. For a time, she seemed still to have great wings upon her back, though those swiftly faded. She was entirely naked. She smiled, revealing sharp white teeth.

'Commissioner,' she said, her voice a purr inflected by the accent of some faraway kingdom.

I nodded dumbly, then croaked out: 'Hello.'

'I have travelled a great distance,' said the lady, 'from a land of forests. My exertions have been many and now I hunger.'

'I see.'

'And so I ask you: may I feed?'

I did not hesitate. 'Yes,' I said. 'Take whatever it is that you need.'

She drew closer, the effect of it all so utterly dreamlike that I wondered whether in some fashion I still slept. She moved nearer, then nearer again. The glorious scent of her. She reached out her arm and took me by the shoulder. She leaned so close to me, so tantalisingly close.

'Who...' I asked, my breathing ragged, 'are you?'

'My name is Ileana. I am being the prophet. I come before one who is greater than me. And I ask, Ambrose Quire – will you serve us?'

No longer having the slightest semblance of self-control, I managed a second, still weaker nod.

And then she was upon me. Her hands were on my form, her face was close to mine and – with a savage joy which I had never before that hour known that I craved – her sharp teeth were cutting at my throat. There was a sweet release and a state of dark bliss. There was a happy suckling. After it was done, her ruby lips still slick with my blood, she took me to the window, her arms about me, supporting me as though I were an invalid.

'All over Europe,' she said, 'the shadow is falling now. We

must prepare for the hour of His return. Will you play your part?'

'Yes,' I said. 'Anything. If only you will do to me again what you did to me just then.'

She laughed with splendid cruelty. 'All in good time. For now, Ambrose Quire, this is what we wish of you. There will soon come a sequence of explosions at the heart of the city. It will be seen as a symptom of your criminal gangs at war. Your task will be to stop all investigation. To stoke the flames of suspicion and mistrust. To be hastening the war that is coming.'

I began, feebly, to protest. 'Ileana, I am a policeman. I am the policeman. My responsibilities... my duties to the city...'

She placed a slender finger to my mouth. 'Are as nothing,' she said, 'to what we have shared. And to what we will be sharing again.'

I let out a rattling, pitiful sigh. 'Yes.'

'Good boy.' She smiled again. 'You are being my very special, my very good boy.'

She held me in her gaze then as she took me wholly into her power. As I watched, she licked the crimson from her lips and shivered in triumph and delight.

MINA HARKER'S JOURNAL

———◆———

29 December. At last, the inevitable has occurred. A great light in all our lives has been extinguished. We have lost Professor Abraham Van Helsing.

There had been some small improvement while Quincey was away, but upon his return from school matters seemed again to decline at speed.

It happened, in the end, very quietly. Both Sarah-Ann and our son were with him.

The death of the Dutchman is, I hope, a mercy, so diminished had he become. Quincey and Miss Dowell came down together shortly after twilight to tell us the news. I bowed my head in expected sorrow, but Jonathan – thinking, no doubt, of all the horrors that he had shared with the deceased – loosed a kind of cry of anguish which he at once made efforts to stifle and subdue.

In an action designed, I suspect, to seem casual, he reached for the decanter and the wine glass. For so many weeks has this sad situation endured that there were few tears from Quincey or from me, but only a grim acceptance of the ways of life and death.

We four went upstairs and, standing together around the bed of the departed, spoke aloud a prayer to safeguard the old physician's soul. And, if only for a moment, I felt the presence, for the final time, of that noble and courageous spirit, quite separate from the shell of his body which lay before us.

There is a very great deal now to plan. A funeral and a memorial service also. I must inform the Godalmings, and I shall send a telegram to them forthwith. We must also take urgent steps to locate Dr Seward. Perhaps Mr Amory can help. I shall suggest offering some manner of reward.

With the passing of Van Helsing, it is as though a grand era has come at last to a conclusion. Why then does it feel to me now rather as if it marks not an ending but a beginning?

Of those darker – and surely half-imagined – fears I have not dared to speak to Jonathan again since Christmas Day.

Later. An odd thing. Quincey has just come to us, shortly before sleep. He says that he is torn into two and that there is something within him driving him to distraction.

I allowed Jonathan to speak to the boy and to take him to bed. It is a father's place to intervene. I wonder whether, in the past, I have not been rather too lenient with Quincey. He is only undergoing, after all, a necessary transformation into a man. I hope that he is sufficiently prepared for that state and that Jonathan will yet prove to be a capable guide. Besides, the business was no doubt evoked by delayed grief concerning the Professor. Surely it must be so?

There are other concerns that I have about my boy. Though I cannot set them down on paper yet.

FROM THE PRIVATE JOURNAL
OF MAURICE HALLAM

——◆——

29 December. And so the young lecher of the gendarmerie has been abandoned and we have moved on. Yesterday saw our arrival in Calais, a port that is bustling and seedy in equal measure. Its close-penned streets are thick with the scents of fish and brine, and with the rank odours of too large a population. To board a ship to England would be the work of a moment but Gabriel, in brusque and taciturn temper ever since our departure from Paris, seems somehow to be waiting for something. He idles his hours away while exhibiting signs of a growing and contradictory impatience. I am happy, as ever I have been, to wait and to obey. I am also relieved to note that there has to date been no recurrence of that horrible pain which felled me in the capital.

There is but a single curious incident to record. It was just beginning to grow dark and we were sitting together inside a miserable wharf-side bar, engrossed in silence, when, without the slightest provocation, Mr Shone threw back his head and began uproariously (though not, it must be said, at all pleasantly) to laugh.

'Gabriel?' I said. 'Whatever is it?'

'The old man is dead. At last!'

'Who?'

'The old man is dead,' he repeated as if oblivious to my question. 'And so the gateway is open. England lies unprotected and unawares, all but begging us – begging us, Maurice! – to ravish her.' This baffling soliloquy done, he laughed once more.

I thought, not for the first time, how very white and sharp his teeth have become.

TELEGRAM FROM LORD ARTHUR GODALMING TO MR JONATHAN HARKER

30 December

News of Van Helsing received with sorrow. Do allow us to help and pay for funeral. We shall be together soon. If only Jack were with us! Carrie still unwell. Often delirious. She woke this morning with a scream and the words: 'He is coming. He is coming home! The one-eyed man is almost here!'

LETTER FROM SARAH-ANN DOWELL
TO THOM CAWLEY

30 December

Dearest Thom,

I thought by now that I would not write to you again till you replied to me for I am awful afraid you have fallen into old habits and bad ways. Weeks without word from you and the press full of strife between the gangs, and your Giddis mob at the heart of it! I fear for you, Thom, really I do.

But I thought I owed it to you, for the love we used to share, to tell you I am coming home to London. Coming home, if truth be told, in something of a flight for I have packed my suitcase and fled from the Harkers' house as soon as I glimpsed the dawn.

My job here is done and the old man has passed over but these are not the reasons why I ran. Oh Thom, you will hardly believe it! I woke in the deep of the night, to find in my room, standing at the foot of my bed, the boy, Quincey. He said nothing but just stared at me. And this is the worst of it – he had eyes of the purest red.

When he saw that I had woken he turned and left. I found I could not scream but only lie where I was, not daring to move, trying to pray but thinking ever of those terrible red eyes.

Oh, Thom, they cut through the darkness. The eyes of some night-time animal. Of some beast.

Even now, as I flee towards the city, I feel them on me still – his hungry, devil's gaze.

Yours, in fear and trembling,
Sarah-Ann

FROM THE PERSONAL COLUMNS OF *THE TIMES*

31 December

MISSING PERSON:
JOHN SEWARD, NOTED ALIENIST, PHILOSOPHICAL THINKER, WIDOWER.

Last seen by his domestic staff on the morning of December the sixteenth in a state of some dishevelment and distress. Seward is almost six feet tall, rather stooped in the shoulders and has dark hair, greying and receding.

His manner is scholarly. He answers to 'Jack'.

A **SUBSTANTIAL REWARD** is to be made available to anyone who can provide useful information as to his current whereabouts.

Dr Seward has many concerned friends who are prepared to be **MOST GENEROUS** in the event of his prompt discovery. Those who have information that they are willing to share should contact Mr R.V. Amory of the Holmwood Estate, Sussex.

FROM THE PRIVATE JOURNAL
OF MAURICE HALLAM

31 December. And so at last is my long pilgrimage ended, my exile done, and I am come home again to England.

We left France under cover of darkness, at high tide. At night, Gabriel was still in the same curiously good spirits that he had displayed in that low bar. Once we were out at sea, his mood seemed to sink and he exhibited some hitherto undisplayed signs of unease at the expanse of water by which we were surrounded. At length, once the worst of the distance was done, we stood together on deck and gazed down at the churning blackness of the ocean. He turned to me and softly (almost sighing) said: 'There will be change, you know, in our homeland. Great and irrevocable change.'

'Oh?' I asked. 'How and when will this come to pass?'

'Why, when I stand at the forefront of the governing power – at the head of the Council.'

'You still have that ambition, then?' I asked. His reply brought no answer, but rather only awoke in my breast further questions.

Suddenly, he seemed to turn quite pale. I felt a firm hand upon my left arm.

'You'll stay with me, won't you, Maurice? Stay with me come hell or high water until the promised end?'

'Of course I shall. Our path is set, dear boy, and I shall follow you wheresoever it may lead. You know that I am pledged to you.'

He gave no reply to this, nor was one needed. We simply stood together as the ship surged on.

After a time, we saw, at first very faint and far away, almost wispy and insubstantial, but then increasing in proximity and heft, those old guardians of our island nation, the chalk cliffs of Dover. At the sight, I felt an odd sense that some circle was within me being ineluctably completed.

The sensation was far from pleasant and seemed to awaken an echo of the pain by which I had been assailed in Paris. Yet time passed, the cliffs drew nearer and before long we were stepping with something of the confidence of returning buccaneers onto the quayside at Dover, back once again on terra firma.

We made the decision to search for accommodation on foot, and had barely begun to find our way free of the maze of the docklands when I became aware that we were being followed – first by one mangy-looking dog, then by another and another until, like some modern-day Pied Piper, we were pursued by a dozen or more slouching hounds.

Although their appearance was bizarre and disquieting, I did my best not to panic. Rather, I merely swore beneath my breath and wondered aloud if the beasts were looking for food. To my surprise, Gabriel stopped short and held up a hand; almost, I thought, like a conductor with his baton. I halted with him. By now, free of the departing throng, we were alone upon a dingy thoroughfare – alone, that is, but for the dogs.

'Gabriel?' I asked. 'What do we do?'

He merely smiled his white, clean smile.

Then more came, slinking out of the shadows, more dogs, and more and more of them.

With a start of horror and revulsion, I saw that there were other creatures amongst the tide which moved now to encircle us. Rats, snakes, spiders, insects, all the crawling vermin of the earth!

Almost without warning the day had taken on a nightmarish aspect, a quality of Fuseli in this seaside town, an intrusion of the Blakean into daylight hours. I gasped in disgust and felt inside me again the pain that I had known in France. I sank to my knees. In spite of my best efforts, for an instant, instinctively, I squeezed shut my eyes. And in the darkness I saw (or thought I saw) several strange things.

They hurried forward, that ramshackle pack, and seemed set to overwhelm us. But then, with a single clap of his hands, Gabriel bade them disperse. They obeyed without demur. All fled back to the shadows. The manner of my friend was now coolly indulgent.

'Gabriel...'

'Oh, but they wished merely,' he murmured, 'to pay tribute...' He helped me to my feet. 'Poor Maurice.'

I was shaking, gasping for breath.

'Tell me,' said Shone. 'Did you see something then? In the instant that you closed your eyes? Some manner of vision or glimpse?'

Painfully, I nodded. 'Yes, but how did you—'

He waved away the question. 'That is not important now. But you must tell me what you saw.'

'A woman,' I said. 'Dark-haired and exhausted. Her face

dappled with blood. She suspects, I think. Even now, she suspects the truth of things, though she dare not bring herself to face it.'

Gabriel Shone tossed his head back and laughed. 'Oh, that is good. That is very good indeed.'

'Why, Gabriel? Why was I shown this thing? What does it mean?'

'It means that the future is intersecting with the present and the past. It means that a great shadow has fallen. And, above all else, it means that He is close now; that His return is imminent; that our Lord is to be reborn.'

'Who?' I asked. 'Who do you mean by that?'

Gabriel spat once and with vigour upon the dusty ground. 'You know his name.'

'I do not.'

'You've known since the forest. Since the castle. Since you were given the Black Grail to drink.'

'No,' I said, as calmly as I was able. 'Truly, Gabriel, I do not.'

Shone smiled, more widely than I had ever seen him smile before. I glimpsed again those sharp incisors. 'You know his name, Maurice. The dread name of our lord and master.'

'I... do not.' In my heart, I knew that I was lying.

'Of course you do. And you shall say it. Here and now. For me. You shall say his name.'

'Gabriel, no. Please.'

'Say it! Damn you! Say it!'

Blood pounded in my temples. My vision spun wildly. My skin prickled with heat.

'Say his name!'

I gasped. I staggered. Yet I could hold it back no longer,

that admission, that acceptance, those three horrible, long-expected syllables.

'Dracula.'

And as I fell again into a swoon, the very last thing that I heard before the darkness was the bleak and terrible laughter of the one-eyed man.

FROM *THE PALL MALL GAZETTE*

1 January (early edition)

LONDON ATTACKED!
IDENTITY OF PERPETRATORS UNKNOWN

At the time of publication, the specific nature of these tragic circumstances has yet to emerge. Nonetheless, this paper has been assured on the very highest authority that in the early hours of this morning an incendiary device of considerable potency was exploded without warning in the eastern end of our metropolis.

The outrage was committed in a Temperance Hall which seems to have been filled to capacity at the time of the vicious assault. Police officials have yet to release details of the number of casualties, yet the toll is believed by our reporters to be substantial and to include (for all that the district contains many displaced persons, European émigrés and paupers) numerous English folk.

Make no mistake – this is an act of unwarranted terror against a peaceful nation, a blow delivered to the heart of our bountiful Empire. This newspaper will not rest or slacken in our determination both to uncover the facts in the case and to insist upon the highest possible penalties for its evil perpetrators. We will print fresh details as soon as possible.

MEMORANDUM FROM SUB-DIVISIONAL INSPECTOR GEORGE DICKERSON TO COMMISSIONER AMBROSE QUIRE

1 January

These are the facts, sir, at least so far as we have them.

Not long after midnight last night, when most of the city was still abroad, a meeting was held just about as far from our sight as it's possible to be, in a Temperance Hall at the corner of Drake Street and Richardson Avenue, on the outer edge of the East End. None of the Force dares step there alone. My intelligence is still imperfect, but it seems as though the meeting was meant to be a peace conference of some kind between the three main criminal gangs – foolish as I know that sounds.

Near as I can tell, it was all in an effort to renew the old agreements and try to keep together what has been falling away between them. The cause of it all is still unknown. None will talk to me save to speak the same nonsense as the kid about bad dreams.

The witnesses, so far as I have been able to sober them up, were all outside when the explosion rocked the district. Any and all inside are either dead or mortally wounded. It seems that a tall man was seen entering the bar minutes before the blast, carrying a brown portmanteau bag in his right hand. This must have contained the incendiary dynamite and he who carried it, unless it went off before he intended, was surely content to die beside his victims.

This should be cause now, sir, for serious concern.

Members of all three gangs were killed but I doubt they will see any justice in that. Each will blame the other – the Sweetmen, the Giddis Boys and the Pigtails – and things from now on are going to escalate. It is my strong advice that we act fast to stop things getting worse. Decisive action, sir, is what we need.

I stand ready, Commissioner, to do my duty. In the meantime, the investigation – as well as our prayers – goes on.

G.D.

NOTE FROM CECIL CARNEHAN TO ARNOLD SALTER

1 January

Arnold,

I am sure that you have heard by now the thoroughly awful news concerning the devastation last night in the East End. Shocking tragedy, many feared dead, a nation mourns, et cetera, et cetera.

On reflection I think that the time may now be upon us when your opinions concerning this drama (and others like it) might be readily received by our readers. I've no desire to be a bore or to ask too much of you, conscious as I am of your advancing years, but might I have, say, five hundred words by nightfall?

Yours, most sincerely,
Carnehan*

---

*The original response to this missive has long since been mislaid or destroyed. Fleet Street legend, however, has it that the message consisted of but a single, capitalised word: YES.

MINA HARKER'S JOURNAL

———◆———

1 January. A multitude of sadnesses continue to afflict us. No sooner has the Professor slipped away than we have lost Miss Dowell also, and in the oddest of circumstances: gone in the middle of the night, without leaving even the tiniest courtesy of a letter of explanation or a note of apology.

Quincey has taken badly this apparent dereliction, being pale, anxious and prone to bad temper. We broke the news to him at breakfast. He heard us out with the most profound ill grace. At luncheon he remained sullen and resentful. To my frank irritation, if not, I fear, altogether to my surprise, Jonathan seems almost as downcast by the absence of our guest as does our son. For my husband has turned taciturn and withdrawn, behaving as though something precious has been taken unexpectedly from him. I suppose, in a fashion, that it has.

He took a drink today at luncheon and then another once we were done.

In truth, I suspect that Miss Dowell's departure has to do chiefly with her mysterious beau in London. Besides, there is so much else at present to occupy and concern us – the wellbeing of Caroline, the whereabouts of Jack and the preparations for our last farewell to Van Helsing. This will take the form of two separate functions: a small, private funeral, to take place on the sixth of January here in Shore Green, and a public memorial service in the church of St Sebastian in the West, in London, on the eleventh. I have shouldered responsibility for making arrangements for both.

There is also a theory emerging in my mind. As much as I try to concentrate upon it – the connections between certain recent events – I find that the details slip away, as if greasy and impossible to hold. Is it possible that something from the outside might be keeping me from resolving these thoughts and from full understanding? Once I would have spoken of these things to Jonathan. Now, after Christmas, I know what he will say. Oh, why will he not listen?

Later. A difficult scene with Quincey, one in which he seemed all of a sudden more like the boy he used to be. He went early to bed but we discovered him (Jonathan by that time half-inebriated) in the dining room, shortly before we ourselves intended to retire, standing in sorrowful silence. For an instant he seemed not to be in the least aware of our presence. Then he blinked, startled and owlish.

'Forgive me,' he said. 'I was dreaming. At least, Mother, at least I think it was a dream.'

'Of what,' I said, more gentle in my manner than I fear that I have been all day, 'did you dream?'

'Of fire, Mother. Of death brought into the heart of the city.'

He fell silent after that and we saw him back to bed, where

he seemed to descend almost at once back into the relative comfort of sleep.

When I left the room I thought that I heard something from far away, from the fields which lie beyond the house. It was like a bark, yet also somehow most unlike...

FROM *THE PALL MALL GAZETTE*

2 January

SALTER SAYS: THE EAST END TRAGEDY WAS NOT INEVITABLE BUT AVERTIBLE

The beginning of a new year ought by rights to be a time of hope and optimism. It should be an occasion for reflection on the year that has passed and an opportunity to consider ways in which we might start afresh. It should be the moment at which we all look happily towards the future.

How sad it is, then, how very sad, that we should instead find ourselves today in a state of mourning. We mourn the lives of innocents who were caught up in the East End conflagration of New Year's Eve. We urge the highest possible penalties to be applied to those who carried out this vile act. We bow our heads and we pray.

Yet should this be sufficient? Should not more difficult questions be asked? How is it possible that so flagrant an outrage could be committed on British soil in the twentieth century? How is it possible that the police forces of London should, through their rank incompetence, permit this terrible thing to happen? There are very grave enquiries which ought to be made into the regime of Mr Ambrose Quire, who stands responsible for so much of the so-called detective work which takes place in our metropolis.

Whatever happened to the accepted notion of an official class which keeps us all safe? Why can honest citizens no longer go about their business without doing so in fear of being caught up in a brutal clash between criminals?

We here at the Gazette would contend that the answer to many of these questions runs very much deeper than merely the internal workings of the police force. Are such failings not indicative of wider problems in our society? Have we not become too timid as a people? Such soft-bellied lives as many now lead leave us open to attack from those who have not the vague and expensive scruples of men like Quire.

So I put it to you now, my friends, that the incident of New Year's Eve was an avertible catastrophe. Had the police done their jobs to a higher degree, had Londoners been stronger in their opposition to crime and had the underworld itself not been allowed such outrageous licence, then the disaster would never have occurred.

Is it not time, then, that we stiffen our sinews? Is it not time that we turn aside from easy moderation in order to establish our security? And is it not time that we consider a radical change of course in how we arrange the affairs of this nation?

FROM THE PRIVATE DIARY
OF AMBROSE QUIRE,
Commissioner of Police of the Metropolis

———◆———

2 January. I have always been a practical, rational fellow. I have stood forever flat-footed on the ground. My watchwords are honesty and probity, and the names of those lamps which have lit my way are Logic and Reason. Yet all these things in recent days and hours have been swept aside. I have been shown the reality which hides behind the surface of the world. I have seen the dazzling horror of how things truly are. I have seen sights which render the tools of the logician and the reasonable man as so much useless scrap.

Another sort of person, upon casting his eyes over the paragraph above, might ask himself whether he were not, in some sense or another, going quite mad. Not I! No!

I have no doubt at all that I remain entirely sane, if hardly without some degree of corruption. This is Ileana's doing – that marvellous creature who has given me such joy by choosing me as her chief source of sustenance.

Ileana, so fair and wise and beautiful. The glory of her hair, the sapphire of her eyes, the wondrous peaks and valleys of her form – these things are what I live for now.

Yesterday she woke me in the hour before dawn. She was sitting on the bed in my chamber, rather as I imagine a wife might or an intimate friend, and she was stroking my face, with a gentleness of which many would doubtless have thought her incapable. I came to only gradually, moving up through layers of dreams like a deep-sea diver swimming to the surface from fabulous depths. As I did so I became aware of my dim surroundings, of the fact that this remarkable woman was again wholly unclothed, due, I speculated, to her having but lately been transformed from one state of being into another.

Her hand was soft to the touch but so very cold. I understand, or at least I think I understand, why this is so yet I am not yet ready to record the truth.

'Ambrose,' she breathed, once full consciousness had been returned to me. 'Ambrose Quire.'

My lips were parched and cracked. I dampened them with my tongue. My voice, when it came, sounded far away.

'No need... my dear, for such formality...'

The darkness covered much of her face. I dare say I was mistaken, though it seemed somehow that at my words an expression of something like distaste crossed her features.

'Just Ambrose,' I said, 'my darling...'

Her expression changed again and she looked upon me with an inexplicable smile. Her teeth flashed in the last of the moonlight. With a wonderful shudder, I glimpsed her sharp incisors.

She leaned down, across my body, close enough to my face that we might easily have kissed.

'The first attack upon your city has already taken place,' said she, and although the import of her words was quite clear, they sounded in that moment, given her magnificent proximity, oddly shorn of consequence. 'A bomb has been exploded in the heart of your underworld. Those bad men will soon become still more brutal and more...' She paused, searching for the right word. 'Rivalrous,' she said at last, rather improbably, it seemed to me.

'Then that,' I said, 'will only escalate matters. It will make this simmering war of theirs far worse.'

She leaned a little closer still and I could feel upon me the weight of her, a solidity at once soft and hard. 'All is as our master desires,' she said. 'Everything is happening that must be happening in order to ensure his return. Do you understand?'

'Yes,' I said, although, in truth, I do not yet fully comprehend, or even, perhaps, wish to.

'You must retard the course,' she said, almost whispering, 'of the official investigation. You must be holding off the law lest they seek to douse the flames.'

'But...' I protested, 'they will suspect me. Until... until you came, my career has been marked solely by competence and skill.'

At this, a single, grave-cold finger was pressed against my lips. 'We need you to stand firm, Ambrose Quire. Matters in your city need to grow far worse if conditions are to be ripe for our master. As it was, long ago, in a realm encircled by the Ottoman Lords, so shall it be again, in this degenerate metropolis.'

'How long...' I murmured as her finger trailed down my face, to my throat, to my Adam's apple and beyond. 'How long will you need?'

'Nine days,' she said. 'That seems meet. Give us nine more days, Ambrose Quire, and after that... nothing at all will be mattering any more.'

I breathed out – a long, rattling, almost painful sigh. 'Nine days,'

I said, and even to my own ears my voice sounded rather hollow. 'If I do all that is within my power, then will you... will you, Ileana... please...' My words dried in my mouth and I felt rush over me, like the arrival of the tide, a lassitude and a powerlessness.

'Yes,' said Ileana simply. 'Yes, I shall be feeding upon you.'

I gurgled out my gratitude.

'Yet I shall not return to your neck. Such a wound may be attracting attention. Instead, I shall find a fresh vein elsewhere.' And she moved down then, down and down my body until, pulling aside the sheets, she found virgin territory, a new vein, and leaned towards it.

There was the glory of her fangs unsheathed, the dreadful expectation, the moment of puncture and then, long dreamed of, a flowing crimson gush.

My lassitude intensified. I could not move. I lay still, my senses surging with delight until a fainting came over me.

The next event of which I was aware was a fierce hammering upon my door not long after dawn. Even then the sound of it seemed to me to be very far away. When I bade the caller enter, I saw that it was my servant come to tell me, with piteous and imploring eyes, that I was needed immediately. There had been, he said, some rank atrocity, a blow delivered to the city.

Of Ileana, my Ileana, there was, quite naturally, no sign. The only evidence that she was not simply the product of some phantastical quirk of my imagination were two neat puncture marks – and, in my heart, a lingering, delectable ache.

Later. When one is given an experience so richly vivid as that which Ileana has granted to me it lends other, more ordinary occurrences a dull and distant quality. I have spent the day numbed, gazing at life as though through a thick pane of glass.

There was much uproar about the explosion in the east. I suggested a calm reaction to the outrage and would take no precipitate action. I sensed disgruntlement at my decision amongst the lower ranks, a suspicion which became a certainty when, in the midst of the afternoon, I heard a brusque rap upon my door, followed, without invitation, by the entrance of that burly American, Sub-Divisional Inspector George Dickerson.

'Sorry, sir,' he said. 'It was not my intention to intrude.'

His words were courteous, studiedly so, yet his manner betrayed what I suspect now to lie behind his professional exterior, that of a roughneck well used to getting his own way.

I waved him in, assuring him as I did so that I stood forever ready to listen to the suggestions and concerns of my subordinates. I hope and trust that my reminding the Yankee of our relative standing in the hierarchy of this place did not pass unnoticed.

Once he was seated, I asked what it was that had brought him to me.

He seemed surprised that I should even ask. 'Why, the bomb, sir,' he said, unable to keep a note of impatience from his voice, 'the dynamite at the heart of the city.'

I pressed my fingers against my temples in order to ward off the approach of that headache which I sensed as, it is said, country folk sense the coming of rain, even when the horizon is unblemished. I said: 'Yes, I thought it would be that.'

The American pressed his advantage. 'I have to say, sir,' he began, 'we have ignored the problem too long. And what is at the moment simply a set of bloody skirmishes will, if we do not take harsh steps to quell it, spiral into crisis. That process, sir, that escalation is already under way.'

'Thank you, Inspector, for your rugged honesty. While I would not go so far as to suggest, or even to imply, that your words expose a certain strain of alarmism...'

Dickerson frowned.

'... I would, however, suggest that for now by far our wisest course of action would be merely to observe the situation and not to intervene.'

'Forgive me, sir, but that is not action. That is inaction. To do nothing will make everything worse.'

'As might our interference in what is purely a conflict between magsmen. So far I have seen no satisfactory proof that there is any real danger whatever to law-abiding civilians to be found here.'

'We cannot ignore this, sir. We must not look away.'

'There are many demands upon our time and attention, Inspector. In our position we always have difficult choices to make. And questions of priority to answer.'

As the American looked at me I saw real anger pass across his face. Then he mastered himself, adopting an expression that would not have disgraced the most dedicated of the Stoics. 'I appreciate that, sir. But—'

'Yes?'

'Should there be a further incident... Should this get any worse. Will you reconsider your position?'

I rubbed my temples again. 'You have my word,' I said carefully, 'that I will most certainly think about doing so.'

He nodded in apparent acceptance before, almost discourteously, turning on his heels. The Lord only knows what he will say to our brothers in the Force. Yet I have a suspicion that events will soon outstrip us and that we shall need only days before all Dickerson's concerns and pious fretting will be as efficacious as is a candle flame at the approach of the glacier.

JONATHAN HARKER'S JOURNAL

———◆———

3 January. Poor Mina. She is at present so very tired and anxious.

In many ways, she is as impressive and indefatigable as ever. In her preparations for the funeral and memorial service for the Professor she is diligent, ordered and calm. In the past few days she has consulted with undertakers, priests and with a chapel in London where we shall soon gather to remember the old man. She has in addition written for him an obituary that is set to appear in today's Times. She has also spent much time in the soothing of Quincey, who seems to be suffering from a sequence of vivid night terrors.

In all these things she is quite wonderful. Yet she appears also to be nursing some wild theory. We have not spoken of it since Christmas Day, yet I do not believe that she has entirely abandoned the notion. It scarcely seems to be in her character – such dreadful, morbid fancies. I hope before long that she sets it aside. It worries me, her state of mind. It concerns me deeply. For it cannot be true what she suggests. It cannot be possible.

Besides, my own thoughts are taken up more often than ought to be the case by the fate of poor Sarah-Ann. I have woken in the night, more than once, frightened for her soul.

FROM *THE TIMES*, OBITUARIES

3 January

VAN HELSING, ABRAHAM

Professor Abraham Van Helsing passed away peacefully upon the twenty-ninth of last month, following a long period of illness. Such an ending seems scarcely just or fair when set against the rare vigour and energy of his life. Indeed, he would not have approved of the manner of his passing and he often expressed the hope that he would perish in the service of some greater cause. Nonetheless, he died surrounded by friends and leaves a substantial legacy, in scholarly and academic terms, as well as in the hearts and memories of those who, like the present author, owe him thanks for years of friendship, guidance and protection.

Born in Amsterdam in 1830, the son of a shipbuilder, Abraham Van Helsing proved himself from his youth to possess a mind of rare clarity and an imagination of striking fecundity, the ideal combination for a scientist. Excelling at school, he hurried to the university in Delft, where he was swiftly established as something of a prodigy.

It was around this time that certain darker rumours began to swirl about him. His closest friends, however, only ever considered such gossip – which was to prove remarkably persistent – as the product merely of envious rivals. Leaving the university in 1851, Van Helsing established himself as a physician, although his areas of research and study already extended into fields considerably wider than those of ailment and disease.

In the third year of his practice, Van Helsing took a wife, Maria Houren, the sister of one of his patients, who was, over the next three years, to bear him two sons, David and Silas.

In 1859, however, when Van Helsing's academic monograph on the correlation between taint in the blood and nervous diseases was attracting attention of an intercontinental nature, a tragedy occurred which was to cast a shadow over the rest of his life. Maria and the children drowned on the afternoon of May the eleventh, 1864, in an accident of the most horrible sort. Bereft, Van Helsing left the Netherlands and took to wandering through Europe, in the course of which he acquired much curious and ancient folk belief. This was when his interest began in the monstrous possibilities of the extension of life by sanguinary means and*

---

* At this point, the clipping of this rather strange obituary by my mother is torn away in my father's journal. Closer inspection reveals evidence of singeing. Odder still, my attempts to locate the original of the newspaper, both in the British Library and at the offices of *The Times* itself, have revealed only gaps in the archives.

FROM THE LETTERS PAGE OF *THE DAILY TELEGRAPH*

4 January

Sir,

Further to that recent and necessary debate in these pages with respect to the continuing and lamentable decline of morals and conduct in the younger generation, I should like to crave your indulgence and add a small item of testimony of my own which will, I believe, shed some welcome light on this widespread phenomenon.

For reasons of personal business, which need not detain the reader, I was last night hurrying home rather later than would ordinarily be the case when I chanced to pass through a somewhat regrettable district in the easternmost quadrant of our capital. There being no hansoms available at such an hour, I had before me no alternative but to make for my destination on foot. Naturally, being of a highly respectable appearance, I endeavoured to render myself as inconspicuous as possible lest I become the object of criminal attention.

As matters turned out, the streets were all but empty and so I was left unmolested. The one exception to this statement was that same encounter which has moved me to pen this epistle. For it was when I passed by the church of St James, a beacon of Christianity amid those heathen rookeries, that I witnessed for myself the most shameful of displays. A young woman, scarcely out of girlhood and (some would say), with her blonde hair and pulchritude, being of considerable personal attractions, ran in a most unladylike fashion from a darkened alley and all but hurled herself at the locked door of the temple, upon which she began, noisily, to plead for entrance. The girl appeared decidedly dishevelled and there was blood upon upon her face – clear symptoms of drunkenness. Her manner was wearisomely frantic, her tone one of coarse agitation.

Both bewildered and unsettled, I stood and watched this unnecessary performance for some moments before a group of pale men of a slightly older generation – no doubt her uncles – emerged and, in the teeth of considerable weeping and much animated objection from the lady in question, dragged her away.

I should like to applaud their efforts in ridding the streets of so egregious a public nuisance. Never in previous centuries have youth and beauty been offered as excuses for poor behaviour, and I fail to see why this state of affairs should be in the least different in the present epoch.

Happily, I returned home unscathed, and I share this incident with your readers solely as a means of detailing the poor standard of the worrying majority of our present young people. Surely, there are difficult questions now to be asked of all those who have responsibility for the young, and of teachers and parents in particular?

Your daily reader,
A Pedestrian

LETTER FROM MISS SARAH-ANN DOWELL TO
DR JOHN SEWARD (ENVELOPE UNOPENED)*

5 January

Dear Doctor,

I wonder if you will ever read this letter for I have heard it said that you are missing now. I have heard you have gone a-wandering, out of London and off to God knows where. If this is true I know it cannot be all of your own choosing. For you would never leave your friends and your work if you was thinking in your right mind. I trust you, Dr Seward, and I know you are a good man. I know you will believe me too when I tell you what has befallen me.

In case you was wondering why I am writing to you now it is to tell you my story and, I am afraid to say, goodbye.

First, you ought to know I left the house in the country where you sent me. I ran away in the night. The old man had passed over and I did all I could. But there was a kind of clumsiness, sir, between the master of the house and me. And there is something wrong with their strange boy. He cannot speak of it but it is there. I want you to know I never thought of fleeing before things got so bad.

I don't think you ever knew, Doctor, that I had myself a sweetheart. His name was Thom Cawley and though he was in many ways a bad one I still believe he had an honest heart. His start in the world was not of the easiest sort and he fell easily into evil company. He ran

---

* I believe myself to have been the first to read this piece of correspondence, discovered in the course of my researches, more than a decade after its composition.

for a time with the Giddis Boys and was well known to the police. Yet he was different when he was with me. He was softer and kinder and he sought only the love which had so long been denied him.

When I left the house of the Harkers, I came at once to London. I sent word to Thom and told him I'd meet him at six the next evening at a place where we'd met many times before, beneath the clock in the railway station at Waterloo. You can hide there, sir, in plain sight. You can hide amid the bustle of the people and pass unseen in that big crowd.

So I stood and waited, sir, and even then I still had hope in me. Time slid by and I grew worried. I waited till the best part of an hour was up. Something in me urged me to go. A voice in my head pleaded with me to run. And I felt my instincts implore me to turn on my heels. I ignored them all, sir. How dearly I wish now that I had listened!

For it was just before seven that I saw him walk towards me out of the mass of people. He smiled with his lips closed and I saw straight away that something was wrong.

'Hello, petal,' he said and he sounded so different, sir, distant and cold. His skin was too pale and in the light of the station his eyes seemed to gleam red, like those of the Harker boy.

I turned and I went to run but Thom had others with him, other men (other things) like him. They surrounded me, sir, and they moved me away, out of the station and into a coach as was waiting. Not one person who we passed seemed to notice what was being done to me.

Thom held me in his gaze all the while. With his red eyes on me I found I could do nothing, neither call out or dash away.

They took me to a low house down East where they keep me locked up. I know now, sir, what Thom and the others are. I know what they've been made into. There are many who would not believe me, sir, many who would call me a silly girl with a head full of old stories, but somehow, sir, I know that you will know I speak the truth.

Yes, Dr Seward, I see what they are – the whole evil nest of them. There is a woman at their head, dark and beautiful. She can transform, sir, into a bat or into mist. I have heard whispers of their plans and though I understand only bits of it, I am sore afraid for my city.

Last night, I tried to escape and looked for sanctuary but they found me and dragged me back. They mean to change me, sir, into you know what. They think I can be useful to them.

There is a certain chapel – St Sebastian in the West – and a certain priest – who it is said I am meant for. My part is already written and they mean for me to follow it to the letter.

I have thrown myself at my Thom's feet but he only laughed and told me it will all be better when I is made like him.

This letter I have given to one of their human servants who cares for them during the hours of daylight. She has agreed to take this from me but will help me no further. She is afraid of them and they are making her rich.

If you ever see this letter, sir, please do what I could

not and run. Run from the city. Run from the creatures. Run from the dark one who is coming.

I am sorry, sir, that I could not love you.

Goodbye, Dr Seward,
Your Sarah-Ann

FROM THE PRIVATE DIARY
OF AMBROSE QUIRE,
Commissioner of Police of the Metropolis

————◆————

6 January. It was at one time a dearly held, albeit an intensely private wish of mine that the cream of these diaries might be presented in some handsomely bound form to the reading public. I had hoped that such a volume might provide much that would be of interest to a general audience. It would shine a light upon all that good work which is carried out by the men of the Force and dramatise those very particular stresses and responsibilities which belong to those who, like myself, dwell at the top of the chain of command.

In recent days, the underworld of the metropolis remains in a state of high anxiety, skittish and quick to anger. Dickerson has been adamant that he should lead an investigatory party to uncover the reasons for these disturbances amongst the tribes. I have, according to my instructions, been successful in the thwarting of his subordinates' ambitions.

I know that by any calculus of morality those obstructions which I have placed before my own men are profoundly wrong. I know too that I am quite helpless in the grip of my mistress and that I have no alternative but to obey. Yet it is also clear to me that what that lady has already wrought – the turning of one pack of savages upon another – is, in its own fashion, rather beautiful; a scouring away of human blight and a necessary amputation of disease.

Yet all of this is prologue to what I have now to confess. My sleep has in recent days been fitful and unsatisfying. Such dreams as those which have visited me are filled with terror and despair and have brought me, perspiring and a-tremble, too often back to consciousness.

In consequence, I have become accustomed to taking a small glass of spirit before attempting slumber, laced liberally with laudanum. Last night, my sleep was fast and without dreams.

I ought to have been suspicious of such an apparent respite, for I was woken deep in the night by an all but intolerable pressure on my chest. I struggled into wakefulness, gasped for air and forced my eyes to see what was before me in the gloom. It was Ileana who sat upon me, her hands at my upper torso, pressing down hard, her palms splayed outwards.

She was in her most natural state. Her mane of hair billowed out behind her. As she saw that I was awake, she leaned closer, digging her nails into my skin. She smiled and showed me her teeth. She moistened her plump lips with motions of her tongue. At the realisation that I was once again to fall under her spell I shuddered involuntarily three times.

Ileana smiled as she placed her slender pale left hand between my legs.

'Poor policeman. So sad a little man.'

I moaned once and was silent.

'You have done well, my servant. I come to tell you there

is to be a second blast. Tomorrow night in the kingdom of the Giddis Boys. Be keeping your men clear and do not interfere. For this you will be well rewarded.'

I moaned once more and shivered in my humiliation. 'Madam, that will only serve to stoke the flames. There will be pandemonium.'

She moved against me. 'And from that pandemonium will come… order. Do not speak now, little Englishman, but nod to show me you understand.'

I nodded.

'Good,' she purred. 'You will obey?'

I nodded once again. In a single expert motion, she was on me and she was piercing a vein and she was drinking, drinking deep.

I sank into delirium. When I awoke she was gone, aside from the marks upon me and the animal scent of her upon my sheets. With the merciful coming of the dawn, I set down these words and wait, in a state of exhilarated agony, for the next attack.

MINA HARKER'S JOURNAL

———————◆———————

6 January. I suppose that what we accomplished this afternoon – the laying to rest of the mortal remains of Professor Abraham Van Helsing in the ground of the churchyard here at Shore Green – ought to have provided to all of us a firm full stop in this difficult stretch of our lives. The occasion ought to have given us an opportunity to mourn, to display our grief by whatever means we thought fit and then to start to piece together again all which we used to have in our small but happy existences. Yet, for reasons which I shall unfold, the event seemed to offer no conclusion, but rather a sense that fate is pressing in upon us and that some dreadful velocity is now being reached. To what destination it all tends I do not dare consider.

The day began in ignominy and ended with a horrid sense of pregnancy. I had made all the arrangements for the interment of the Professor, thinking it best that this be a small, private affair to precede the public memorial to be held in London on the eleventh. As matters turned out, the ceremony was far too sparsely attended, marked by the absence of lost friends.

Poor Jack is still amongst the missing (where is he, I ask myself ceaselessly, where is he, where is he?) and Miss Dowell,

I sense, has left our lives for good. I had hoped to have by our sides Lord and Lady Godalming (for surely Arthur would want to mark the passing of that great Dutchman), yet I was in this to be disappointed. Shortly after ten this morning, two hours before the funeral, I was at work in my study when a brisk tap upon the door heralded the arrival of the maid.

She announced that a gentleman was waiting to see me, having come up that morning from Sussex.

'Is it Lord Godalming?'

She shook her head in a tight, nervous semi-circle.

'Well, who, then?'

'He said his name is Amory, miss.'

I bade her send him in and she scurried away to accomplish this instruction.

When I saw Mr Amory again, as he stepped with visible melancholia into the room, dressed in black and wearing an armband in honour of the day, a wave of something like disquiet washed over me. That noble manservant seemed tired, lined and drawn, traits which I doubted had been fostered in him merely by the journey from his county to ours. Even his broad shoulders seemed slumped at the weight of events and his frame, which I should choose to characterise as displaying a kind of muscular stoutness, seemed to have been whittled down. He said: 'I imagine you must be surprised to see me, ma'am, come to this house alone.'

'Not to the degree which I would like,' I admitted. 'Am I to take it that you are here as a representative?'

'That is so, ma'am. Lord and Lady Godalming have sent me in their stead.'

'I see.'

'Naturally, they also send their most abject apologies. I fear that for them to have come here today, for my mistress in particular, would have been most unwise. They despatched me with a letter to explain their failure to attend.'

He drew from his pocket a slim manila envelope. Inside was a note from Arthur as clipped and formal in tone as one would expect of a man of his breeding, yet which seemed also to me to contain behind every stately syllable the intimation of a scream.

That letter I have retained and pressed between these pages.

LETTER FROM LORD ARTHUR GODALMING TO JONATHAN AND MINA HARKER

6 January

My dear Jonathan and Mina,

You will by now, having seen Mr Amory arrive alone, have guessed the sad truth that Carrie and I shall not be with you at today's event, a dereliction of my duty of which I am most heartily ashamed. I fear that you may also by now have divined the reason for our absence. My poor Caroline has not rallied since the loss of our unborn babe. Indeed, she has grown only steadily worse since last you were with her. I fear that her mind has begun to loose its moorings and that she drifts even now into a realm from which it will be a terrible challenge indeed to bring her home.

Where is Jack Seward? There is no specialist in England to touch him! If only he were with us now, then I surely should not feel so acutely that my wife as we know her has begun to fade from my sight. She shouts often and calls out shrilly. She suffers from bad dreams. She cries when she wakes and has taken to stalking through the house during the hours of darkness. My servants – young Ernest Strickland in particular – have been both tolerant and compassionate, but their efforts have yet to prove efficacious in the soothing of my wife. In spite of all of these peculiarities her behaviour troubles me most greatly when she is simply quiet and still, for she wears at such moments an expression of near-absolute vacuity as though she is the subject of some horrible process of hollowing out. It is as if the essence of her is departing and leaving behind only a husk.

Those quacks and apothecaries whom I have summoned assure me that this is natural and to be expected. They are to a man, however, both frightened of me and great lovers of my money, and so I suspect that they tell me only what they think I wish to hear.

My friends, I hope that you will forgive me for telling you of our travails at such length; I wished you to know that our failure today was not of our own making. I cannot leave her now. I shall do all that is within my power for us to be with you in London for the memorial service. Until then, please know in what high esteem I hold you all and how much your friendship means in these difficult times. Lay the old Dutchman safely in the ground. I shall say a prayer for him today in memory of how he once saved us all.

I remain your loyal friend,
Art

MINA HARKER'S JOURNAL

———◆———

6 January ★ *Continued.* After I had read Lord Godalming's letter, I folded it, returned it to its envelope and placed it upon my escritoire. Mr Amory was watching me with some concern.

'Thank you for bringing this,' I said.

''Twas no trouble, ma'am. No trouble at all.'

I drew in a long, contemplative breath before I allowed myself to speak my mind. There is something inherently trustworthy in Mr Amory. He has a quality which all but invites the giving of confidences.

'Is it very bad with them?' I asked. 'As bad as Arthur says?'

'I fear, ma'am, that the noble lord may, doubtless from a wish to spare you, have held back the worst of the situation. The mind of my mistress is almost entirely shattered. In some fashion it does not seem to be capable of healing. Just when she appears to be on her way to recovery there is a sudden, inexplicable relapse.'

There lay between us a gravid silence.

An awful thought began to form itself; disquieted, I thrust it away.

'Ma'am?' Mr Amory seemed to me to be at once both inquisitive and concerned. 'Mrs Harker, there is another matter which I must discuss with you. It has to do with your missing friend, ma'am. Dr Seward.'

I began to ask Mr Amory to explain. Yet before I could say more, the door to the study was thrown open. Jonathan entered. Dressed in black, he ought to have seemed sufficiently smart for the ceremony which awaited us. In some fashion, however, for all that his tie was well-knotted, his cuffs held neatly together with silver links and his face clean-shaven, there was about him a frayed quality, an air of dishevelment. To me the cause was, sadly, quite plain — a bottle of strong drink, taken, no doubt, under the pretext of requiring additional moral courage for the duties which lay ahead. I frowned at the sight of him, and I dare say that he saw my disapproval writ upon my face.

'I'm sorry,' he said, 'for interrupting.' His gaze passed on to the manservant. 'Who is this?'

'This is Mr Amory,' I replied, no doubt rather tartly, 'of whom you have often heard me speak.'

'Of course,' said Jonathan, somewhat glibly. 'You are most welcome, sir.'

'I am here,' said the butler, 'to represent my master and mistress, Lord and Lady Godalming.'

My husband softened. 'Then you do them — and us — great credit. Mina? It is almost time to leave now. Everything is ready and all is prepared.'

As he spoke, another slender figure stepped into the room — seeming almost to glide into our presence. My pale, thoughtful boy, Quincey.

'We should go now,' he said with that too-mature brand of earnestness which is his most familiar manner. 'For the Professor is waiting.'

We all agreed that this was so, and we practically processed out of my little study into the hallway beyond and to the drive where our carriage was waiting.

As we reached the door, Mr Amory drew near to me and said in a low voice: 'Ma'am? The question of Dr Seward. I would truly be most grateful if we might discuss it later.'

'We shall. After the funeral. Though I think I may judge from your tone that whatever news you have is not good.'

He looked levelly at me. 'Later then, ma'am. Let us talk of such things later.'

Jonathan ushered us around the carriage. Shortly before he himself embarked I saw that he took a swift, deep swig from a silver hip flask which flashed briefly in the light in its journey from coat pocket to mouth and back again. This receptacle safely secreted, he joined the three of us and urged the driver to depart. I looked with disappointment yet without surprise at my husband, who would not return my gaze.

I wish to speak to him again of that theory which still takes form in my mind. Yet I cannot. I dare not. He is more fragile than I believe he knows. The drink is but a symptom of something greater which lies, perhaps, in us both.

The funeral service itself was a mean, perfunctory thing, quite unworthy of the life our dear friend had led. We four – we Harkers and the redoubtable Mr Amory – were the sole mourners.

The priest, our local Reverend, Jackson St Clair, is a rake-thin, desiccated man in whom I have never seen much evidence of hope or charity. He had not known the Dutchman and so was able to rehearse only those biographical particulars with which I had myself provided him.

As he spoke on in his drab, querulous tones, and as we

managed an inexpert rendition of a single hymn, I surveyed the faces of our meagre congregation. Mr Amory, resolute yet labouring beneath the strain of responsibility; my husband, his skin pouchy, perspiring despite the chill of this wintry afternoon; and my son, who struck me as now not as sullen or as withdrawn as he has seemed in recent months, but rather suddenly and startlingly vacant.

His face was blank and – a thing of subtle horror – almost without character. He seemed distant during the service, as though he were present in purely physical terms. At the time, I believed that this was merely his method of bearing the sadness of the day, just as I had my busy list of tasks and Jonathan, regrettably, his hip flask.

Now, however, as I write, I am no longer sure at all.

After the service was over, we went outside, into the graveyards, to watch the coffin lowered into the earth. This sight was as bleak as ever it was. The vicar, who is evidently upon the cusp of a head cold, snivelled as he spoke those ancient words which accompany interment.

As is traditional in so grim a scene, a thin drizzle began, the rainwater oddly slick and even viscous, like oil on one's skin.

Jonathan moved to stand a little closer to me, so close, in fact, that I could smell the liquor upon him. As the coffin was lowered into its allotted place by four glum pall-bearers, I found myself regretting our choice to lay Van Helsing in this rustic spot.

I took one step farther from my husband's side, closer now to Mr Amory, and in that moment I lost sight of my son. I looked but I could not see him. I wonder – oh, how fervently I wonder – whether, had I paid closer attention, I might not have stopped (or at the least alleviated) that shocking thing which followed.

The coffin which contained the body of our old friend had been lowered into its allotted place and the pall-bearers stood back. There was a moment of respectful silence before the vicar was to intone the last words of the ritual. Yet this quiet was broken not by the oddly indifferent tones of the man of the cloth, but rather by the sound of my son making a noise which lay somewhere between a whimper and a gasp.

I turned to look, and saw that Quincey was now paler than ever before. He did not speak. He seemed to sway, to and fro, upon his feet. Before any of us could catch him he staggered and fell heavily backwards.

At once, Mr Amory and I were by Quincey's side. My husband looked on with an expression of dumb horror. I reached out. I touched my boy as he lay on the damp grass. I saw that he was shaking, his whole body thrashing and flailing, in the grip of some paroxysm or fit. Mr Amory held him firm as shudders wracked the boy's form.

'Quincey,' I murmured, 'my dear one. Be still. Be still now, I pray you.'

His mouth was flecked with foam and spittle. His eyes pivoted wildly in their sockets. He moaned once, twice, three times. The vicar and the pall-bearers stepped forward, meaning to offer their aid but Mr Amory bade them keep their distance so that the boy might be granted space. Jonathan looked down at us, blinking as though he had been rooted to the spot.

Then my child fell still. His eyes looked up now towards the heavens and he spoke in quiet, earnest tones of absolute sincerity.

'The south has been set to burning, in the service of his design. And know this...' His eyes moved downwards. Quincey trained his gaze at us, but it was as though there were nothing of him at all in the look: merely a blankness, more hideous than ever before. 'He is coming soon to claim me. Unless I find the strength to fight it.'

Quincey gave a final, convulsive shudder. His eyelids fluttered shut and the boy lay still.

In the aftermath of this incident there was a horrified silence in the graveyard until, from somewhere unseen but nearby, a colony of rooks rose squawking into the sky, their cries sounding to me horribly like human laughter.

FROM *THE PALL MALL GAZETTE*

6 January (evening edition)

FRESH OUTRAGE COMMITTED AT HEART OF CITY. MANY WOUNDED AND FEARED DEAD.

As we go to press, news has reached our offices of a major conflagration in the south of the city, in the vicinity of Vauxhall. Early reports remain confused, yet it does seem probable that an incendiary device was exploded in a busy thoroughfare. The region has a reputation as a stronghold of that notorious criminal gang known as The Giddis Boys.

Has the war between criminals exploded once again into the broader life of London? If so, then it has burst its banks to encompass the lives of the innocent, for the blast will doubtless have claimed lives of the law-abiding as well as those of the law-breaker.

Details have still to emerge, but if the suspicions of this newspaper are correct then we say this unto the authorities and His Majesty's Government: something must to be done to stem this tide of gang violence – done swiftly and without compunction. More will follow soon upon this subject, in our popular new leading column: 'Salter Says'. No doubt our correspondent will have much to say.

MINA HARKER'S JOURNAL

———◆———

6 January ★ *Later.* The rest of the day and that evening have passed in an atmosphere of profound gloom. The Professor is buried. We saw the first of the earth placed upon the coffin. It is devoutly to be hoped that, in spite of the dramas which have attended his laying to rest, he is now at peace.

Mr Amory, who has been a constant source of wisdom and support, remains with us. As I write, he slumbers upstairs. My husband, meanwhile, is by now almost certainly in his cups, for he has taken himself to the drawing room and closed the door behind him. I have no wish to interrupt him or even, if truth be told, to be at this moment by his side. As I passed by that room an hour ago I heard emanating from within a deep, dull, whisky-sodden snore.

As for our boy, he has recovered. After his swoon in the graveyard we brought him to the vestry, where he was revived. He seemed exhausted, yet he showed no sign of remembering much of his fit. Certainly, he displayed no memory at all of those peculiar words which he spoke before he fainted. He appeared quiet and thoughtful enough at supper and without any visible sign of distress.

Nonetheless, it has become clear that he is far from well. I would keep him with us, away from the school, and seek out the advice of expert physicians. These recommendations I shall make to my husband when he deigns to emerge from his stupor.

Earlier, dear Mr Amory looked in, his face drawn and fatigued. He asked me if we could speak 'on the most urgent matter, concerning Dr Seward'.

I smiled weakly at this kind fellow. 'Is it to be more bad news?'

He frowned. 'I fear that may be so, ma'am.'

'Then may we speak of it tomorrow? I am not sure that I could bear any more disaster now.'

I saw from his expression that the butler understood. 'I can wait one night more,' he said. 'But, ma'am, it ought not to be left for any longer than that. Every hour that we delay may bring tragedy closer.'

'Tomorrow,' I said. 'I give you my word. You can tell me everything in the morning.'

He agreed and left, and so our little house is all abed. Dear me. What a long and difficult day it has been.

I shall sleep deeply and well tonight, I know it. I shall not dream.

FROM THE PRIVATE JOURNAL
OF MAURICE HALLAM

———————◆———————

7 January. For a week now I have been more unwell than ever before in all my misspent life. Not once in that septet of days have I found myself to be in my perfect mind. Such persistent misfortune should suffice as an explanation for my distressing absence from these pages.

My condition is said by Gabriel to be a form of tropical fever, no doubt picked up in the course of our wanderings. The symptoms are delirium, extreme physical weakness, a febrile temperature and, on several unpleasant occasions, a tendency to hallucinate.

Mr Shone and I have not spoken of what passed between us at the docks on the day that we returned to England. We are both Englishmen, after all, and we understand very well the power which lies in omission and in a kind of shared forgetting. We have known almost from birth (for society has long celebrated its potency) the awful potential for dominion which lies within the lacuna.

While all that is unspoken has settled around us, our relations have undergone a sequence of subtle modulation. He has never been more the master, and never have I been so dependent upon him. We have moved into a hotel of the expensive but discreet kind at the fashionable end of Charlotte Street. We have a small suite of rooms, each adjacent to the other and linked by one adjoining door, which is generally kept locked.

The décor is that of bourgeois luxury, and since my palate has always favoured decadence, I find that I am here altogether at home. At the least, I have found it to be a fine place to be so wretched an invalid.

It has all been a thoroughly ugly experience, wearisome and dull. Gabriel, however, has been most kind, attending to me often and consulting several specialists who have prescribed much bed rest and intimate attention.

Every night, late in the evening, Gabriel visits me in my chamber and insists that I drink a foul-tasting medicine, a thick, soupy draught which he promises will aid my recovery. The tincture is sour and metallic – but I do as I am bidden and I drink deep. I obey Gabriel Shone in all things and in all ways. For surely – how he could not? – he has my best interests at heart.

Gabriel himself has been busy. In England he is become all energy and verve. Of exactly how he has occupied his time, and precisely to what his considerable ambitions might amount, I know not. Yet I am sure that the focus of his attention is no longer simply the seeking-out of pleasure but rather some species of business. I hear voices from the room next door: voices of serious men, voices which seem to me to speak of the great professions, of the Bar, the House, the Synod. Voices, above all, which are saturated with money and influence.

On only two occasions has the door which connects my room with Gabriel's been left unlocked and ajar. The first was three days ago. With a remarkable effort of will, in considerable pain and tortured by fever, I rose, ungainly and without speed, from the bed and took myself to the far side of the chamber. Silently, I peered through into the room beyond and saw there Mr Shone surrounded by men of the gravest sort, all dressed in raven black. One, absurdly, had with him a large and elderly Irish wolfhound. Gabriel himself seemed more sombre than ever he had before – upright and sincere, listening to his guests with almost courtly attention and with a gracious ease as he received their enquiries and compliments.

I recognised none of these visitors, but I do believe that I know the type, men who are born to power, those who, through all manner of systems and levers, rule the Empire (and the kind of men, let it not be forgotten, who once made this country so thoroughly intolerable for me, and those who are like me). I said nothing to Gabriel of what I saw, but merely returned to my sickbed.

The second occasion when the door was left open and unlocked was but an hour ago, and even now I do my best to persuade myself that what I saw was only fancy or imagination, a vision conjured wholly by my illness. As before, I heard voices from the next room – one Gabriel's, but the other that of a woman. Something in their low, conspiratorial tone urged me to pay close heed. Rising on rickety legs and with blood singing in my ears, I crept to the door and strained to see.

The vision that awaited me was hideous indeed, and surely – surely, if there be justice and sanity at all in this world of disharmony and sin – cannot have been the truth of things. Nonetheless, I believe that I saw with Gabriel Shone, dressed in all his respectable finery, and standing beside him, far closer than propriety would ever allow, one hand held against his ruined eye, the nightmare figure of the Transylvanian woman, Ileana.

Gabriel sighed and chattered softly at the lady's touch, and I experienced a curious certainty that something passed between the two of them at this weird contact. There was also in that place a most unexpected scent – that of smoke and burning, although no fire was lit.

Neither of them saw me, or so I believe, and so I crept back to my invalid place, clammy and afraid, though, somehow, not altogether surprised.

Although I try to reassure myself that what I saw was an hallucination, I believe that I know the reality of it. As to its broader significance, I cannot be certain, though I have several theories, all of which lack the slightest comfort or goodness. As I write these words I wait – for Gabriel to come through to me, for my evening draught, for my dark medicine. I hope only that ingestion brings peace, sleep and a portion of merciful forgetting.

FROM *THE PALL MALL GAZETTE*

8 January

SALTER SAYS: A GLIMMER OF HOPE AMONGST THE YOUNG

It will come, I dare say, as small surprise to many of you that I have for some years now exhibited towards the younger generation an attitude of something not so very far from despair.

Those who are now under the age of forty seem to me too often to be a pampered and indolent lot. Born into an Empire which has provided for them, they nonetheless chafe ungratefully against it while accepting all its bounty. Having done nothing at all to build the world as it exists today, they criticise their elders and take the gifts of our society for granted. They are also – and almost to a man – far too lenient and forgiving when it comes to the criminal classes, speaking with doubt of the death penalty and looking back upon the days of public executions with wearisome squeamishness. For the consequences of such moral cowardice one needs look, I fear, no further than the recent carnage in London.

However, it is my very great pleasure to be able to tell you today that there is at least one representative of that generation who gives me cause for hope. The name of the young man in question is Mr Gabriel Shone. He is lately returned from an expedition across Europe with some bold new ideas as to how to govern our ailing nation.

For inspiration, he has reached into the past and proposed a return to the more robust methods of our forefathers. In this he has shown a rare perceptiveness and acumen which is a credit to his youth.

The young man was once the ward of the late Lord Stanhope and, as such, has inherited his benefactor's seat in the Council of Athelstan. From his temporary home in a well-known hotel on Charlotte Street, Mr Shone has held court, receiving notable parliamentarians, residents of the back benches, a large number of Whiggish donors, a brace of journalists from the better sort of newspaper, at least two members of the current Cabinet and, most often, his mentor and friend, Lord Tanglemere.

Let us hope that they all take heed of the words of this impressive young gentleman and that his own generation are inspired by his example. It seems likely that Mr Shone may one day seek election – unless, of course, there be any means by which he might obtain influence over the state by swifter means. It is a pity that at present the Council itself holds only ceremonial power. What a force for good it might be if it were allowed again its old responsibilities. Just imagine what could be achieved if the singular Mr Shone were ever to stand at the head of it!

TELEGRAM FROM SUB-DIVISIONAL INSPECTOR GEORGE DICKERSON TO CHIEF INSPECTOR MARTIN PARLOW (UNANSWERED)

8 January

Please, sir, forgive this wire. I guess you have troubles of your own. But the city is in danger. Two bombs. War brewing amongst the gangs. Quire worse than useless. If you can, sir, come back to us. London needs you.

LETTER FROM MINA HARKER TO
LORD ARTHUR GODALMING

9 January

Dear Arthur,

I do hope you will forgive me for not writing sooner. Our lives now seem blighted. Not only those of our circle but in the wider world too. Such terrible news from London. So many innocents lost without reason or good cause.

I understand entirely the reasons for your absence from the funeral. How is dear Carrie? I think of her often and pray for her too. If there is anything that lies within my power to help, please do not hesitate to instruct me. If only matters were different I should come at once to the estate to be by her side.

However, I am unable at present to leave my own house. Quincey has not been well. At the end of the service, just as the coffin was being lowered into the earth, he suffered a mercifully brief though most frightening fit, the cause of which remains unclear. Yesterday, he suffered another, smaller such incident. As you may well imagine, we are concerned. I am not certain whom we should consult first – a physician or an alienist. If matters persist we shall take him to the hospital in Oxford, for our local doctor is too fond of the bottle. For now, we keep our son close to us and hope that these difficulties will pass.

Jonathan is, of course, as concerned as I – he sends his salutations to you both – though I do not think that I shall be speaking too grievously out of turn when I say that recent crises seem to have awoken in him much of his old fearfulness. On occasions too numerous, he has taken recourse in the worst of remedies.

Are we to see you both at the memorial service on the eleventh? It would be wonderful, assuming only, of course, that Lady Caroline is well enough. Somehow I feel that once the service is done with and the Professor remembered with all due propriety, our lives will begin a new, brighter and more hopeful stage.

My dear friend, there is another matter, another strand in our web of sadness, of which I must inform you. It concerns the question of the whereabouts of poor Jack Seward. The excellent Mr Amory, whom you were good enough to send as your emissary and representative, was, almost from the moment of his arrival, eager to speak to me of our missing companion. Yet, in consequence of multiple difficulties, it was not until late in the afternoon of the day after we had laid the Professor to rest that Mr Amory and I were at last able to speak in private in the study.

It was meant that my husband should join us but, as matters turned out, he was in our bedroom, exhausted (he said) and sleeping away the afternoon.

'Mrs Harker,' Amory began as he settled his considerable bulk into the armchair facing me. His eyes filled with sorrowful concern. 'I have received a goodly number of replies to that advertisement which we placed in The Times enquiring for information concerning Dr Seward. I believe that the Yard keeps an open file on the disappearance, yet experience and instinct both suggest to me that we should expect little enough assistance from that quarter.'

'I sense you are right, Mr Amory. But tell me, pray, how many responses have you received?'

'Just a shade over four dozen, ma'am. And it gives me no pleasure to say that the great majority of them have evidently been sent by pranksters, by the deluded or, in some cases, by the palpably lunatic.'

He looked away, as though he were embarrassed or, in some obscure fashion, ashamed.

'You may as well as tell me the whole of it, Mr Amory.'

'But, ma'am—'

'I am not as other women, Mr Amory. My stomach is strong. I have seen and endured much.'

'If you are certain.'

'Quite certain, thank you.'

It was a cold day and our house has never succeeded in retaining much heat, yet Mr Amory was perspiring visibly. He wiped at his forehead with his great right hand before he spoke again. 'Many of the letters are crude, ma'am, and many are cruel. More than one said that the doctor was roasting in H— and others that he had in some fashion been... made rotten... by an... overindulgence in pleasures of the flesh.'

In reaction to this, I did no more than raise an eyebrow. 'The world is full of strange correspondents,' I said, 'and, sadly, of mad people also.'

'That is assuredly true, ma'am, yet it seemed to me that there was an oddly standardised quality to these missives, as though they had been sent not by individuals, disparate and without connection, but by a group, or controlled by some organising power. In reading that strange sheaf of correspondence, I felt on more than one occasion the distinct sense that I was in some way being mocked.'

'I sympathise, Mr Amory. Yet amongst this unpleasant flotsam, was there anything more solid? Any useful detail?'

Your dear old manservant nodded. 'There were two letters, ma'am, which I believe to be genuine and which I hope may help us yet.'

'What were they?'

Mr Amory reached into a pocket in his old, dark, well-preserved jacket and pulled forth two folded sheets of paper. 'Here,' he said, 'you may peruse them for yourself.'*

---

* Having traced originals of the letters which my mother was handed by Mr Amory on that chill afternoon, I reproduce both here in their entirety for ease of comprehension.

LETTER FROM MRS ELIZABETH DRABBLE
TO MR AMORY

Undated

Dear Mr Amory,

I saw your advertisement in the newspaper and I think as I have seen your man. I am a cook in one of the great houses at Ely and I was on my way to perform my evening duties on the Friday before Christmas, walking from my little cottage to the manor house. In the gloom of the afternoon, I passed by some barren ground which borders the fenland. This is by way of being my 'short-cut'.

It was on this lonely path I met him who I think was your man. I took him at first for a common vagrant so idle and bewildered did he seem. But as I drew nearer I saw that his clothes were too fine for that and his ways too nobby. In other respects, he looked just like your description.

When he stopped me I was fearful he would ask for money, of which I had none. He seemed nervous and fitful. He seemed lost but frightened too. Though all that he asked me in the end was whether I knew the way to Wildfold.

Eager to be done with the talking, I said that I had heard of such a place but that I knew it to be half a county away in Norfolk (not so far, as I had heard tell, from Cromer).

He thanked me and I think there was more he would have wanted to ask but something I saw in his eyes scared me then so I pushed my way past and hurried on.

I looked back once and saw that he had not moved at all but still haunted that same spot.

I am not in the least wise embarrassed to say that I have not walked that way since. I never saw the man again. I hope this letter of mine may be of use to you. I am a Christian woman and I pray for that poor man's soul.

Yours sincerely,
Mrs E.B. Drabble

LETTER FROM HORACE BARING-SMITH TO MR AMORY

Undated

Dear Sir,

My attention has lately been drawn to your advertisement concerning the present whereabouts of the noted London specialist, Dr Seward. Whilst I cannot be altogether certain that it was indeed that roving gentleman whom I encountered in the course of my duties shortly after Christmas, it would not surprise me to learn that I had done so.

Now, whilst my name may be unfamiliar to you, my rank and occupation will surely not be. I am a station guard in the employ of the railway terminus in the city of Norwich. My duties and responsibilities are plentiful and I bear them all with the solemnity that they deserve, without neglecting to maintain that demeanour of friendly knowledge which has enabled me to rise to the top of my profession.

It was in this capacity that I was approached as I patrolled the platforms of the station on perpetual lookout for those who require my aid and expertise (and for the less desirable sort who would seek to use our station for reasons of shelter, beggary or worse).

I was approached shortly after noon by a man of dishevelled appearance who fitted nonetheless the description which you have circulated. I remember that he struck me at the time as being a superior sort of person who had, no doubt through no fault of his own, fallen on evil times.

I felt a deal of pity at the sight of him and I care not if any think me too tender-hearted for such an admission.

He had money, for he clasped fiercely in one hand a pound note as though it were a gypsy charm.

'Can you tell me, good sir,' said he, 'how I might get a train to the town of Wildfold?'

With patient kindness I said: 'Wildfold, sir? You must get the train to Cromer, sir, leaving shortly from platform three. Your stop is the thirteenth.'

I drew my big, old-fashioned watch from my pocket in order to effect a consultation. The thing was a present, dearly loved, from my father (a decent man and a clever one for all that he had had little education).

'Seven minutes, sir,' I said. 'That is all the time which is left to you.'

The stranger thanked me with much warmth. I found this pleasing, for folk can be discourteous indeed to men of my position. He left me and walked away. Something in me bade me follow him, and I watched as he went to the third platform and boarded the train which hissed and panted there, readying for departure.

The gentleman then passed from my view and from my life.

I feel in my heart that this traveller was indeed Dr Seward and I hope that my testimony is of some material assistance to your finding him. Of course, if you were able to remember me in any future account of your search, then I should be most grateful.

I remain, sir, your obedient servant,
H.R. Baring-Smith

LETTER FROM MINA HARKER TO
LORD ARTHUR GODALMING

9 January

Continued. Once I had read these letters I passed them back to Mr Amory, who looked at me with grave severity.

'You think that these are real?'

'I do, ma'am, yes.'

'Then I am inclined to agree. But why would Jack be seeking with such determination to reach this Wildfold?'

'I cannot say for certain, ma'am. Though I am from that part of the country myself and spent the first fifteen years of my life there. Wildfold has always had a certain reputation. It seems almost to attract, ma'am, strange stories.'

'Indeed?' I said, thinking how odd it felt – almost impertinent – to hear stately Mr Amory speaking of his earliest days. 'I fear that I have never heard of the place and that it conveys nothing at all to me.'

'Ma'am.' Mr Amory looked towards the floor as he spoke. 'I do not know the full particulars, or anything like them, of what befell you all in the last century. Yet there have been moments when my master has confided in me and told me something of the outline of the truth. And those stories which I heard long ago about Wildfold are... in accordance with certain of those fragments with which Lord Godalming has entrusted me.'

A long silence yawned between us. To delve any further

into the past seemed, I think to us both, to be dangerous.

Then, very quietly, I said: 'What do you propose, Mr Amory?'

'Ma'am, I have some outstanding leave. I should like to suggest that I take that holiday in the vicinity of Wildfold in the county of Norfolk and that, if I should find him there, I bring Dr Seward home again.'

Oh, Arthur, he struck me at that moment as so noble and so implacable!

'Thank you,' I said softly, 'for all that you have already done, and for that which…'

He completed the sentence: 'For that which I am yet to do?'

'Have you no doubts?' I asked. 'No uncertainties? I have an inkling that the journey may prove to be a dangerous one.'

'I feel, ma'am, that this is to be my role in events and that I can do no better than to play my part to the hilt.'

'Thank you,' I said. 'Will Lord Godalming allow it?'

'He said that he would, ma'am, though I am sure that the cause should only be strengthened were you to write to him yourself. As to the prosecution of my own duties, I have the utmost faith in the capabilities of that admirable young mastermind, Mr Strickland.'

So this, dear Arthur, is the final reason for this letter of mine. Will you give Mr Amory leave to search for Jack? I feel certain somehow – with something of my old intuition – that such an action is both necessary and just.

I do hope that you reply in the affirmative.

My love to you and Carrie always,
Mina

PS. If Mr Amory should go to Wildfold, can you urge him to take care? And to mistrust all whom he meets. Tell him to look for men's reflections in mirrors and to watch for shadows which move of their own volition. You may think me mad (my own husband would seem to hold a view not so very far removed from that opinion), but I fear that there is more in this matter than we have at present fully understood – or dared to face.

TELEGRAM FROM LORD ARTHUR GODALMING TO MRS MINA HARKER

10 January

Letter received with thanks. Amory may pursue suspicions with my blessing. May the Lord grant him success. C a little better today. God willing, we shall see you tomorrow in London. We surely have much to discuss. A.H.

RECORD OF CONSULTATION KEPT BY
DR ISAAC HOROVICH OF OXFORD GENERAL HOSPITAL

10 January

Patient: Quincey, a boy of twelve, brought in by parents Jonathan and Mina Harker. Boy has suffered three 'fits' or 'attacks' in which he is seen to shake and flail. Some rolling of eyes. Paroxysms. It is said that he has muttered numerous strange remarks when in this state. No history or evidence of epilepsy. Parents both concerned. Husband capable of hysteria.

At their urging, I examined the boy thoroughly. No physical cause. I asked if he had been under strain and they said that this was so. Slow death of beloved family friend. Difficulties at school and, I deduced, at home. The father clearly drinks. Privately, I suspect the boy is either faking or in the throes of a transient phase which will pass very soon. I was happy to prescribe a restorative syrup. All seemed calm once we were done and I sent them on their way.

One curious postscript: as he was leaving and once his parents were already beyond the threshold, the boy leaned close to me and whispered in my ear.

My wife, he said, has never loved me and has of late been unfaithful to me on five separate occasions.

Dumbfounded, I watched him go, too shocked to comment. Of course, this was mere fantasy on his part since he can know nothing at all of my own recent domestic unpleasantness.

Nonetheless, I should be most grateful were I never to receive the Harkers into this institution again.

FROM THE PRIVATE DIARY
OF AMBROSE QUIRE,
Commissioner of Police of the Metropolis

———◆———

11 January. Time was I would wake early in the morning, hurry down to breakfast and make haste to the Yard to begin a day heavy laden with responsibility. Time was I would fill my life with duty and strive to uphold my vow as an officer of the law to protect the peoples of the city. Time was, I was a policeman and a person of honour.

Nowadays, I am a coward, a vassal, an agent for the enemy. Yet the dreadful paradox is this: I have never once been happier or known joy in greater quantity than I do today. Such is the nature of habit at its most seductive; how much better do I now understand the helpless actions of the lotus eater, the laudanum addict, of he who reaches too frequently for the syringe.

This morning has been something of a case in point, a sequence of incidences which typify my life as it is now lived.

It was almost eleven (hours after I would generally rise) when I was woken in my bedroom, woken by a cool touch upon my forehead and by the gentle brushing of a nipple against my unworthy lips. I was dreaming of infancy, yet it was with sudden urgency, at the realisation another was present in the chamber, that I clawed my way as fast as I was able into complete consciousness.

I knew at once who it was – the intruder, the night-prowler, she of the bat and the mist. His dark herald, bringer of agonising joy.

I reached out hungrily with my tongue. She arched her back. Her breast moved out of reach. I caught her scent – something of spices, of the evening air and of freshly turned earth.

Lying happily beneath her. I murmured her name. 'Ileana...'

She looked down with a look of great disdain. 'It is not being long now,' she said. 'There will today be a double-event. For this you must stay silent. You must be thwarting any efforts to investigate.'

'But...' I tried to move but found that legs and hips and arms would not obey. 'I cannot stave off the others for ever. The American grows ever more indignant.'

She smiled at me, that devil-goddess. There was no true humour in the look, for her laughter is the laughter of malice.

'Be silent, Mr Quire,' she said. 'Be silent and be doing as you are told. For after today... none will be able to stop us.'

I gasped. 'Very well. My dear. Yes. But would you... Could you...' I tried to flex my neck at the moment, hoping to entice her with a vein.

She snarled at the sight, which was, I dare say, a pitiful one. 'You wish me to feed?'

I succeeded in a nod.

'Later, maybe,' she said. 'If you are being the best of all possible boys.'

In an instant she was gone. She slid back into the shadows and became as one with the darkness.

At the Yard they must be missing me. I shall rise in a moment and dress and do what I have been ordered to do. But I have yet to move. After Ileana left, I lay here in my bed. I wept as I wrote.

And a very few moments ago I heard, like the sound of distant thunder, the first of the explosions.

FROM THE PRIVATE JOURNAL
OF MAURICE HALLAM

———◆———

11 January. My life has not been one which any honest man could describe as having been free of vice or sin, yet surely I can have done nothing so monumental as to deserve those rich and vivid punishments which are visited now upon me. The gods, it seems, are fickle to those who love them best: every good deed is punished as much as every trespass.

I believe, yet cannot be certain, that four days have passed since I summoned sufficient strength to hold a pen and inscribe my thoughts. In the hours which have slipped by since last I offered my testimony, my apparent illness has only intensified. I languish in this fine hotel. I hear many voices and much laughter and I am aware, but vaguely, of all the apparatus of business being done in that chamber which is adjacent to my own.

Pleasure? I have known it not at all. Joy has been a stranger to me. The only fragment of goodness has been my nightly visitation from Mr Shone, when he has sat beside me and coaxed me to sup from his chalice. That medicine is as thick and as vile as ever, yet still do I drink of it. Gabriel assures me that it is for my own good and that it will, given time, bring about my healing.

To ask whether or not I believe him in this is surely, by now, unnecessary. For his words, though honeyed and sweet, disguise, as I have always known, darker things.

This has been the pattern of my days: to sleep and to dream, and to hear the distant words of serious men, and to be visited in the night by Gabriel, and to be made to drink. Given sufficient time, even strangeness can become ordinary and the outré grow routine. Nothing has changed since we first came to Charlotte Street – until, that is, this morning.

It was shortly before eleven when I woke. Although the drapes are heavy, thick and expensive, a little of that clear, bright, cold sunlight which is unique to the English winter succeeded in creeping in to illuminate the room. A single shaft of sunshine lay directly upon my closed lids, enjoining me to wakefulness.

When I opened my eyes I saw that I was not alone. My visitor was not known to me. She was a slight, young, blonde woman, no doubt pretty but also, it seemed to me, the victim of some recent assault, for her face was begrimed and dirty and her hair in disarray. Upon her soiled dress were stains which I took to be sanguinary. Her eyes had a hunted, harried look.

She was pacing up and down at the foot of my bed, looking with anxiety towards the door which led to the adjoining suite.

'Are you awake?' she asked.

I tried and failed to form the necessary words in response.

'I'm Sarah-Ann,' she said, in answer to a question that I would have asked had I been able, 'and I'm here to save you if I can.'

I managed to reply only with an inarticulate gurgle.

Then this young woman, this Sarah-Ann, was by my side. She lifted me out of my bed and helped me to stand, for all that my legs trembled at the exertion. She urged me towards the door.

'Don't worry,' she said. 'Mr Shone is away. At the memorial service. They're all distracted. Today is the day of the double-event.'

I must have seemed to her to be bewildered, for she sounded surprised and even frustrated at my failure to understand.

'I know what they're planning,' she said. 'I did what they asked. And I know what they mean to do to you. When I escaped I knew I had to rescue you.'

We were now by the door of my room. She opened it and we stepped out into the corridor beyond. It was quiet and deserted. Miss Sarah-Ann held tight my hand and pulled me onwards. From far away I felt the whisper of a breeze. I sensed it then – like a caged animal upon the hour that its keeper makes his first and only error – the distant prospect of my liberation.

I croaked out two words: 'Thank you.'

At this, the woman gave me a brief, broad smile and I saw how she must seem to men who are not of my persuasion.

'This way now. We should take the staircase. I do not trust the elevators here.'

Down the corridor we went, until at the end of it, Sarah-Ann pushed open two glass doors and we reached a tall, winding flight of stairs.

'We are on the third floor. But we must hurry if we're going to have the slightest chance.'

Down those stairs we went. I was breathless and weak. Something surged and roiled in my stomach. Yet Sarah-Ann hurried on and drove me forward. I sensed at the sight of her that she was a woman who had but lately learned of those reserves of courage and resilience which lay within her. Still we passed no resident or official, a fact which, I see now with all the unbearable knowledge of hindsight, ought to have appeared significant.

As we went, Sarah-Ann did her utmost to explain. Some of her words I believe that I understood. Many others were to me without meaning.

'They kept me underground. But they did not make me like them. Not yet. They need humans. Folk who'll help them in the mortal world. And I did it. I did what they asked. They gave me no choice, sir, for I escaped once before and they dragged me back. I did what they asked and I seduced the priest and I made sure a bomb was planted inside, hidden in a suitcase. The service today, sir. They'll all be killed. Except for the boy. He'll survive the flames. They've timed it, sir, timed it till they're all inside and they'll blow them to kingdom come.'

Now we had reached the head of the second staircase. I had to stop. With awful desperation, I sucked in air. I shook. My guts roiled in distress. By some miracle I forced from my parched and wretched lips a single, fractured sentence.

'You said... madam... something about me...'

There was in her expression both pity and distress.

'Don't you know, sir? Haven't you understood?'

I groaned my response.

'You were chosen, sir. Long ago, right back in Brasov.'

'Chosen,' I wheezed, 'for what?'

'Sir, you were chosen as the womb.'

She might have said more, but then there came from somewhere in the building overhead a great, shrill cry, terrible to hear, as of that of some monstrous bird, fierce and maddened.

'They've seen that you've gone! Run now, sir. Run for our lives.'

On we went without speaking, fleeing desperately down the stairs.

Behind us, and closer than before, we heard again that hideous shriek.

At the very moment when I had begun to believe that I might bear the ordeal no longer, we reached the last of the steps and Sarah-Ann flung open another set of double doors. We emerged into the reception area (oddly darkened) of this grand hotel. Here at last were people to be seen, those employed by the establishment itself and those who were entering it as temporary residents. There were perhaps as many as thirty of them and, upon our entrance, they turned to stare in our direction.

We must have made for the oddest of sights – a foolish old man in his night-shirt clasping hands with a blood-stained young woman. The distinguished men and elegant women in that vast lobby gaped at us with what I took to be understandable surprise.

Only too late did I realise the truth of it: that these were not ordinary people and that it was not so much surprise I saw in their wide eyes and open mouths but something very like amusement. Worse still, hunger.

The group of them turned as one and, like mechanical things, moved in a tide towards us.

At the sight of their approach, my stomach roared and convulsed in exquisite agony. Poor Sarah-Ann let out a scream filled, I thought, with absolute despair. She has escaped them twice. I feel certain that there will be no third occasion.

I held her hand as tight as I could while the creatures

approached us. For creatures they assuredly are, and not humans any longer.

I need not name them. I have long suspected their existence. All those European tales – every one – was formed from truth.

'Forgive me, sir! I'm so sorry!' called out the young woman as she was ripped from me by the crowd, their eyes glimmering, their sharp teeth glinting in the gloom. I found in that moment of absolute horror an unexpected dignity.

'Forgiveness is not needed,' I said quietly. 'I understand how it has to be.'

Then the girl was torn away, screaming again, and was subsumed by the voracious mob.

What will become of her I cannot say. When last I saw her she was still alive, yet it is my suspicion that she will not long remain so. Surely, when we see her again she will be not living but rather un-dead?

As for me, I was held fast by several of the creatures. Their leader appeared to be a sommelier. He was a young man, prematurely fat, his eyes dark and selfish.

He touched the side of my face and hissed, a lisp discernible in each of his words. 'There wath nether any needth to run away, Mr Hallam. We will bring anything you needth to thor room.' His skin was cold. He caressed my forehead, and what ensued was a merciful sort of darkness.

When I awoke I was back once more in my bed, as though no disturbance had ever occurred. Horrible and vivid was my failed escape, yet as I lie upon this rich, exalted pallet it has the qualities only of a dream.

I know now what I have long only suspected: that I am a prisoner here in this place and that I am in some fashion being prepared. As a sacrifice, perhaps?

I remember the words of poor, doomed Sarah-Ann and I begin to sense, I think, something of the whole truth.

There is an awful kind of happiness to understanding that one's path is set and that one's destiny has been written. I feel rather as must a victim in the days of the Aztec and the Inca have done as they were shepherded by high priests to the stones where they would be slaughtered to propitiate their thirsty deities. There is to it all an unanticipated peace.

So I lie in my bed, and I wait for Gabriel to return and raise the chalice to my lips and enjoin me to drink the serum within. Too weak to move, I mean to play my part before the end. And I am conscious also, all around, of a process of acceleration. Every element of the design is moving into its allotted place, in readiness.

It is shortly after dark. Shadows are lengthening. Hours ago, I believed that I heard the sound of distant explosions. There were screams also. The air is thick with fear. Fires of every sort are rising here. London, she is aflame. She is being scoured clean in preparation for that which is coming.

MINA HARKER'S JOURNAL

———◆———

11 January. For many years, the events of a certain terrible time in my life have seemed very hazy and far away. I have thrust aside all thoughts of our ordeals, pushed them to the very back of my mind, until every awesome and impossible sight I had witnessed – from the ruination of poor Lucy and the horrid interventions of the Transylvanian to the nosferatu women who surrounded me as I stood in the ring of fire – became faded memories, as if from a book which had been left for days out in the sun. Such a wilful act of neglect on my part, urging those violent recollections to sink into abeyance, has allowed me both to retain my sanity and to have grasped at a little real happiness.

Jonathan, I believe, who saw in that castle worse things even than the rest of us, has in his own way tried to carry out a similar process. Yet lately – and more than ever after the dreadful events of today – those old memories have been returning to me more colourfully and more vividly than they have for more than a decade.

I believe that I know the reason for this resurgence. Indeed, I think that I have known in my head since my journey from the Godalmings – since poor dear Lucy warned me as I slept.

The past few days have been trials indeed. Quincey suffered another of his fits. Although he recovered swiftly enough we took him to the hospital in Oxford. I do not think that the doctor there believed us. Our son has been quieter than ever since. He is afraid and in mourning, yet he also has about him (and this I do not care to examine too closely at present) an odd, disquieting air of expectancy.

Dear Mr Amory left us yesterday, to go to Norfolk and to Wildfold so that he might carry out his mission concerning Jack Seward. My husband drinks too often and I have myself been subject to bad dreams. Nonetheless, and in spite of all of these difficulties, I had hoped that today, the day of the memorial service for Van Helsing, would serve to bring us together and to purge some of the worst of the feeling that lies between us. I had hoped that it would be an occasion of healing as we gathered to celebrate a beneficial life. How wrong – how very wrong I was.

We caught an early train to the city this morning, down to Paddington station. The journey went by mostly in silence. I attended to some outstanding correspondence. Quincey either gazed from the window or else drew with a pencil in a notebook he had brought with him for the trip.

Twice I asked him to show me what it was that he was sketching. Twice he snatched the book away before I was able to see so much as the outline of his illustration.

'I'll show you,' he said, 'only when it is ready, Mother.'

After these rebuttals, I did not ask again.

Jonathan sat largely in silence, though his eyes were bloodshot and he was often to be seen perspiring in a most unhealthy manner. I knew the cause and chose to say nothing, but only waited for the liquor to leave his system. A fine party we must have seemed in our carriage, a family all dressed in black, not speaking one to the other, the air between us thick with resentment.

At the London terminus we ate a late breakfast and hailed a hansom to take us to the church. I began to think of old times as we clattered through the streets. I thought of London as she had been when we had known her well, back in another century. I saw, as any visitor to the metropolis surely must, how much the city had changed and, in certain places, how she had stayed the same.

There was to these observations of mine what might be called an ordinary poignancy, as might any woman think when her youth has long been parcelled up and put away. Still, there was something else I felt as I watched the avenues, alleyways and boulevards roll by, as my husband's eyelids drooped and as my son attended only to his notebook – a sense that the whole of London was ill at ease and afflicted by anxiety.

It was as though the place were waiting for something.

We reached the church of St Sebastian in the West, at the apex of Warren Street, a squat building with a touch about it more of fortress than of temple. Before it was the road, beyond it a patch of grizzled public land, a small urban wilderness beloved by the disreputable and the transient.

Still, this had been stipulated in the Professor's will and so I had seen that his wishes were fulfilled. Other people were already there, gathering outside like crows. There were former students and colleagues of Van Helsing's. There were old friends and acquaintances and those to whom that wise old Dutchman had offered aid. Some I recognised, though most I did not. A few I knew only from newspapers – the detective

Moon was present, mingling with a group of university men, as was the philosopher, Judd.

The priest came out to greet us. He was a younger man than I had expected, and would have been a handsome one had he not allowed corpulence to take root.

'You must be Mr and Mrs Harker,' he said, 'and Quincey also. Welcome. Welcome to you all.'

His eyes seemed rather glazed and he appeared, for a priest for whom such occasions were surely as regular as rain, oddly distracted and vague in his manner. I wondered if the man had been drinking, though none of those other indications were present with which I am now more familiar than I should prefer. There was a wild instant when I felt a distinct urge to turn around and leave that church, to climb aboard the cab again and take my family out of the city and back towards safety.

I believe that my instinct was a true one and, for all that it might at the time have caused surprise or offence or distress, I wish now with all my heart that I had found the courage to act upon it. Yet the moment passed and I shook away that strange presentiment, for what appeared to be the happiest of reasons.

The little knot of mourners parted to reveal two guests whom I had not spied upon alighting: Lord and Lady Godalming. They smiled and made their way towards us.

Arthur looked so very tired. He seemed lined and older than he has ever appeared before. There was a stoop in his gait which, pitiable in a man of such former athleticism, only added to the impression of age and fatigue.

Carrie, although the strain was not so marked in her appearance, appeared somehow far worse than her husband. She had been cleaned and bathed for the occasion and was dressed with her usual expensive finesse, but her movements were slow and exaggerated, as though she were a woman walking underwater. Her eyes were very big and wide but they seemed devoid of curiosity.

She walked through the world as though she were barely cognisant, her every word and action those of one who follows directions in a script.

'The Harkers!' she said as they drew near to us. 'How wonderful to see you all again.'

Her speech seemed almost slurred. I wondered, with an idleness that might look almost callous set down on paper, what drug had been used to calm and sedate her, and how she might behave were the influence of the dose to wear off.

Arthur and my husband shook hands. Quincey gazed at us all, his sketchbook underneath his arm, and murmured a bashful 'Hello'. Arthur took his wife's hand and held it tightly.

'Shall we go inside?' he asked. 'There are places set aside for us in the first pews. And we have much to discuss.'

At this we stepped into the church, little realising that, within the hour, we would be reduced in number by the worst of events.

We took our seats at the front of the congregation. I have never before today found any Christian church to feel narrow or oppressive, thinking them instead to be places of sanctuary and calm, yet I fancy that St Sebastian's will forever remain in my memory as the exception. We sat quietly as the pews filled up behind us.

Lord Arthur took his wife's hand in his and held it. She gave not the slightest indication of knowing that he had done so, so pliant was she and uncomprehending. Nonetheless, the gesture was a kind one, meant to offer comfort. I wondered if Jonathan might do the same for me. He did not.

Quincey cast his eyes towards the ground and clutched his book. I thought how saddened would the dear old Dutchman have been to see us so fractured and reduced. Those respectful murmurings which had filled the air turned to silence as the priest walked up the little aisle and approached the lectern.

He seemed unsteady on his feet, and when he reached the place from which he was to address us his face was damp. His voice was high and ill at ease. At the sound of it, I saw, to my surprise, that Carrie leaned forward, her posture now one of apparent concern, the first movement of her own accord which I had seen her make that day.

'Good morning,' he said. 'We are gathered here today for the saddest of reasons, yet must there be joy also. We mourn the passing of a dear friend, just as we celebrate the consequences of his life and seek comfort in the resurrection which is coming and which surely shall be his.'

He passed the back of his right hand across his forehead, no doubt to wipe away the perspiration that still gathered there.

'Yet today we shall give thanks for the mercy of the Lord. He has seen fit to gather our friend into heaven where, even now, he sits bathed in love and in light. For Abraham Van Helsing did the Lord's work upon earth, so it is only fit and just that he should now be receiving his true reward.'

Something struck me as peculiar in the phrasing of that last sentence which, in combination with the odd nervousness of the man, served to accentuate my anxiety. He spoke on for a few minutes more, careful in his dispensation of platitudes. As he did so, it seemed to me that he could meet no individual gaze within the congregation and that his eyes slid often towards the floor.

In time, he finished and bade us stand.

'We shall now sing the first of our hymns,' he said, and for an instant I thought that I detected in his voice a note of suppressed exultation. 'The day Thou gavest, Lord, is ended.'

Music began to sound from the church's pipe organ, at which we all got to our feet. For a very short time after that, I began to feel more settled in my heart. There is to that hymn a stolid sort of comfort, and as the words rang out something of my anxiety began to ebb away. We sang the first verse:

The day Thou gavest, Lord, is ended
The darkness falls at Thy behest
To Thee our morning hymns ascended
Thy praise shall sanctify our rest.

I glanced to my right to observe my family and saw that both Jonathan and Quincey were singing with diligence. At the sight, I allowed myself the frail hope that damages might yet be repaired, misunderstandings and injustices overturned.

We sang the second verse:

We thank Thee that Thy church, unsleeping
While earth rolls onward into light
Through all the world her watch is keeping
And rests not now by day or night.

It was only at the conclusion to this stanza that the occasion moved swiftly towards tragedy. Carrie stepped forward a single pace, her head cocked exaggeratedly to one side, as though she were an animal sniffing the air. She turned and began to make her way along the pew, towards the aisle. Her husband reached out to her but she shook off his hand quite easily. With weird determination, she pressed on.

Everything was performed with an energy and vigour of which I would have thought her incapable. All this happened with extreme speed, yet does it seem to me in recollection to have happened also with a horrible leisureliness, an all but balletic sense of deliberation.

Carrie reached the aisle and looked wildly about her. The music ground on, but plenty now were no longer singing and were instead staring at the aristocrat's wife. There were the seeds of a commotion.

The Reverend looked at her with an emotion in his eyes which one would not have expected – not concern or surprise or irritation, but panic. Lady Godalming ran to the back of the church.

Arthur followed, as, more hesitantly, did Jonathan. No more than seconds had gone by.

Caroline ducked beneath the last, untenanted pew. She was at that moment a study in indignity, a half-crazed riposte to all those antique notions of how a lady ought to be.

She emerged from the darkness with a brown battered suitcase. Her mourning dress was covered in dust and cobwebs. Her pretty face was daubed with dirt. The organ ceased to play and the singing stopped.

There was a moment's absurd silence in which all present stared at Lady Caroline. She opened her mouth as though she meant to speak, to offer some explanation for all this eccentricity, only to close it again and run from the chapel.

'Carrie!' Arthur cried. She did not look back or show any indication of having heard him, but only ran on.

Arthur and I were the first to follow her out onto the street. She was before us, still clutching the suitcase, loping ahead. She moved not towards the road but out into the patch of waste ground. She reached the centre of it – I realise now, to minimise the danger to the rest of us – and called out seven desperate words.

'Stay back! All of you, stay back!'

Something in her voice meant that we all, unthinkingly, obeyed.

'Darling—' Arthur began.

'Carrie!' I called out.

Her next words cut us short; it was by this time already too late. 'Don't you understand?' she cried. 'Don't any of you see? He is returning. He wants his revenge and he wants – he wants his boy.'

As these words were spoken I felt a hand brush against mine. I looked down. It was Quincey, gazing at me with a childish fearfulness in his eyes such as I have not seen there for years. His sketchbook was clasped tightly beneath one arm.

Carrie held the suitcase high about her head.

Arthur shouted: 'Carrie, please! Stop this. Come back to me.'

'You are the vessel,' she shouted, nonsensically. 'Poor child – you are to be the vessel.'

There was surely more that she would have said, but at that moment two things happened simultaneously. The first was that Quincey fell suddenly to the ground, his eyes pivoting, drooling from the mouth, in the grip of one of his terrible fits. The second was more fearsome still.

The suitcase which Lady Godalming held above her head exploded. The bomb that was within it did its vile work. And all then was fire and smoke and terror, as if every evil thing that we had ever dreaded was coming now to pass.

FROM THE PRIVATE DIARY
OF AMBROSE QUIRE,
Commissioner of Police of the Metropolis

———◆———

11 January. ★ *Later.* When the distant sound of that explosion roused me to uneasy consciousness, I felt at once more entirely awake than I had done for weeks, since before the time when I first embarked on this dark path. It occurred to me with sudden yet undeniable force how derelict I have been in my duties, how far I have allowed myself to fall and how entirely I have been seduced by a creature who is very much less than human.

At the memory of my collusion and betrayals, I felt only a burning shame. I knew at once where I had to be and what I had to do – back at my desk in the Yard, at the helm of the ship, leading and inspiring my men.

At the time I mistook this clarity of thought for a form of liberation. Only now, at the very end of things, have I understood that it was only ever a part of the trap.

I stirred from my bed. I rose. I called for my valet, I rang my bell and received no response to either summons. Puzzled, I called out again and still heard not a thing. Indeed, the house struck me as being far quieter than it ought to have been at such an hour.

Feeling a growing certainty of disaster, I had no choice but to wash and dress myself. Examining myself in the mirror I thought I looked a little better, though I was still unshaven and there was about me a quality of the unkempt and unloved (her residue, I suppose, her mark).

Thinking of that muffled conflagration which had roused me, I felt again the necessity of action. For had not Ileana, her soft, yielding flesh mere inches from my own, spoken of some double-event?

I hastened to leave my quarters. Before I did so I called out once more for my valet, or for any of the servants. No answer came. Perhaps I ought simply to have left the house straightway, hailed a cab and gone at once to my offices. Maybe then I might have eluded her. I doubt it, but I must at least acknowledge the possibility. Instead, at the resurgence of my old and, I should like to think, inherent decency, I chose to search the house before I left.

I do not now have time, for the clock is surely running down, to recount in any detail that increasingly frantic quest. There are no hours remaining in which I might delineate my hunt through every room and every hallway, or to itemise my dread. It must suffice simply for me to state that I found them in the end, all together in the scullery. All four of my servants were dead and had been stacked, in a parody of neatness, one atop the other. Each was pale, their skin quite white, all drained of blood. I saw that the floor about them was unmarked and that wherever was now that life-stuff which once had coursed through their veins, it was no longer upon my premises. I tried (truly, I did) to say a prayer for those poor lost souls but nothing would come. The words simply died in my mouth.

I turned away and fled, out into the day.

In the street I was overcome by a sensation of fearful bewilderment which would once have been anathema to me but which in recent times has become too familiar.

I should have called for somebody to take me to the Yard. Instead, I yielded to instinct and began to walk in the direction of the heart of the city. I knew the way of old. I was as a homing pigeon, my head and feet and soul all knew best where I belonged – these, I suppose, were my foolish and ruinous thoughts as I began the final trek. I hoped that something might yet be done to invert my treachery and that justice could still be carried out. If hopes they were, then they were empty ones: empty, frail, meritless.

I hastened on through the streets in the grudging light of a January afternoon. It was still daytime, yet the darkness seemed to possess a sinister eagerness to fall earlier even than is the case in the very deeps of winter. Shadows lengthened all around me with unnatural speed, as though minutes were ticking by faster than science allows. Even the temperature seemed to decrease and, though I had dressed myself well, I began to shiver in my coat.

I pressed on. The going began to grow harder and more difficult, the act of forward motion itself more strenuous. Every step was a struggle. The phenomenon is not easy to describe to one who has not undergone it, except, perhaps, to say that it felt as if there were some great cord, elastic but invisible, wrapped about my midriff, and that the more I struggled forward the more insistently I was pulled back. I cannot say for certain how long this sensation went on, but I do know when it was (dusk) and where I stood (at the corner of Bleighley Avenue) when the true cause of it was revealed to me.

As the shadows clustered around I heard in my ear a voice I had come to know well, with its European vowels and foreign insinuations, its promise of the dense forest and the deserted high road.

'My Quire, my Ambrose, you will not be running now.'

Ileana was present and she was not present. She was absent yet she was by my side. She seemed like smoke, or like the sound of a distant melody. Her voice was a whispering hiss.

'I am to be giving you your final duty, this thing you will perform for us in exchange for all our boons.'

I fought against it. If ever there is some account to be made of these sad events, I wish it to be known and understood that I tried at the end to fight them. I attempted to run but I made no progress. I endeavoured to call out but my mouth would make no sound. I did all that I could to push her from my mind, only to discover that she had taken up residence there long ago and now controlled it utterly.

'You will be taking this,' she said, 'and you will be placing this beneath your desk and you will be waiting for your...' She paused, the spectre of Ileana, as if to relish some moment of amusement. 'Your martyrdom.'

At the end of this sentence I felt something heavy arrive in my arms, I cannot say from whence – a large brown suitcase. Quite how this was achieved I am unable to say, except to remark that I am reminded of sundry claims by certain psychics and table-rappers to do with the possibilities of materialisation.

I knew what it was, that case, and what it signified. Had we not, after all, received accounts from previous attacks of the blast being preceded by the entrance of some unfortunate with just such a receptacle in tow?

'Be going now,' said Ileana. 'Be going to do His work.'

There was a period of brief, thick darkness and the next thing that I knew I was alone again. Ileana was gone and I was mounting the steps to Scotland Yard.

I walked indoors, my men parting before me. I must have cut a strange, dazed figure, and I dare say there was many a glance of surprise, distaste or incredulity thrown in my direction. It was only then, I think, as late as that miserable promenade into my office where I sit now and write these last words, that I finally understood how absolute has been her tenancy in my mind and how entirely lacking I have become in matters of free will. For with every step I took, although I was raging and screaming within, I could make not a sound, nor could I dissuade my feet from moving so much as a fraction of an inch from their preordained path. I have become a silent prisoner in my own body. This is the price for the pleasures that the Transylvanian brought to me. This is the vampire's bargain.

The brown case is beneath my desk. I know with what industrial malice it seethes. I know how this must surely end and there is in that a certain, black-hearted freedom.

I shall have this journal taken from me to the post room and sent at once to George Dickerson in the hope that he may yet circumvent their plans. I am resigned to the fact that I shall never be forgiven, by him or by anybody. But I seek no redemption. I am damned and, worse than that, I understand that I have been so for a long, long time.

FROM *THE TIMES*

11 January (late edition)

LONDON ROCKED BY DOUBLE OUTRAGE

The city is tonight deep in mourning following the successful detonation of two separate bombs, both thought to be part of that sequence which has already sown so much fear and horror. The first, seemingly smaller, device exploded at a memorial service for the late Dutch professor Abraham Van Helsing in the church of St Sebastian in the West. That many more casualties did not result is thought to be due to the courage of the attack's sole victim, Lady Caroline Godalming. Further details and a full obituary will follow as the facts become established.

The second incident occurred late this afternoon and though, at the time we go to press, details remain elusive, reports would seem to indicate that a substantial portion of the offices of Scotland Yard have been destroyed, numerous casualties being sustained within the ranks of our constabulary. The Commissioner himself, Ambrose Quire, remains amongst the missing. The very worst is feared.

We shall present to you at the earliest possible opportunity a full account of this most nefarious of outrages. In the meantime we pray for the souls of all those who perished, and we pray also that vengeance may soon be wrought upon those malefactors who would commit such evil deeds.

DR SEWARD'S DIARY,
(kept by hand)

———◆———

11 January.[*] The first thing that I knew when I came at last –
after who knows how long? – back to full consciousness was that
I stood alone in some abandoned field. The sky was growing
dark, the earth was cold and barren, and it seemed impossible to
me that anything at all might grow here. Nothing human was
with me. Rooks and crows overhead. The sighing of the wind.

Have I been mad? I think so, or at least I have existed in a
state not far from that condition, one allied also to dreaming.
I have read of such things in certain obscure journals but had
always dismissed them as a combination of superstition and
misdiagnosis. My own recent experiences have proved me quite
wrong. Even after all the horrors that I witnessed as a young
man, it would seem that my mind still remained closed to the
worst extremities of the world.

I can recollect the journey which led to me this place only
dimly. Much of it was done on foot, though there were trains

---

[*] The date is an estimate. The doctor was not in his right mind when he wrote these
words. I reproduce them here with his express permission.

also and people. There were odd conversations which I cannot recall and an inexplicable urgency which lingers with me still. Yet there is little else. I have not been myself, I think. No, I have not been myself at all.

The diary was a trap, I see that now, meant to remove me from the board. Yet I sense another hand at play also, one which offers much wisdom and support if only I can find the strength to help myself.

I have been sent here, to this place, for a reason. And so I will go on. I have a journey to make. And a crucial part to play.

It may be my imagination but I do believe that I can hear now, from somewhere far away, the sound of the distant sea.

FROM *THE PALL MALL GAZETTE*

12 January

SALTER SAYS: ENOUGH IS ENOUGH – THESE HORRORS **HAVE** TO CEASE

Another horror has been forced on us all, another miserable occasion for tears and for prayers. This time the enemies of our nation have struck twice in one day.

My friends, this state of affairs cannot continue. Why was our police force so thoroughly inadequate as to actually find itself the successful target of this latest outrage? How can such evil-doers roam free? How is it that the wife of a peer of the realm is executed, in all but name, in broad daylight at the very heart of London and nothing at all can be done?

How much longer can we, the people, be asked to bear this disgusting assault upon our dignity? How much longer can we be expected mutely to endure? I put it to you that the answer to that question is: not a moment longer! Not a minute, sir! Not a second!

From this time forth we must chart a new course. It is now plain to all of us here at the Gazette that the current way of doing things is simply not up to the task of protecting our Empire. The modern methods of our leaders have been exposed as being altogether without backbone or merit. Would it not behove us to look towards the past as inspiration for how we ought to conduct ourselves? Why do we not now reach once again for the solutions of previous centuries? I am only a humble scribbler, but I have lived a long while on this brave little island and it seems to me that such an approach is the only sane response to the crisis.

As to exactly where we ought to begin, I leave that to smarter fellows. Still, even a man as ordinary as I has heard whispers of the growing influence of the Council of Athelstan. Even I have heard of the Tanglemere Faction. And even I – like, I dare say, a good many of you – have lately begun to wonder whether the Council might not do a very much better job than that mob of floundering incompetents who stand at present at the helm of state.

JONATHAN HARKER'S JOURNAL

◆

12 January. Somewhat to my surprise following the appalling events of the day, and having completed an entry in her journal, Mina fell almost at once into a deep slumber.

She had said to me after the tragedy at the church, and once the news of the second bombing had reached us, that she wished to speak to me in detail and at length. I feared I knew the topic. She sees connections between things which do not – which cannot! – possibly exist. All is coincidence, appalling coincidence.

He is dead. He is dead. We saw him crumble into dust.

I confess myself relieved that Mina went so immediately to sleep – a sleep so profound that she could not easily or lightly be roused. Now I wonder about the nature of that sleep – especially after my own experience.

Five hours ago, at a little after ten, I lay down beside my wife and did my utmost to close my eyes. Yet even that seemed beyond my powers. The darkness would not come. My mind was filled with rogue thoughts and wandering concerns. I was beset by unwelcome memories and strange theories of my own – by one in particular.

How often in recent weeks have I thought of Miss Sarah-Ann

Dowell, and of what might have befallen her? Something in the business of her disappearance – not so very different, perhaps, from that of my friend Jack Seward – has long struck me as significant, though I cannot say quite why. Nor can I explain the reason, as I lie in the gloom of an unfamiliar hotel room, why two names ought to have come to me.

The first of them? Sarah-Ann's distant beau: Thom Cawley.

The second? The name of the criminal gang to which that young man was affiliated: the Giddis Boys.

It was with these unpleasant details in mind that I stole in silence from the bedside, dressed myself as swiftly as I was able and stepped with quiet purpose from the room.

For too long have I been a passive recipient of tragedy. Something is bearing down upon us and I must stir myself to uncover the truth.

When I entered into the hallway which lay beyond the marital room, I strode in the direction of the staircase which would lead to the lobby and to the promise of the city beyond. Yet I was stopped before I had moved a dozen paces by the voice of my son.

'Jonathan?' he said. His voice sounded strange to me, deeper than before.

'What do you mean by addressing me so?' I asked. 'And what do you mean by being abroad at such an hour? I had thought you asleep. You have not, I trust, suffered another of those... attacks?'

'No, Father. I have not. But I could not settle. Poor Lady Godalming... The things we saw today.'

I relented a little at this. 'Try not to linger on such moments. Sleep if you can and tomorrow the world may look a little brighter.'

'You don't understand, Father.'

'Then tell me,' I urged him. 'Tell me what it is that ails you. For your conduct has for months now been most... bizarre.'

He looked at me with a frail hope in his eyes. 'I want to tell you,' he said. 'But it is as though... I am not always permitted to do so. As though I am a prisoner in myself. I have tried to explain... more than once.'

'What do you mean?' I said. 'Has this to do with school?'

'No,' he said. 'It concerns nothing that is without at all. Rather, it relates to what is within me.'

'Did we not speak of such matters?' I asked. 'When Miss Dowell was still amongst us?'

He shook his head. 'This is of another sort. There is a kind of war within me. Between two fathers. You, Jonathan Harker, and...' He said no more. I sensed that he wished to speak on, yet was he silent.

'I don't understand,' I said. 'You know I am your father.'

'Yes. Yet in a certain sense there is – is there not? – another...?'

I felt a surge of anger. 'What is this? Who have you been speaking to? Who has been speaking to you?'

'Nothing, Father... nothing which has form.'

'Your mother? Is this your mother's work?'

'Most assuredly not.'

I looked down at the boy and, confronted with the evidence of my disapproval, he averted his gaze.

'Father?' he said. 'Father, what happened the year before my birth? What happened to you and Mother then?'

'Go to sleep, Quincey,' I said, as coldly as I could. 'Go to sleep and let us not speak of this again.'

He grimaced. 'Father, please—'

'Enough. I care to hear no more of this. You are fatigued, I think, and prone to wild imagination. Now: sleep.'

He turned to go back into his room and I began to walk away. Then he called after me, and there was in his voice a cunning which made me – for an instant – despise him. 'Where are you going, Father? Whom do you seek?'

I turned around, meaning to chastise him. Yet when I did so, his door was closed and the hallway was empty again.

It was with considerable relief that I stepped briskly out of the hotel and emerged onto the street. London rarely sleeps. It is in a constant broil. I was unsurprised to find plenty of street life in evidence before me.

We are staying in Bloomsbury, not far from Russell Square. My head filled with unpleasant questions but I was determined to begin my quest. I left the hotel behind me and headed south, towards the river and the district of London which was, in secret matters at least, ruled over by the Giddis gang.

In the past, I have been cursed with too exact a memory. After tonight, I wonder if the reverse might not now be the case. For I can recall little of my long walk to Vauxhall. There are in my mind only flashes and impressions. I remember the streets, narrow and dark. Some of the cries of the night people, of invitation or of despair. After a time, I remember the river, and it was when I crossed the bridge which yawns above the water that my memory seems most detailed and exact. I can still hear the noisy, hungry rush of it.

Afterwards, I came to where I thought that I was meant to be, in a long, low street filled on every side with establishments of dubious sorts, all selling liquor in spite of the lateness of the hour. I dare say that I stood out against this vista, neatly dressed as I was in clothes of mourning. Or, perhaps, my long walk had rendered me as draggletailed and seamy as my surroundings.

I remember stepping into three separate taverns (if one can dignify them with the name) and buying strong drink in each before endeavouring to make my enquiries. I spoke quietly and in circumlocutions, though without the least success.

In the fourth house, I was more plain-spoken, my demeanour no doubt aided by the draughts. Having purchased another grimy glass, I asked the barman, a thin-faced, perspiring fellow, if he knew of the Giddis Boy called Cawley.

He held up his hand, dirty palm outwards, in a brisk, definitive gesture.

'But you recognise it,' I pressed. 'You do. You recognise that name.'

He leaned across the bar, with odd, nervous energy. 'Get out,' he said. 'That's my advice to you. Get out of this place and go back to your home.'

'I mean nobody any harm.'

'No doubt that's true. But there are plenty here who'll mean great harm to you.'

I was about to press my advantage and question the fellow further when I noticed that he was gazing at something behind me, close to the door by which I had entered. As soon as he understood that I had seen his expression, he cast his eyes towards the ground. I turned in time to see a figure dart from the doorway and out into the thoroughfare beyond.

It was not the figure of a man, however, but rather that of a woman. Even from the merest glimpse of her, I knew her at once. Recognition gave me more gladness in my heart than I know how to express.

Gladness and guilt also. Oh, but there was guilt in great quantity. I dropped my glass and ran after her, out onto the street beyond. 'Sarah-Ann!' I called. 'Sarah-Ann!'

She did not stop or slow her pace, or in any way acknowledge my proximity.

'Please!' I cried out. 'Please stop!'

She did not. She ran on, and I followed as she turned hurriedly left and plunged into a darkened alley. I did not hesitate but followed post-haste, my heart beating madly, an awful optimism rising within me at the thought that I might, even now, be able to save her.

I remember running, yes. I remember hoping. I remember my body quivering at the exertion. I remember her blonde hair swaying and disappearing into darkness.

And after that I remember nothing. Nothing at all.

I woke early in the morning, disrobed and beside my wife once more. For the briefest moment I attempted to persuade myself that my experience had been nothing but another dream. The most cursory inspection, however, showed grime upon my skin, and grazes also. I did not panic and I kept my head. I made sure that I washed thoroughly before Mina woke. I dressed most quickly. We are to leave London today and return home. It feels miserably like a retreat.

I have said nothing to her about the events of the night. She has shown no indication thus far that she even noticed my absence.

What is happening to us? Dear God, but what is happening to us all?

I cannot – I will not – believe the very worst.

FROM THE DIARY OF
ARNOLD SALTER

———◆———

15 January. It has been a good day. I have not had a chance to write much in here for some weeks, such have been the demands of the Gazette. Numerous pieces* have I penned for that resurgent organ, arguing not only for the harshest possible penalty for those malefactors who assail our capital city but also for a wide-reaching reconsideration as to how we conduct ourselves as a nation. Time and again, I have made the argument that we should return to first principles: strength, courage in our convictions, and the willingness at certain times to behave in a way that the weak or indecisive might choose to see as ruthless.

Words have fairly poured out of me. I have not written in years with such fluency and ease. And readers have responded well. The mailbag, I am told, is bulging with messages of approval.

This afternoon I went to Fleet Street – at the summons of no less a personage than Mr Cecil Carnehan – and I have to say

---

* In this, at least, Mr Salter did not exaggerate. In the present volume, I have elected to reproduce only a representative sample of his oeuvre.

that the experience was an altogether pleasant one. Greeted at the door by an attentive clerk, brought up to the office of the deputy editor with great fanfare and pomp, ushered at once into his presence and presented with a glass of good wine, in spite of the earliness of the hour – I was treated in other words with all the deference and respect to which my rank ought long to have entitled me. How very different from my last visit here!

Once the clerk had left us and I was seated opposite friend Carnehan, the junior newspaperman leaned forward in his chair. He too had a glass of wine in hand. This he held out before him in a toast.

'Well, Mr Salter…'

The young pup paused after this, no doubt expecting me to insist that he refer to me henceforth by my Christian name.

D—n me if I would allow him that satisfaction!

I simply took a sip and waited.

'Mr Salter,' he went on at last, 'I wanted to ask you here today to offer you my most hearty congratulations.'

I was modest and I was magnanimous. 'Most kind.'

'Our circulation has increased markedly since your column started to appear in our pages. Never let it be said that I am a petty fellow, nor one who cannot admit when he has made a blunder.'

I smiled.

'So I am happy to say, sir, that you were right and I was wrong. There is indeed a public appetite of the most pronounced sort for opinion of your kind. Indeed, your analysis has made you more famous than ever before – and us all a good deal richer.'

'I am only glad,' I said, 'that you saw the truth of things in the end. Besides, it is your support that has allowed me to ascend to such a position. You should not be too hard on yourself, Mr Carnehan. It was your wisdom that saw the value of my words... eventually.'

'Thank you,' he said. 'And I want you to know how much we at the Gazette all value your work. Truly, you are one of the family. Should there be anything you need from us... Anything at all...'

'Most kind,' I said. 'But you need not worry. I am a simple sort of man who enjoys simple pleasures. I cannot easily be bought.'

He seemed relieved at my words.

'And I am not about to leave you, Mr Carnehan, for some other, richer, older newspaper. The Gazette's in my blood, sir. Rest assured, you have me for as long as you need me.'

The young fellow smiled. 'Then that is really very good.'

'Good health,' I said and swallowed the last of my wine.

'Allow me,' said Carnehan, 'to refill your glass.' This he did most deftly, leaning towards me over his desk. When it was done, as if he were frightened of eavesdroppers, he murmured: 'Now there is something that I have been meaning to ask you.'

'Anything.'

'Your friends...'

'Now, what friends would those be?'

He hesitated, then pressed on. 'The... Tanglemere Faction...'

I grinned, said nothing and took another hearty swallow of the wine.

'Well...' Carnehan went on, quiet as a mouse, '... whatever you want to call them.'

'I do know,' I said at last, 'who you mean.'

'What do they want? I mean – what is their ultimate objective?'

I wondered for a moment how much to tell him. Would he be able to manage, as I have managed, those passing but unsavoury emotions of guilt and uncertainty at the spilling of blood, even in so fine and necessary a cause as this? No. The very question is ridiculous. A cub like Carnehan, like much of his generation, is not used to the making of difficult choices, nor to the living with them. And so in the end, I told him only a sliver of the truth.

'They want first to stoke the flames,' I said. 'Then they want to set the land to burning. And once it's over, we'll all build a better, finer kingdom on the ashes of our mistakes.'

DR SEWARD'S DIARY
(kept by hand)

————◆————

15 January. Four days have passed since my own spirit was first returned to me. There is still much fog in my mind. Yet I have walked on, out of the last of England, and towards the sea.

I write these words on a beach where I have made my temporary home, amongst the sand and stone and driftwood.

I know that I have not been well – that I might, in fact, have belonged most properly in the care of the asylum itself – but I know also that I am recovering. Day by day I feel a little stronger.

There is a small town nearby which is, in truth, barely more than a village.

Its name – of course – is Wildfold.

I have stolen there after dark and scavenged some meagre sustenance. I am still emerging slowly, getting stronger and realising in increments what must be my purpose.

Much has happened, I am sure, in London and with the people whom I love. Yet I know that my place is here.

How do I know this?

It is because I have seen them, here, in this far-removed

place. I have seen them glide amongst the shadows, seen their weird infection start to spread.

I should have seen it earlier. I should have realised from the first. A great and potent force has set itself against us, all but invisibly at first, but growing now in boldness and determination. It fancies itself all-wise, I think, yet it cannot be. Surely it has made a mistake – even a small one? Perhaps – yes – perhaps my survival is already proof of that.

FROM THE PRIVATE JOURNAL
OF MAURICE HALLAM

———◆———

16 January. The whole world seems now to be in uproar. It must be so if I can sense it even here, alone in my sickroom in my luxurious eyrie.

I wonder sometimes if my body – that ruined failing engine, choked, filled with tar and fog, nearing the end of its period of usefulness – might not act as a metaphor for the ills which assail the nation. For within me something stirs and flails and thrashes. I know its name, though I dare not speak it often. It is eager to emerge and it is hungry to be born, but as we approach the point of parturition it struggles and causes me much agony. Its haste to return means only pain; pain and the certain knowledge of the imminence of my mortality.

It began, or so I realise now, from the moment when we entered the Transylvanian citadel and I was made to drink from the Black Grail, though pain of the physical sort did not announce itself until Paris. It began in my belly, deep in the guts of me, but now it surges, quite unfettered, throughout the whole of my system.

I sleep often and I dream much. My hours of consciousness

decline daily. Yet still news reaches me of what is happening in London and beyond. I believe that from those scraps of intelligence I see something of the pattern, the shape of the thing which is coming.

Every night I am visited and every night I am made to drink from the chalice. The fluid that it contains (I dare not speculate as to its foul ingredients) is dark and oily. I swallow it down.

Some nights it is Ileana who brings the chalice, her manner cold and curt, as though I am the child of a woman whom she despises. At other times it is either one of the creatures who turned to gaze at me and Miss Dowell as we stood in that infected lobby or else it is one of the human servants, one of those dark-clad persons who dress so finely and well. Tonight, however, it was Gabriel who came and bade me drink. After I had done so he sat with me awhile.

'Is it important to you,' he asked, 'that you understand the reasons for all of this? Why it is so imperative that we bring him back? Why so much sacrifice is needed?'

I said that none of this I needed to know and also that no explanation could possibly be sufficient.

He sighed. There was in him an odd dreaminess which I had not spied for many weeks. 'When you first met me,' he began, 'I had no purpose. I had no goal save for the receiving of pleasure. I loved only beauty. But mine was an ideal love. It lacked discrimination. I was looking, as I believe you knew, for a mission. He has given that to me. He has given me that purpose.'

I heard my voice, speaking as politely as though I were back at some grand soirée of the '90s, how happy I was that he had found for his existence so meaningful a trajectory. Of the bitter and sardonic tone with which one might imagine such words to have been infused I heard none, but only a kind of wistful resignation.

'When he comes back,' Gabriel continued, 'everything will be better. I see that now. I understand. The corruptions of modernity. We have made ourselves so plump and soft and weak. Do you not see, Maurice?'

He touched me upon my forehead, his fingers lean and too cool. 'Soon now. There are but a few more steps to be taken and then... Well...' He gurgled in oddly infantile happiness. 'The White Tower... Strigoi... The dawn of a new dark age.'

FROM *THE PALL MALL GAZETTE*

17 January

SALTER SAYS: WE DEMAND ACTION OF HIS MAJESTY'S GOVERNMENT

On too many a recent occasion I have found myself wondering what our forefathers might have made of the conduct of our government during the present crisis, only to conclude that their view would be one of profound disappointment. Four outrages have we seen in the capital since the turn of this year, and our gored police force stands now leaderless and in disarray. The underworld is said to be at war with itself and the ugly effects of that conflict have been felt often, and to their great cost, by the ordinary populace.

A sense of terror and of lawlessness is to be found everywhere upon our city streets. It is plain to all that the situation cannot be permitted to deteriorate any further. We have long since passed the point in this intolerable situation at which conventional solutions and modern thinking might still provide a helpful point of reference. To that end, I cordially invite the government to institute at the earliest opportunity a state of emergency, resulting in a temporary transfer of power to that noble, incorruptible and famously decisive body the Council of Athelstan.

We hope and pray that our political seniors will see sense and make this vital decision.

To do otherwise would be to risk further chaos and disarray, as well as the fury of the people. Should they flinch now from this necessary choice, then posterity – as well as those aforementioned forefathers of antiquity – will be bound to judge them with severity.

JONATHAN HARKER'S JOURNAL

———◆———

19 January. Something happened to me. Did it not? In that low alleyway in the territory of the Giddis Boys on the night of the eleventh? Surely I saw Miss Dowell, and surely I was confronted by something else in that place? But what was it? What was its purpose with me? And why can I not now remember? Why is there in that portion of my memory only blackness and oblivion? What am I not being permitted to recall? And why can I not face the truth?

Mina has asked often to speak with me alone but always I find a reason not to do so. Always I evade her. When I am near her, she sleeps to a degree which seems all but unnatural.

I drink too often. Dear God. How much longer can this go on? Without the storm breaking?

LETTER FROM LORD ARTHUR GODALMING TO JONATHAN AND MINA HARKER

20 January

Dear Mr and Mrs Harker,

I write, with something of a heavy heart, to inform you of my future plans. Following the laying to rest in the grounds of my estate of my dear wife, Caroline, and in the wake of those events which have beset us in recent times, I have reached a decision which may well strike you as disagreeable. In light of our long and complicated association, I ask only that you try to think the best of me.

Within the next few days, I mean to leave the country. Your own family aside, England has nothing for me now. I am surrounded by death and decay. Even this fine old house, once the locus of considerable joy, seems to me to be a dreary place. I have prayed often and with considerable fervour in the hope of discovering some cause for those disasters which have dogged us. I have received no answer or guidance save for the odd, persistent sensation that enlightenment shall be granted to me only if I leave our realm and strike out for fresh territory.

So I intend to wander awhile, throughout Europe and perhaps beyond it. I shall take only one companion – my excellent young servant, Ernest Strickland. My remaining domestic staff will ensure the upkeep of the estate during my absence. My hereditary responsibility to the Council of Athelstan I mean now to lie fallow. You may understand this more clearly when I say that I do not care at all for the direction in which this country is being steered by His Majesty's Government, and by what the press are calling 'the Tanglemere Faction'. The King's continued silence on these things strikes one also as ominous.

Please, my friends, do not attempt to dissuade me from this action. I am certain that mine is, for now, the best and wisest course. We shall all see one another again – of that I have no doubt – though I am at present far from certain as to quite when and where that reunion will take place. I shall think of you and pray for you often. You must not do the same for me, unless, of course, you wish it, but I beg this of you: please do not consider me a coward.

Your friend,
Art

LETTER FROM LORD GODALMING TO
LORD TANGLEMERE OF THE COUNCIL OF ATHELSTAN

20 January

My lord,

I take no pleasure in the necessity of this missive. Nonetheless, I must be plain: please accept this letter as representing my irrevocable wish to offer my immediate and permanent resignation.

My motives for this abdication are two-fold. The first concerns the tragic death of my wife, at the hands of one of those devices which have of late struck at the heart of our capital. The second has more immediate relevance. I do not care for the course which this Council has in recent months appeared to have charted for itself. Although founded in antiquity, I had thought it long understood – as did my father, from whom I inherited my place – that it was in the modern age to be thought of as a ceremonial committee only and not as a body which should ever again possess any real constitutional power. Recent efforts at the highest levels of the body politic to place true power in our hands in the event of some unspecified emergency strike me as perilous and profoundly undemocratic. I wish to take no part in an organisation which can countenance such medievalism.

I trust that you will accept this resignation as final. I mean to leave the country at once and I shall take steps to ensure that I cannot, for some time, be contacted. It has been my utmost pleasure to serve with many of you and I wish you well.

Nonetheless, if I may, I should like to leave you with the following exhortation. Please resist all efforts to alter the present nature of our Council. To accept the temptation of a reversion to older times would be to risk overturning much that is good in our present system, as well as the righteous wrath of the people. I only wish that I could find still within me the strength to fight upon their behalf.

Yours in sorrow,
Lord Arthur Godalming

MINA HARKER'S JOURNAL

———————◆———————

21 January. I am troubled not by Lord Godalming's actions
– for they are, in their way, perfectly explicable – but rather
by their apparent urgency. It is as though his processes of
thought have become subject to some unnatural process of
acceleration. Indeed, it is as though we have all been pushed
in our lives at great and unsolicited speed down the worst
of all possible roads, from the death of Van Helsing to the
disappearance of Jack Seward to the behaviour of my husband
to Quincey's fits and queer behaviour. The same procedure
also seems to be well under way beyond the circumference
of our circle.

Why, after all, have the gangs of London, for so long
capable of a form of wary coexistence, fallen to fighting
amongst themselves? Why have the explosions in the
metropolis grown at such speed and with such ferocity?
And why have the press taken to arguing with such
insistent urgency for power to be transferred into the hands
of this Council, which has for years been little more than a
decorative archaism?

The possible answers to all of these questions are becoming

clear. If Jonathan will not help me, then I shall act alone.

For were we not warned? Did he not make the promise, long ago? That he would spread his revenge over centuries?

DR SEWARD'S DIARY
(kept by hand)

————◆————

21 January. Much has been returned to me these past few days: memories and fragments of the journey which brought me to Wildfold, and of the diary which began my mental descent. I begin to sense the outline of a larger design. I can see the ways in which all of us have been hamstrung and distracted – me by obsession, Arthur by poor Caroline, the Harkers with their own domesticity and the Professor by mortality. And what is emerging once more from the darkness, onto centre stage, while we five are all so ruinously debilitated? We know his name, of course. We know it of old.

He is not yet, I think, quite returned to us, though his spirit grows hourly in strength. Evidence of his imminence is all around us. For Wildfold is infested.

Today I caught and killed one, down by the edge of the sea. It was a profound cruelty ever to have changed him, for he was old and in possession only of one leg. His sticks had been taken from him and I came across him at twilight wriggling along the sand. His face was contorted into an expression of painful, hopeless hunger. His lips were pulled back to reveal sharp teeth and a froth of crimson saliva. He wheezed helplessly and gasped pathetically for breath (although, of course, he has no longer any need for air or lungs, or for internal organs of any kind).

I approached this benighted creature, saw him for what he was and gazed down at him. His arms flailed and reached for me. He gurgled and whinnied and sighed. I had with me a long wooden stick (for I have taken to having about me at all times now such an object), its tip whittled to a sharp point.

How wonderful it was to feel again the old sense of certainty and passion, as I drove the stake into the heart of the creature! After all these long weeks of befogged confusion, I thrilled again to the old dark passion. The vampire on the beach let out a single, short, anaemic shriek, then began at once to turn to ash. The ease of the execution was almost disappointing to behold.

I left the remains of the blood-sucker where they lay, knowing that the waters would cover them soon enough, and walked back to the makeshift hide amongst the trees which is, for now, my home. As I went, I became almost at once aware that I was being followed. Swiftly, I seized a fresh stick from the ground and snapped it smartly in twain.

'Come out!' I called. 'I know you're there.'

There was now no sound or movement of any kind. I hesitated, only for a moment.

'Show yourself!' I called again, gripping the stake hard in my hand.

Without warning, I heard a soft voice close by.

'Don't shout. Don't call attention to yourself. Their hearing is far better than ours.'

I whirled about to confront the stranger, only to stumble

on the woodland floor and stagger to the ground. Panting and afraid, I looked up.

There was a woman standing over me – human, much to my relief. She was dressed in mannish clothes, of green and brown, and held in her left hand a long curved knife which showed signs of recent use.

'Who are you?' she asked. 'You're not nosferatu.'

'My name is Dr John Seward.'

'Seward?' She seemed to recognise the word. 'Seward the London alienist?'

'The same. You know me?'

'I've been expecting you, yes. Or rather one of you.'

'Who exactly are you?' I asked.

'I'm Ruby Parlow,' she said. 'And we have much work to do.'

JONATHAN HARKER'S JOURNAL

———◆———

22 January. We have retreated home to Shore Green. I have not been diligent in the keeping of this journal, as I know that I have not been diligent of late in too many matters. Since the horror in the city, Quincey has grown still worse. His fits are daily now and wholly uncontrollable. It seems almost as if he is lost to us – engaged in some private internal battle between order and chaos, hope and despair. We simply have to make the boy comfortable and wait for each attack to pass. We have not sent him back to school, but have kept him here with us until this dreadful season in our lives has passed.

What happened in London has, of course, affected us all. Poor Arthur. Poor Caroline. I understand that there was a small private ceremony which laid that troubled lady to rest only yesterday. We did not attend, nor were we expected. Arthur knows our troubles.

When well, Quincey seems to find solace only in his drawing. He is forever in that sketchbook, though he has yet to show us so much as a glimpse of any fruit of his labours. That secretive side of his nature he gets, I fear, from me.

Matters came to a head this evening, before supper, when

Mina visited me in the drawing room. Here I sat alone, and I dare say my wife had some notion that I had already taken recourse in the bottle. I cannot blame her for such suspicions, given my recent conduct, and I think that I was pleased and even a little proud to see her note that I was still quite sober and engaged merely in reading today's Times, which brought bad news from London, with all its talk of emergency powers and martial law, of the Tanglemere Faction and the Council.

At Mina's entrance, however, and upon observing her resolute expression, I set the paper down.

'My dear?'

'Jonathan,' she began, 'there is a conversation which we must have tonight.'

'Concerning Quincey?'

'No. At least, not exclusively so.'

'What then?'

'You know,' she said. 'You know of what I speak. And this is your last chance, Jonathan Harker, to listen and believe.'

I cannot bring myself to set down every detail of what she said. Her argument was overwhelming, detailed and precise. Only certain leaps of logic were made – enough to permit a reasonable rejection of her claims though not so many, perhaps, as to make that position inevitable. Some of this must have shown upon my countenance.

'You still do not believe? Even now? After everything?'

'Mina...' My tone was quietly imploring. 'We watched him die. We made certain of it. We were unstinting. There can be not the slightest doubt.'

It was as though she had not heard me. 'He would want to take his revenge,' she said, with a horrible sort of mildness, 'don't you think? If he ever came back. He would want his revenge upon us and – yes – upon England too.'

'Mina,' I said, reaching for an acceptable means of unstitching her contentions, 'did we not watch as he turned before us into dust?'

'But how do we know?' she asked, her eyes burning with self-belief. 'How do we know what truly constitutes death for one who is un-dead?'

Her words hung heavily in the air.

Then something like bitterness stole into her eyes. 'Oh, but you are too frightened to accept the truth. You must find your courage, Jonathan – the courage of the man I used to know – before it is too late.'

I rose to my feet. 'Give me time, Mina. You have to give me more time.'

'There is no more time!' she said, all but in a fury. 'We have already delayed too long. We have to face the truth of what is happening and we have to face it now!'

'Please excuse me,' I said. 'I do believe that I shall take some air.' My tone was cooler than I had intended. I had no wish for her to notice how much I trembled at her words, or how damp was my collar with perspiration.

I turned and walked away. Indeed, I left our house and stalked out into the gloom of the evening, little caring where my feet took me, to the edge of the village of Shore Green.

Exhausted and in distress, I sit alone on a patch of common land. Here I write and I think and I try my utmost to remember.

MINA HARKER'S JOURNAL

———◆———

22 January. The Count is returning.

My husband knows this too, yet he cannot bring himself to accept the truth of it. A part of me has always understood that, while he is not a bad man, Jonathan is certainly a weak one. He thinks too well of people. He looks for goodness and hopes for the best. He does not care to examine what lies in darkness. This makes him easy prey for malefactors of every kind.

I only pray that he finds the necessary strength within him. We shall all need much courage in the terrible days to come.

After Jonathan stormed out, I looked in upon Quincey. He was sleeping, quite soundly it seemed. That sketchbook he still clasped tightly in one arm.

I left my son and went to the study. Here I took a very modest drink and then applied myself for an hour or more to prayer. I prayed for wisdom and for guidance, as well as for that strength which will soon be necessary. I prayed for the souls of Caroline and Van Helsing and I prayed for the safe return of Jack Seward and Lord Godalming. Above all, I prayed that we shall prevail. I prayed for victory.

Whenever Jonathan returns and whatever he believes, we must make all preparations: the garlic and the holy water, the knives and the crosses. If I have to do this alone then I shall.

JONATHAN HARKER'S JOURNAL

——◆——

22 January. ★ *Later.* At last. At long last I see it. Though I must be swift, I have now to set down the moment of revelation.

I have resisted the truth for too long – to spare my sanity, yes, but I fear that the delay has placed us all in the gravest danger.

My long walk from home took me to the site where the people of Shore Green celebrated Bonfire Night, a little more than two months ago, for all that it seems that a lifetime has flowed by since then.

The marks of the conflagration upon which I assume they burned the guy were still faintly visible on the ground, a rough ring of scorched grass. Seeking sanctuary, I took myself to the midst of it and sank upon the earth. Here I endeavoured to put together in my mind all those events which have assailed us in recent months – the slow death of Van Helsing; the madness of Lady Caroline Godalming; the attacks upon the city; the resurgence of the Council of Athelstan; the disappearance of Miss Dowell.

All of these seemed at first to be altogether fragmentary and without connection. Yet as I thought harder, as I brought to bear that same logic which Mina had demonstrated, something like a pattern began to emerge.

Still I writhed away from it. Still I would not accept the truth.

I rose to my feet, meaning to go home and beg Mina to reconsider. Yet as I rose up I bore witness to a hideous phenomenon. The scorched earth around, the circuit of charred grass, seemed to burst into flame.

Nor was it any ordinary blaze but rather a weird, capering blue fire.

I stumbled backwards and cried out.

In the distance, it seemed to me that I heard the sound of laughter, far away now but coming ever closer, and sounding to my ears unbearably familiar.

In a fury, I smote the side of my own head. 'Face yourself,' I muttered. 'Face yourself!'

And then I saw it – that which my own memory had treacherously kept from me. The truth of what I had witnessed in that alleyway ten nights ago – a most vivid and horrific vision.

The beauteous Sarah-Ann had been upon her knees, transformed and despoiled. Her eyes were dancing with crimson malice. Her teeth were sharpened to points. Her every movement had been made redolent of the forests of Transylvania. And above her, with its great wings outstretched, there had stood some terrible raven-haired fiend. Such a terrible tableau: two vampiresses locked in unholy embrace!

No wonder I fled the scene. No wonder I forced the horror from my mind, like some demented hotelier rejecting an unwelcome guest. No wonder I sought solace in forgetting.

I screamed aloud my rage and horror.

Still the laughter echoed in my ears and still the blue flames capered before me.

I ran through it to safety. The heat was pure and terrible.

Whatever demoniac fire it was did not scorch me but rather filled me up with energy and purpose.

I hurry home now, back to Mina and my son.

Dear God, I would do anything not to be too late!

MINA HARKER'S JOURNAL

———◆———

22 January. ★ *Later.* I was still praying when I heard Jonathan return.

The door was flung open and I heard him dash into the hallway.

'Mina!' he called. 'Mina, my love!'

I heard such hope and wonder in his voice that I hurried to my feet and ran out to meet him. He stood before me with his arms opened wide, his face set in an expression of manly determination such as I have not seen upon it for more than a decade.

'I have been such a fool,' he said as soon as he saw me. 'I have been wilfully blind!'

'But now you see?'

'Yes,' he said. 'I believe you. You have made all the right connections! Indeed, I have witnessed some proof of my own.'

We were close now to one another, almost touching.

'Then what do we do, my love?' I asked.

'We fight him,' my husband said, and I thrilled at the sound of his resolve. 'We do what we did before. A new crew of light! We fight him, we track him down and we kill him all over again.'

'Yes! But we must hurry. He seems still stronger this time

than ever before. His ambition grows daily. And he wants – oh, Jonathan – I do believe that he has designs upon our son.'

'All these things are true,' Jonathan said. 'You are, as ever, quite right. And, my dear Mina, we will sever again that monster's head from his body. But before then – before so much as a single moment more should pass...'

'Yes?' I asked. 'What is it, my love?'

'I have to give to you, my dear, a thorough, a comprehensive and a most unstinting apology.'

'You... need not apologise to me.'

'Mina, I must! Love of my life, I must!'

He seemed in his words almost to be delirious.

'Not only for my recent recalcitrance but for all that came before. For my taking strong drink. For my neglect of you and Quincey. For my foolish gaze and my wandering affections. For not worshipping you every day that I am given with you.'

He was trembling now, poor fellow, and there were tears in his foolish eyes.

'Enough,' I said. 'Enough now. Let it all be done with. Let us say no more.'

Instead of speaking, I stopped his mouth with a kiss – our first in many months – and, just for an instant, I do believe that we were happy.

Our embrace was interrupted by a loud, insistent knocking upon our front door – the kind of knock of which it is said that it might wake the dead.

My husband and I stepped hurriedly apart.

'Jonathan?'

Before he could reply, the knocking came again, fierce and inexorable.

'Jonathan, who is it?'

'I...' My husband looked down at me then, and there came into his eyes a horrible species of panic. 'I...'

Without saying more, he swayed, tottered and then crumpled, insensible, to the ground. I crouched down and saw that he was breathing but that he seemed lost to some unnatural swoon. I shook him but he did not respond.

When the knocking came again, I rose and took from about my neck the pretty silver crucifix which hangs there. Clasping this in one hand, I stepped with trepidation towards the door, my head full of fear and foreboding.

When I reached the door, determined to avoid any suggestion of timidity or appearance of weakness, I opened up with a flourish, positioning myself firmly on the threshold so that, were the visitor to be an unwelcome one, he might feel discouraged. I hope – although the truth of it scarcely matters now – that the boldness of my posture disguised the fear which crept and clawed inside me. The figure whom I then confronted was, though covered largely by the dark, a most familiar one – the stout form of Mr Amory.

His face lay in shadow but I sensed that he was smiling.

'Mrs Harker,' he said. 'I hope most sincerely that you will forgive my calling upon you at so late an hour, and for being so very noisy about it.'

'Did you find him?' I asked softly. 'Dr Jack Seward?'

'Oh, I found him, ma'am, yes. Him and all his new friends.'

'Then where is he?' I asked. 'How is he?'

'It's a long, strange story, ma'am. Won't you let me in so I can tell you everything?'

A pause fell, one in which the hideous truth of the situation became to me undeniable.

'Mr Amory,' I said.

'Yes, ma'am?'

'I do not mean to invite you in.'

'Why ever not, ma'am?' His tone was flat and flecked with menace.

'Because I am very much afraid that I know what you have become.'

He did not reply but only stepped forward, out of the darkness.

Poor Mr Amory. I saw at once what had been done to him, for he was now deathly pale and his eyes were violently bloodshot. He peeled back his lips, hissed and grinned, displaying the proof that he was no longer a man at all but had rather become a creature. He moved forward, far faster and with a greater degree of agility than ought to have been possible in a man of his size and age.

'I'm very sorry,' I said, 'but I cannot allow you to come any further.'

At this, I held out the crucifix, at the sight of which the vampire shrieked and shrank back. I clutched the cross and held my ground. A few moments later, having grown accustomed to the nature of our confrontation, the thing which now went about the earth in the form of poor Amory stepped forward once more, as close to me as he dared, somewhat in the manner of a dog approaching a blazing fire.

'The master is returning,' he said, his tone now almost wheedling. 'He is coming to the White Tower. And once he is there he means to take his revenge.'

'I do not doubt you,' I said, with the greatest degree of

nonchalance I could summon. 'Yet you may tell him this: that we all of us will fight him with all that we have for every inch of ground, and that in the end we shall surely triumph.'

A look of savagery crept onto Amory's face. 'Oh, but your precious crew is broken. The Dutchman is dead. The lord is in exile. The alienist is mad and your own husband is lost.'

'We will reform,' I said. 'We will be stronger than before.'

'Ha! On our side is all the machinery of the state. On yours... merely broken threads.'

'We have enough,' I said, as stoutly as I could.

'Oh, Madam Mina,' said the blood-drinker then, his eyes glittering with malice, 'but you have far, far less than you believe.'

Only an instant or two was to pass before I was made to realise with sickening force the truth of his words.

'Mother?' I heard a voice from behind me, oddly calm in its timbre.

'Go back to bed, Quincey,' I said, not turning but keeping my eyes trained upon the nosferatu. 'Go inside and lock your door.'

I heard my son move closer.

'No, Mother. I cannot do as you ask. Besides, it really is awfully rude to keep a guest waiting upon our threshold like this.' Quincey raised his voice. 'Mr Amory? Do come in.'

The butler scuttled forward.

'Quincey, no!' I whirled to confront him. Still I held that crucifix outstretched, but my own son with dreadful strength knocked it from my hand. It clattered to the ground. Quincey's eyes were blazing red – crimson, the colour of hot coals, of scarlet berries in the snow.

When he spoke again his voice sounded older and deeper than before; it seemed to possess some horrible sense of resonance. 'My father is coming,' he said, and I heard from behind me the ugly giggle of the Amory creature. 'My father is coming for us all.'

I began to scream then, but it was already too late, for I felt the hands of Mr Amory at my arms and shoulders as something damp was thrust upon my mouth. A swoon came upon me, and as the dark rose up to claim me I heard the sounds of weeping – from whom, even now, I cannot be certain.

JONATHAN HARKER'S JOURNAL

———◆———

23 January. I can recall nothing at all after that knock came at the door, mere moments after my reconciliation with Mina. For those missing hours I have only darkness and imagination.

Instead, I woke in my own bed again this morning to an atmosphere of profound and unusual stillness. From the quality of the light that streamed through the window I understood at once that I had slept for far too long. From the complete silence of the building I realised that something was very wrong. I rose hastily to my feet, my motions groggy and uncertain as though the floor had become a sea. I had to clasp the back of the chair for support so that I did not tumble to the ground. I had to take several deep, steadying breaths to right myself and ensure my balance.

This achieved, I called out: 'Mina! Quincey!'

I heard in response only the dull echo of my own voice. I moved out of the study and into the body of the house. I called the names of my wife and child once more but the sound discomfited me, so I did not do so again.

As I entered the hallway I felt a chill breeze and saw that the door stood wide open. This was ominous enough, but there were clear signs that a struggle had taken place. There was a dappling of blood upon the carpet and a spray upon the wall.

There was to the scene a horrible quality of theatre – as though the tableau had been arranged for my edification. I noticed a book open upon the ground. I cannot say why it should have arrested my attention then, amongst the more obvious relics of violence, but as I peered more closely I saw that it was the volume in which Quincey had of late spent so much of his time sketching.

A gust of wind drifted through the door and, as though with invisible fingers, riffled through the cream-coloured pages. I caught glimpses of numerous illustrations – all odd and troubling to me, evidently the product of a warring mind.

The book stopped turning then and I was confronted by an illustration of almost uncanny detail, drawn in dark ink, the exact replica of a face I have long striven to forget, that of a very tall old man, dressed all in black, with a long white moustache. It was a precise replica of the Count himself as I had first seen him standing upon the threshold of his castle, long ago in the country of Transylvania. Another page revealed him in the process of transformation, from something like a man into a column of mist. The evidence by which I was surrounded became to me overwhelming, so much so that it took all my resolve not simply to sink to my knees and howl.

Instead, I turned and went back upstairs to my son's bedroom.

'Quincey!' I called out. 'Quincey!'

I opened the door to his room without knocking and saw that, curtains drawn, the place yet lay in darkness.

There was in the bed, discernible amid the gloom, the outline of a figure.

'Quincey!' I shouted, now at least as angry as I was afraid, suddenly filled with righteous but impotent fury. 'Quincey!'

The answer that I received from that figure beneath the sheets was an unexpected one – at once horrifying and thrilling.

It was the sound of female laughter. It was a tinkling, giggling glissando.

'Who's that?' I said. 'In God's name, who's there?'

The figure moved – or, rather, writhed – beneath the covers, then cast them aside.

She unfurled herself and sat up against the headboard, her every movement both languorous and suggestive of energy suppressed.

'Sarah-Ann? Is that you?'

Her blonde hair fell about her shoulders. Her skin was milky white. She arched her back and rose with liquid motion to her feet. As her eyes flashed red, she hissed and bared her teeth, and I understood what she had become.

Oddly – or, perhaps, not so very oddly as all that – I felt at this realisation not the slightest trace of surprise but only a form of acceptance.

'This is what you have dreaded,' said Sarah-Ann Dowell as she glided towards me. 'But it's also what you have longed for.'

I could not move so much as a muscle, so absolutely was I transfixed.

'All my days I was wanted... by men like you. I was pawed at and leered at and touched. But now – at last – the power is moving away from your sort and towards... folk like me.'

I wanted to cry out, to apologise and to make a full confession. I am sorry, I wanted to say. I am so very sorry.

But my lips would form no words, nor was I able to make a single sound.

And then? Why, then she was upon me, that new vampiress, tearing and rending and drinking her fill.

FROM *THE PALL MALL GAZETTE*

27 January

SALTER SAYS: A NECESSARY JUDGEMENT

For some time now has this newspaper been critical of the actions of His Majesty's Government.

Too often in recent weeks have our elected leaders appeared to be merely indecisive in the face of concerns of the most pressing sort. Rising discontent in the capital and a tide of motiveless violence was met with little more than platitudes. Warfare of a sprawling, vicious type amongst the various criminal gangs of London received a response from the constabulary which appeared to move from the slipshod to the simply impotent.

Although it behoves no one to speak ill of the dead, it must be stated here that the late Commissioner, Mr Ambrose Quire, was feckless and derelict in his duty. Finally, in that dreadful sequence of costly and deliberate conflagrations which has beset the capital, we have witnessed from our representatives the behaviour of a toothless dog which, under the whip of an unstinting master, whimpers, quails and lies still. All these lapses on the part of the authorities have been regrettable. They have proved costly to a horrible degree and they will not lightly be forgotten.

Yet now is not the time to dwell upon the errors of the past. Rather it is to the predicament of the present and the challenge of the future that this newspaper looks. It is with considerable pleasure and not a little pride that we are able to salute the decision that has been taken today to cede direct control of London to the Council of Athelstan. The emergency bill has served its purpose at last.

This step is born of necessity, and we are certain that while it surely was not taken lightly it represents the only appropriate reaction to the current emergency. It is our fervent belief that, with the application of those special, particular and unique powers which lie within its purview, the Council will be able to restore order far more swiftly than might otherwise be practicable. If the campaigning of this column has in any way provided some degree of expedition of this temporary transfer of power, then we humbly take our bow.

Far be it from us to proffer any further advice, but might we not suggest that the most logical first act of the Council would be to take complete control of both the police and the military who are at present within the confines of the city and, with immediate effect, to declare martial law?

Only so firm a judgement will restore to the people of the metropolis true faith in those who stand at the helm of the great ship of state. That this suspension of recent democratic process is only temporary may freely be acknowledged to those doubters and cowards from whom we shall shortly, and with wearying inevitability, hear.

It cannot be stressed too strongly, however, in the face of such objection that the instatement of the Council in its proper place can only be accounted a victory for the ordinary law-abiding citizen and a triumph for all who wish to see this mighty nation soar once again to its awesome and appointed destiny.

LETTER FROM THE SECRETARY OF THE COUNCIL OF ATHELSTAN TO SUB-DIVISIONAL INSPECTOR GEORGE DICKERSON

28 January

Dear Mr Dickerson,

This letter is written to you both with pleasure and with regret. The pleasure was brought about upon receipt of news of your survival in the wake of the recent devastation at the Yard. As you will doubtless be aware, the damage caused by the bomb was widespread and multifarious. It has been gratifying to discover that some of this city's most trusted servants in the force have been spared.

The regret, however, is occasioned by the following necessity: the immediate termination of your terms of employment. Your rank, office and all associated powers are hereby revoked with immediate effect. On this matter, we have taken advice and it is felt that your failure to prevent the attack by your own superior upon your own headquarters, coupled with your status as an alien in our nation, renders your present position untenable.

This city stands upon the precipice of disaster and to guard its ramparts we need only determined, capable and, above all, patriotic Englishmen.

Might we recommend that you return to the United States of America at the earliest opportunity, where your reputation can (one presumes) more easily be repaired? Here your survival has rendered you the leading representative of a failed and soft-bellied system. You will, we are certain, appreciate the fact that things in London must change, and change swiftly.

Yours sincerely,
?*

on behalf of G.D. Shone
President-Elect of the Council of Athelstan

---

*There is a signature here but it is an illegible scrawl.

LETTER FROM LORD ARTHUR GODALMING TO JONATHAN HARKER

31 January

My dear friend,

I write these words – who knows if you will ever read them? – amid fury and tumult of every sort. All around us is chaos. The worst of all our fears has shape and terrible form.

As I promised in my letter of the twentieth, I have left England in the company of my servant, Strickland, and set out for the Continent. I had hoped to wander, to explore and to seek some manner of peace.

I prayed often that, across the sea, we might escape the shadow's reach. Yet it would seem that our doom is already set.

At Dover, travelling incognito, we obtained passage on a vessel of German origin. Our captain was a lean, heavy-lidded fellow named Delbruck whose usual demeanour was of exaggerated suspicion.

This very morning we were shown to our cabin by a suet-faced mate and ordered, in crude English, to stay away from those areas of the ship which contained its cargo. Strickland and I were to be allowed on deck only at Delbruck's discretion.

Exhausted, as if in the wake of fever, the two of us fell asleep in that little space. Consciousness fled with unnatural swiftness.

I was woken by a hand upon my shoulder, shaking me, firmly but gently, back into reality. A picture of bleary concern, Strickland stood over me. It was immediately apparent that the ship was moving at a pace suggesting that we were already at sea.

'My lord? Do you hear that?'

A child was crying somewhere nearby. Whether it was boy or girl, I could not discern, nor was the age of the unseen individual at that time clear.

We looked at one another for a moment as we listened to those sounds of evident despair. Before either of us could speak, all other noise was drowned out by a single continuous roar.

Seconds later, our vessel lurched violently sideways. We were both hurled to the floor and, in the melee of the event, my instinctive thought was that capsize (at the least) was now inevitable. Then, with a second, counteractive surge we seemed to right ourselves. Strickland and I rose to our feet. From overhead, from somewhere on deck, we heard the frantic cries of the sailors.

It was towards those shouts that we now moved, departing the cabin and racing towards the open air. We arrived to greet a scene of near-absolute confusion. The deck shifted beneath our feet. The surface was slippery and treacherous. White water churned and sluiced to either side of us, fierce spray drenching us repeatedly from the moment we appeared. All around us darted harried, desperate crewmen.

'What has happened here?' I shouted. 'What is the meaning of all this?'

Not one of the mariners replied to my entreaty, or so much as slowed their efforts in order to acknowledge our presence.

Then we heard a voice – of the most unexpected kind – rise up behind us.

'What we are witnessing now is only an after-effect.'

We turned to discover the speaker and, my dear old friend, I tremble now to admit to you the truth. For it was none other than—

'Quincey?' I cried. 'My God, whatever are you doing here?'

Your boy seemed almost entirely without emotion. 'I came to find you, my lord.'

'What do you mean?'

'I've been fighting a battle all this time. I was not permitted to speak of it. But now I know which side has won. We must move this ship around, my lord, and go back to England.'

'In God's name, why?'

'Surely you know?' said Quincey. 'To greet my true father now that he has returned.'

As he spoke, a new wave struck the side of the ship and we were all sent sprawling. Before it happened, at the end of your boy's words, I saw his eyes, in a moment of uncanny horror, flash a terrible kind of crimson.*

---

* The letter ends here. Subsequent events made its completion decidedly impracticable.

FROM THE PRIVATE JOURNAL
OF MAURICE HALLAM

———◆———

31 January. I lie still in my bed in this hotel, tended by servants, visited but occasionally by Mr Gabriel Shone and comforted not at all. Something dreadful grows within me, of that I am certain. It swells. It buds. It hungers for egress.

Each word that I write costs a good deal in effort and pain. This pen is too heavy in my hand. My eyes are become treacherous things. Time is made slippery and frictionless again, and is full of pitfalls.

I feel as must have the great tragic heroes as the final act approaches – Hamlet upon learning of the proximity of Fortinbras; the Scottish thane glimpsing impossible movement amongst the trees. One cannot turn away now, nor seek to escape. The momentum is all, my destiny is set, and so it behoves me merely to speak the lines that are required and stand where my director asks me to stand. I can sense them, as of old, my audience gathering upon the other side of the curtain. I can sense their agitation and rising excitement as the denouement draws near.

My last bow will not, I fear, be a pleasant one, but it must needs be most memorable. As I lie here, drugged and weak, looking back upon my plentiful mistakes and counting my regrets, I can at least number the following fact as something like a comfort: I shall not lightly be forgotten.

MINA HARKER'S JOURNAL

———— ✦ ————

Date unknown. I am again with Jonathan. Things seem different. We are together in a garden, a lush and fertile place which, although striking and beautiful, I do not seem to recognise or recollect.

We are sitting alone upon a wrought-iron bench. It is warm (surely the height of summer) and the air is filled with the incense of English flowers and with the drowsy, comforting drone of bees. All is delight and easy comfort. All seems fair and well. Jonathan takes my hand and smiles. I see now that he is very much younger than when I saw him last. I look down and find that my own hands are smooth and quite unlined, just as they were once, before Transylvania and all that came afterwards, back when I was but an assistant schoolmistress and Jonathan merely a solicitor's clerk.

'Mina?' he asks. 'Mina, my dear?'

Even his voice sounds different – oh, how could I ever have forgotten! – so full of kindness and good humour and the subtle intimation of desire. There is not a trace of that near-constant vexation and fragility which has come to mark so much of his speech.

'Yes, my darling?' I feel almost giddy with the quiet thrill of the moment, its wealth of hopeful possibility.

'I asked, my dear, if you would consent to be my wife.'

'My goodness, Jonathan, nothing would make me happier.'

He seizes my hands and kisses them. 'Oh my love. Oh my dear one.'

Suddenly, I pull away. 'No.'

'Mina?'

'No,' I say again, more firmly. 'This is not how it happened. This is not how it should be.'

He smiles in understanding. 'You mean, I think, that we should not be alone at such a moment as this? That there should be present some friendly chaperone?'

'I do not think so... no... that is not what I meant...'

'Mina. Please. Be not afeared. For we are not alone. Nor shall we ever be. He is always watching. See for yourself. Please. Turn around.'

Without speaking, I do as I am bidden. I turn and look behind me and I see, watching us from a distance, a single dark figure. He is forming, I realise, forming out of what seems to me to be a pillar of mist. The sight grows in definition to reveal a man, very ancient, dressed all in black, with a long white moustache and an air of inextinguishable malice.

For an instant, I do not recognise him. Then, as realisation rushes in, I understand with horror what is happening and, unable to stop myself, I loose a panic-stricken scream and—

It was at this moment that I awoke, still screaming, from the most vivid dream of my life. I gasped and struggled to breathe and became only gradually aware of my surroundings.

Just how long had passed since my encounter with the transformed Mr Amory and that hideous realisation concerning my son I cannot be certain. I felt weary – unaccountably so – from which I deduced that I had been drugged for some considerable period.

As to precisely where I was, the place felt thoroughly unfamiliar. It was very dark indeed. Nonetheless, I did not wish to remain for a moment longer in that most undignified sprawl in which I had recovered consciousness. It was, I dare say, quite an ungainly process, but I got, all the same, to my feet. For a moment I tottered, weakened and unsteady after my prolonged sleep.

My movements were still hazy and leaden and my processes of thought must have been equally impaired, for I was about to call out into the darkness, for help or attention or to ask the whereabouts of my son. Such efforts would have availed me nothing.

No sooner had I drawn an uncertain breath and parted my lips in order to speak than a great bright light was shone upon me. I blinked hard and squinted before I was able to see something of where I had been placed – for I saw now that I stood upon a kind of low stage, a long, narrow dais which had about it also something of the transept.

I became at once aware of the presence of spectators – two rows of men, unspeaking and in shadow.

All appeared to wear some form of ceremonial dress, elaborate robes which possessed a quality of the Masonic. One in particular, who stood in the midst of them, seemed to draw my attention: a lean and weathered man, patrician in aspect, who had by his feet an old Irish wolfhound which stood upright and alert. The man himself wore a look of triumph, and there was something in the posture of the animal which seemed somehow to suggest the same.

I glanced downwards and saw that I too had been dressed in some elaborate robe. At the thought of how this might have been achieved, I experienced a spasm of disgust.

'Why are you watching?' I called out to this audience. 'What do you want with me?'

No answer came. The men simply looked on, staring silently. A few wriggled forward in their seats, leaning and peering, I supposed, that they might see me better.

A voice came from the pool of darkness at the far left of the stage.

'Mrs Harker? Mrs Mina Harker?'

I answered with as much decorum as I could muster, given the profound grotesqueness of the circumstances. 'I am she.'

The speaker came out of the shadows to join me in my pool of light. He was a tall, swaggering young man, dressed in the same robes as those in the audience (although his seemed rather grander than the rest). He would have been handsome had it not been for the black patch which he wore upon his left eye.

He was not alone. By his side there sloped an older man, rotund and florid-faced, perspiring heavily and trembling. This second figure moved only with what was evidently the most profound difficulty. An exemplar of that grossness which can be visited upon the human form, his every step was accompanied by a piteous whimper.

The final element in this vision was the fact that there was about his neck a metal circlet, and that the older man was being led by the younger as though he were some recalcitrant beast.

'It is fine indeed to see you so well, Mrs Harker,' said that one-eyed man. 'From the first he told me that he wanted you to be present for his rebirth. In spite of it all, he thinks so very highly of you.'

'Who are you?' I asked. 'And what is this place?'

'Why, I am Gabriel Shone and this is the Council of Athelstan. You stand in the depths of the White Tower, at what is now the centrifugal point of power in this great nation.'

'You don't understand,' I said. 'You can have no conception of the force you are bringing back to life. The absolute nature of his evil!'

'Believe me, madam, I know exactly what it is that I am doing.'

He looked down at the corpulent figure by his side. 'Is it ready now? Is it almost ready to be born?'

In response, the man in chains could only moan. Gabriel Shone gave a conniving smile. 'I shall take that as being in the affirmative,' he said. 'So – all rise.'

He held out his free hand, at which, as though they were mere puppets, each member of the Council got to his feet, standing with the solemnity of mourners at a funeral.

At the same moment, I felt strong hands reach from behind me and hold me tight. I struggled but could not move. My captor was a woman. I could smell the strange, sweet scent of her. I could hear the rustling of great wings.

'Welcome, Ileana,' Shone said. 'You are just in time to witness the second coming. This dark miracle.'

The fat man moaned again. This time a small trickle of blood emerged from the left-hand side of his mouth.

'Long,' purred the female voice from behind me, 'long have I been waiting for this moment.'

I felt the touch of a smooth tongue against my neck. I could not help myself but cried out, at once disgusted and… something else.

The fat man made another sound, of horror and despair. More blood came from him, trickling down his lips and chin. He fell to his knees and he groaned again. This sound aside, all was silence. Every spectator looked on without speaking. More blood came from the fat man's mouth, and more. He convulsed, then threw up onto the ground what seemed to me a half-pint of it, crimson falling upon the floor.

He repeated this involuntary action. He was crying, I saw, and plump tears coursed down his face.

Something like a laugh escaped Mr Shone. Those slender, powerful hands which held me squeezed still tighter than before, flexing, I thought, with excitement. Once again the fat man heaved blood upon the ground, and then once more. The floor swam with blood and filth. He screamed, a wet and guttural sound, as one final convulsion came.

Yet more blood upon the ground. The sight and smell of it was repugnant beyond belief. He sighed and fell sideways, exhausted and drained, surely, I thought, unto the point of death.

Shone seemed disappointed. 'Where is it?' he asked. 'Where is he? What is to happen now?'

'Wait,' said the female voice behind me. 'Wait, Mr Shone, and be understanding at last the truth of the thing.'

Then something occurred which, even to one such as I, who has seen so much, would hitherto have seemed impossible. The blood that lay upon the ground began to move, to move of its own volition, to join together into a greater whole.

It moved then with hideous purpose towards the figure of Gabriel Shone, as though it were an animate thing, some foul creature of nightmare. Shone gasped and stepped backwards, but he was in this too late. For already the blood-thing was upon him, moving to his feet, his legs and torso, before speeding – one might almost say scampering – towards his face.

He had time to scream only once. The light of realisation flickered instantaneously across his features before the blood-creature surged into his mouth and nose and eyes. He sank to the floor, convulsing. No new sound came from me, nor from those ranks of silent watchers. He thrashed upon the ground, his head now covered, rippling with blood. As he struggled, the floor around us shook and quivered. A moment more – that was all it took – and the obscenity was over.

The tremor in the earth stopped at the moment that the figure upon the ground ceased to move. There was everywhere stillness.

In the distance, I heard the fat man moan.

The woman spoke up. 'Master? Master, are you returned to us?'

She released me then and stepped before me. I caught a glimpse of a tall, dark-winged, inhuman creature.

'Master?' she called again.

And at these words the man on the floor rose to his feet. He seemed different from before. His very body itself seemed to have been altered. He was taller and leaner and still more purposeful. His face was smeared with blood. But then – with a sensation of bone-deep horror – I saw the truth of it.

With his hands, the man wiped away the blood. He was smiling now. He was laughing.

As he cleaned his face, piece by piece, I saw a new, a different countenance revealed. An aquiline nose. Saturnine features. A high brow. Two bright eyes. A long dark moustache. Sharp white teeth.

In seconds it was done and I saw who it was who stood before me, in the place Mr Gabriel Shone had so lately occupied.

'Count...' I breathed.

Yet I could not say more, for in a single savage movement, and with a roar of feral appetite, the vampire was upon me, and in me, his incisors at my helpless neck.

I tried to scream but I could not. Then, as my own blood pumped from my vein and into his mouth, I yielded entirely to sensation, feeling only the dark satisfaction of complete despair, the certain knowledge of the totality of our defeat.

PART THREE

THE
SHADOW
CLAIMS
ITS OWN

FROM *THE PALL MALL GAZETTE*

1 February

CITY SHAKEN – EMERGENCY PERSISTS – MARTIAL LAW GOES ON

At the time of going to press, London remains in a state of the most dire emergency. Unrest amongst the criminal gangs has continued in the wake of the near-absolute destruction of Scotland Yard and the loss of numerous lives, including that of Commissioner Ambrose Quire. In necessary consequence of these extraordinary events, the Gazette has recently learned that martial law is set, for the immediate future, to endure while supreme metropolitan control remains in the hands of the Council of Athelstan.

In addition to these horrible escalations, the city was last night assailed by what appears to have been a minor, though most disruptive, earthquake. Its effects were felt across the majority of the metropolis and even some distance beyond. It is believed that the epicentre was located somewhere upon the north bank of the Thames, in the approximate region of the Tower. Considerable damage has been reported in the Houses of Parliament and several persons have already been declared missing. There are rumours, as yet unconfirmed, that Mr Gabriel Shone, scion and heir to the late Lord Stanhope, and the current head of the Council of Athelstan, is amongst that number. If these reports are true, then a great hope for the future has been snuffed out long before its time.

Of course, your Gazette will be the first to bring you all further news of these most disquieting developments – as well as copious judgement and sagacious conjecture upon the topic, to be supplied by the irreplaceable Mr Arnold Salter.

JONATHAN HARKER'S JOURNAL

———◆———

2 February. I believe that a day or so has passed since his return. Only this – not more than a few dozen hours, although that time has felt to me like an eternity. Matters of chronology are so difficult now to discern. I am reminded, horribly, of those long weeks that I spent during the last century as a prisoner of the Count.

Here in Shore Green, I am become again a captive. I write these words in a rare moment of relative liberty, by the flickering light of a candle stub.

Sarah-Ann – or, more properly, I suppose, the creature who was once Miss Dowell – has placed me in the cellar, often chained and bound like a beast. She feeds regularly upon my blood, being careful never to transform me but only to use me to take what she needs. I have been made ragged and filthy. My body has been punctured repeatedly. My every limb and muscle aches. There is scarcely a vein within me which the vampiress has not tapped. Yet I myself – and perhaps this is some small species of victory – have drunk not a drop of anything stronger than water.

I see little sign in her now of the sweet girl that she once was. For Sarah-Ann has become remorselessness personified and appetite incarnate. She visits only to drink and to sup. She speaks barely at all and I sense that she has been ordered here to keep me under lock and key. As to what the Count's plans may be – the extent of them – I dare not imagine. I am a playing piece that has been taken from the board at the present moment to be held in reserve for some future piece of villainy.

Oh Mina, my Mina – what has become of you? And Quincey? Where are you now? I pray for the wellbeing of you both. I have implored my Lord God for forgiveness, for succour and for aid. I have offered my own life in exchange for those of the two people upon this Earth whom I love more dearly than any other. Yet my prayers are left unanswered. With every passing hour that I spend in this gloom-haunted dungeon, I rot a little more and slip ever further into degradation.

Mere hours ago, something terrible took place. Sarah-Ann was feeding upon me, astride my prone and helpless form. I was weakened almost to insensibility. Yet the earth, very faintly, did tremble and shake beneath us. I wonder now whether that was the moment at which he came back to the waking world. Certainly, I seemed to feel an alteration in the atmosphere, a sense that something material in the substance of the world had changed.

At these sensations, the Dowell creature lifted her head from my breast. Her expression was a mixture of delight and disgust. 'Ten days,' said she. 'That is all it will take. Ten days before the city belongs – body and soul – to Him.'

'No,' I protested. 'Surely this is some manner of nightmare?'

'Maybe it is, Mr Harker. Maybe it's a nightmare which

started, long ago, in Transylvania. One from which you never really woke.'

Before I could reply, she bared her teeth and bent towards me once more. As she resumed her exsanguination, I moaned and shivered in absolute despair.

FROM THE PRIVATE JOURNAL
OF MAURICE HALLAM

———————◆———————

2 February. How very strange a thing it is to have established the imminence of one's own extinction only to discover, at the very moment of one's doom, that salvation is, in fact, to be one's own while death has been granted to another.

Of those minutes which followed my expulsion of that dark spirit which had been growing within me since Transylvania (since, in fact, that long and terrible night in the Castle), my memory has retained but little. I find that I am able to recollect only moments – the transformation of poor Gabriel Shone into an entirely different order of being, the approving faces of the Council at the screams of their female captive, and the thick, bright blood which poured from her, smeared, in curiously painterly fashion, across the floor of the temple.

The human body and mind, I have concluded, is capable of experiencing only a finite quantity of horror. Soon afterwards, my own limits were reached. It is my suspicion that I fell into a deep faint. Certainly my next recollection is of waking in darkness, having been laid out upon some unfamiliar divan. I knew not where I was and I could discern nothing at all of my surroundings, uncertain as to whether I had been placed in a boudoir or a cell.

I was capable of but a single realisation: that I was not alone in that place and that what was in there with me, watching over me, was something very far indeed from human.

Two bright eyes. Those were all that I saw of him then – a pair of red gleams, like burning embers in the gloom.

I struggled to sit upright, pulling the blankets to my chest with an almost comical chasteness, like a character in some popular farce.

Still those shining orbs observed me; still I felt myself the object of their dread scrutiny.

'Who's there?' I asked. 'Who are you?'

A voice issued from the blackness. It sounded deep and ancient but it was also possessed of a certain quality of creaking and wrenching, as though tongue and larynx had not been used for many years. The diction of that aged, unseen speaker was formal and quaint and there was to be found also in his language the trace of a Slavonic accent. Yet it was ever the eyes which held me. It was they which scintillated and compelled and made my senses reel.

In all our conversation I do not think that I saw them blink even once.

'You know what I am,' he said. 'For it was you, Maurice Hallam, who brought me back. It was you who rendered unto me form and breath. You who first saw the outline of my design.'

I could not bring myself to look away from his gaze. 'I know you,' I said, making in that moment the only choice which seemed open to me, the only sane judgement which would ensure my survival. 'Yes, I know you well... my master.'

'Name me,' said the voice, with an awful, quiet deliberation.

'You are,' I said swiftly, 'Count Dracula.'

'You understand this land, I think, Maurice Hallam?'

'Master, I was an exile from this country for more than a decade. But I do believe I know it still.'

'You know its ways. Its needs and its wants. You understand how to speak to its people.'

'Perhaps, yes. Perhaps I do. Why... my master... do you talk of such things?'

Those red eyes showed no flicker of reaction. 'I would rule this island awhile as, in times past, I have commanded nations.'

'You want to rule London, Count? England?'

'More.'

'The Empire? This is what your resurrection has been about?'

Those eyes observed me coldly. 'It is but a facet of my plan. It is but an element of my revenge.'

'Then what do you want of me?'

'Listen well, my good and faithful servant. Attend carefully to me.'

I breathed in, endeavouring to settle my nerves. 'Master, I shall.'

'For this now is what I would have you do...'

And, although I could not see it for myself, I somehow knew from those crimson eyes, as he spoke the words that followed, that he had begun to smile.

FROM *THE TIMES*

3 February (early edition)

'THE COUNT' ANNOUNCED AS NEW AND RIGHTFUL HEAD OF THE COUNCIL OF ATHELSTAN

It is the solemn duty of this newspaper to report a change in the governing structure of that Council which, at present, holds necessary control over our capital. Following the disappearance of Gabriel Shone, believed lost in the recent earthquake, the identity of his heir at the head of the Council of Athelstan was announced today. Known only as 'the Count', this figure, of uncertain royal extraction, is said to bring to his position considerable knowledge and expertise in the fields of statecraft and legislature. It is understood that his accession to the role has been met entirely unopposed by all other members of the group. Lord Tanglemere, head of what has been referred to colloquially as 'the Tanglemere Faction', is reported to have been the controlling force in the crowning of the newcomer, citing the sincerity of the personal beliefs and convictions of the Count as being the chief reason for his swift accession.

The new Secretary to the Council of Athelstan and the personal spokesman to the Count, Mr Maurice Hallam, remarked to this reporter, at the temporary base of operations which has been established at the Tower of London that: 'The Count is most certainly the finest individual to lead the Council at this most troubling and difficult of times. His tenacity and wisdom will see the nation safely through curfew and martial law.'

It has been said that there are plans afoot to increase the boundaries of the state of emergency beyond the limits of the city, perhaps even to encompass the whole nation. The King has to date remained silent as to these new constitutional arrangements. Further details will be forthcoming shortly.

MEMORANDUM BY LORD TANGLEMERE*

3 February

How privileged we were to witness for ourselves tonight the glorious realisation of a dream. In the secret temple beneath the Tower, the first full meeting of the Council was held since the ritual of the thirty-first, the palpable success of which the whole nation is coming now to know.

We arrived early, properly robed according to tradition, and we waited patiently for his arrival. We gentlemen of duty and of honour. We patriots who long for order and dominion. We sat in our appointed places and in our established rows, our heads bowed, filled up with gratitude. The atmosphere in that place combined excitement with what I do believe I might most accurately characterise as a species of prayerful gratitude.

There was little conversation. We all knew why we had gathered and what we had come to see and to achieve. Indeed, it is most striking to me how little of this affair has ever needed to be defined or expounded amongst ourselves. When one is amongst one's peers and when one's aspirations are in common, explanation is needed so very rarely. Posterity may be surprised at how little of those events which have led to our present state of happy restoration were set down upon paper. We gentlemen of the Council know better, however – that

---

* In the course of my researches, I have uncovered no evidence that the Council of Athelstan ever kept records or minutes of their numerous boards and meetings. Such secrecy, of course, is entirely in keeping with their objectives and modus operandi. Who knows now what occurred in those convocations? This is the only extant documentation which I have uncovered: a rare eyewitness account of the triumph of the Count.

the wisest conspiracies are those which are, in least in part, instinctive and unspoken.

These thoughts, or something like them, passed through my mind as I waited.

And then, all at once, he was amongst us. Not since the age of Scripture can so many have witnessed at one time a miracle. For the Count appeared first as a column of mist, seething from the shadows and billowing in that ancient, subterranean room. Then: a weird cohesion as mist shifted into man, the impossible making of a tangible thing of what had hitherto seemed amorphous.

There he stood, the Count, the new head of our Council. Tall, strong and saturnine, dressed in sombre black and having about him a quality of manful leadership such as the world has not known for centuries.

'Welcome,' he said, 'my dear friends.'

We all rose to our feet. Blood sang in my ears. I am not sure that I have ever felt so gloriously alive, nor so utterly convinced of the justice of my own actions. How much better is everything shortly to become, how much more noble and fine!

'I wish to speak to you,' he said, 'of my strategy for this island.'

The Count then made a gesture with his hands (what long, tapered fingers he has, what sharp blades of nails), and out of the darkness scampered his creature, Hallam. He had in his hands a sheaf of paper and hurried to one side of the Count. He spoke up, relishing his moment centre stage.

'The Count has ordered me to read to you his declaration

concerning his plans for the future of England.'

For all his obvious faults and failings, the fellow has an excellent speaking voice, most pleasing to the ear. There may even be some (though I, of course, am not amongst them) who would profess it to be more euphonious than the Count's own, admittedly accented timbre.

'First,' Hallam went on, 'there is much to be said concerning curfews and the treatment of those who willingly and knowingly flout our rules...'

I shall not record here the details of that speech in full. In fact, I am not certain that I could do so even if I wished it. For although I agreed with every word – the need for a universal return to a purer, simpler morality; the re-ordering of society upon approximately feudal lines; a more warlike approach to international relations – I find that I am unable now to recall the specifics of the piece.

Once it was over, we all applauded. We pounded our hands together in feverish joy. The Count himself stepped forward.

He smiled, lips pressed tightly together. 'Thank you, my friends,' he said, 'for placing your trust in me. Keep faith. Follow orders. And all shall be given to you in time.'

This said, he vanished again in a stream of mist.

The Council began to leave then, one by one. There will be drinking tonight, I expect, and much celebration also. I had intended to join them, for I feel ourselves to have earned champagne. Yet I felt a soft hand upon my shoulder.

'Wait here.'

I turned, to see Hallam, grimacing up at me.

'What did you say?' I asked.

'You must wait,' he said again.

'I do not take orders from an actor,' I said.

'Yet you must do so from him. And he orders you to wait.'

Hallam turned and walked away, with altogether more alacrity than one would have expected from so corpulent a man. I do not like him, but I respect more than anything he for whom the actor speaks.

I waited. Until the others had left and the temple was empty, I closed my eyes as though in prayer.

Some minutes later, as I had expected, the silence was broken by a jagged chuckle from the darkness. I got to my feet and looked about me. The temple was empty.

'My Lord?' I called. 'You wished to speak with me?' How he had been hidden from our sight I could not be certain, yet he emerged then out of some dark corner of the room.

'Count...'

'You have done well, my servant,' said our lord and master. 'You have done much in our name. And so you need now to receive your reward.'

'But my Lord,' I said, 'I ask for no reward.'

'Fear not,' he said. 'I would have you at my side. It is a place that you have earned.'

'My Lord,' I said, 'I am more than honoured.'

He stepped towards me and for a moment I caught a scent of something far away: the cold clean air of the Transylvanian forest.

The Count breathed heavily. 'I need sustenance also.' He seemed to shake a little as he spoke. 'I hunger.'

'Of course, my Lord.'

'I am not yet quite whole,' he breathed. 'I need what is within the boy. My vessel. I need what the Rite of Strigoi will yet prise free.'

'I'm not sure that I understand,' I said.

The Count smiled and I saw his teeth. At their proximity, I felt both wonder and fear in equal measure.

'You need not do so,' he said. 'You need ask no questions. You need seek no understanding. You need now only serve my will.'

He did not hesitate then but bared his teeth, hissed and threw himself upon me. A dark and dreadful pleasure ensued. I shall never forget the first sensations: the puncture, the drawing out, the suckling...

And now, I realise that I am changing. I am being transformed from the inside out into something so much better than ever I was before. And what is taking place within me even now is being done also unto this nation.

MEMORANDUM FROM REVEREND T.P. OGDEN TO DR R.J. HARRIS

4 February

Headmaster,

I write to you this night in a state of great concern. I have prayed at length for guidance. This memorandum would seem to me, for now, to be the best and wisest course of action.

Headmaster, I am worried, almost beyond measure, as to the spiritual wellbeing of our boys. You will already, I fancy, have an inkling of what it is that I speak. For days now there has been amongst the pupils a growing sense of unease and disquiet. I am sure that you cannot have failed to notice this yourself, for all that you have of late been sequestered in your office upon so many occasions. Much of what has occurred I have tried to explain to myself as the understandable result of those recent events in London which have so arrested the country's imagination. It is clear that we stand at a point (at the very brink!) of national crisis. It is natural enough that such things should affect our cohort of intelligent and perceptive young men.

But there is something more at work here. Of this, I am quite certain. There is in our midst some alien element, some invader.

The seeds of hysteria have taken root in our school and are already bearing dreadful fruit. Matters came to a head during our evening service in the chapel. It is generally a quiet, respectful occasion but tonight there was a febrile quality to the atmosphere even before we began. The boys seemed restless and ill at ease. There were more whispers and hushed conversations amongst them than is either customary or permitted. It seemed to me as I stood before them in the pulpit that there was to be spied a kind of collusion between them too. There were numerous looks, you see, Headmaster – knowing looks and glances.

Even before I began to speak, I experienced something I have not known since my earliest days in the gown, the schoolmaster's nightmare, the sense of one's influence over the boys starting to weaken, the first notes of a total loss of control.

The prayers, however, proceeded much as ever they do, as did our hymn and my short, pithy reading from Ephesians, in which, I am proud to report, my voice cracked only once.

My hands were shaking as I spoke and I was forced to grip the sides of the lectern in order that my state of anxiety should not become apparent. It is my belief that several of the boys were able to detect this.

As I spoke on, there was an increase in muffled conversation and sly glances. There came too to be apparent an unprecedented tendency towards tactile communication in the pews, a hideous, thoroughly inappropriate corporeality.

It was not, however, until we all rose to recite together the Lord's Prayer that the chaos began in earnest.

Still trembling, I invited the recital to begin. From the start, the prayer was tainted. As one, the boys twisted the words, first into something which sounded like burlesque before becoming vile and ultimately blasphemous.

'Our Father,' they chanted, 'who art now in England. Dreadful be thy name. Thy kingdom come. Thy dark will be done. On Earth as it is in Hell.'

There was more, Headmaster, which I dare not set down here – more of the most frightful and abominable language, more invocation of the very darkest of forces. By the end, the boys were screaming it, screeching and whooping with a dreadful admixture of terror and delight which was altogether chilling to behold.

At the finish of it, the chapel had become a site of wicked baboonery of the most shameful sort. I ran, Headmaster, for the door, and as I hurried along the nave a single cry went up amid the boys.

'The master is coming!'

The air was thick with hysteria and giddy panic.

'The master is here!'

A fever pitch was reached. There was weeping and fainting also. And, Headmaster, there was blood. They were causing each other harm and they were glorying in it.

I ran to my study and I locked my door. I have prayed at great length and now I write these words to you. Oh, Headmaster, what is to become of us? What is to become of us all?

MEMORANDUM FROM DR R.J. HARRIS TO REVEREND T.P. OGDEN

4 February

My dear Reverend,

Thank you for your message, and for the memorable and vivid nature of its descriptions. I am grieved, of course, to hear of your ordeal.

Nevertheless, I think that I shall be able to set your mind at rest. Be not afeared, Reverend. For something wonderful has come amongst us.

Allow me to explain. I returned to my office after luncheon today intending to spend the afternoon in clearing up a number of outstanding administrative matters which have bedevilled me since the start of Michaelmas. If any time were to be left to me after the completion of this task, I meant to resume my study of the Emperor Caligula, upon whose rule of Rome I am preparing, as you may recall, a substantial monograph.

The winter light was weak this afternoon. The shadows were long and it seemed in my study already to be growing dark. I sat behind my desk and set to my labours, yet I did so with the distinct, and initially unpleasant, sense that I was not in that room alone.

A few minutes into my duties, I looked up from the ledger, my fountain pen in hand, to see a stranger standing at the far end of the study, indistinct and wreathed in shadows. He was a tall, moustachioed man and he was dressed from head to foot in black. At the sight of him, I began to cry out involuntarily, yet did the sound die in my throat.

He moved forward carefully, keeping to the dark places of the room and eschewing the pale slivers of sunlight. His manner was courteous and old-fashioned. His accent was inflected by the sound of the furthermost reaches of the continent.

'You will forgive me, Herr Harris, for my interruption.'

As he approached I found myself unable to move from my chair; I was rooted there. 'Who you are, sir?' I asked.

He sat down before me, his every movement as lithe and elegant as that of any jungle cat. 'I am a... relation,' he said, 'of one of the boys who is in your charge.'

'Indeed?' I asked. 'And which of them might that be?' I found that I was perspiring and that I felt the onset of a headache.

The figure in the chair presented me with his piercing gaze, at which, on instinct, I looked away. 'His name is Harker.'

'Of course,' I said. 'I know the boy in question. And you are his... uncle?'

'I am a guardian of sorts. A second father.'

My heart galloped.

'Where is the boy?' he asked.

I breathed out with some relief. 'Not here,' I said. 'Harker never returned to us after Christmas. There was, as I understand it, a series of family tragedies... A great deal of unpleasantness. No doubt his parents have made other arrangements. As is their prerogative.'

A series of fierce emotions passed like stormy weather across the visage of my guest: fury, wonder, self-satisfaction, laughter. 'What a sadness you describe,

Herr Harris. How much the boy has suffered.'

'Hardship, loss and sudden death are all a part of life,' I said stoutly. 'It is well that the boys learn these truths at the earliest opportunity.'

The stranger smiled. 'Herr Harris. I am in agreement with you.'

'All the world,' I went on, warming to my theme, 'is made up of those who rule and those who obey. The order of things is most naturally pyramidical, with the most successful at the top of it. We encourage all our charges to climb as far and as fast as they can towards the top.'

The visitor smiled again, more widely than before. I noticed for the first time then that there was something singular about his teeth. 'How very right you are.'

'Thank you,' I said. 'But I am sorry that I have no better news.'

'All is well,' said the man. 'I shall seek him out without difficulty. There is a splinter of me within him. He lacks the strength to conquer it, of that I have no doubt. And so it will draw him to me.'

'Forgive me,' I said, 'but I am not certain that I understand.'

Those white teeth flashed again. On this occasion, I thought that I saw something else also: the crimson flicker of his tongue. 'You understand, Herr Harris, more than you think.'

At these words, I saw something in my mind: an image, as clear as any one saw in a gallery. The Harker boy in an unspeakable ritual which meant to draw out of him that secret portion of spirit, placed in him before his birth, which will make the creature whole again. I started in horror at this waking nightmare.

The man in black smiled, as if he knew what I had seen. 'The Rite,' he murmured, 'of Strigoi.'

'Yes,' I said, still half lost in the dream. 'Now that you mention it, I do believe that I have heard that name before.'

The creature peeled back its lips. 'I am bored now, Herr Harris. And I hunger also. Would you be so kind as to… open a vein for me?'

The boys spoke the truth, my friend. The master is indeed amongst us. And in his wake, I see now that the world is once more being set aright.

FROM THE PRIVATE JOURNAL
OF MAURICE HALLAM

———◆———

5 February. It would doubtless surprise almost all who have known me, yet it would seem that I have been made for the political life, and it for me. The bureaucratic exercise of power is now as natural an operation to me as once was soliloquy and the gracious receipt of applause.

For decades I have considered myself a being of the spiritual realm, of air and not of earth. Yet now, in this unexpected and unsought encore, I find that my métier is in truth the terrestrial sphere and that I thrive in regions of the purely material. Working as a spokesman, go-between and diplomat I find that I have been uniquely prepared by my time upon the stage. As in the theatre, all in politics is showmanship, greasepaint, misdirection and flair.

Outwardly, perhaps, in this city as in me, little enough has been altered. The people still eat and work as ever they did. They go about their business just the same. Only in the atmosphere of the metropolis is the transformation discernible – a pervasive sense not simply of fear but of some subtler shift, of a return to an older way of thinking and a simpler ordering of life.

The state of emergency continues and so, as it must, does the rule of the Council. The Count stands at the head of it, although he speaks always through me. The mechanism of the state itself has not been changed in any way, yet control of these levers has, with cunning and determination, been delivered into the hands of him whose return I unwittingly ensured. In the days that have passed since the resurrection, however, those who believe that they were born to rule have begun to comprehend the degree to which they have been outwitted.

This afternoon, shortly after dusk, the Prime Minister came to call upon us.

I was waiting to greet him – a tall man with a prominent forehead as would interest any student of phrenology and a large moustache which seemed to hint of some suppressed ambition upon seafaring lines.

'Prime Minister,' I said, and bowed my head in a kind of ironic supplication. 'You are most welcome here. The Count is sleeping now but he will be delighted to receive you at his earliest convenience.'

The politician's face turned a deep shade of damson. 'Insolence,' he said, and the word was laden with fury. 'How does this cuckoo dare to treat me so? The Council was never established in order to advance the ambitions of some European despot.'

I gave a casual smile such as I might provide to some notorious curmudgeon at the Garrick. 'What a pity, Prime Minister, that you should feel as you do upon the matter. Yet I fear that the rules of succession in the Council are quite clear. The Count has come to his position by entirely fair and logical means.'

The man bristled. 'Those means may very well appear to be so. But you and I both know that there has been chicanery and devilry at work. I have tried to see the King upon multiple occasions. My way has been barred. I have my suspicions, sir, as to the truth of all this! Aye, sir, I do!'

I gave merely a faint smile at this tirade, as if mildly embarrassed. From somewhere below us, from one of the deeper levels of the White Tower, there then came the incongruous cry of a wolf.

The statesman seemed appalled.

'Ah,' I said. 'So the Count has awoken. He will see you now.'

The politician only gazed at me.

'This way, sir,' I said. 'Please.'

'But… that was a wolf, was it not?'

'Escaped from London Zoo. After which he hastened, with all the speed of Mercury, to the Tower. You need not fret, Prime Minister. You're quite safe. The beast is tame. At least when the Master walks abroad.'

There is something rather dreadful in seeing a man who was born to the easy, gilded life of influence made to tremble with such ease by one for whom the getting of power was an altogether more strenuous affair, whose spirit has been forged by centuries of struggle. At that moment, the wolf howled once more, as though to issue summons, and at the sound of it I watched any willingness to fight drain from the face of our Premier.

'Come along now, Prime Minister,' I said, my manner that of an indulgent nanny to a hesitant charge, to which the old statesman murmured his assent and capitulation.

I turned, he followed, and together we walked down dank stone steps to the lowest level of the White Tower. Once we had descended, we waited before the great door which seals that subterranean room which I have come to think of as the crypt.

I knocked. No answer was to be heard, yet a second later the door creaked open. It did not surprise me in the least to note that it seemed to achieve this feat of its own volition.

Darkness waited upon the other side. I looked to the man beside me and saw that his face was white and perspiring.

'Stand firm, Prime Minister,' I said. 'I recommend that you do as I did and simply accept the inevitability of change.'

A voice came from the darkness, deep and ancient. 'Prime Minister. Enter freely and of your own will.'

The politician looked at me rather plaintively.

'Go,' I said, not unkindly. 'For the Count is amongst us now. An ant may as well try to resist the turning of the wheel.'

He did not reply, save with a stoical nod. A moment after he had crossed the threshold, the door swung shut behind him. I waited outside for only a little while.

Once the screaming started, however, I found that I could bear only a moment of it and hurried away. Alongside those cries, I heard also, and somehow still more unpleasantly, the sound of high female laughter.

Later. Of course, the Count would never be so reckless or so hungry as to cause even the smallest permanent damage to that august official. He may have toyed with the Prime Minister for a while. He may have filled him with terrified awe. Yet he would never have gone so far as to drink from his veins, nor so much as pierce his papery aristocrat's skin.

The Count's survival, for so many centuries, has been founded, I believe, upon knowing when stealth might best be employed. Still, the Prime Minister is now the Count's creature, as surely as am I and as was poor Gabriel.

I saw our Premier pass from the outer walls of the Tower some hours ago. His movements were a little more stilted than before, his eyes a little more fixed and staring, but there were no further indications that he – like all of us – has been placed in thrall.

FROM *THE WESTMINSTER PRISM*

6 February

PRIME MINISTER OFFERS FULL SUPPORT TO THE COUNCIL AND THE COUNT

The Prime Minister, the Right Honourable Earl of Balfour, today declared his full support for the continuance of the present state of emergency in London and for the retention of control over the metropolis by the Council of Athelstan. Furthermore, although he did not name the present leader of that Council, he affirmed his trust and loyalty in the figure who stands at the head of it.

Speaking in Chequers to a small, select band of journalists (including your reporter), the Prime Minister spoke upon a variety of topics, including the recent devastation caused to the Houses of Parliament, which has, he says, rendered the buildings out of reach for the present time. He touched also upon those numerous souls who are still missing in the wake of the tremor which shook the city five days ago. Responding to several questions upon these matters of significance, he declared himself delighted to support entirely the temporary and interim control over the city of the Council and its leader.

'I have met he who commands the Council,' our Prime Minister said, 'and I have the greatest confidence in him to steer us through this crisis. According to the ancient laws of our people, I cede all power over London to his Council until this catastrophe is eased. Once normality has been restored, so shall the usual order of things resume.'

The Premier seemed in himself to be a little tired and drawn, although there was no mistaking the strength of that faith which he holds in the Count. He would answer no further questions and retired early to bed. It is said that he will remain in his country residence until the worst is over. If many of us who were present felt rather as though we had seen some shift of significance in the ordering of our national life, there was none of us discourteous enough – or, perhaps, sufficiently courageous – to speak such a thought aloud.

FROM THE DIARY OF
ARNOLD SALTER

———◆———

7 February. 'You must be most encouraged,' said Lord Tanglemere, 'at the progress of events.'

'I suppose that I am, my lord,' I said. There must have been a note of uncertainty in my reply for, once I had spoken, the nobleman grimaced. He gulped.

'You don't sound sure, Mr Salter.'

The location of our conversation was, once again, that drab little tea-room in the shadow of the Museum on Russell Street. The place was deserted. It was almost twilight and the drapes were pulled, yet even in the gloom my companion seemed ill at ease. He winced often, as though it were high summer and bright light was streaming in, and not the depths of winter at all. Perhaps he is unwell. Certainly, he looked more drawn and haggard than I had ever seen him before. There was an unhealthy pallor to his skin. Whatever the nature of his malady, it seems in some fashion also to have affected his dog. For the animal lay at some distance from its master, shivering and fretful.

These things I noticed anew as I thought about how best to answer the man's accusation.

'I am,' I said at last, 'very happy to think that this country might at long last be returning to its proper course.'

'Yes, yes, yes,' Lord Tanglemere drawled. 'We have all heard that from you before. But what are your doubts? I know that you have them.'

'My lord,' I said, 'I have no doubts whatever concerning the direction of our new government's policies. But it seems to me that there has been a great deal of pain. A fair amount of death. And there is – is there not? – an awful kind of fear abroad at the present hour?'

Tanglemere smiled a tight-lipped smile. 'Such things did not appear to concern you in any of our previous tête-à-têtes. Nor have any such matters arisen in your public writings. It is a little late now – do you not think? – for such moral palpitations?'

'You are right, of course, my lord.' Somewhere in the kitchens a kettle whistled and sang. 'I meant only to acknowledge the cost of all of this. The sacrifice in blood and treasure.'

Tanglemere seemed unmoved. 'Such things,' he sniffed, 'would not be necessary had our recent leaders only possessed better judgement. The blood is on their hands, not ours.'

'Quite so, my lord. Well said.'

The wolfhound made a thin, keening, whimpering sound. Tanglemere hissed through clenched teeth, and at this instruction the animal fell silent.

'I trust, Mr Salter, that you are not in any way losing your nerve?' There was clear contempt in every syllable.

'No, sir,' I replied, at military speed.

The door to the café was opened and the bell above it jingled. The newcomer was revealed to be a florid-faced yeoman sort who stamped over to a table at the far side of the room. Within moments, a bustling maid was at his side. At all this commotion, Tanglemere glowered, as though he found such disturbances almost painful.

Once the stranger was settled, the nobleman leaned across the table. 'Your work is not yet done.'

'I should hope not, my lord.' I tried to smile but failed.

'The new order is in place but it is not yet entrenched. The people, Mr Salter, must be reassured. And, like you, they must not be permitted to harbour any room for doubt.'

'I understand. I can write more. I can explain to them. I can urge them to keep the faith.'

'Of course you shall. But you will do even more than that. Mr Salter, the time is almost upon you.'

'Time?' I said. 'The time for what?'

'Why, the time for your interview. The time for you to meet him, face to face. The time when you must confront the nature of that which you have helped to bring back into the world.'

'Truly?' I said. My voice quivered. 'Is that time truly come?'

'Oh, it surely is,' said Lord Tanglemere. 'And it is an experience from which you will not walk away unchanged. Indeed, the encounter will likely prove... transformative.'

He smiled then. The light in that place was bad. The other customer called out. The dog whimpered and cried. I was distracted. I must have been mistaken. Surely? Surely I cannot have seen what I thought I saw.

His teeth. D—n me – his teeth!

FROM *THE PALL MALL GAZETTE*

8 February

SALTER SAYS: JUST WHO *IS* OUR NEW FRIEND, THE COUNT?

The decent, honest, God-fearing people of this nation have for some time found themselves to be profoundly disappointed in the quality of their leaders. Too often have we seen the strength and wisdom of elder days overturned in favour of policies which have done nothing to elevate the common man and have instead laid us all open to threats of the most horrendous kind. The recent upheavals in London have been more than proof enough of that. Now, however, and at long last, things seem to be changing. The issuing of martial law, the ascension of the Council of Athelstan and the instatement of that figure known as 'the Count' seem to have brought about the beginnings of a new golden age.

Speaking as a Londoner, I have never felt safer or more content in the metropolis. Speaking as a man who has been alive long enough to see things in this country go from bad to worse, I feel instinctively pleased at the news – and the evidence – that a gentleman of such substance stands now at the head of state.

Yet who is this enigmatic figure who has captured our attention and our good wishes? Who is he who has come to set this country aright, with assistance, of course, from certain decent Englishmen – the nobleman Lord Tanglemere, the young heir Mr Shone and his amusing friend, Mr Maurice Hallam? What is his own history, and how does he see so clearly the faults and failings of the apparatus of the Empire?

It would seem that I shall soon be able to provide you with answers not only to these but to a plethora of other questions. For who do you think has received his invitation to the White Tower, and to an audience with this remarkable figure, but your own humble correspondent?

Having been brought up to remain modest, no matter the circumstances, I take this not as any reflection upon my own writings but rather upon the wisdom of the Gazette itself

– the only periodical in Britain to have seen to the heart of this situation right from the start. I have been but the mouthpiece of the ordinary fellow on the street. My friends, it would seem that at last our words have been heard and our prayers answered.

The Count is waiting to give me whatever knowledge I desire. It is an opportunity I mean to seize. Yet I wish you all to appreciate this fact: that I shall be entering his presence not as an individual but as a representative of us all. You will hear from me again very soon, at which time I shall be the bringer of all sorts of marvellous truths.

JONATHAN HARKER'S JOURNAL

———————◆———————

8 February. Today, at last, I seized my opportunity.

As has been, since his return, the pattern of my life, I woke upon the floor of my own cellar, ragged, ill-used and debilitated. Yet I soon became aware that I did not appear to feel altogether as drained as I have in recent days. Indeed, I even felt something like my old vigour rising once again within me. At first, this was to me a source of puzzlement. Then I saw the reason why.

The vampiress, poor Sarah-Ann, lay in the corner of the room. She was not as she has been.

This house is an old one and I fear that in recent years I have rather neglected its maintenance and upkeep. For such slovenly disregard I was now unexpectedly proud. Due to the crumbling nature of the place, and thanks to the quirks of providence, a shaft of sunlight had found its way into that place of shadows, clear, bright and unforgiving.

Sarah-Ann lay beneath and seemed almost pinioned by it. I would not go so far as to say that it caused her pain, yet she was evidently rendered most uncomfortable by its proximity. The un-dead care not for any evidence of the day. The Count was ever able to walk about in it unscathed; newer, younger vampires are, I have come to believe, very much more sensitive to the light. She moaned softly, and murmured some words which were unfamiliar to me.

I rose, feeling stronger than before, and hurried to her side. She did not stir herself at my approach, but only whispered.

I reached her. I stretched out my arms towards her.

'It has me,' she said, and then again: 'It has me. And so I could not feed.'

I felt pity for her then, but also a chill determination to do what was necessary. I grabbed her shoulders and wrenched her upright. As I did so, she made lunges, all of which I was able to parry, for the lack of sustenance had weakened her as much as that abstinence had fortified me. She moaned as I dragged her towards the steps of the cellar. In this, I may have been brutal. I dragged her up towards the main body of the house. She fought me but I held her back.

Daylight streamed towards us as I swung open the door into the hallway. She screamed, not only at the sunshine but also at the realisation of what had to happen next.

I hurled her to the floor. I cast around for something which might be used to despatch the creature, finding in the end a stick by the doorway. In the time that it took to achieve this, she scrambled to her feet and charged towards me. We fell together upon the floor and tussled. She hissed and bared her fangs, but she never made a mark upon me. Sensing victory, I fought back as fiercely as I have ever fought, giving her no quarter.

There was a kind of battle going on within her. For, after several minutes of this inconclusive combat, she loosed a madwoman's giggle.

I took up the stick and plunged it down towards her.

My days in the cellar had made me weak, however, and my first blow went wild. It grazed her but did not penetrate the skin.

She screeched in rage and frustration.

'Wait!' she called out. 'Wait!'

'Sarah-Ann,' I said thickly. 'I have to do this. I have to set you free.'

'Jonathan,' she said, and I saw that there was blood trickling between her teeth. 'He is coming through now.'

She screamed once more, went limp again, and then her very countenance seemed to take on a different shape before my eyes. Her features had not been changed in themselves but there was a marked alteration in her demeanour, as though another intelligence spoke through her.

'Mr Harker.' The voice that emerged from the ruby lips of sweet Sarah-Ann was one which was familiar to me, for all that I had not heard it in years. There was no forgetting its European sibilance, its angular vowels and brisk consonants.

I held my nerve. With one hand I pushed down Miss Dowell and with the other I kept tight hold of the stake. The old devil, that quintessence of wickedness, spoke blasphemously to me through the mouth of the woman.

'Mr Harker, it has been too long since last we met.'

'Count,' I replied, as levelly as I was able. 'I am afraid that I cannot say the same.'

'I found, Mr Harker, that I did not care for the manner of our parting so many years ago.'

'On the contrary, I thought it altogether just.'

The girl's face was contorted in a trice into a mask of rage. 'You fool! You dared to pit yourselves against me! Yet did I not say – did I not promise you all? – that I would take my revenge?'

I could not bring myself to look away. 'You said a lot of things, Count. I can hardly be expected to remember them all.'

The old man laughed with Sarah-Ann's larynx, the effect of it disgusting. 'Now your Professor is dead. Your alienist is mad. Your woman whom you love is by my side. Your country has delivered itself willingly to my command. And the child – my son! – shall stand soon at my right hand.'

I could bear this no longer. 'I am coming for you,' I said. 'I shall kill you again, Count. I shall kill you just as many times as it takes!'

With this, I brought the stake down hard upon Sarah-Ann's breast. She cried out, convulsed once, sighed and passed beyond this world. As she died the true death, her features arranged themselves again into those of that sweet innocent of whom I had thought so very highly.

I kissed her once. Just once, I swear. Upon her beautiful red lips.

This done, and without compunction, I severed her head from her body. It took considerable effort and a succession of five separate blows. Yet these things were necessary. More than necessary. Sacred.

She is free now. She is with the angels.

There is much I have to do. I must find my son. I must rescue my wife. And I must do all that is in my power to wipe that vile abhorrence from the face of this earth.

FROM THE PRIVATE JOURNAL
OF MAURICE HALLAM

———◆———

9 February. I have found myself in the past few days thinking often of seduction. Not that any carnal pleasure has of late been mine – not, indeed, since long before the familiar form of Gabriel Shone was eclipsed by that of the Transylvanian. Rather, such a line of thought has been in me inspired by the plentiful victories of the Count.

As any successful lothario well knows (and there was a time, at the dawn of the '90s, when I might justifiably have been considered a pre-eminent example of the breed), one always proceeds upon the assumption that one's quarry wants, in truth, to succumb, for all that he might protest to the contrary. Something in his soul cries out to be conquered; something within him pines to yield up its sovereignty to another. Indeed, this secret trait, this yearning for capitulation, is at its most pronounced in those who affect an outward display of robust independence, in those who declare themselves most adamantly to be inviolate.

Given certain recent miracles and reversals, I have come now to believe that cities – even the greatest of them – harbour this same furtive desire. How else to explain the Count's remarkable success? The people of the metropolis must, in some dark, untended quarters of their hearts, have craved his dominion.

London is almost entirely under his control. The country shall surely follow, as, in time, must the Empire. And after that? Well, it seems to me that death has only honed the Count's ambition.

Later. My master is nothing if not cunning. He has arranged for himself an ideal manner of existence, almost a simulacrum of his old life in the easternmost region of our continent. He lies in state in this tower's crypt, like a spider – as the old saying goes – at the centre of a web. His power grows daily – hourly! The government has fallen. The King is silent. And there is nothing that anyone can do to staunch his rise.

Yet how does he feed himself? How does he live? This it has taken me some time to deduce, for he has confided in me not at all concerning that aspect of his strange existence, believing, rightly enough, that I still possess a modicum of squeamishness. The truth I discovered shortly after twilight.

Was I meant to see it? I think, perhaps, that I was. To witness the spectacle, and to understand in full the nature of that enterprise to which I am now inextricably secured.

My own quarters have been placed at the very top of the White Tower, as far away as might be possible from those of my master. Much of my work is daylight work and so it has been easy enough to turn my face away from the excesses of his authority.

I was attending to some business in my room and wondering if I might not justify retiring early for the night with the great oak door bolted securely behind me, when I caught from the hallway beyond the same sound that I had heard four nights before – high, gay female laughter. There seemed, however, to reside within it no genuine mirth. I found myself instead riveted to my chair in an aggregate of curiosity and fear. Laughter came again, followed by the sound of its maker moving away from my threshold. Driven onwards by some unhappy desire, I crept to the door, opened it silently and stepped out into the corridor. There, just ahead of me, I saw, disappearing around the corner, the figure of a woman in a long dark gown: Ileana, queen of the Transylvanian forest. Curious, I followed.

We descended to the next level of the tower. She was sufficiently slow as to allow me to keep pace with her, but just swift enough to stay at the periphery of my vision. It was a pageant, artfully arranged. Once again, as I followed, I found myself considering the question of seduction.

Down and down we went, farther from the light and into the lower reaches of the tower. At length, we came to a door that was locked and bolted, the shuttered gateway to a cell.

I paused at the edges of the corridor and peered around the wall to see how Ileana would proceed.

From around her neck she pulled a single iron key with which she unlocked the door. It opened with a creak. The silence that followed was horrible. She gave an odd, soft cry, something like a bird call. This she did three times.

Out of the shadows, three men stepped. I knew none of them as individuals yet I felt certain that I knew the type all too well – low and vulgar men who loiter outside the law, survivors, I supposed, from that triumvirate of gangs which for so long, before the coming of the Count, had ruled over the city.

They were evidently not in their perfect mind. Lulled and

silent, they walked with stilted, trance-like motions. These beguiled men followed Ileana as, having taken care to lock the door behind her, she led them away. I could guess well enough where it was that they were bound.

I walked a few more steps. I hesitated. I walked on. I came to the door that led to the crypt, and there I paused awhile. For I heard from beneath me precisely what I had expected: the frantic screams of those men who, awaking at the last moment from their trance, did so to realise that they faced the murderous eyes of one who stands far above them in the great chain of predation. I felt at that moment, for all that I knew them to be low men, a twinge of sympathy that their lives should be ended with such a flourish of horror.

More screams came, a terrible quiet, and then something unexpected, the laughter not only of Ileana and the Count but of another – another woman, the sound of her mirth, laced, I thought, with madness.

I fled, unable to listen to the inevitable sounds of feeding. These words I write barricaded again in my own apartment. I have thought much concerning what I saw and heard tonight. I have issued to myself many justifications, rationales and vindications.

Certainly, none of those men will be missed. If – as I suspect – my master has turned the criminals of the city into a larder, London will surely be only the better for their absence. In serving his own appetite, he may also have drained the metropolis of its most visible manifestation of sin.

Yet I have asked myself this also: what is the point of life when it has but one texture, when the scarlet thread of transgression is removed? What is peace and security if it is brought about solely by the sword? What place have these methods in our new century? And more pertinent even than these: to whom will the Count turn for sustenance when his stock of recidivists is exhausted?

JONATHAN HARKER'S JOURNAL

———◆———

9 February. A day has passed since I escaped from captivity. One day since I set Sarah-Ann free.

I had thought first to make my way to London where, it seems, the heart of this madness lies. Having disposed of the body of my gaoler, having bathed, dressed and made myself respectable once again, I left the house at Shore Green. I packed into a satchel a few essentials (that bloodied makeshift stake included) and I went on foot to the railway station.

As soon as I reached the village, I realised with horror the scale of the task before me. For while I have been held captive the world has shifted around me. England herself has altered. There is something in the air now which was not there before – a kind of weary, watchful acceptance of the new order.

I walked through the village with as great a degree of discretion as I could muster and made my way towards the station. As I did so, I attracted many looks of suspicion. Men and women whom I had known turned their gaze away from me. Doors were slammed at my approach and shutters pulled hurriedly down. A memory reared up – of my approach to Castle Dracula, of the fearful peasantry who had wanted to play no part in my story, they who wished only to survive at any cost. It was, I thought, as though the past were in some fashion first impinging upon and then colonising the present.

How swiftly has this spread, and with what devilish speed! If it is so here in Shore Green, who knows what it must be like in the city?

I held my head down and hurried on. I must not succumb to fear. I must only go on. All must now be swift, decisive forward motion. Quincey and Mina need me – as, perhaps, does England.

At the station itself I was met by a locked gate and a surly signalman who stood before it, his fat arms folded and his bewhiskered face set into an expression of constant disapproval.

I held up my hand in greeting. He gazed at the gesture in distaste.

'Station's closed,' he said, and the words hung heavily between us.

I waited for an explanation, though none seemed forthcoming. 'And why is that?'

He gave a sour smile. 'I couldn't rightly say, sir. No, I couldn't rightly say.'

'But I need,' I said, 'to get to London.'

'Then you'll have to go by another way. Won't you, sir?'

'How, if not by train?'

He took his time before replying. 'By horse, sir. Or by carriage. Or by foot. After all, those things all used to be just fine, didn't they? There wasn't no need for the railway in my grandfather's day. Or for any motor cars neither.' He looked almost affronted at what I had said, as though there were something offensive in the very notion of swifter transportation.

I turned without replying and stalked away, back towards the village.

The fat man called after me. 'Mr Harker, ent it? Mr Jonathan Harker?' He laughed – an awful, knowing chuckle. The sound of it made me shiver.

I did not go back to Shore Green in the end but struck out into the countryside. I felt that I needed to get clear of the place and not tarry a moment longer. The Count, after all, through Sarah-Ann, knew of my earlier whereabouts.

I still meant at that time to go to London. I was striding around the edges of a farmer's field, on a complex route which would, I hoped, lead me eventually to the city of Oxford (from where my journey to London might surely be less conspicuous), when I heard a voice in my head.

The voice was real and not the product of my imagination. Of that, I am quite sure. I have seen many peculiar things in my life and I have long ago learned how to distinguish dream from reality. This was assuredly in that second camp.

The voice was one which I had not heard for months. It was that of Professor Abraham Van Helsing.

He spoke just one word to me. No, rather a name than a word. A proper noun.

'Wildfold.'

I stopped short and whirled about. I was alone in that place. No human was with me. In the undergrowth something stirred. There was a flurry of anxious bird calls.

'Who—' I began, but in my heart I knew the answer to my question. My voice sounded ridiculous in this desolate place.

The Professor spoke again. I felt his presence as strongly

as if he had been standing at my side. 'Wildfold,' he said again, and then he was gone.

Knowing that he had departed, I fell to my knees and began to pray. I begged for forgiveness and I sought succour. I declared myself a sinner and I asked for guidance. I humbled myself before my God.

When I rose, I had a new destination.

I go now, as swiftly as I can, to the place that was named, moving largely at night, keeping myself out of sight. There may be further perils ahead of me, but I am determined to reach it.

So I travel in secret. I travel in fear. And I travel with vengeance in my heart.

LETTER FROM CECIL CARNEHAN TO ARNOLD SALTER (ENVELOPE UNOPENED)

9 February

My dear Arnold,

I felt compelled to write to you. I have, perhaps, in the past been a trifle haughty as to your abilities and unjustly dismissive of your many achievements.

I want you to know now I am quite happy to admit my mistakes and oversights. Finally I understand. At last, I see the truth of things. There was a time – and you will forgive my candour – when I thought your opinions merely useful, a means by which to attract older readers and increase sales. Now, however, as a direct consequence of an encounter which I shall relate, I truly believe, in my very heart.

The last week has been unusually hectic. While as a newspaperman I have found it exhilarating, as a patriot I have found it troubling. At least, until tonight.

It was late and my stint at the office had been a long one. Having pursued my labours for the day to their limit, I took myself down to the Strand and to a Turkish bath there, a place I have come to frequent. There is (or, at least, there was) something soothing in the experience.

As is my custom, I spent time in each room of the house. The last, as you may be aware, is filled with steam – great, billowing clouds of it which put one in mind of the worst of the city fogs. The result is, typically, cleansing and so it proved tonight, albeit in a different way.

I sat alone in the final room, the steam surging around

me, coiling against the walls. I breathed in deeply through my nose, and as I felt my skin prickle pleasingly I cast my mind over the events of recent days: the uproar in the underworld, the ascendancy of the Council, the chaos at the heart of the Empire, and the sudden arrival of that gentleman who seems now to stand at the peak of it. I turned matters over and over, trying to see the pattern. There were, I concluded, certain possibilities in it, all of very considerable gravity. I wondered what we had let in – indeed, what we had invited in – without ever understanding its true nature. And I wondered also, dear Arnold, about your role, about how much you really knew and how much you understood.

At this moment, when you were uppermost in my mind, I realised that I was no longer alone in that steam-drenched space. I could make nothing out. I could hear nothing at all. I was aware just the same that something in that room had changed and now held a new presence. I sat quite still and listened.

'Hello?' I said, although my words sounded puny, foolish things. No answer came, and so I assigned the incident as an example purely of my imagination. Still feeling ill at ease, I rose to my feet and meant to leave – and then I heard emanate from the fog a low chuckle.

'Hello?' I said again, an edge of fear no doubt by now quite audible in my voice. 'Who's that?'

A voice issued forth – European in accent. 'Good evening, Mr Carnehan.'

'Who are you? Who's there?'

The voice came again, resonant with distant lands

and half-forgotten knowledge. 'You know who I am, Mr Carnehan.'

'I…' A sequence of thoughts, each more dreadful than the last, tumbled through my consciousness. 'I…'

The voice rose to a roar. 'YOU KNOW WHO I AM, MR CARNEHAN!'

'Yes,' I said, very softly. 'I know.'

As I watched, I saw a figure emerge from the mist. I should make it clear that this was not an instance simply of a person walking into view, but rather of a creature seeming to materialise out of the steam.

(You will remember all the old stories, Mr Salter. You will know the many forms that their kind can take.)

I watched, frozen in fascinated fear, as the dark man came into being. His eyes blazed like hot coals; his form was all sinew and muscle. My ears rang as though there were some great and violent sound nearby, although the room was silent. My stomach clenched. My nose began to bleed.

'Count…' I breathed and, without understanding precisely why but acting solely on instinct, I found myself upon my knees.

'I wished to seek you out, Mr Carnehan. I wished to thank you for all that you have done. And I wished to ask you one question.'

'Anything…' I murmured.

'Would you like to be for ever as you are now?'

I could not bring myself to look up. Yet I murmured 'Yes' all the same.

And then it was upon me – the ancient thing, that

DEAD thing – and it was draining me of all my life and vigour. The pain was beyond imagining, but I invited it. Indeed, I urged him on. I begged him to continue.

He left me there, like offal. But when I awoke again, I was changed.

So you see, Mr Salter, I do finally comprehend. I understand the change that has swept over our island. And, you will be gratified, I have no doubt, to hear that as I write I am filled up with savage joy.

Yours,
Cecil

PS. I do believe I shall write the editorial myself tomorrow. The people deserve, after all, to hear the truth – or, at least, as much of the truth as their sanity can at present stand.

FROM *THE PALL MALL GAZETTE*

10 February

EDITORIAL: WE WELCOME THE FIRM, SAGACIOUS LEADERSHIP OF THE COUNT

Ten days have passed since the Count took control of the Council of Athelstan and, by extension, London herself. During that time, he has restored order. The curfew has endured and the state of emergency continues.

Nonetheless, the metropolis feels safer than it has almost within living memory. The spirit of the place seems calmer now and more at ease. Reports of crime, of almost any kind, are greatly reduced. There is a security to our lives which feels apt and welcome, as though we, as a people, are relearning the lessons of our forefathers and returning to a simpler and more contented time.

The means by which the Count ascended to his present position may have been forged from crisis, yet he is building a better future on the ashes. Not for nothing, we suspect, has he attracted the enthusiastic support of the highest in the land – not only the so-called 'Tanglemere Faction' but the Prime Minister himself, the Earl of Balfour. The King's continued silence may be taken, we think, as tacit approval.

Might we then humbly suggest that the period of emergency be prolonged and that the Council remain in control until its wider objectives are achieved? Might we also suggest that the realm of its influence be extended? London ought not to be a fortress, after all, but rather an example to the rest of the country, and to the Empire that lies beyond her.

As Mr Salter has written time and again in these pages, society has been crying out for leadership of a robust sort. For too long we have pined for safety and for certainty, for determination and resilience. It is, perhaps, an accident that such leadership has been provided by a man about whom we know so little. On this score, we expect to learn very much more upon Mr Salter's imminent return from the White Tower.

Yet it would seem to all of us here at the Gazette to represent an error to try in any fashion to thwart the Count when he has achieved such happily productive results. He is a figure of inspiration to us and one to whom we all owe a great debt. Besides, who would dare to cross him now?

PERSONAL MEMORANDUM BY FORMER SUB-DIVISIONAL INSPECTOR GEORGE DICKERSON

10 February

I do believe we're the only fellows left in this afflicted nation who'd dare now to cross the Count.

I write this beside new friends. We all carry satchels filled with stakes and holy water. The scent of blood is in our nostrils and in the course of the past few days we have gotten ourselves quite an appetite for the killing of vampire-kind.

But I'm getting ahead of myself. I'm letting my yarn run away with me. I should begin, near as dammit, at the beginning.

The day after the Yard burned down I got myself a parcel in the post. It had inside it the diary of Commissioner Quire. No note or explanation. I read the thing real quick, disturbed but not, I guess, surprised. I'd seen and heard too much by then not to have suspicions of my own. Though I don't believe I'd imagined the reach of it. Oh, but he was useful to them! Wasn't he? Old Quire.

A day after I got the diary I was sent a letter which threw me off the Force on the direct orders of the Council. I felt no shock. Anger, sure, and outrage too, but by then I'd seen the direction of things. I understood the tide was coming in and the rain was pelting down but that we'd all been so distracted by the colours of the horizon that we'd not noticed the water pooling by our feet.

What could one man do? The Council controlled the state. The darkness controlled the underworld. The police force was routed, gutted, gone. All was in disarray. But by then I'd started to see that it was a chaos which was meant. Which was planned and designed.

I drank that night. Too much. I slept. And when I slept I dreamed.

Till then I'd never given much thought to my dreams. Never paid them mind. As a policeman – what the British call a peeler or a crusher – I always had to deal strictly in reality. In facts and clews.

But somehow, the way the world is now, dreams seem more important than before. Even to a fellow like me.

In fact, I've got a theory as to why this could be. I think they're his element. I think, in some queer way we don't fully understand, the Count is a creature of dreams.

So that night, as I dreamed, I saw Parlow again. Martin Parlow who left London just before everything went bad. Parlow, my mentor and friend, who went home to a town called Wildfold to see his daughter and bury his wife, a good man and a fine Jerry who vanished and who never came back.

In the dream he stood on a cold grey beach, on dark stones in twilight. The sky was clouded. The sea whispered behind him. In the distance, there was the ruined hulk of some ship left ages past to rot on the shore.

He smiled. No humour in it. 'The answer's here, son,' he said. 'Everything you're looking for. It's in Wildfold. With me.'

At this, I started to ask what he meant, only to realise

that in the dream I couldn't speak at all but only listen.

'Wildfold,' he said again. 'That's the only chance we've got to stop it. So you'd better hurry. Don't you think so?'

He nodded, just once. Like old times.

'Spit-spot,' he said, and winked.

Then the dream ended, sudden as a blade.

I woke up and found the earth around me shaking. As I came back to consciousness, the tremor subsided. I knew what it was, having spent some years in California, though I did not know the cause. I did know, however, just where I had to be. And what I had now to do.

It was still dark when I left my lodgings with a single suitcase and a heavy walking stick and started on foot for the station at Liverpool Street.

The streets had changed. They had had a different quality, ever since the first explosion. I'd seen it in the criminals – in the swell of hostilities between the Pigtails, the Giddis Boys and the Sweetmen. Folks were swifter to anger. They were hungry for violence. There was everywhere a fearfulness and a sense of dread.

Yet even knowing these things I was still much struck by the emptiness of the streets that morning. By their desertion.

There were folks abroad of course, though I did not see their faces. They clung to the shadows and hid themselves in alleyways and cloaked themselves in darkness. I gripped my stick and hurried by. Occasionally, I heard voices but they were always from a distance.

Often I felt sure I was being watched. Strange eyes

looking over me. Twice I heard laughter, shrill and desperate. Once, from the shadows which clustered around a doorway in a row of tenements, I heard a murmured invitation. I ignored it and strode on. There was broken glass underfoot, and trash left to rot in nooks and corners. When I passed a hole-in-the-wall tobacconist I heard from within a shriek of dreadful pleasure, fearful agony in every note of it.

Thoroughfares and crossroads were all but empty and reeking of menace. From somewhere very far away I heard what might have been a scream. I had meant to hail a cab but I saw not a one, their absence adding to the sense of desolation.

As I approached the district in which Liverpool Street is contained, dawn came up and the streets stirred into something more like life. I started to see other travellers making their way towards the station. A stream of passengers, all laden down with suitcases and bags. Some had children. Some carried large and heavy possessions. One family had a canary in a cage. No one spoke. The mood was grim. Everyone – I felt certain – was trying to escape, though I doubt that any of them, if asked, could have told you just what it was that they were running from.

In the last half mile before the station loomed into view I was followed. Not by a beginner but by no expert neither. Once I paused and turned my head and caught myself a glimpse of my pursuer. It was a young man, lean and pale. I had seen him somewhere around. That much I knew. But I could not have told you just when or where.

I got to the station to find the place teeming with folks

who were trying to get away, decent, honest citizens, fearful and worn down.

At the sight of this ragged congregation, I was put in mind of the Good Book and its words about the separation of sheep and goats. I wondered which we were, those of us in flight. Then I realised that I got the parable all wrong. These people were sheep sure enough, fleeing from the city. But it wasn't goats that we were giving up London to. It was wolves.

The trains were already starting to fail. No room for everyone. The guards did their best but there wasn't enough space for us all. The taking of tickets and the checking of documents looked to have been entirely abandoned. Everyone was yielding to a herd instinct, to a yearning for escape. The crowd grew restless. No violence. Just tears and lamentations. In the air, panic rose.

I was a lucky one. I helped a family on board a train bound for the country and was ushered on in their wake. As I clambered up I saw my pursuer – a dot in the sea of faces. For a moment as I saw him, his name swam to the front of my memory. Then it – and he – were gone.

I entered a compartment that was already all but full. I stood – the seats having long since been taken – gladly yielding my place to a family with a brace of yowling kids. I stood instead in the corridor beyond. All of us were men out there, all shoulder to shoulder. All of us were trying not to be afraid. The atmosphere was thick with desperation. No one spoke yet our eyes told their own story.

We waited till at last we heard the frantic whistle of

the guard and the slamming of the doors. A moment later the carriage swayed and the train began to move. With too much effort, we pulled away as the engine broke free of the station.

'Thank God,' muttered several of those present. 'The Lord be praised.'

As I looked about that gang of strangers – all those relieved and hopeful faces – I realised that one of them was not in truth a stranger at all.

The pale young man, scrawny and down-at-heel, saw that my eye had lighted on his and he gave me a secret smile. He moved towards me, elbowing his way through the knot of travellers.

Folks complained. They even swore at him but he was persistent. Just his presence seemed to have punctured the mood of fragile hope.

At last he reached my side. He gave me a sneer.

'Don't recognise me, do you, copper?'

I saw that he was even younger than I'd thought. Barely more than a boy, for all his angry swagger.

'I think you followed me,' I said. 'God knows why.'

'No. From before then. From before... everything.'

I looked at him. He grinned wildly. At last his name came to me... 'Thom Cawley.'

'Well done, Yankee. Smart as a snake, ain't you?'

'What do you want?'

He laughed – a sour snorting.

'I want you to kill me, Mr Dickerson, sir. 'Cause if you don't...' He smiled and at the sight of it, any doubt I might have had left about his sanity utterly dissolved.

'Cause if you don't, I'm going to have to murder everyone on this train.'

As his smile widened to reveal clean white fangs, I started to understand the nature of the situation. And even then I moved too damn slowly.

At the words of Thom Cawley, panic in the crowd spread like wildfire. There were shouts and screams and curses. There was the start of a stampede. And there was the voice of that hoodlum, now made into some alien thing, above the sounds of fear.

'Please, detective. End it for me! They give me my orders but I don't want to do it.'

Truly, the boy was in pain.

'Please!' he shouted one more time and bared his teeth again. 'You know what you have to do!'

He gave a moan of agony before lunging at a man who was struggling by him, sinking his fangs into his neck and clamping down hard. There was blood. The train surged on.

Cawley disengaged from the guy and hurled his twitching form to the ground. When his eyes met mine amid the rushing chaos, I saw they were full of pleading.

Unable to stop himself, the little gangster stretched out a hand to seize another victim.

At last I acted. At last my old instincts were returned to me. In one motion, I took my stick and broke it on my knees. I discarded half and kept the other. I took the boy by the neck and thrust him to the ground.

He gurgled, almost as though he found it pleasant.

'Go on,' he begged. 'You know what to do!'

'Why?' I shouted.

'Because I can't bear it...' There were tears in his eyes. 'I don't want to live as a monster.'

'No, I mean why were you sent? To kill all these people?'

'To make an example of them. To scare the rest into staying.'

'Why?'

'He's got plans for us. Plans for us all. And that's why. That's why I want to—'

I had no interest in hearing any more. I brought down the stake hard into his chest. He screamed, like a child. I guess I hadn't been forceful enough. So I did it again. Even harder than before. Smashed bone, ripped skin and gristle. No scream this time. His eyes rolled upwards. No more breath.

Already tired, I got to my feet. I saw a mass of frightened faces. And then in the distance, from somewhere in the train, we heard the sounds of screaming.

'There's another one,' I said to the throng. 'There's another goddamn vampire on this train!'

More screams. Panic. Chaos. The engine churning onwards. The bloodied stake, gripped tightly in my hand.

What I knew next was this.

It was later that same day. Evening. Full dark. I was in the country, in a field beside the railroad track. The earth was cold and hard beneath me. My body was in agony, my arms still trembling in the aftermath of exertion. As I came to, I glanced down and I saw that my suit was covered with spreading islands of blood.

There was a smell of burning on the breeze. As I rose to my feet I saw the cause. The train on which I had left London was burning like a torch. Even at a distance I could feel the heat of the flames. I could hear their crackling.

As I stepped forward, hoping that someone might still be alive inside it, I heard a voice – a woman's voice – from the shadows.

'Everyone on board is dead, sir. You did your best. But they were many and you are but one man.'

I turned and saw the speaker. She was a young lady, small, demure, dark-haired and full-lipped.

'My name is Ruby,' she said. 'I think you knew my father. Welcome to Wildfold, Mr Dickerson. And welcome to the heart of the resistance.'

Without saying more, the young woman turned and vanished into darkness. With only the inferno of the train before me, and the long, empty line of the railroad tracks, I saw no alternative but to do the same.

'Wait!' I called. But she would not slow her pace. I followed. Away from the track we moved, down a steep incline and towards a line of trees. For a time the light from the burning locomotive cast dancing shadows on the ground, but they faded soon enough as we approached the copse.

'Where are we going?' I asked again to the girl who still kept several paces ahead of me. 'Where are you taking me?'

This time she replied, though her answer was of damnably little use. 'You'll see soon enough. Hurry now.'

As we passed through the trees I became aware of

something else: of how close we were to the ocean.

A long, low beach of stones lay before us and the dark sea stretched beyond.

The train and the horror of it seemed far away. There was only the taste of salt on my lips and the roar of the waves in my ears.

'Come on,' said Ruby. I guess I must have paused to take in the vista. 'Or else we'll miss it.'

She stepped onto the beach and strode away.

For a time we walked along the shore together. The sea seemed to me to be unruly, as though there were a storm somewhere far away or else some freak ruction in the deep. Waves crashed, clawing at the ground. There was a sound of stones, skittering and tumbling one over another, cascades of rock, sand and silt.

'You said you were the resistance!' I cried. 'Surely there's more of you?'

'Of course,' she said, only to add a moment later: 'But not many.'

We rounded a curve in the landscape and passed onto a stretch of beach which had not been visible to us before. It was then that I saw it: another fire, bigger and even more dramatic than the one I had seen on the railroad tracks. It was a fearsome bonfire, a vast blaze, like something out of Scripture.

'What is the meaning of it?'

'It's a pyre,' she said. 'But it's a kind of beacon too.'

'Who lit it?'

'We did,' she replied, with a queer sort of jauntiness. 'The doctor and me.'

As she said these words, I saw a dark figure moving against the flames. A bustling silhouette. I did not know him but even from a distance he was troubling. There was something too agitated in his motions. Something close to crazed.

As we came nearer, our footsteps crunching on the beach, his outline grew more plain. There was something about him of the priest. But not of those polite vicars and meek curates of this country. Not, at least, unless they had been driven into a state of exultation close to madness.

Rather, dressed all in black, severe and ascetic-looking, he was much more akin to the wandering preachers I knew in my childhood. Wild-eyed prophets, forever seeking alms or a congregation or both, they who criss-crossed the great plains of Utah in the last century.

'Doctor!' called out the woman by my side. The man beckoned us forward. At last we reached him. The wall of flame was vast and intense. The fire hissed and spat. I saw timber there, being consumed by the inferno, but there were other things too. Other, half-familiar shapes.

The stranger held out his hand. I saw now that he had been badly injured. Half his face had been torn away, as if by a single, brutal swipe from some terrible claw.

'Hello! I'm Jack Seward,' he said. 'You must be George Dickerson.'

I told him that I was. 'You knew that I was coming?'

He nodded. 'We saw your approach in our dreams.'

'And I prayed,' said the young woman. 'I prayed to

God to send us help.'

'Seward...' I began. 'You were missing. Ain't that right? Your friends wanted to send out a search party.'

The scarred man nodded once. 'It was a long, strange road which led me to this place.'

'I should like to hear what happened.'

As if in reply, the fire sent up a shower of sparks.

'Maybe I shall tell you,' said Jack Seward. 'But not, I think, tonight. For we have other work to do.'

Ruby Parlow interrupted. 'Is it almost time, then? Is it almost here?'

'Is what almost here?' I asked. 'What exactly are you folks waiting for?'

Seward smiled – a smile of unsettling calm. 'We're waiting, Mr Dickerson,' he said, 'for that.' And he flung out his right arm towards the ocean. 'See! See there!'

His face was illuminated by the crazy flickering of the flames. I looked out across the water and I saw then what he meant. A tall ship weaved wildly out at sea, listing in the water then hurtling on towards the shore.

'She's in trouble,' I hollered. 'Unless she's righted she'll be wrecked.'

'There's nothing we can do,' said Ruby, 'except to pray.'

'I expect she will be wrecked, Mr Dickerson,' Seward said. 'But there will be survivors. One in particular. One who will change the course of all our destinies.'

'Who is it?' I said. 'Who the hell's on that boat who's so important to you?'

Seward sighed, as though the answer should be obvious. 'Who else?' he said. 'But Dracula's child.'

★

That ship was wrecked and there was nothing we could do to stop it. We bore witness, the flames hot at our backs, as the vessel tilted, foundered and, with a roar of splintered wood and metal, sank.

Once the ship was down I ran to the water's edge, scouting for survivors. I shouted in the hope that they could follow the sound of my voice. Behind me, Seward and the woman stood like guardsmen. In the end, rising out of the dark water, I saw just three people – two men and a boy.

I waded in as far as I could and helped them struggle ashore. I urged them to safety and they stumbled up towards the bonfire's edge. Seward greeted thcm as though in a kind of rapture: 'Arthur! Quincey!'

The older man took the doctor in his arms.

'Jack! Thank God. Thank God, you're safe. But... your face.'

'It's a long story. I dare say you've one of your own to tell.'

'Yes, I suppose that I do.' He motioned towards the stranger. 'This is Strickland. Without him, Quincey and I would be dead.'

'I'm George Dickerson.'

He looked me over, then smiled. 'Of course. The policeman. The American policeman.'

I found that I was grinning back. We shook hands. The boy – Quincey – was smiling too. For an instant, I allowed myself the possibility of hope. Then Ruby spoke up again. She has about her, in spite of her age and sex, the most terrific sense of authority. Truly, she is her father's daughter.

'Gentlemen!' We all turned to look at her. 'We need to make plans.'

'Plans for what, ma'am?' I asked.

She looked me straight in the eye, unblinking. 'For the final battle,' she said.

JONATHAN HARKER'S JOURNAL

———◆———

10 February. I am unable to recall any previous occasion on which I have exerted myself for so prolonged a space of time, or forced upon myself such relentless and unforgiving endurance. For a day and a night I have walked without ceasing. Often, I think that I have even walked while half asleep, my feet trudging ever onwards, my body obeying my will even through the mists of unconsciousness.

I have moved steadily east, following where I can the railway tracks and, in their absence, both my instincts and the stars. As I have moved through the counties of England, I have done my utmost to draw to myself no attention and to lie low. Wherever possible, I have kept out of sight. As before, I have felt that thoroughly unsettling sense that the country herself is shifting, that she is undergoing a process of reversion. Never have I felt so perpetually at risk in my own nation, not from one singular threat but from many.

Everywhere there persists a quality of hunger, as if appetites which have long been forbidden are now being permitted to break free. The shadow of the Count has fallen over us all, and now is the time at which we understand what other forces lurk in the shadows.

It was growing dark for the second time in this desperate trek of mine when I saw a stretch of dense and gloomy woodland. I was by then (or so, at least, I believe) at the edge of East Anglia. I had been following the line of the railway for ten miles or so as those tall lines of elm and ash rose up about me.

It was late and I was exhausted. I had seen no trains for more than an hour and there was a stillness in the air, a hush in the twilight which seemed to me almost soothing. For the first time in too long I no longer felt watched.

I kept walking onwards, my determination undimmed, but then I stumbled. I gasped and righted myself only to stumble again. My knees were giving out in protest at how I had used them. My legs ached and sang with pain. All the long days of my imprisonment and enforced inactivity now paid bitter dividends. Far away, in the forest, I heard the plaintive, questioning call of an owl. I lay for a moment upon the earth, quite helpless. I felt horribly exposed. If a vampire had found me in so vulnerable a position, my life would not have been worth a farthing.

I made up my mind. I needed rest and sanctuary, if only for an hour or two before I pressed on towards the sea. I rose with great difficulty to my feet and staggered a short distance into the woodland, far enough in that I could not be seen from the tracks. Masked by trees, I found a kind of concave undulation in the ground, carpeted by dead, dry leaves.

Into this happy bower I collapsed. Sleep came almost immediately, my body grateful to be granted rest.

The last thing that I remembered before slumber was the cry once again of the owl, closer this time than before.

★

I was woken some hours later – exactly when I know not – by a pair of voices. One belonged to a man and the other to a woman. Both were evidently young.

'Who is he, do you think?'

'Poor fellow looks exhausted.'

The sound of them was pleasant and kindly and, though I have learned of late to mistrust once more such effects, trustworthy also.

I opened my eyes and scrambled to my feet. I fumbled in my pocket and brought out a makeshift crucifix which I had constructed on the road.

The two strangers laughed – a noise which might have been eerie in that dense, unpeopled woodland but which, to my ears, was oddly and even charmingly musical.

'Fear not,' said the man.

'We are not like them,' said the woman.

In the grey light of the moon, I examined this pair of visitors. They were still younger than I had thought. Neither can have been more than twenty-one. He had dark hair and she had fair. They were dressed in the rough pragmatic clothes of village folk and they had about them an air of smiling hospitality.

Still suspicious, I stepped closer, the cross outstretched.

Neither of the young people flinched from my approach.

'Smile,' I said grimly. 'Show me your teeth.'

Both did as I had asked. Without embarrassment or shame, I peered closer and saw that their teeth were entirely human.

'No fangs,' said the boy, and both of them laughed once more.

'Who are you?' said the woman.

I stepped back. 'Jonathan Harker.'

'Pleased to meet you, Jonathan Harker,' she replied. 'My name is Julia and this is my brother, Joshua.'

'Hello, Mr Harker.'

I nodded warily.

'So you have met them, I think,' Joshua said. 'And killed some of them to boot?'

'The un-dead? I have, yes. More than I know.'

'Then you should tell us,' said the girl. 'These are dangerous times for sleeping out in the open. In the hours of darkness you should not travel alone. We live not far from here, sir. Won't you come home with us?'

Full of foreboding, my mind still clouded from sleep, I hesitated.

'Please, sir,' said the girl. 'It's not safe out here. We wouldn't be able to live with ourselves if something terrible befell one who slumbered almost upon our very doorstep.'

She smiled with all the sweetness of untarnished youth. Her brother clapped me manfully upon my back.

'Come back, Mr Harker. You must be safe. In such dark days as these we all should take particular care of one another.'

I agreed that he was right and I allowed myself to be led away, deeper into the forest, farther from the line of the railway and into darkness.

'They can be killed then, the blood-drinkers?' asked the young woman, with an enthusiasm which I thought rather unbecoming.

'Yes,' I said. 'They are powerful but they can be defeated. If one understands such few frailties as they possess.'

'Can you show us?' Julia said. 'Please, Mr Harker, can you show us how to kill them?'

As she spoke, I realised that I was already lost. I whirled around, striving to regain my bearings.

'Hush, Mr Harker,' said the girl. 'No need to fret. We know the forest and we understand its ways. We will see you safely out of it once daylight comes.'

As we walked on, I heard rustlings and scrapings around us, and more than once what I took to be footfalls. The trees creaked. There was in the bracken a rustling.

'Are we—' I began, but the siblings cut me short.

'Only animals,' said the brother.

'Stay with us,' said the sister, 'and you will be quite safe.'

'Wait,' I said.

'We must hurry.'

'No.' I stopped to pick a piece of dead wood from the ground. On my knee, I broke it swiftly into two: a pair of new stakes created. I held one in each hand, knowing that, in the line of work to which I am once again committed, one can never have too many weapons.

'Now,' I said. 'Now we may go on.'

It was not long, and not without considerable relief, until I saw a small cottage, dirty-white, appear out of the gloom.

'Home,' said Julia as she led me to the door.

From inside, I smelled something cooking – some lean meat. At the scent, my belly roared its approval.

'Come inside,' said Joshua, and I did as I was bidden.

At first all was as it ought to be and everything was as appearance suggested. The house was a snug little home, warm and dry. The smell of cooking intensified within and hung most pleasantly in the air.

'We still have some supper,' Julia said sweetly. 'If you would like to eat before you rest.'

'Rabbit stew,' Joshua said with insistent joviality. 'Her specialism.'

A feeling of doubt and suspicion was growing in my breast. Who would not be suspicious in such a situation? Even a child, weaned on fairy tales, would recognise the threat. Yet at those words, I felt a little reassured. Besides, I truly was exhausted.

'Thank you,' I murmured. 'I should be most grateful.'

Within what seemed like moments, I was seated at the table and a steaming bowl of stew was being set before me.

The scent of it was quite delicious.

Joshua and Julia did not sit beside me but rather remained standing. Both rocked slightly upon their heels, an expression, almost identical, of happy expectation upon both of their faces.

At the sight of this, a fright rose up in me again and I became cognisant of great and imminent danger.

This perception I endeavoured to disguise from my hosts.

'Try it,' cooed the woman.

'Might I,' I said smilingly, 'be permitted a knife and fork?' Only a spoon sat before me.

'For stew?' said the man. 'There is surely no need.'

'Nonetheless. I have... a weak jaw. In case of gristle... The tenderness of my teeth... I am sure you understand.'

Julia smiled, altogether without humour. She went to the sideboard and brought out a knife and fork, both of which looked blunt and speckled with age. 'Here,' she said, with no particular grace, and placed them before me. 'Now will you try my cooking?'

I reached for the knife and took it.

'Please,' said the woman again, and there was now an audible quality of brittleness to her voice for which I did not care. 'Please, sir, do not be so discourteous as to reject our hospitality.'

I looked at her then, and at her brother, and I saw in their eyes an awful, but not a supernatural, kind of hunger. I felt a sickening wave of fear, mingled with disgust.

By my expression, they saw that the charade was almost over. Joshua sighed.

'Could we not just kill him now, my love?' he said. 'I am sure that together we could overpower him. He is old, look, and weak from his walking.'

I pushed my chair backwards and staggered to my feet. I pushed the stew to the ground. The bowl shattered and the food, which by now I was quite convinced was in some fashion drugged, poured sluggishly onto the floor.

'Why?' I asked. 'Why would want to kill me?'

The young woman sighed, then shrugged. 'Because we like it,' she said. 'Because we've always been curious.'

'And,' remarked the young fellow by her side, 'because, nowadays, we can. This is his world now, Mr Harker. He permits many things. And so our time is come around.'

They ran at me then, both together, their every motion speaking of murderous intent. Why? There was to it no rhyme or reason save for some base desire to kill.

Both were evidently human – but they represented the very worst of our kind, twisted and thoroughly without hope. As they surged towards me I felt a rising within me of fury and outrage.

All that we have suffered, my family and our friends. Mina gone, our son lost, our friends scattered, mad or dead. That these young panthers should dare to stand against me now! I felt a certainty then, an ardent belief in the necessity at that moment of absolute brutality.

I thought of Mina and Quincey, and poor Sarah-Ann, and of all those who have been sacrificed, and I seized the knife and gave myself up to my rage. It was a brief but dreadful battle. I do not care to set down its every detail, even if I were able to recall them through the tidal waves of fury.

Suffice to say that shortly afterwards, I left their house torn and bloodied, and that two cadavers lay within.

I make no apology for this. It was done in self-defence. They were as maddened beasts and I had no choice but to destroy them. A brisk search of their dwelling-place revealed to my disgust that I would not by any means have been their first victim. How many others had they lured to the slaughter?

And why? What darkness within urged them to commit such horrors? I have no answers, though I am sure that the revival of the Count has only emboldened them, they and others like them. I did not rest in that frightful house, nor did I dare to sample any food or drink.

Instead, I walk on, more certain than ever of my purpose and mission. We have to stop him. We have to kill the Count. We have to set things right.

Onwards, then. Onwards to Wildfold.

PERSONAL MEMORANDUM BY FORMER SUB-DIVISIONAL INSPECTOR GEORGE DICKERSON

10 February

Continued. Back when I was a kid, my pa took me to a ghost town. It was an old mining settlement out on the fringes of the desert – a place where the ground had failed to provide much of anything, where every seam had turned out to be a false lead, where what glittered in the dust was only broken glass.

Folks had drifted. All the diggers and the prospectors were gone, along with the few shops and shacks which had sprung up to service their scanty needs. It was empty when we passed through it. Just shuttered storefronts, sand, rubble and tumbleweed. Nothing human was left, but even as a child I felt just the same that something had survived, that something was watching us with unfriendly eyes. I recall that I was most relieved when we left and moved right along. I suppose my father meant to teach me a lesson by taking me there – though quite what it might have been I cannot say.

I thought of that abandoned place when our little group – the girl, the doctor, the Lord, his aide, his son and me – left the wind-whipped beach and walked into Wildfold. It was a small place, of fisherfolk and farmers, the kind which can be found, in different forms, on most every coast on Earth. In summer I dare say the place would look pretty enough, but at night at the end of an English winter it was only desolate.

More than that, it had the same atmosphere as

the ghost town of my younger days. It was a place where strange shadows fell. Where things slithered and shuffled just out of sight. After we walked up the beach, we came to the harbour and passed into the high street.

We were heading (mostly, I guess, on instinct) for a little flint church at the heart of the town. Many doors were closed and many windows were boarded up, as though the inhabitants had left of their own free will. Other, gaping entrances and shattered panes told a different story. For a long time there was only the sounds of the sea and of boots on stone.

Mr Strickland and me were at the back of the party. Strickland was a small, thin young guy, loyal and hardworking. I liked the man. I wish he had not died so hard.

'Inspector?' he said.

'Not any more. Just plain George now.'

'Of course. Forgive me.'

I shrugged. 'Ain't nothing to forgive.'

'I have two questions for you, George.'

'Just two?'

'Well, many more than that, of course. This whole business – this entire, wretched affair – raises so many questions for us all. But as to you, here tonight, I have but two enquiries.'

'Then shoot.'

'First, what led you to Wildfold?'

'I was invited here.'

'Who by?'

'By an old friend – in a dream. And as to who sent that dream... who the hell knows?'

He seemed not in the least bit surprised by my admission but just nodded. 'Yes. We were brought here the same way. Lord Godalming – he was shown things in dreams. Told to trust the boy and to return to England. He'd meant to leave, you see, to depart the country altogether and go wandering abroad, for as long as the mood took him. But then... the storm... the ship... Crossing became impossible.'

I think I only grunted at this. 'What was your second question?'

He looked away. 'I... wouldn't want to sound foolish. In such days as these one's imagination has become distinctly skittish.'

'Strickland, please. Ask me whatever you damn well please.'

'Do you think, since the beach, that someone's been following us?'

I stopped. I held up my hand.

Ahead of us, the others walked on, almost at the church. I looked into the darkness. Nothing. Only the hiss of the sea.

But there seemed to me to be something all the same – something wrong, something which the quick eyes of Mr Strickland had seen and recognised.

'Do you feel it too?' he asked. 'That sensation of being stalked?'

I didn't reply but just peered into the gloom. For a long moment there was nothing at all. And then...

He must have been so hungry. That is what I have come to believe.

Attracted by the sounds of our voices, he must have crept out of whatever shallow pit he'd been hiding in, and tracked our progress till his compulsions overwhelmed him.

The vampire roared out of the darkness, moving far faster than should have been possible. Hands stretched out like talons, lips peeled back to show fangs like razors, and gleaming eyes which spoke of appetite. In a flash of horror I saw who it was: my old friend, Martin Parlow – hollowed out and made into a monster.

Strickland was closest, so the creature took him first. With a wretched hissing sound it threw itself upon the Englishman and sank its teeth into the exposed part of his neck. Strickland cried out.

I whaled on the creature. I pulled at his fat form, releasing Strickland. He fell at once upon the ground, crimson pumping from his neck.

I had my old mentor held tight. Parlow thrashed and groaned in frustrated fury. I forced him around – gripped him by his lapels. He grinned madly up at me. His lips were flecked with foam and blood. He laughed, moist and gurgling.

'In my eyes, Dickerson,' he said, 'you see the future.'

I made my right hand into a fist and I smashed it hard into his plump face.

He only laughed again.

'Oh, but it's a wonderful thing,' he said. 'Being like this. All them years of abiding by the law. Trying to keep order. When all the time I could have been this way. It's glorious. You should try it, Georgie boy. Let yourself be transformed.'

I held that filthy creature tight in my hands. 'How…?' I said. 'How could you have allowed this to be done to you?'

'No choice,' the vampire spat. 'No choice is given. But when she stopped me on the lonely road – the dark woman, the beauty who sent me here – I found soon that I wanted her to change me. In the end, we all want it.'

His words – his filthy lying words – stopped. He writhed and hissed in my hands.

'Stand back.'

These words were spoken by Dr Seward, who appeared from behind me. Outstretched before him, he held a silver crucifix. The Parlow-thing wailed.

He thrashed against me. I held him firm. Then Seward was by him, pressing the cross to his right cheek. There was a smell like burning meat.

'Hold him down,' Seward snapped and, with pleasure, I thrust the vile creature to the ground. It roared and protested. Too late.

From somewhere, Seward had a stake and hammer and in an instant the thing was pushed into Parlow's chest.

The vampire screamed, a keening, unearthly sound. On my right, the aristocrat, Arthur, appeared. He had a knife and in six strong motions he succeeded in severing head from body. It was hard work. His face shone with sweat.

Once it was over, he looked across at Seward. 'Like old times, Doctor.'

Nearby, poor Strickland lay in a spreading pool of blood.

The girl was by his side, her face grave and full of sorrow. As she rose to her feet, I noticed that she could not bring herself to look upon what remained of her father.

'Dead,' she said simply. 'With Mother now.' Her courage impressed me.

Lord Arthur surveyed the scene. 'We cannot tolerate this,' he said. 'We simply cannot allow it. I ought never to have left this country. I should never have abandoned her. I should have stayed and I should have fought.'

I spoke up. 'There's still time enough for that, sir. There's still time to fight.'

'Then I shall go to London,' said the Englishman. 'I shall destroy the vampire-king or I shall perish in the attempt. Who's with me? Eh? In Strickland's name and in Caroline's and in the name of all those who have been destroyed by the monster, who is with me?'

'Me,' I said. 'I am.'

Seward: 'Me too.'

Ruby: 'Of course.'

We turned towards the kid. Young Quincey.

It was a queer sight, for he did not seem to be paying us the slightest heed. Instead, he stood with arm outstretched, pointing towards that little flint church.

'There comes another,' he said. 'The crew of light is not yet complete.'

None of us replied. Without asking why, we found ourselves doing just what the kid wanted, staring at that damn kirk.

As we watched, the door was thrown open. I sprang forward, ready for action, expecting another blood-sucker.

'Wait,' said Lord Arthur. 'Hold fast, Mr Dickerson.'

Out of the door stumbled a man in his middle years, brown-haired and pale. He looked fretful and tired – the kind of fellow who lives on his nerves. At the sight of all of us, however, and of the kid in particular, his face creased into a broad smile.

'Jonathan?' called out the nobleman and the doctor almost as one.

'Father!' shouted the boy.

They ran then, father and son, practically into each other's arms.

And for a brief, sweet moment, there even seemed to me to be a scrap of hope still left in this world.

FROM THE DIARY OF
ARNOLD SALTER

———◆———

11 February. I used to believe that this country had been infected by a poisonous, fast-spreading disease, and that the name of that infection was the twentieth century. In order to fight it, I looked for a cure. But, given the events of recent days, I wonder if the remedy might not be very much more contagious than the original malaise.

Oh, I went to the Tower to ask my questions, of course – just as the Gazette had promised its readers, and just as I had promised Tanglemere that I would. I walked into the White Tower all puffed up, all dressed in my finery and with a kiss from Mrs Everson still glowing on my cheek.

It was Mr Hallam who met me – a fat, florid, self-important man and a clear lover of perverted telegraph boys if ever I saw one. He is not as the Count is, or as the rest of them. He, amongst us all, is still human.

I remember the fireside stories and the folklore. Is there not often one who is unchanged and is kept mortal in order to help them? Isn't that right?

In any case, I shook the man's hand and followed him inside.

He led me down – too far! – down into the depths of this place. He led me into a room of shadows and told me to wait. I was about to round on the man and d—n him for his impudence. When I turned, I saw that Mr Maurice Hallam was already gone.

Then the voice stole out of the darkness, deep and rich and ancient.

'Mr Salter?'

'Yes,' I said. 'I am here to interview the Count.' I was trying to sound tough but I sounded only young, like a mere stripling. Next to him, I suppose that is exactly what I am. Which of us is not?

Next I heard a scuttling sound, as though there were some animal in the room. There was a hopeless scuffling before silence fell again.

'Who is it?' I said. 'Who's there?'

'I wanted to thank you, Mr Salter,' said that deep, strange voice again. 'For all that you have rendered unto me.'

'I'm... not sure...' I began, only to be cut short as he stepped forward out of the gloom and stood mere inches from my face.

He was tall and very pale, with a great moustache and a high forehead and a quality about him of nobility. I looked into his eyes and saw in them my death.

I had never seen the man before but somehow I knew him well.

'You have seen me in your imagination, I think, Mr Salter,' he said, as though he had in some fashion read my thought. 'Lost as you were in all your dreams of England.'

'What are you, Count?' I asked, and once again my voice piped like a boy's.

He smiled. I saw his incisors, but I felt no surprise and I did not flinch from them. I was mesmerised, held fast like a mouse before a cobra.

'I am the culmination of your deepest desire, Mr Salter. I am the past and I am the future. I am Alpha. And I am Omega.'

There was much more I wished to ask him, but it was already too late. He fell upon me, sank his teeth deep inside and drank his fill. It is my curse that I can remember the experience in precise and visceral detail. I remember how painful it was – and how horribly pleasurable also.

When I woke, a day and a night had passed and I had been changed. There will be no more words from me. I am no journalist any longer but only his creature. I dwell, like him, in darkness. I feed on what is given to me – on those criminals and reprobates he keeps penned in this place. I follow his orders, those of Mr Hallam and those of a raven-haired beauty whom I suspect to have killed as many men as the worst tyrants of history. There is another here also – another of his kind – though they have yet to speak to me.

I wait for sustenance and for my orders. Such is now my existence: hunger and obedience. He has some particular task in mind for me, he says – a small but vital part of his design.

As I lie amongst the dead my thoughts run often towards the past, of my Mary and the life we shared. Above all, I wonder about the part that I have played in bringing this new world into being.

What would now be different, I wonder, had Tanglemere not swayed me from self-murder? How might a great many tragedies have been averted if only I had found the courage to jump?

DR SEWARD'S DIARY
(kept by hand)

————◆————

11 February. Dear God, may it not yet be too late to set the world aright. The good Lord willing, may we yet beat back that shadow which has fallen over us all.

Three essential facts must be recorded:

(i) A crew of light has been established. Jonathan Harker stands at the head of it. Lord Arthur Godalming, the American policeman, Dickerson, Ruby Parlow and I are its constituents. Young Quincey – for reasons which remain opaque – is our conscience and our guide.

(ii) We have decided to attack the Count directly during the hours of daylight. We shall locate his base of operations and find where it is that the vampire lies. We shall drive a stake through his heart and sever his head from his body.

(iii) To that end, Lord Godalming, Ruby and Quincey himself have gone to Ely, where they will establish a base of operations and acquire an arsenal of weapons for use against the Count. It is from that small city that we shall make our final approach to London.

Before the others left, we buried Strickland and what remained of Ruby's father. He made, I fear, a most ugly cadaver, for his chest was staved in and his head had been quite separated. After a ragged and impromptu funeral, we all stood together in the church and prayed devoutly for the strength to carry on, and to execute all that must still be done. These words complete, the others began the journey to Ely while Jonathan, Mr Dickerson and I stayed here, pledging to join them as soon as we might.

We had some bloody labours before us. Wildfold had been infested and we volunteered our services to rid ourselves of what remained of the taint.

It took us many hours to achieve that end. Much of it was carried out in the grimmest of silences. For safety's sake, we went together from door to door. While it was light we found plenty who were sleeping and dragged them out into the day. Those numerous executions which we had to carry out we did without the slightest pleasure. On every occasion, as the head was severed at the neck, the vampire's features regressed to those of some earlier time. So far as I am concerned, let the historical record show what it may: our acts were not unconscionable ones. We have done no killing in this place but have only set poor souls free.

I wish to dwell no longer than is necessary on these sad duties. Nonetheless, there are four further items of interest.

(i)   I do not think that I have ever seen Jonathan Harker in quite so energetic a state. For so long have I known the drowsy toper of Shore Green, this fresh rendering of the man strikes me as entirely original.

(ii) I have been thinking again about the effect of the Renfield diary upon me. I said as much to Mr Dickerson as we dragged an elderly vampire out into the day and removed her frail bony head from its scrawny neck.

'I have theorised,' I remarked, as we cast the writhing creature down upon the ground, 'that it was a kind of trap. One that was left behind for me long ago.'

The conversation enjoyed a hiatus as Jonathan brought down the blade.

Once it was over, the American said: 'You think that the vampire can do such a thing? You believe he was thinking so damn far ahead of himself?'

It was Jonathan who answered, though I was thinking as much myself.

'Consider his extreme longevity, Mr Dickerson. The Count does not see time as we do. He is thinking always of the future and the past.'

These thoughts made us sober. We said no more but only laid the body aside for the pyre and moved on.

(iii) I have learned what became of poor Sarah-Ann. Jonathan told me that he set her free, just as we have given the poor wretches here their liberty. I deduce that there is much that he has not told me. I shall pray for her soul, and also for my own. For did I not send her to the Harkers? Did I not place her in harm's way? Merciful God, is there no end to my foolishness?

(iv) One of the faces today will haunt me for as long as I live. It was a small boy. He cannot have been more than eight or nine years old when he was changed. The creature he had become cried, as a human being might cry, when we dragged it from its nest in the schoolhouse and beheaded it. With his last breath he begged us to spare his life. For all our grand talk of war and of justice, I shall not forget the true cost of the Count's appetite and avarice. I shall not forget the sound of a child crying out for mercy in the last moments before his extinction.

FROM THE PRIVATE JOURNAL
OF MAURICE HALLAM

———◆———

11 February. I have in this place – in this White Tower – become in all but name a prisoner, held captive at the heart of this great city as was Jonathan Harker, all those years ago, confined in that distant and sin-draped castle. Such, at least, is the story that I have heard often at my master's knee.

My work continues as the Count's power grows. I am allowed egress only upon occasion, to deal with the government or with the newspapers or with some other tedious representative of the people. I am, as I have come to understand, what I was always meant to be: the Count's voice in the wider world. Yet, in the wake of those ten days which established the foundation of his influence, more and more of my time is spent in solitude in my quarters.

I find that I am beset by drowsiness. The influence of the vampire swells daily as the bounds of his kingdom grow. Each twilight brings with it some fresh emissary, come to pledge their allegiance.

I can do nothing. I can barely bring myself to stir from this room – barely bring myself, indeed, to set down even these thoughts. I think often of the choices that I have made in my life which have brought me to this pass. I know that I am become his creature, that I am mired too deep for there to be any prospect of redemption. This I mourn, yet I know, in truth, that I have now so much for which to atone that any true restitution is impossible.

But wait. A knock upon my door. The voice of Ileana. I am summoned to the crypt. The master has some new and dreadful task for me to perform. More – I pray – later.

DR SEWARD'S DIARY
(kept by hand)

——————◆——————

12 February. Our work in Wildfold is now complete. That village is no more.

These words I write upon a train, speeding towards Ely. We have attracted many glances of hostility. I dare say we smell of perspiration and unhappy labour, of smoke and of blood. Yet no man has tried to stop us.

How very odd it is to be abroad once more in England, now that the shadow of Dracula has fallen so absolutely upon it. Our journey has been quiet and without incident. The railway service, it seems to me, has never been better or more reliable.

Nothing is said aloud. No overt indications are visible that there has been a coup d'état in our democracy, only, perhaps, in the people a certain quality of the lulled and cowed, an acceptance of the new reality.

Although we have been largely left alone in our carriage, we three have found ourselves with little appetite for conversation. Yet when Jonathan drifted into sleep (of, it seemed to me, the most fitful and unhealthy kind), my American companion leaned forward in his seat and said, almost in a whisper: 'You saw him, didn't you? Back in the old days?'

There was no need for me to ask for him to clarify the object of his sentence. I checked to see that Jonathan still slumbered before I replied.

'Only twice,' I said. 'Once, in London, when we had run him to ground, when he pledged to seek revenge against us all. And then again, in Transylvania, in the last moments before his death.'

'What was he like?'

I took a moment before replying.

'Doc?'

'I think it is most probably a mistake,' I said, with as much calm detachment as I could muster, 'to think of Count Dracula as being in any way like us. He may once have been human. Yet he has passed long ago into something quite different. A whole new species.'

'Then it is your suggestion, sir, that his motives are completely different to those of ordinary men? That he is entirely unpredictable? What I have heard called a loose cannon?'

'Oh, on the contrary. I have come to believe that his motivations are clear cut. Indeed, they are driven by the very nature of his distance from our race.'

'Go on.'

'Well... he is profoundly lonely. He is consumed by it. He hungers, I think, for a kind of connection, although its mode of expression is curious indeed. Some of us – he would contend, I think, the best of us – he wants to make into something like him. In point of fact, he did just that to a most spirited young lady of my acquaintance. Others – the least of us – he sees only as subjects or food. The Count is a feudal creature at heart. He seeks now, I suspect, to return to some simpler time.'

'To a time, you think, when he was fully human?'

'It is possible,' I said. 'More than that – it is likely... But these are only speculations. Mere theories. And in the end...'

I could find no more words after this, and the American gave me a look of odd concern. 'Jack?'

'Well, I suppose none of it really matters now. Who he was or why he acts as he does. All that I really care about is tracking him to his lair and sawing his head from his body.'

Dickerson nodded in gruff acquiescence as the train thundered onwards and as Jonathan stirred and groaned, the victim, no doubt, of bad dreams.

FROM THE PRIVATE JOURNAL
OF MAURICE HALLAM

———◆———

12 February. I believe that I have just strength enough to set down what occurred last night, after I was summoned from my chamber. How cruel a mistress is long life, how playful a sadist!

For the first time since His return, the crypt was illuminated. This had been achieved not by candlelight or by electricity but rather by a strange blue flame, the source of which I was quite unable to discern. It lit the close, dank walls of the crypt with a weird azure light that lent the scene something of an artistic quality, as it had been arranged, perhaps even for my own benefit, by some poor, lost artist of the Bedlamite persuasion.

In the centre of the chamber stood, upon a pair of raised daises, two wooden coffins. Both were closed, yet I did not have to dare to look inside them to feel certain that they contained at least some necessary residue of earth from the homeland of the Count. Between them, in the manner of a latter-day Cerberus, crouched the wolf.

Dracula himself, dressed all in black, stood at the centre of the scene. At his side stood Ileana.

'My Lord. We are well met.' I gazed deeply at the ground.

It does not do to look for any longer than is necessary upon the dread face of the vampire-king.

'Look at me.' His voice, deep and terrible as ever, nonetheless possessed, I thought, some additional quality, some frayed element, some new, disquieting note.

I had no choice but to obey. I raised my eyes and steeled myself to look upon him.

He seemed older than before. His moustache had grown more white and there were lines upon his face which I had not seen before.

'My servant. You have done well.'

'Thank you, my Lord. I have done only that for which fate has moulded me.'

'Does our power grow?'

'It does, my Lord. The country is with you. Though I note that the King has yet to offer his support.'

Ileana smiled. 'The King is sleeping often now,' she said. 'He is... as once was my poor Ambrose.'

'That is good. And yet...' Dracula seemed then almost to stagger a little where he stood. It was a moment of fragility entirely without precedent. 'My body is not as strong as I had hoped. My true nature is as fire within it, burning through this mortal flesh. I need...'

'Sustenance, my Lord?' I said. 'Surely your larder of the criminal classes has yet to run dry?'

At this, the beauteous Ileana bared her teeth and hissed.

'I require complete restoration,' said the Count. 'I must draw succour from the only one still living who bears my imprimatur.'

'How, my Lord... will that be brought about?'

He smiled. 'In the days of the last century, I placed a portion of my essence within a certain woman who passed it to her child. For years this inheritance has been rising within him – my vessel. At any moment it shall overwhelm his human nature.'

'My Lord,' I said, 'I think I know the name of this boy. I do believe that I can guess it. Was his mother not brought before the Council?'

'Silence,' hissed Ileana again. 'You shall not speak of her.'

'The mother is not of your concern,' said the Count. 'Only the boy.'

'What would you have me do?'

'Ileana is to bring him to me. He shall be with us soon after midnight tomorrow. And in that potent hour which falls before the dawn we shall perform the Rite of Strigoi.'

I frowned. I thought of a moment, months past, when we had stood amongst the gypsies. Had Ileana used that strange word then? I believe that she had. For how long has every detail of this black scheme been laid?

The vampiress smiled dangerously. 'You know of the Rite, my friend?'

'I know,' I said, 'at least I believe that I know – that name.'

'The Rite will take what is within that child,' said Count Dracula, 'and place it once again in me. I shall be made whole.'

Ileana purred beside him, in happy expectation of this eventuality.

The Count continued. 'Such is the duty of a son to his father. The young must be sacrificed as was the child of Abraham, long, long ago.'

'My Lord,' I said, 'what must I do?'

'You must, upon his arrival, prepare the boy for the Rite.'

'And what...' I swallowed with discomfort. 'What will that task entail?'

★

Dear God, that I should ever have asked that question! For, once I had spoken, the Count moved closer, and he told me the dreadful truth of the thing — those awful depredations and unspeakable violations.

Can I do as he demanded? Can I find it within myself to make those blasphemous preparations? Surely, surely I cannot. Yet I have no alternative should I wish to ensure my own survival.

How fortune mocks us! For I had fondly imagined that I could go no deeper into damnation. Instead, in the wake of the Count's instructions, I understand that all this while I have been standing merely at the brink of the abyss.

DR SEWARD'S DIARY
(kept by hand)

———◆———

Later. We arrived this afternoon in Ely, during that tepid hour which lies between two and three. Four facts of significance have become apparent. While we have been in Wildfold, Arthur, Quincey and Ruby have found themselves accommodation in a small boarding house, run by an elderly woman by the name of Smallbone. During our absence, they have acquired a deal of further weaponry. Not only holy water, garlic, stakes and hammers, but much along more conventional lines also, including five pistols and a brace of knives. For who knows what human allies the vampire may have drawn to his side, loyal to his dark majesty and willing to do anything in his service?

The malaise in our nation which has, since my escape from Wildfold, been evident to me continues to spread and to deepen. Here in the streets of this formerly quiet and well-ordered place there is a tangible sense of suspicion and fear. Like ink dispersing through water, the influence of the Count is spreading, tainting all that it reaches, bringing out in every man and woman the very worst of themselves.

We are none of us immune to this dreadful effect. Poor

Quincey, for reasons about which I should prefer not to speculate, seems to me the most grievously affected. He has not been well, I gather, in recent days. There have been attacks – fits – of some unspecified sort. He seems to be maintaining his equilibrium only by a massive effort of will, as though he is engaged in some secret battle for his own sanity.

But this is unnecessary detail. I must face the truth. No longer can I try to evade reality simply by a process of compartmentalisation, placing all disagreeable facts and suspicions into ordered lines rather than face their ramifications. Why have I not learned this lesson yet? Surely the course of a human life ought to demonstrate development? Yet have I made the same mistakes my whole existence, replicating in ravaged middle age the same errors that I committed as a very young man.

Enough now. This is how the tragedy unfolded.

We dined together in a small inn by the river. It was a council of war. We made plans for a stealthy approach to London, after which we were to inveigle ourselves into the metropolis individually and unseen, aiming to penetrate the White Tower in which, according to the press, the Count had made his stronghold. We planned to travel in the hours after sunrise, when the powers of evil are at their weakest.

These schemes seemed to me sensible, practicable and well-considered.

All have now been rendered obsolete.

Still, we allowed ourselves in that repast the possibility of hope. Wine was drunk. Quincey took a small glass and the liquor loosened his father's tongue, just a little.

'I think,' Jonathan confided, 'that Mina must have been taken to London too. There was ever a connection between the Count and her. As to its specifics, I do not permit myself to think. She will, I'm quite certain, have formed a cornerstone of his revenge.' As he spoke, his face was white and drawn in a mask of determination. I noted also that he took pains to drink no more than one glass and to refuse all offers of replenishment. Something in him has shifted for the good, at least, though it is surely scarce worth the cost.

Dickerson was, according to his nature, more eager than the rest of us to hasten to the city. He feels a certain guilt, I think, that he missed the slow corruption of his superior, the late Mr Quire. Ruby, however, seems most able to calm and to soothe our fiery American friend. She provides a welcome note of grace and reason to our band.

She spoke with wisdom and pride for some minutes, giving us a kind of impromptu homily as to the necessity and urgency of our work and of that divine advocacy which she believed to be at the back of us. After she had finished, she said: 'Close by, gentlemen, is God's house. And so I suggest that we pray together there for the strength and wisdom which we shall surely need in the battle which lies ahead.'

We all agreed with these sentiments.

'A fine suggestion,' said Lord Arthur, speaking, without thought, for the whole party. At his words, the rest of us nodded and murmured our assent.

'Then let us leave,' said Ruby. She rose from her seat and we all followed suit. Godalming settled the bill and we filed together from the tavern. There was a valedictory air to our procession, almost as though we knew even then that things were closer to their conclusion than we had thought.

We walked in silence to the cathedral, through streets that seemed at once to be both deserted and observant. We saw ahead of us the welcoming glow from within the temple – candlelight filtered through stained glass, identifiable at once as uncomplicatedly beautiful, even to one such as I who possess but a scientific gaze.

As we came close to the great door of the place, I found myself at the tail of our group. Jonathan, the girl, the nobleman and the American strode ahead, each purposeful in his or her differing manner, while I hung back with young Quincey.

'You must be strong,' said I to the lad. 'Your father has survived a great ordeal. And I have seen at first hand the remarkable resilience of your mother. You shall all be reunited. Of that I have no doubt.'

At this, the young man gave me a melancholy smile. How much older he seemed at that moment than his true age! A world away from the boy who, only last year, played as happily as an infant with that poor kitten. How difficult and strenuous is the process of growing up.

At that moment, we reached the threshold of God's house. There being no sign of any other worshippers, the others went inside. At the instant that they did so, however, the Harker youth touched me on the shoulder.

'You go on, Jack,' he said. 'I find that I don't feel altogether well.'

'Oh, but that's to be expected. You are tired and you are anxious. Perhaps dear Ruby is right and a spell in the cathedral will soothe you in that regard.'

'I just need a good night's sleep.'

'Come now. Just a few words of prayer.'

'No,' he said, more firmly than seemed necessary. 'No. You go on. I shall see you soon enough.'

'Back at the boarding house?'

He bowed his head. He would not meet my eyes. I wonder now – was he trying to tell me? Was he trying to warn me of what was even then fast approaching?

'Thank you, Jack,' he said. 'For everything you've done. You've done your bit, you know. You've more than played your part.'

'I'm not sure what you mean.'

'Without your actions, the infestation at Wildfold, begun by poor Mr Parlow, would by now have spread halfway across the county… like some raging virus.'

'I only did what many others would have done.'

'And… more than that.' He smiled weakly. 'All through my life you've offered me a kind of alternative model. A different way to be – quite at right angles to my parents.'

'Quincey,' I said, 'you're speaking really rather strangely. Are you sure it's only tiredness and this headache? I'd hate to think that you'd picked up some fever at sea. Or that, weakened by fatigue, you were sickening for something.'

'It will pass. I am sure of that. Give my apologies to the others, won't you? Most especially to my father.'

'Of course.'

'Thank you.' He nodded, his every gesture now freighted with weariness. 'Good night, Jack.'

'Good night.'

He turned, and was swallowed up by darkness. I went on, into the light, little knowing that we were but minutes from disaster.

FROM THE PRIVATE JOURNAL
OF MAURICE HALLAM

———◆———

12 February. ★ *Later.* Not long now. I am expecting soon the arrival of two visitors: Ileana and that poor, sacrificial boy.

Naturally, my thoughts have been engaged by the nature of my orders, of those terrible things which it seems that I must do in order to prepare the child for the Rite of Strigoi. I have grappled with my conscience, or at least with what remains of that withered thing. My choice is, at least upon its surface, a simple one: whether to obey the horrible commands of my master or to defy him and so confirm my own extinction.

As I sat and pondered these things, not more than a few moments ago, I closed my eyes and steepled my hands together. I suppose that I drifted into something almost like prayer, a thing that I have not dared attempt for more than twenty years. I think that in the silence I reached out and called, silently, for help.

Unexpectedly, an answer came. From the shadows at the corner of the room, I heard the whisper of a voice, one that I have not heard in its true form for too long.

It was that of Gabriel Shone.

Shone, not as he was after his corruption, not after we

entered the gates of that foul castle, but before, in Brasov, when he was still unsullied.

He spoke three sentences as I sat with eyes shut and head bowed.

'Fight, Maurice. You must fight now as I did not. Capitulation, you have my word, shall lead you only to hellfire.'

I opened my eyes and turned towards the sound of the voice, hoping with great desperation that he might still be there, in however transitory a form, shimmering and spectral.

Yet was there nothing to be seen but shadows. As, I think, was always to have been my destiny, I am now left alone to make my choice.

DR SEWARD'S DIARY
(kept by hand)

————◆————

12 February. ★ *Continued.* Five of us kneeled at the head of the cathedral nave, before its altar, pledging ourselves, body and soul, to the fight against the Count and imploring our Creator to assist us in that noble endeavour.

Ruby's gracious, confident voice led us in our prayers.

'Merciful Lord,' she intoned. 'We who lay ourselves before you as humble sinners ask now for your guidance and your wisdom in that task which lies ahead of us. The chief agent of the Adversary, of him whom you cast down from the heavens, has been returned to the world of men. The evil-doer, that commander of the legions of the damned, sits at the centre of our earthly empire, seeking, we believe, to rule absolutely over us, and to institute in the name of his satanic master a new dark age. Give us we pray all hope and sustenance as we strive to defeat him. And if our lives be lost in the enterprise, please gather our souls to your side.'

She paused, as if she were surprised at being caught up in the emotion of the moment. 'Amen,' she murmured.

We all said the word, Jonathan, Arthur, George Dickerson and me. 'Amen.'

'I'm not quite sure,' Ruby admitted, 'where all that came from.'

'The words were fine,' said the American.

'Thank you,' she said, and smiled dazzlingly.

None of us moved but all sat in quiet reflection, contemplating the enormity of the task before us. Then we heard, quite clearly, from somewhere not far from the cathedral, something like a scream, composed in equal parts of terror and grotesque delight.

'What was that?' Lord Arthur asked, already rising to his feet.

'Come on,' said Dickerson. 'No time to wonder.'

He ran, without saying more, down the nave and towards the door. I followed, with Jonathan, Godalming and the girl at my heels. As we did so, it came again, that weird, haunting sound, this time accompanied by something else: a dreadful strangulated noise of exertion, like foxes in the night.

In the end, it was the policeman who led us to them. We found them in the cloisters, standing together in the shadows. So swiftly did events unfurl that I caught only glimpses – mere dreadful glimpses – of the whole scene.

Quincey Harker was standing beside a stone wall. Behind him stood a woman – or, rather, not quite a woman. She was, or had been, very beautiful – that much was clear – but she was monstrous also, for when we interrupted she was (I have come to believe) half-transformed into something like a gigantic black bat.

'Quincey!' I shouted. 'Get away from that thing!'

One taloned hand was upon the boy's shoulder, yet he did not seem to be struggling or trying to escape. Rather he accepted that proprietorial claw as though it were proper and just.

'Son!' Jonathan called out. 'Come to me. Run away.'

'No,' said Quincey in a small, determined voice. 'This is what has to happen. Ileana has come. She has to bring me to my... other father.'

Poor Jonathan went quite white at this. 'No,' he muttered. 'No. No.'

Quincey said more: 'I must be prepared. You see? For the hour before the dawn, when the Rite of Strigoi will be performed.'

'Get away.' This was the policeman. The girl, at his side, was murmuring some prayer or incantation.

'Get away,' said Dickerson again to the woman whom Quincey had called Ileana, 'you foul abomination. Get away from the goddamn boy!'

She called out in response – the same strange keening cry that we had heard from within. It was caused, I realised then, by pain as much as by exultation: the agony, I supposed, of constant transformation. Her form shuddered, shifting now ever closer to the bat.

Jonathan could only look on – pale and afraid.

It was our American ally who leapt forward, towards the boy, as the vampire writhed behind him. He meant, I suppose, to drag Quincey free of her grasp. As matters turned out, he did not even reach him.

'Stay where you are,' young Harker said. 'You cannot stand in the way of destiny. Do you not remember? When Van Helsing fell? His last words to me? I am to be the vessel.' As he spoke, I saw that something glinted in the darkness – a revolver, filched, no doubt, from our arsenal.

'He's armed!' I called out, but it was too late.

'Come here,' said the American. 'Come to me!'

'Please,' said the boy. 'I beg you, come no further.'

'You have to step away from that creature,' the American cried. 'Right now!'

The vampire-woman was now almost entirely bat – a vast, monstrous, freakish sight.

'I'm sorry,' Quincey said. He pulled the trigger on the revolver in his hand. The sound of the detonation was brutal in that holy place.

The policeman stopped, as if hesitating, then fell with a horrid slump towards the ground. Within seconds, Ruby was with him, on her knees at his side. He was bleeding. I could see that even in the gloom. She placed her hands on his chest, in an effort to stop the flow.

With a shriek, the gigantic bat soared into the sky. There was clasped in her hands the slender figure of Quincey Harker. As in some fantastic nightmare, they rushed into the distance. It sounds absurd set down, but that truly is what happened.

'Look at me.' This was Ruby to the former sub-divisional inspector. 'George, look at me. Please. Please. Keep looking into my eyes.'

Still the blood poured from him. Surely his life hung in the balance.

Another noise came then, as we gathered about that courageous man – a single sob of absolute hopelessness and despair. At the sound of it, I turned to see tears coursing down the grizzled cheeks of my old friend, Jonathan Harker.

'We have to go then,' he said. 'You heard my son. He spoke of the hour before the dawn. The Rite of Strigoi. We have scarcely any time. We have to race against the night.'

The American tried to speak, a horrible gurgling struggle. 'Go,' he said at last. 'Get the boy back. Stop them before the dawn.' He took a breath then forced himself to go on. 'And, once and for all, kill that vampire bastard.'

JONATHAN HARKER'S JOURNAL

——————◆——————

12 February. My worst imaginings have come to pass and all that I can do is to bear witness to them.

If only I had listened sooner. If only I had dared to understand. If only I had been more courageous.

I watched helplessly as my son was taken from us by a creature whom I recognised as being a vampire of the oldest sort – a Transylvanian hellion like those brides I once met beneath the castle of the Count. The American policeman, Dickerson, lay helpless upon the ground and it was thanks only to the diligence and expertise of the young woman, Ruby Parlow, that the bleeding in him was eventually staunched.

As to whether that gentleman still lives, I know not. When last I saw him, he was still breathing, although every inhalation sounded painful and perilous. The lady, by his side, bade us fly and blessed us as we went.

'He would not wish you to stay! Go, gentlemen. Hunt the creature down. Rescue the child!'

So we ran, we three – Godalming, Seward and I – away from the bloody scene at the cathedral and into the road beyond.

Already I was panting with exertion, pushed by events

almost beyond endurance and desperate now to save my son at any cost. Our mood was both grim and frantic.

'We have to get to London!' I cried, as crazed and unmanned as, I dare say, any father has ever been.

The road was empty and dark. Indeed, the whole of the town seemed abed and slumbering. There was no sign of life. If beings of a different order patrolled the night, then we saw no sign of them.

'How?' I cried. 'How are we to get there?'

It was Arthur, our natural leader, who opened his mouth to speak. Quite what even his money and influence might have achieved in such a situation, I cannot say.

Whatever the nobleman's suggestion may have been, however, I never learned it, for at that instant two lights emerged from the blackness and we heard the leonine roar of an engine. We watched as it slid forward – a great, high four-seater thing, gleaming brass and chrome. A single figure sat behind the wheel, burly in aspect, goggled and dressed in all the apparel of the motor-car enthusiast.

It seemed at first like salvation. I raised an arm.

'Stop!' I shouted. 'Stop!'

The vehicle rolled on. The driver bent his head as if in concentration and gave not the slightest indication of slowing his speed. He had surely seen us three, yet he appeared determined to ignore us.

Panic to a still greater degree gripped me at the thought that the fellow might not stop. In the end, it was Seward who thought the fastest and who flung himself in front of the approaching automobile.

With a shrill whinnying of brakes the car came to a grudging halt. The driver called out: 'Clear the way. Clear the way, I say!'

There was a touch of Scots to his voice. An educated Edinburgh tone. He tore off his goggles. 'I said, clear the way!'

Seward stood his ground, even lifting his chin a little in order to suggest pugnacity. 'I am very sorry, sir, but I cannot do as you request.'

The man snarled. 'What are you talking about? What is the meaning of this?'

I stepped forward and hurried to the alienist's side. 'I'm sorry,' I said. 'I'm very sorry, but we need to get to London.'

'Are there no trains, sir?'

'Please,' I said. 'My boy has been taken. He's been kidnapped! And something terrible will happen to him if we don't reach the capital by dawn.'

At this, the fellow behind the wheel looked, one might say forgivably, sceptical. 'Nonsense,' he said. 'You men must be drunk. Or worse. The whole thing sounds to me like a melodrama from the popular stage.'

Arthur joined us then. All three of us stood in the path of the motor car. His voice cleaved the sound of the engine. 'It is the Count, sir.' His words rang out. 'The same man who has taken control of the apparatus of our state has taken my friend's boy. And we mean to get them back. First the boy and then the nation. Indeed, I believe the two to be connected.'

The fellow behind the wheel squinted.

'Loan us your car, sir,' Arthur implored him. 'I give you my word that I will recompense you most generously. Or better yet. Join us. Join us in London at the White Tower and see that tyrant brought low!'

The driver pursed his lips. He stroked the end of his nose three times in evident contemplation. 'No,' he said at last.

At this, we all three gazed at him, quite dumbfounded.

It was Jack who found his voice first, being the one amongst us who was most accustomed to conversing with lunatics. 'Do you not understand, sir? The severity of what has been described to you? The taking of the boy? The wound at the very heart of our democracy?'

The fellow touched the underside of his chin again. 'I know nothing of the boy, sir,' he said, choosing his words with a maddening deliberation. 'I know none of the complexities of that dilemma, whatever they may be. But I do know this... I approve of the Count.'

At this declaration, Godalming swore, cursing with a vigour and ferocity which would have shocked even the most jaded of his colleagues in the House.

'Well, you may choose to adopt that tone, sir,' the motorist went on. 'But I dare say that I am only speaking aloud what many folk are thinking. We like what the Count has done. We approve of the course he is charting for the nation. And if the cost of our security and success is at times a little unpleasant, well, I expect that's only natural. Indeed, we should give thanks that at long last we have at the helm a man who is capable of making the most onerous decisions.'

There would have been more of this, of that I have no doubt, but with this latest broadside my patience had come to an end. Quickly, while the driver still pontificated, I ran to the side of the car and dragged the prating fellow from his seat. He struggled and spluttered in outrage.

'How dare you, sir! How dare you manhandle me like—'

I silenced him with an uppercut. He whimpered, sighed once and went limp.

'Well done!' cried Arthur. Seward nodded, more stoically, in recognition of the necessity of my action.

Lord Godalming took charge. 'Put him somewhere safe,' he said. 'I'll take the wheel.'

With impressive expertise, he leapt aboard the vehicle and began to turn the motor car around in preparation for the drive to the capital. Wordlessly, Jack and I lifted the heavy stranger to a point where he lay in the shadow of the cathedral, sheltered from the elements and under its protection.

'I'm sorry,' I said, once we were done. 'I am afraid that I saw no alternative.'

On the road, Arthur sounded the horn, its high-pitched klaxon a note of wild clamour resonating in that deserted place. 'On board!' he shouted. 'We have to hurry!'

Grateful, fearful, full of foreboding, the alienist and I ran to the vehicle and climbed up. Seconds later, we were moving swiftly, heading as quickly as we could to London, a distance of more than eighty miles.

Words must have been spoken during that hectic journey, though I can recall scarcely any of them. Arthur, grim-faced behind the wheel, scrutinised the road ahead while Jack Seward sat beside me, doing his utmost to ensure that I did not succumb absolutely to despair.

We careered first around country lanes and then along more urban thoroughfares, the first spokes that led to the hub of our nation. We moved at speed past places which had, until then, seemed wholly innocuous and without sin: Newmarket, Duxford, Bishop's Stortford, Harlow. All the while, the engine roared in complaint at the plentiful demands Arthur placed upon it.

I dare say that we thought – though none of us dared to

vocalise it – that there was something horribly reminiscent of that final hunt of the last century, when we had tracked the Count to his lair. Then we had been in Transylvania and the vampire was desperate and fleeing before us. Today, we were in a corrupted England in which Dracula seemed unassailable.

We raced through the night, struggling to beat the dawn, down through Epping, Chigwell and Ilford, as the landscape waxed and changed about us – from the starkness of the country to the outposts of the city, the rural to the gloweringly industrial.

I have never before been driven with such rapidity. As it occurred, an awful phrase returned to me, a line I had heard many times in my unhappy sojourn in Eastern Europe.

'The dead travel fast.'

In the early hours of the morning, as we entered the outskirts of the metropolis, rain began to fall. With it we heard thunder and felt the onset of a storm.

Jack Seward shouted above the clamour of the engine.

'Surely this is the Count's doing?'

I could only nod. As the rain began to hurtle down, all Arthur's concentration was needed to circumvent the challenges of the road.

'The correct term,' bellowed the alienist, 'is a "micro-climate". I've long believed that the vampire-king is capable of creating such phenomena through force of will alone.'

As if to lend credence to his theory, a fork of lightning lit up our path ahead, like a warning. The dawn seemed close then: too close, it seemed to me.

'Hurry!' I shouted. 'We have to hurry if we're to save my son from damnation!'

FROM THE PRIVATE JOURNAL
OF MAURICE HALLAM

———◆———

12 February. ★ *Later.* She did not knock upon my door but simply thrust it open: Ileana, draped in some black shroud, and holding in her arms the prone and insensible body of a young man whose name I knew to be Master Quincey Harker.

She laid him upon my floor. He seemed so very small and fragile.

'There,' said the vampiress. 'You know what must be done. You will be preparing him now for the Rite.'

I bowed my head, as though in acquiescence.

'The Count and I have preparations of our own. I shall be returning within the hour.'

'Madam,' I said. 'You may rely upon me.'

The creature gave me a look of absolute contempt and made haste towards the door.

'Ileana?'

She turned her crimson eyes upon me. 'What do you want, little Englishman?' said she.

'I wanted only to know,' I said. 'For certain, you understand.'

'Know what?'

'All those months ago, when you met Mr Shone and me, in that tavern at the boundaries of Brasov… did you know then what was coming? How Gabriel would be used? What part I had to play?'

Her cruelty was effortless. 'He knew. He has always known. For this is his revenge – not only upon the Harkers but upon the whole of your race.'

'So I never really had a choice?' I asked. 'I was always to be a pawn.'

She seemed to be profoundly uninterested in my questions. On the floor, the boy appeared about to wake. He groaned and stirred. Ileana looked down at him, as might a farmer at a piglet. 'Do as he said. Prepare the boy.'

She glided from the room and I was left alone with Quincey. He groaned once more. I sighed and, with a muttered profanity, yielded to my fate and set about doing that which had to be done.

DR SEWARD'S DIARY
(kept by hand)

———◆———

12 February. ★ *Continued.* As we sped out of the east, it soon became apparent that we were driving through something almost like fog. By this, I do not mean that the fog was of a literal sort (although a storm did indeed begin to brew) but rather that the night took on an oppressive, choking air. It was as if the atmosphere itself possessed a thickness, as though we were passing through some awful substance which clouded our minds and sapped our resolve.

I believe I was a good deal more sensitive to this than were my companions. Perhaps the effects of that hideous journal upon me have yet entirely to depart. Certainly, I felt more faint and ill with every passing mile.

The land told its own story. It seemed to me that there was an unfamiliar neatness to things, a well-ordered quality which might in itself not be thought of as sinister but which, given its context, seemed to me profoundly ominous.

Neatness, yes, and starkness too. And quiet. An awful, pervasive quiet.

We saw few other vehicles on the road, and such people as

we passed darted into shadows or averted their eyes as we drove past. It was just as I had seen on the train: there was a horrible incuriosity abroad, and an unspoken fearfulness. More than once, as we progressed towards our destination – as even the engine seemed to struggle more than ought to have been the case – I found myself reminded of the panorama I had seen on only one occasion, years before, in the course of my excursion to the wilds of Transylvania. It is as though – and I tremble even to write the thought upon the page – the distant place, their conduct and customs, is becoming now our own.

As we came upon the outskirts of London, a storm descended. Thunder first, then rain and lightning. The tempest had only begun when I called out to Jonathan that I considered the phenomenon to be the work of the Count. He seemed to agree. Arthur said nothing but bent closer to the wheel. The car was being pushed to its limits. The road was treacherous. At that moment I thought it more than likely that an accident might yet be the thing to foil our intentions.

I was about to speculate aloud as to the parameters of the abilities of the Count – and wonder if they had grown since our last encounter – when something unforeseen occurred.

We were upon some grim road, surrounded on either side by patches of bleak and sleeping grasslands, when all at once a shape blundered into the road before us: a bulky shadow in the gloom.

'Watch out!' I cried, but it was too late in such conditions even for a driver as experienced as Arthur to swerve in time, and so our car was struck. The sound was not a pleasant one: a deep, dull and somehow fleshy thump.

Lord Godalming swore briskly and fluently. He applied the

brakes. We skidded to a halt. The tyres squealed their complaint against the rain-slicked surface and for a moment I wondered if the vehicle itself might not be about to be upended. Once the car stopped, I leapt out.

'What was it?' Arthur called. 'Did you see it?'

'An animal?' Jonathan replied, raising his soft voice to be heard above the storm. 'A deer?'

'No,' I said, speaking with grim certainty. For I had seen precisely what it was that had struck us. 'No, it was a man!'

'I never meant to hit him,' said the aristocrat. 'You chaps saw that, didn't you? How he all but hurled himself in front of us. There was no alternative. No time for me to change course.'

Jonathan shivered in his seat. 'It was a tragedy, Arthur. We both saw it. But we cannot afford to tarry now. We have to leave this and go on. To the White Tower.'

Arthur was appalled. 'No, we cannot. We must not. If we abandon our principles now – if we abandon our decency…'

'But my son. Lord Arthur, the fate of my son's soul hangs in the balance!'

I stepped adroitly from the car. 'Wait here!' I cried. 'Just for a short while. Let me see if this unfortunate fellow still lives.'

'He can't be.' This was Jonathan Harker. 'We all heard the sound of it. The poor devil's body will already be cooling in the rain.'

'But Arthur's right!' I said. 'We need to see for sure.'

I hurried back to the place where the person had been struck. Still he lay upon the earth where he had fallen. I drew near and crouched down beside him. Swiftly, I reached out to take his pulse. The skin of his neck was clammy and cold. No blood stirred in those veins.

'I am terribly sorry,' I murmured. 'I am really very sorry.'

He was a stranger. That much was clear. He was a large man with a sizeable belly. I should say a septuagenarian. He was untidy and ill-dressed. There was dirt and mud caked upon him. A few days' growth of beard sprouted in unbecoming patches. I thought him most likely a vagrant or a wanderer.

I spoke again, pitching myself against the tempest. 'If we had more time we'd give you a proper Christian burial. But I'm afraid that, for now, this must suffice.'

I lifted him up by his shoulders and dragged him as swiftly as I could to the side of the road. It was horrid work, and far less than any man deserved, yet I could see no alternative. Poor Quincey needed us.

The body of the stranger was light. Suspiciously light. That alone should have made me realise.

My grisly task accomplished, I turned around and waved to Jonathan and Arthur. 'It's done! We must hurry on.'

Yet I was barely able to speak the last word of my sentence before I was knocked flat to the ground. Something was upon my back, pinioning me. I knew what it had to be and I appreciated the dire nature of the peril in which I now found myself. There were fingers tight at my throat and a hissing in my ears.

I kicked furiously back and, for a second, succeeded in flinging my assailant away from me. I stumbled upright and, through the merciless rain and against the distant bellow of thunder, saw the true nature of my opponent: the man from the roadside revealed as un-dead, his lips peeled back to reveal grotesque fangs, delirious hunger in his eyes.

I shouted desperately over my shoulder in the direction of my fellows. 'Vampire! Vampire! Vampire!'

I cursed myself for a fool for not having brought from the car any of our store of weapons.

For a few moments, the monster and I circled one another. The creature gave a harsh and bitter laugh and, at the awful sound of it, I understood that whatever experiences had brought him to this place had not merely vampirised him but driven him irreparably insane.

'I know you,' said the creature. 'Seward. The perverted alienist.'

'Then you have the advantage, sir!' I cried.

The fiend laughed again. 'You know my name.'

'I assure you I do not.'

It hissed. 'Salter. I was once named Salter. I was celebrated and beloved. I was the tribune of the people.'

'I'm sorry,' I said, 'I really don't think I've ever heard of you.'

This seemed sufficient to enrage the creature. It ran at me, full tilt. I stepped aside, only for the vampire, with unholy dexterity, to hurl itself sideways against me and pinion me once again to the ground. I felt its foul and rotting breath against my face.

'Liar. Damned liar. You will never reach London! I will not permit it! I will do my duty and see that you never see my master again.'

I struggled, but his strength was inhuman. I screamed, more in fury than in fear, at the thought that my journey might end here. The blood-drinker lifted high his head, his fangs bared, and brought his mouth down hard upon my neck.

I screamed as his teeth punctured my skin. I screamed still louder when the monster was pulled from me by force. The hands of Jonathan and Arthur were upon him and they dragged him from me.

As they did so, his teeth were still in me. He bit down as

they dragged him away. Much skin and flesh was torn away from me. Blood pumped faster than before, spurting obscenely into the air.

I struggled upright, clamping my right hand to the left of my neck. My fingers at once grew slick with crimson. My vision swam. I saw just enough to glimpse Arthur hold down my attacker and, through the driving rain, Jonathan raise a stake above Salter and drive it down into his heart. I heard that wretched creature shriek in desperation.

'My master! My master!'

Then all unnatural breath left his body and he sank, shrivelled and reduced, back upon the ground.

I slumped down too. The blood seemed unstoppable. Darkness swam towards me. I saw my friends run in horror towards me. I heard their words of passionate concern.

'Go on!' I called out to them. 'In God's name, go on. You must save your son.'

I do not know for certain whether they even heard me.

FROM THE PRIVATE JOURNAL
OF MAURICE HALLAM

———◆———

12 February. ★ *Later.* The boy groaned on the floor before me. His eyes flickered open. I stood before him and gazed down. How innocent he still looked. How tender!

'I am so very sorry,' I said.

'No,' the boy murmured. There was blood on his face, I saw now, and I thought that several of his teeth had been broken. 'You have done nothing beyond what has been written for you. The Count is so very strong.'

'Quincey,' I said. 'The Count is indomitable.'

He spoke to me then with a weird, beguiling knowledge. He knows of the workings of this place – the prisoners, the larder, the dark woman from the forest. And he made to me certain unexpected suggestions and recommendations of the most curious kind. He urged me to make a decision of my own, and as he talked he seemed to see into my very soul. I felt a little as might a Pharisee when the child in the temple spoke, far beyond his years, of ancient secrets and of the hidden truth of the universe.

Once he was finished, I breathed in deeply. I was shaking profoundly, as if palsied, all over my body.

'You're sure?' I said. 'You're absolutely certain?'

He gave a terrible smile. His eyes flickered briefly crimson. 'I am.'

I could stand no more. I ran from the chamber, out into the tower beyond, and set about doing that which the boy had asked of me.

JONATHAN HARKER'S JOURNAL

———◆———

12 February. ★ *Continued.* We did what had to be done. We did our duty and did not flinch from it.

Poor Seward was already unconscious. Arthur ripped off his jacket and tore up its sleeves, cursing all the while the excellence of his tailoring. These strips he applied to the doctor's wound, pushing it hard against the skin in an attempt to stop the bleeding. The fabric was soon soaked with blood. I had no notion as to whether there was any chance that he could last the night. The only fellow amongst us with medical training lay before us, bleeding and faint.

Together, we helped the injured man back towards the car and lifted him carefully within.

'We go on?' Arthur cried.

'We must!' I shouted. 'We have no choice!'

Arthur took the wheel once again. Seward had slumped upon me, dead to the world. I held down the cloth against him, though it soon grew still more sodden and useless. I spoke no words of comfort to him, for I knew not what they might be.

We drove away at speed. The remains of the vampire Salter we abandoned, without a shred of shame or regret, to carrion.

That crazed journey continued. On we went, into Newham and Leamouth, skirting as best we could around the docks, and then on into Wapping. The rain grew torrential, the sky shuddered with thunder and the storm surged. We were all of us soaked and shivering. I muttered a prayer beneath my breath and reached, for comfort, for those weapons that we had managed to bring with us, a mere fraction of our arsenal: a stake, a hammer, a crucifix and a phial of holy water, scarcely enough to deal with the most minor demon, let alone he who stands at the head of that number.

Pray God, I thought, let my son be safe. Pray God, let my wife still live.

I was lost to these miserable thoughts when I heard Arthur call out: 'There it is! You see?'

He was right. For out of the rain and the darkness loomed towards us the great structure of the Tower. Beside me, poor bleeding Seward groaned.

'There's light,' said Arthur. 'Light all about.'

I saw what he meant: the familiar vision of the turreted tower seemed to shimmer with strange blue light. The effect, against the darkness, was thoroughly bizarre, yet I found at the sight of it that there was within me a strange urge to laugh at this thought: that it resembled nothing so much as a pudding at Christmas, when it has been doused in brandy and set aflame.

As Arthur steered the car to a halt a short distance from the White Tower, I understood for the first time that something must already have gone awry with the Count's design. For fleeing from the Tower itself streamed dozens of furious men. Prisoners, I thought, escaping – a mob in a state of dangerous excitation. The mood was akin to that of a riot, to some act of civil disobedience which would be ended by gunfire. Yet we had no choice but to go into the very heart of it.

We stepped from the car, leaving Seward in place. I bent down towards the alienist.

'I'm sorry,' I said. 'But you may yet live, old friend. All may still be well.'

There was no time for any better farewell than that.

Many strangers flowed by, calling out in mingled terror and wrath. I have learned since that they were all members of the city's criminal classes – the worst of the gangs, the Giddis Boys, the Pigtails and the Sweetmen – that every one of them was a thief or a killer or worse.

Several of them, seeing the vehicle, stopped their flight and ran towards us, their faces clenched and filthy. One of them called out to his fellows and they rushed in our direction. We were too surprised to offer much resistance. There was a brief, brutal struggle before the car was taken. Too many of them clambered on board, the effect of it horrid and bizarre.

The car disappeared then, swerving wildly away, with poor Seward still within it. He lay quite insensible, his body limp and unmoving.

'Come on,' Arthur shouted. 'We need to get inside. He would wish it.'

I hesitate now to admit the truth: that I spared not a glance for the vehicle or for that dear friend of mine who lay trapped within it. It seemed to me that my course was altogether clear and absolute.

I made my choice without hesitation. I must try to save my son at any cost – even if, I see now, some part of me already realised that I was far too late.

We ran towards the White Tower, forcing ourselves against the tide of those who fled from it. We must keep our wits about us. Exhausted as we were, we must battle on against the crowd. Had we faltered even for an instant we might easily have been trampled underfoot.

Some were fleeing but others were staying to fight. A pitched battle was still in progress between the vampires and the prisoners. The blood-suckers were winning but the convicts were fighting hard.

There were many human bodies to be seen, strewn about the courtyard. We passed men in the scarlet robes of acolytes who lay sprawled upon the ground, their faces masks of blood and gore. As we dashed past, one of them cried out. A crude and splintered stake had been thrust partially into his body. He seemed in some fashion to be familiar.

'Help me! Help me in England's name!'

Arthur and I looked at one another. For a moment, we stopped.

'Tanglemere,' he said. 'My lord.'

'Yes, yes,' said the stranger upon the ground. 'Lord Arthur, help me!'

Lord Godalming shook his head. 'Vampire,' he said simply. In a gesture of contempt I had never before seen in him, my friend spat once upon the face of the creature. It snarled and hissed.

Then Arthur reached down and, with a terrible calm, pushed the stake further into the creature's body. It screamed its last.

As it did so, we saw a dog – an Irish wolfhound – leap through the throng. It reached its master's side and, with what felt like a gesture of revenge, bent towards him and began to lap up the blood which pooled around him.

Godalming and I said no words but simply ran on.

We reached the gate to the Tower. 'In here!' I shouted. 'We must follow the light to its source.'

With a terrible shriek of rage, she came out of the shadows, half-flying directly at us: the vampiress, her great black wings beating frantically against the air. She launched herself at Arthur and flung him downwards. She hissed and raised her head high into the air, white fangs flashing in the night.

Arthur thrust her aside before his skin could be punctured. He flung a phial of holy water and, with a shriek of agony, she drew away.

'Damn you!' she screamed. 'Damn you all!' And she swore, loudly and at length, in what I took to be her own language.

Godalming scrambled up. He had the stake and hammer. He pinned her down.

'Run!' he shouted to me. 'Save your boy!'

He had the creature on the ground. She laughed bitterly. 'Too late!' she cried. 'You are being far, far too late for that!'

I ran on, into the Tower. Behind me, I heard the scream of the vampiress and the awful sound of a stake being driven, with horrible relish, into her dead flesh.

Inside, the strange blue flame was more vigorous and potent. I saw from where it seemed to emanate and I followed.

Down, down, down I went in that awful edifice, down to the catacombs of the place, to its lowest and most subterranean levels. From outside, I heard the cries of the criminal rioters and the thunder of the storm. Ahead, the blue light seethed and tantalised. As I ran, I grew weary and short of breath. I ached and in my mouth I tasted blood. In my mind, I cried to God for aid and prayed that I might not, even then, be too late.

At last, I realised I could go no farther. The dank stone passageway before me led to only one place, to where everything had been tending: the crypt. It was only as I burst into that abysmal room that I realised I had upon my person not a single weapon: that Arthur had already used them against she who had been known as Ileana.

I shall never forget the scene that awaited me in that ghastly place, where the blue flame was at its most unnerving and vivid: a bleak and horrifying cellar, in which two coffins had been raised upon daises. One of these was open, its occupant loose; the other remained closed.

Count Dracula: reborn and reconstituted, though less suave and more feral in aspect than I recalled, was upright, his teeth bared, leaning against the figure of my son, who endeavoured with one hand to push the creature away. Both seemed weakened and exhausted, like bareknuckle boxers at the end of the most testing bout of their career.

'Get away from him!' I shouted. 'In the name of Jesus Christ, I command you to step away from my son!'

It was the use of that name, I think, which caused the vampire to obey. He stepped back and turned to gaze at me with mad triumph in his eyes.

'Herr Harker,' he said. I trembled and shook as if palsied. 'How fit it is that you should be here once again. Here to witness the zenith of my revenge!'

The vile thing smiled and I saw my son's blood smeared about his predator's teeth.

'I don't think so, Count,' I said, mustering a bravado that I had failed to bring forth since I was a very much younger man. 'I do believe that I've seen your larder escaping from this place.

And your lieutenant is even now having her head removed from her body by a certain old friend of ours.'

'Bah! You know nothing of what you speak. I shall find new victims. And my true lieutenant still lives!'

'It is over,' I said. 'All your dreams of conquest. Your dreams of a new dark age. Now give me back my son.'

'Your son?' The vampire laughed, and the sound was like wrenching metal. 'Rather he is our son. He has but a little of you in him, but so very much more of me. So it was planned. So it was meant to be. He understands his inheritance. He welcomes it!'

Quincey stepped forth then, to stand between the two of us, between that dark master and me, his true (if flawed and foolish) father. 'Wait,' he said. 'Wait.'

I said, simply: 'Quincey?'

'The Count speaks the truth,' he said. 'I have come to understand that in some manner, a portion of him was placed inside me, before my birth, through poor Mother. I have indeed a terrible inheritance. And all these long days I have fought against it.'

'I know you have, my boy,' I said. 'I see that now. How difficult it has been! How nobly you have grappled!'

'But,' he said, 'I shall do so no longer. For I understand that I have to accept my true destiny.'

The vampire laughed repulsively. 'That is very good. Quickly now. There is yet time to perform the Rite of Strigoi. I need that essence which resides in him to be placed within me. I must live on.'

With a weary gesture, as of one very much older than his years, Quincey shook his head. 'Oh, but Count,' he said. 'You don't understand. In truth, Mr Hallam never prepared me for the Rite. It was he who set the convicts free.'

The vampire hissed, as though these things were to him but minor irritations.

'And I see what it is that I have to do. You remember, Father, Van Helsing's last words to me? You are to be the vessel. That is what he said. And I finally see now what he meant – that I was born, Count, to contain you.'

For the first time, I saw pass across that loathsome killer's face an intimation of fear. 'No,' he said. 'No, no, no. You have only barely held that splinter of my essence since your birth. You would never possess the necessary power to hold all of me.'

'But, Count,' said my son, 'I have long been praying to one who does.'

'No. No! He would not intervene!'

'But He will,' I said. 'I have faith in that. And I have faith in my son. And I have faith in our family!'

Quincey stood in a posture of supplication, his eyes open, gazing upwards.

The Count set himself against him. 'You are mine,' he said to Quincey. 'We are part of one another.'

Instantaneously, my boy seemed to falter. 'No...' he said. 'I rebuke you. I rebuke my inheritance.'

Yet he did not sound certain.

The Count pressed his advantage. 'Accept your destiny,' he said. The air in that Stygian place seemed to crackle.

Something passed then across the face of Quincey. A horrible expression, a vile leer of sinful hunger. It seemed as if a shadow had fallen over him, an impression of profound evil.

'Fight it!' I cried. 'My dear Quincey, fight it!'

The boy rallied. He seemed to push back against the invader

and, within seconds, his face was as it had been before, resolute and human.

'No,' the Count cried. 'I shall not be defeated so. Not by a boy! This is not how this age can end.'

'You defeat yourself, Dracula,' I said with feeling. 'For evil always does. It overreaches itself. It contains within its greed and lust the seeds of its own downfall.'

The vampire screamed in absolute rage. As he cried out, he began that dark miracle of transformation: not into a bat but into a churning column of mist.

'God be with us!' shouted my boy. 'God be at our side! God help us now!'

As he spoke, the blue flame grew brighter. It seemed to swell and ripple. And the mist – strange as it sounds to relate – began to curl away, not towards the doorway or down into the crevices of that place but rather, as if compelled by some mighty force, towards the figure of my son. The light grew fiercer and I thought I heard, as though from very far away, the sounds of something almost like voices, raised in majesty and praise. All was cacophony and fear and raw, rippling power.

It ended very quickly. The mist – that which now contained all that was left upon the earth of the vampire lord – was dragged into Quincey, into his mouth and his eyes, into the very skin of him. My son shrieked and whinnied in pain, a scream of pure horror. Once, the mist seemed to move away from him, to seek frantically some escape, but the forces arrayed against him were, at the finish of it, too strong.

Within a minute, it was done. All the mist had vanished into my own boy's form. The light flickered and dimmed and, outside, the storm itself seemed to cease. There was silence, then, as though something great and terrible had been snuffed out.

Quincey, who had but moments before seemed as adult and as commanding as a soldier twice his age ran, like a child again, into my arms.

'I'm so sorry,' I said. 'I'm so sorry, my boy.'

'Father,' he said, and how my heart swelled to hear him call me so, 'you need not worry. All is quite well. All will be well again.'

How sad it is to think of how wrong he was, how utterly mistaken. As I write, my eyes flood with tears.

For no sooner had he spoken this sentence, than we heard from behind us the dreadful sound of wood moving on wood. We turned to see the lid of the second coffin start to move aside, manipulated by whatever horror it was that dwelt within.

But surely, I thought desperately, surely the Transylvanian woman, Ileana, is dead.

The lid was thrust away then and that which had lain within it sat upright. In that moment, she seemed more beautiful and more terrible than I had ever seen her before. Her dark hair curled about her shoulders and her eyes gleamed scarlet.

Quincey cried out in horror: 'Mother?'

'Mina?' I said. 'Oh God. No. Mina?'

And my wife looked across at us and she licked her lips and she smiled in greeting. Her teeth were white and pointed and her fangs were dripping with blood.

'Welcome,' she said. 'Welcome, my beautiful boys.' And she laughed a laugh of horrible despair.

EPILOGUE

FROM *THE PALL MALL GAZETTE*

1 March

EDITORIAL: AFTER THE STORM

Almost a month has gone by since the fall of the Count and the restoration of civilian law to the peoples of this nation. Yet still we lie in disarray. Suffering has been widespread and bereavements have been many. This period of agony has been acute and without precedent. Nonetheless, we have to stand firm. We in this great country of ours must do all that lies within our power to rebuild and to grow stronger than before.

It is a source of sorrow to those of us who are presently engaged at this newspaper that any words of ours may, in however minor a fashion, have contributed to the inevitability of the catastrophe. At this distance, it may be observed that a regrettable tendency crept into those who stood at the helm of this publication, one which, in defiance of the traditions of the Gazette, slid swiftly from a state of commendable open-mindedness into one of outright credulity and even gullibility.

Reader, you may be assured that the new regime is quite different from the old. The editor at the time of the unpleasantness has been removed from his post without the least compunction. That correspondent with whom he was most readily associated (and whom we need not name here) shall never again return to these pages. You have our assurance that in the future this publication, eschewing the reckless appeal of mere opinion, will cleave strictly to fact and to truth.

And as the Gazette regathers its forces, learning from the mistakes of the past and moving with courage and determination towards the future, so too must the nation itself.

LETTER FROM LORD GODALMING TO THE COUNCIL OF ATHELSTAN

15 April

Gentlemen,

Following our meeting of the fifth of this month, I should like to reiterate and to make official our determination, in consequence of long and meticulous discussion, to dissolve the Council of Athelstan.

In the end, after much debate, you will recall that our decision in this matter was unanimous. Many of you have but lately inherited your positions in direct consequence of actions taken by the Council in the days of the reign of the Count. In spite of some reservations expressed by newer members, I trust that you have come now to appreciate the necessity of this judgement.

The Council is a relic of antiquity and must be set aside. We are creatures of the twentieth century and any such outmoded systems as these must be left at long last to sink into abeyance.

Although I am now in law the head of the Council, I intend to call no further meetings, nor to use that old constitutional power for any reason whatsoever. This verdict stands until my death.

To end upon a note of optimism, why should there ever come again so dark a period as that which we have endured? Surely all that lies ahead of us now is light, goodwill and necessary progress?

Yours, in hope,

Lord Arthur Godalming

EXTRACT FROM A LECTURE, GIVEN BY DR JOHN SEWARD
TO THE CLUB FOR CURIOUS SCIENTIFIC MEN, ENTITLED
'ON THE EXTERMINATION OF VAMPIRIC NESTS'

13 August

My friends, what an honour it is to be standing before
you today – an honour not just because of the wisdom and
sagacity of this society to which I am most gratified to
have been admitted, but also because, not so very many
months ago, I believed that my death was inevitable and
that no more breath was to be granted to me by my maker.

I speak, of course, of the dreadful events which bedevilled
this country in the winter of 1903 and in the early months
of this year. Upon this subject I have begun to observe
in recent weeks a kind of shared forgetting amongst the
populace: a decision, unspoken yet widespread, not to
discuss the details of the disaster but rather to let them
slide into a kind of gentle amnesia, to allow all wounds to
heal over and the waters to cover the earth.

Gentlemen, I am not prepared – nor shall I ever be – to
collude in such a fashion. We must remember and respect
our history, even the very worst and most bloodstained
of it, lest we doom ourselves to repetition. And this is
why I have come to speak to you today: to educate and
to remember.

I wish to tell you in particular of the work that we have
done in the aftermath of what, after all, was tantamount
to an invasion of these shores – namely, to seek out and
eradicate every nest of the vampire horde which remained.

The best known of these was the little seaside town

of Wildfold to which the policeman, Parlow, had been sent to seed and overwhelm. Yet this was far from the only instance. We understand but little even now of the biological means by which the virus of vampirism is spread and sustained. We know all too well, however, those methods which must be used in order to ensure its absolute eradication.

This was long and bloody work. Yet did a small team, with myself at the head of it, set to our labours with determination and zeal. Although the exercise was in essence one of necessary brutality, I did my utmost to attend as closely as I could to the science of the business. During this time, as we moved from village to village and from town to town, I kept a detailed notebook. The death of every victim of the nosferatu plague is listed within, alongside the manner of their demise. For we must never forget the sacrifices made by so many to keep this country safe.

We must remember those who have gone before us just as we must keep up our guard against a resurgence of the un-dead.

I should like to present you now with fifteen separate findings from my recent encounters with vampire-kind. Your patience will be appreciated; I shall take questions only at the end.

J.S. BARNES

FROM THE BIRTHS – MARRIAGES – DEATHS COLUMN OF
THE DAILY TELEGRAPH

9 September

MR G.W. DICKERSON AND MISS R.S. PARLOW

The engagement is announced between George, son of
Ephraim Dickerson of Utah, USA, and Ruby, daughter of
Martin Parlow of Wildfold, Norfolk.

FROM THE DIARY OF
QUINCEY HARKER

———◆———

6 November. Till now, I never thought I'd keep a diary. In my family, decisions like that often don't seem to end all that well.

But today seems an appropriate time to start. Why not? For things seem better now, and safer too. And today marks my thirteenth birthday, as well as the anniversary of the evening, one year ago, which began the most horrid run of events in all my life.

The past few months have been at the same time full of incident and also, to be honest, rather boring too. The house at Shore Green has been repaired and we've all moved successfully back in. We have no servants now, for reasons which, I suppose, are obvious. Poor Miss Dowell is never mentioned, though I think of her often. She was so very kind.

Worse luck, I have been sent back to school where I am now obliged to spend all the term-times. I suppose it's not so bad. Somerton's a decent enough place and I find I quite enjoy the routine. I like the learning. Occasionally, I seem to have in my mind more answers than I ought. Strange thoughts and images enter my head, as though from some set of olden days, from before even my parents were born. I say nothing at all about them to the beaks. It wouldn't do, I think, as has held true for every schoolboy in history, to seem to have too much knowledge.

Strangely, I have come to enjoy sports much more now than ever I used to. I still do not much like team games, but I have come to relish running and athletics. I find that it is easier when caught up in exertion not to have to think too hard. Such spare time as I have I tend to spend nowadays in the school chapel. I have much to pray about: lots to thank God for, but lots to ask Him for too.

But tonight, I have special leave to come home for this anniversary dinner. We are expecting many guests and it is an exciting thing indeed to imagine our old, isolated house filled up again with the sounds of merriment.

Lord Arthur is to come, of course, and he'll have Jack Seward with him. The pair of them have finished their tour of the country in which they rooted out a number of similar (if smaller) nests to those which we discovered in Wildfold. I am given to understand that it was rather bloody and wearying work, though, of course, both of those chaps carried it out with great aplomb. The doctor is returned now to practice. It took him a few months to recover from his ordeal last year but he bounced back in the end, almost as good as new. The noble lord, meanwhile, has returned to his responsibilities in the upper chamber.

The American detective, George, will be coming too. Father says that he is still very weak and is now in a Bath chair. He's going to bring a friend with him – Ruby Parlow. They are to be married after Christmas.

And there is to be another guest. One upon whom I insisted. It is my birthday, after all. Arthur made the arrangements. He greased the wheels. There are advantages, he says, to being an important man again.

So that old actor, Mr Maurice Hallam, will join us, at least for the first half of the evening. It is a long way from his prison and he will have a gaoler at his side at all times. I want to thank Mr Hallam for what he did. There is still a lot of good in him, I think, even if he himself does not quite believe that to be true.

I wanted us all to be together tonight, all of us survivors. It seemed important somehow. Unusually, Father agreed with me. We shall all raise a toast to the late Professor – and to the memory of those who are no longer with us.

Later. What a happy evening, the happiest of the year by a long stretch. All attended. We'd arranged for food and drink to be brought in from the village, and a very merry feast it was.

Arthur and Jack were both on good form, and my father was pleased to see them. I think the alienist may be contemplating getting engaged himself, although he did not say as much to the assembled company. As to who the lady may be, we've none of us any idea.

George Dickerson arrived after them, pushed into the house in his chair by Ruby Parlow. I thought they seemed really rather contented. I apologised profusely and in full to the American for what I had to do to him on that terrible night in February.

'Now, you needn't worry yourself about that, young fellow,' said the man in the Bath chair. 'You only did what you had to do. Truly, I see that now. And I raise my hat to you, Master Harker, for your courage and good sense.'

'But, Mr Dickerson,' I began, 'all the same...'

'You need say no more,' said Miss Ruby Parlow quickly. 'Trust me. He understands.'

George beamed up at me, a shade too enthused in his agreement.

There would have been much more that I wanted to say but perhaps it was for the best that we were interrupted then. Mr Hallam arrived next, a stern, stout, bald man at his side whose pockets always seemed to jangle when he walked. The actor shook my hand very warmly.

'You did the right thing, Mr Hallam,' I said to him as soon as I laid eyes on him, for I have not been allowed to see him in his prison cell, nor have I been permitted to write. 'I owe you my life. This whole nation, sir, owes you a very great debt.'

He smiled sadly. 'Ah, Quincey, my dear, I may have done the right thing upon one occasion, yet has there been a near-infinity of instances when my personal judgement has been immensely poor.'

'I'm probably too young,' I said, 'to know this for certain, but I think that learning good judgement, however late and whatever the cost, is one of the reasons why we were given life in the first place.'

At my reply, he seemed surprised. 'I hope you are right, young man. I really do.'

The captor at his side gave me a strange look and took several steps away.

My father came downstairs then and bade us all go through to dinner. We obeyed, and we had such a lovely feast. Conversation flowed very naturally and it felt to me as though a process of something like healing was taking place all around us. Father, I noticed with quiet pride, took not a drop of strong drink all night.

It was only after the eating was done that Mother was finally brought up. She does not care now for the sight or smell of food as we know it. She waited in the shadows of the cellar till we were done.

All present were very pleased to see her, though they seemed understandably nervous in her presence. The men (save, of course, for George Dickerson) rose when she entered. Oddly, she seems younger now than she used to be, and more powerful too. She moves with a feline grace.

'Thank you all for coming,' she said, dazzling them with her charm. She might almost have been any matron welcoming her guests. She took her place at the head of the table, beside my father. Our guests relaxed substantially, if not entirely.

'I should like to propose a toast,' said Arthur, 'to all our absent friends.'

'To the Professor,' I said.

'To my father,' said Ruby Parlow.

'To Caroline,' said Lord Godalming stridently, 'and to Mr Strickland also.'

'To that fool Quire,' muttered the American. 'And to young Thom Cawley.'

'To Miss Sarah-Ann Dowell,' said Dr Seward, almost too quietly for any of us to hear.

We all fell silent at this awful litany of names, at the realisation of quite how many had been lost.

A few seconds later and the aristocrat tried to lighten the mood. 'Charge your glasses,' he said. 'And let's toast to the future!'

We all took a fresh drink and raised our glasses into the air.

'To the future!' we cried. 'To the future!'

'My dear?' This was my mother. She looked imploringly, almost desperately, at my father. 'I am thirsty also. I know it's not quite what we agreed but... may I?'

My father turned his gaze meekly from the others and looked with adoration into her eyes. 'Of course. Of course you may, my darling Mina.'

And then, as I have seen now a hundred times, she took his pale, stippled hand in hers. He pushed up his shirt sleeve with ease, for he no longer troubles himself to don cufflinks, in order to make possible such necessary access.

With practised ease, my mother found a vein. Of course, everyone looked away or consoled themselves with a swig of their liquor. But we heard it. The sound of the vampire-queen taking sustenance from the only place from which she allows herself nowadays to drink. My father was very good and placid, though he whimpered once or twice before the thing was done.

Once it was over and my mother had wiped her lips, conversation started up again. At first, it was fitful and uneasy, but it grew soon enough in confidence and volume. There was a clinking of glasses, a pleasant hubbub and even, after a while, some sporadic, hesitant laughter.

It was, I thought, almost as if nothing out of the ordinary had ever happened here at all.

EDITOR'S POSTSCRIPT

———◆———

It has been an interesting, if often melancholy, journey that I have taken in the collation of these documents. Much that I have read during this process I found both difficult and troubling, yet I have replicated it all here as completely as possible so that the entire truth of the business might at last be known.

As to why I have done so now, just as our country goes to war, I have a further explanation to present. I have volunteered for duty in this new conflict and I am to leave for France in the morning. When – or even if – I shall return, I have not the slightest knowledge or presentiment. This bundle of papers I shall despatch to a trusted publisher before I depart.

I have a confession also. For many years, that which by the power of prayer I took within my soul in the catacombs of the White Tower has lain dormant and still. It slumbers. It dreams. From time to time, perhaps unwittingly, it has shown me certain inexplicable things. To date, I have been able to contain it. With the coming of this war, however, I have felt an increasing restlessness. That which is trapped within me scents the coming bloodshed. It longs to escape and be loose in the world, and I fear that it has already begun to scheme.

For this reason, you must heed my warning. I am fearful that my prison will not hold him for very much longer. There is a new savagery rising, one which will seem to him to be the most perfect of habitats.

Put simply and in the plainest language: Count Dracula is hungry again.

Lieutenant Quincey Harker
Dover
13 October 1914

ACKNOWLEDGEMENTS

———◆———

The author would like to thank:

My agent, Robert Dinsdale.
My editor, Craig Leyenaar, Jo Harwood and all at Titan Books.
Ben and Michael for their wit and companionship.
My parents and brother for their love and support.
And Heather, of course – my own Mina Harker!

ABOUT THE AUTHOR

———◆———

J.S. Barnes is the author of three previous novels – *The Somnambulist, The Domino Men* and *Cannonbridge* – as well as numerous audio originals for Big Finish and Audible. He has taught Creative Writing internationally for more than a decade and is a regular contributor to the *Times Literary Supplement* and the *Literary Review*.

THE SILENCE
TIM LEBBON

In the darkness of an underground cave system, blind creatures hunt by sound. Then there is light, there are voices, and they feed... Swarming from their prison, the creatures thrive and destroy. To scream, even to whisper, is to summon death. As the hordes lay waste to Europe, a girl watches to see if they will cross the sea. Deaf for many years, she knows how to live in silence; now, it is her family's only chance of survival. To leave their home, to shun others, to find a remote haven where they can sit out the plague. But will it ever end? And what kind of world will be left?

**NOW A GRIPPING NETFLIX MOVIE
STARRING STANLEY TUCCI AND KIERNAN SHIPKA**

"Lebbon develops a believable and intense narrative that is certainly a must have for any horror enthusiast to add to their collection" *We Love This Book*

"*The Silence* is a chilling story that grips you firmly by the throat" *SciFi Now*

"A truly great novel with a fresh and original story" *Starburst Magazine*

SOON

LOIS MURPHY

On winter solstice, the birds disappeared, and the mist arrived.

The inhabitants of Nebulah quickly learn not to venture out after dark. But it is hard to stay indoors: cabin fever sets in, and the mist can be beguiling, too.

Eventually only six remain. Like the rest of the townspeople, Pete has nowhere else to go. After he rescues a stranded psychic from a terrible fate, he's given a warning: he will be dead by solstice unless he leaves town – *soon*.

"Lois Murphy's *Soon* is an exquisitely written, atypical post-apocalyptic/horror story that smartly focuses on the characters/survivors without sacrificing story/thrills/scares. Like the nightly mists, *Soon* will linger."
Paul Tremblay, author of *The Cabin at the End of the World*

TITANBOOKS.COM

For more fantastic fiction, author events,
exclusive excerpts, competitions, limited editions and more

VISIT OUR WEBSITE
titanbooks.com

LIKE US ON FACEBOOK
facebook.com/titanbooks

FOLLOW US ON TWITTER AND INSTAGRAM
@TitanBooks

EMAIL US
readerfeedback@titanemail.com